FINAL PLAY

A Novel

MICHAEL TROY

For my wife

Like rivers, cities, moon craters and forest fires,
oil fields exhibit a curious pattern.
A small number of the world's fifty thousand fields
hoard a vastly disproportionate share of the oil.
Fifty fields, each with over five billion barrels,
hold nearly half the oil ever discovered.
The supergiants.

In the four decades following the war we discovered forty.
Over the last four decades, using advanced technology
and over a trillion dollars,
we found four.

Like rain on the desert,
oil has fueled an explosion of life,
propelling the world's population
from one to over seven billion in just 160 years.

And now we are using three barrels for every one we find.

"Oil is found in the minds of men."
—Wallace E. Pratt, honored as
the Grand Old Man of Exploration at
the International Petroleum Exposition of 1976

TABLE OF CONTENTS

CHAPTER 1

POWDER KEG

Arctic Ocean
Soviet Drift Station SP-19
July 18, 1975

The melting of the ice floes that began each year in early June
would slowly and inevitably reveal all manner of things gone
missing over the winter, including that day the famed Soviet polar
scientist Dr. Gennady Pleskov. He waved to Oleg Lazarev from across
the ice just as the young geologist had finally coaxed his crew into the
bright Arctic night.

"Jesus, not another," said Lazarev, his fingers scrambling into his
pocket for the prayer rope. At first they were very occasional visitors,
good for a fright but forgotten the next day like a bad dream. Now,
after weeks of being wet, cold and awake, the stench of his misery was
sucking them in and they were thick as Siberian flies. Yesterday the
bully from his Leningrad judo club had jumped him in the mess tent
at breakfast. At midday a boat of bloodthirsty Swedes had chased him
down an open lead as he paddled away in the kayak, screaming. After
dinner he was off by himself sobbing when his father surfaced in the
sounding hole to announce that he had not drunk himself to death
but in fact been drowned in the Vuoksa River by an evil water spirit.
Beware the *vodyanoy*, he said, before sinking back into the abyss. And
now this, a *polyarnik* appearing out of nowhere in a white fur parka,

the kind given out only by Brezhnev himself for distinguished service in the North. Of course Pleskov would reappear now. Lazarev's desperation to complete that morning's task, the sole purpose of these two wretched months on the ice, was bringing in the demon like a polar bear on a colicky seal pup.

Pleskov's life-long research partner, a dull, second-rank hydrologist by the name of Ostrovsky, pulled up short and swung his head from side to side like a tired pack animal. "Another what?"

"Pay no mind, Lev Arsenevich," said Lazarev, forcing a smile and slapping Ostrovsky on the back. "You just keep picturing the look on Lipatov's face when you tell him how you helped me." Ostrovsky shoved Lazarev's arm away and scanned the horizon. Mid sweep, he stopped short. The hydrologist pulled down his goggles, wiped at soggy eyes with damp leather mitts and peered into the distance. It was two in the morning and the low sun was glaring right through the thin cloud cover, casting dark gold over the usual rainbow of blues. Easterly winds whistled softly over echoes of distant, cracking ice. There was nothing to be seen in any direction but soggy floes, the tiny, far-off tents of their drift station and now this inconvenient figure reclining near their old campsite, hailing them like a cab.

"A sip for all from my flask once we clear another five hundred meters, how about it?" said Lazarev. "I'd say we earned it." Ignoring him, Ostrovsky raised up his hands and bellowed like a drunk. "Yes! Our brother has returned. Oh, he has returned at last!"

"What are you talking about?" said Lazarev, twisting every which way. "I don't see anything." But Ostrovsky was already gone. "That?" Lazarev yelled after him. "Trust me, Lev Arsenevich, it's not the Pleskov you remember." The other seven members of the crew stumbled after Ostrovsky like zombies.

Fear crushed Lazarev's chest like the hands of a vodyanoy driving him down under dark waters. He dropped to his knees and held the prayer rope with trembling hands. "Lord Jesus Christ, Son of God, have mercy on us all." Again and again. A few moments of this feverish contemplation stayed the vodyanoy just long enough for him to stagger over to his sled, heave his Kalashnikov rifle up onto his shoulder and follow them.

When he caught up with them Ostrovsky was laid out in a shallow pool of water, weeping and cursing and pounding his fists, splashing water all around. Beside him was Pleskov, who upon closer inspection proved to be real flesh and blood, though frozen. He lay back on the ice, propped up on his left elbow. His right hand was extended, reaching for help that had never arrived. His skin had a purple tinge and his eyes looked gray and soft like petroleum jelly. The left side of his face had endured some horrific trauma and was smeared with dark blood. Beyond this, he was remarkably well-preserved. He still had his paunch, his trim mustache and his prized sable jacket. But he also had a chain locked around one of his ankles, the other end of which was likewise locked to a stake which now lay idly on the ice, but which by the looks of it had once been driven deep into the pack.

"As if we needed proof," said Lazarev, bent over and gasping. "Is this not why you decided it was so very, very important to help me?" He pounded a mittened fist into the palm of his other hand. "Immediately after we are finished and not one second later we are carrying poor Dr. Pleskov back to camp. Then we'll see what Lipatov has to say for himself. We are agreed, yes?"

"No," said Ostrovsky, his wild eyes leaping from man to man. "Already Gennady Dmitryovich has waited too long for justice." And with that he loped off back to the sleds.

In the popular imagination, as fueled by breathless Soviet press reports, the men and women of the Arctic drift stations were near-mythic heroes, elite scientists who dared to ride the fragile pack ice as it churned along with the Transpolar Current from the East Siberian Sea up into the unrelenting cold and darkness of the Pole. Relying only on their superior intellects, model collective behavior and sheer grit, these brave polar explorers, or *polyarniks*, would often as not pop out the other side of the Arctic basin near Franz Josef Land or the

Greenland Sea with vast treasure-troves of scientific data, everything
from deep-sea soundings and salinity measurements to atmospheric
temperature and pressure readings. From the moment the first drift
station began its dramatic nine-month journey from the North Pole
to the East Coast of Greenland in 1937, led by a tiny, peasant fire-
cracker named Ivan Papanin, the Soviet public had been thrilled by
tales of survival at these extreme outposts. The Arctic never failed to
stir the Russian imagination. Its icy northern shore was the longest
coastline of any country in the world, a grand white façade for a land
that truly faced north. Other countries might border the Arctic, but
the region belonged to no one but Russia. And so the challenges of
Arctic exploration were deemed fitting tests for the New Soviet Man
and by all published accounts the polyarniks passed them again and
again with ever greater acts of selfless heroism. But the fact is these
reports served ideals other than the truth, and the reality on the ice
was often quite different, as it was now for the polyarniks of *Severnyi
Polyus-19*, the nineteenth 'North Pole' drift station.

Contrary to what readers in Moscow or Odessa would have expected, the polyarniks dreaded summers far more than winters.
Temperatures could dip sixty degrees below zero on a typical winter's day, but their cold-weather equipment was quite good and in a
pinch there were always hot drinks, warm stoves and the cozy refuge
of sleep, lots of it. From May to August, however, the sun shone continually and regular sleep was impossible. After two weeks of tossing
and turning the polyarniks became irritable, sluggish and decidedly
self-centered. After two months without sleep they were also suffering from memory lapses, headaches and hallucinations, and if you
looked at them crosswise they would knock you silly without even
remembering or feeling badly if they did. The summer did bring
warmer weather, of course, but too much of it. Temperatures hovered around freezing, usually just above, so that over the course of
the summer all of the snow and much of the ice on top of the floes
would melt, leaving their camp a soggy mess in the middle of an icy
swamp. Buildings teetered perilously on ice pillars as the exposed ice

melted away, clothes and bedding were constantly damp and impossible to dry and meat and vegetables rotted because they could not be kept quite cold enough. The dampness also clogged the skies with nearly constant clouds and fog, which contributed to the generally foul mood.

But as Lazarev had learned repeatedly even at his young age, things could always get worse, and indeed the polyarniks were required to cope with the fact that even this thin gruel of an existence might be snatched from them at any moment. It would be expected that in winter the pressure from freezing and expanding ice could shoot ridges twenty meters high before a man could wake up and roll out of bed. But wind and land and currents also played with the ice, and the floes could split open or buckle at any time, winter or summer. Sentries were posted at night to listen for cracking ice, food was kept near sleds so it could be moved in an instant and escape holes were cut in the roofs of tents. And on this day, a storm in the east had been generating high, sustained winds, and the resulting pressure had turned the pack ice under SP-19 into a powder keg.

There were also more deliberate threats. Polar bears were attracted to the noise and smell of the scientists and would come hunting at any sign of activity. They were pervasive year-round, although the constant summer light gave you more of a sporting chance. In the winter they were invisible, silent killers. Every team out working on the ice had to dedicate an armed man solely to spot bears.

And for the duration of the summer, there was no relief from the misery and danger. From deep in the Arctic pack ice, the polyarniks' only escape route was through the air, and from May until October drift station runways were unusable lakes of icy water. Lazarev and his three special machines had been the unfortunate cargo on the last flight in for the season.

And so, with the polyarniks beaten nearly senseless by sleep deprivation, wrapped only in wet, cold, scratchy wool and terrified that the ice would rip open under their feet or a bear would catch them without a rifle, there had been no rational discussion for weeks. In the best of times, their innate Russian maximalism would whip them casually from one extreme to the other. But now, tempers flared constantly over trifles and a broken magnetometer, a missing chess set and the last can of nuts had all provoked major crises. Two months into the punishing summer season, at two-thirty in the morning, with the sun's glare painfully bright behind the never-ending fog and clouds, all twenty-two members of SP-19 had descended into madness.

Lazarev bolted after Ostrovsky and promptly slipped and fell face-first into a pool of ankle-deep freezing water, banging his nose on the ice and his rifle against his ear. The front of his jacket and pants went from damp to soaking, and cold water surged in around his neck. As he struggled to his feet the water ran down his chest, and from there around his seat and down his legs. For all the good his clothes were doing, he might as well have been naked on the ice.

  With his body temperature dropping, his nose and ear throbbing and water dripping from his hood into his eyes, Lazarev fought a losing battle against panic. If he started to blubber again, he may not be able to stop. And in less than three hours, whether he was ready or not, the Soviet Ministry of Geology would be detonating a large seismic charge deep under the permafrost of northern Siberia, at a site south of Tiksi. By which time, in order to avoid learning the nature of the 'severe consequences' planned in the event of his failure, Field Geologist Oleg Lazarev and his able partners from the Arctic and Antarctic Institute must have lowered to the continental shelf under the Laptev Sea three specially-constructed ocean-bottom seismometers. Not all the way down, because of the currents. They would be dropped the last meter or so at precisely the correct moment and then the cable played out from the winch for seven minutes, no less, until the seismic waves from the explosion had been fully recorded and then some. The drop sites could be any three of his choosing, as long as they formed a roughly equilateral triangle having no less than 850 meters on a side.

Straightforward, his supervisor Yuri Telnov had told him. A five-month vacation with those slackers at the Arctic and Antarctic Institute and only one mindless task to complete. I have to stay here and explain to Moscow why for the past four years we haven't discovered a single major field in all of West Siberia, at a time when the West will pay us any price we ask. You should thank me.

Lazarev checked his watch. They had gotten a late start after he had to drag them all out of the mess tent and then listen to his team argue about exactly how stupid it was that he wanted to bring the heavier winches, how his division of the teams was plainly reactionary and why there simply had to be some scientifically sound method developed to determine who should pull which sled. If Radio Moscow could be believed, it was now two hours and thirty-seven minutes until detonation. His initial estimate for the time required to travel to the sites, blow the holes, clear the remaining ice, assemble the tripod and winches, power up the seismometers, check their calibration and lower them to the hold position was three hours and fifteen minutes. This did not include the distraction of finding a dead colleague. Either way he was in trouble.

When Lazarev reached him, Ostrovsky was untying the seismometer from his sled. It looked like a small yellow keg set into a metal latticework shaped like a car tire. Ignoring Lazarev's pleas, he picked it up and flung it across the ice. Lazarev heard a jingly rattling sound as it hit the floe.

"Lipatov must answer for his treachery," said Ostrovsky. "No doubt we will find the chess set as well once his tent has been searched. All will be made right."

Pleskov had disappeared in a major snowstorm about a week before Lazarev's arrival. Notwithstanding the obvious explanation, everyone seemed to assume that Lipatov, the head of the station, was responsible. Being the new arrival and an outsider, no one bothered to explain to Lazarev why this was and he didn't ask. Given the lofty stature of the two, Lazarev assumed there had been a passionate scientific dispute that went too far, over competing theories of Arctic salinity changes, or the mechanics of Arctic-Atlantic heat exchange, something of that nature. Perhaps even fraudulent data, or the right to name some prominent underwater feature. But from his eventual allies in the Pleskov faction, he learned that after five years on the ice together the two scientists had in fact become blood enemies over a half bottle of Dr. Pleskov's plum brandy that had gone missing in January.

From the Pleskov faction he learned the facts of the case were indisputable, and the Lipatov denials outrageous. First there was the very public argument over the brandy only the week before. Then, the day after Pleskov's disappearance and before the storm had even subsided, Lipatov ordered a hasty move of the entire station due to unspecified ice risks. Most shocking, as the days went on Lipatov refused to even notify the Institute in Leningrad about the disappearance, claiming it would reflect poorly on the whole station and why risk that unnecessarily, as if silly old Pleskov had just gone walkabout in the middle of the Arctic and would return when he was done sulking. And then, after the last flight of the season had left, what could be done? Even if they wrested the radio away from Lipatov, what would they say? Pleskov disappeared in a storm, we have no body, but we think Lipatov killed him? Send help in October? In the meantime, what would they do with an enraged Lipatov and his allies? Because of the threat of fires, there were no locks on any of the doors. They couldn't confine anyone. They couldn't protect themselves.

So no one said anything to Leningrad. They just waited for October and simmered to a boil.

Lazarev watched in horror as Ostrovsky tossed his electric winch, its heavy batteries and his tripod onto the ice next to the seismometer and started dragging the empty sled back towards Pleskov.

"Don't settle for half measures, Lev Arsenevich," said Lazarev, jogging beside him. "Think about how Lipatov will feel if you return with Pleskov *and* we have completed this project. It will destroy him!"

"How can you think about your experiment?" said Ostrovsky, not stopping. "No. We are going to march into that camp with Pleskov behind us, raising his fist at Lipatov, speaking the truth to his crime. All of us, now, together."

"All of us?" Lazarev's sleep-deprived brain sluggishly seized on the scope of his problem. The only way Lazarev had been able to round up the eight men he needed to make three three-man teams was to exploit the conflict between the Lipatov and the Pleskov factions. While Telnov had told Lazarev there would be plenty of assistance at SP-19 to complete his simple project, Lazarev in fact found that the only way he could get any help at all was to convince the Pleskov faction how much they could irritate Lipatov by helping him. Now they had found a better way.

For whatever reason, Lipatov did seem dead set against Lazarev and his project. He drafted Lazarev into all sorts of activities that became curiously dangerous, in the course of which the geologist had been abandoned on breaking ice floes, knocked into open leads while carrying heavy equipment and so routinely left unprotected by the assigned bear watcher that he had taken to carrying his own rifle at all times. They all seemed in on it. Lazarev was unable to seek further counsel from the Ministry on his situation because Lipatov controlled the radio and as a matter of policy denied all attempts at "frivolous" communications, which is how all of Lazarev's requests were regarded.

Lipatov's antipathy towards Lazarev certainly arose from bureaucratic conflict at levels far higher than Lazarev would ever be able to see or understand, like thunder in high, dry storm clouds. He was just a pawn in the usual interagency blood feuds, the constant wars for greater turf and resources fought by claiming responsibility for successes and blaming others for failures. That Lazarev, a very junior member of the Ministry of Geology, was even allowed to conduct MinGeo research at an Arctic and Antarctic Institute drift station was remarkable. The Institute jealously guarded its exclusive right to conduct polar research and its flagship drift stations. And SP-19 was their golden child. Due to the vagaries of the polar winds, currents and ice conditions, each drift station met with varying degrees of success in its attempt to traverse the Ocean and explore new frontiers. But against all odds SP-19 had danced and weaved with the currents through the most sought after sectors of the Arctic for over five years. It had ridden the Beaufort Gyre into the Amerasian Basin, sliding right up against imperialist American waters before sweeping out through the Eurasian Basin and the East Siberian Sea and then curling back through the Laptev Sea, where Lazarev joined it in May. Next stop certainly the Pole. It was the grandest of grand tours of the Polar sea.

Although exactly where he was at the moment Lazarev couldn't say. With great relish, Lipatov had advised him that because of the threat of interference by American forces, particularly high given their bold foray into the American end, the exact location of SP-19 was kept secret. He would be provided with the location data, continually and accurately being recorded by Lipatov's team he was assured, upon his return, once the station had safely drifted on. But Lazarev didn't care, he would leave that to Telnov. He just had to get his seismometers on the bottom.

Lazarev watched the backs of the polyarniks as they left with Pleskov, who mocked him with a wave from the back of the sled.

At their final meeting before Lazarev flew off to the only place further north than Siberia, his supervisor Telnov made a point of telling him a story about Baibakov and Stalin. It was July 1942 and the Nazis were storming through the Caucasus on their way to seize Russia's prolific oil fields on the Caspian. Hitler's generals were so confident they presented him with a birthday cake with a map of the inland sea, complete with a frosted Swastika over Baku which the dictator reportedly cut out and popped in his mouth. Baibakov, at the time a young petroleum engineer in Baku, later to become the Soviet oil commissar and then head of all economic planning at Gosplan, was brought before Stalin and told to seal up the wells. Pointing two fingers at Baibakov's head, Stalin told him, "If you can't stop the Germans from getting our oil, we will shoot you. And if we can't reopen the wells after we throw the bastards out, we will shoot you again." As the mean little Telnov pointed two fingers at his head, Lazarev tried to remind himself that they didn't manage people in the Soviet Union quite like that anymore. That said, failures were still not received well and always required a scapegoat. And based on his experiences in MinGeo, and at SP-19, Lazarev could imagine far worse consequences than being shot. Which may be why Baibakov could remain a great fan of Stalin. The only thing Lazarev didn't understand is what this all had to do with finding oil, the responsibility with which he and Telnov were tasked by the Ministry of Geology. Baibakov had convinced Stalin not to invade Iran after the War by telling him they would find all the oil they needed in Siberia. As appalling as it had been, that's where he wished he were right now, thought Lazarev, back in Siberia finding oil.

Lazarev pointed his rifle over the heads of the deserters and fired. Ostrovsky turned and yelled at him, something about seeing him in hell with Lipatov. Lazarev lowered his rifle and aimed it at them. "Don't think I won't shoot you all!" But they turned their backs and continued on. Except for one. Grigory, the youngest in camp, was holding his hands in the air. "Don't shoot!" he cried.

Two and a half hours later one seismometer was on the bottom, and Grigory was paying out the cable from the electric winch at the side of the hole, all while trying to ignore the gun at his head. The heavy wire ran from the electric winch staked in the ice up to a wheel suspended from an iron-legged tripod set up over the hole, then down into the sea. The water was impossibly deep, thought Lazarev. They were supposed to be over the continental shelf. The bottom should have been at three hundred meters, not over fifteen hundred. With the ice drifting at the high end of the usual two to six kilometers per hour, they might not have enough cable. Damn it all, they should have brought the bigger winches. Lazarev checked his watch. "Two more minutes," he said.

Why seven minutes, he wondered? Russian crust was hard, and the sound traveled well. They had to be less than fifteen hundred kilometers from the source, and the leading edge of the seismic pulse would reach them in less than three minutes. They would be listening to nothing. And what kind of charge were they using? It would have to be massive. Nearly asleep on his feet, Lazarev dreamed of the sound waves traveling down to the molo, the boundary between the earth's crust and its molten core, and back up to the surface, again and again, for thousands of kilometers. The image was hypnotic.

"Oleg Maksimovich, has that not been seven minutes?" said Grigory. "I think we're dragging on the bottom."

Lazarev jerked awake, but his first thought was that he was still dreaming. A nightmare, in which the cable was taut, and the idiot boy was letting the instrument drag on the bottom. But then he realized how cold he was, and that they really were about to lose the seismometer. He yelled at the boy and lunged over to start the winch, in the process tipping the tripod back on two legs only, leaving the other leg suspended over the hole, but only for an instant before it slipped out of its socket in the crown and disappeared into the water. What? He hadn't screwed it in properly! He was so tired he couldn't even remember putting it together. What had he done? The tripod was teetering and in danger of falling over and being dragged into the hole. Without it, they would never get the seismometer out. With one hand on a tripod leg, Lazarev slipped the rifle off his back and stuck it in the socket where the leg had fallen out. Then he yanked the tripod over and set it on this short, wobbly leg.

"Wind, Grigory, wind!"

Grigory hit the switch as Lazarev held the tripod together. The wet cable started to sizzle around the spool. Oh, this was too good to be true, Lazarev thought. Maybe everything would be fine. After all, what could they say to him? The resources weren't at all what they had promised, and he had performed heroically in the circumstances. Waves of giddiness rolled over him, and they were so strong he wasn't really bothered by the fact that Grigory suddenly zipped out of his field of vision. But then Grigory screamed. A close, coherent, terrified scream.

Lazarev did not look, he just held tighter onto the tripod. It was balanced too precariously, the current was too strong. He couldn't let go, much less take out the rifle. Grigory kept screaming. "What do you want me to do?" Lazarev yelled back, still not looking. "I cannot lose the package, can your selfish mind not comprehend this?" He gripped the stand as he listened to Grigory's howls mix with the sound of splintering bone. "Stop screaming at me, there is nothing I can do! Stop it, stop it!" Grigory seemed to try. His cries faded to guttural moan, then there was only the sound of ripping muscle and tendon, like the sound of someone tearing up a carpet.

The seismometer broke to surface. Lazarev grabbed the wire and swung the instrument onto the ice. Then he pulled the tripod off the hole, yanked out the rifle and spun around. The bear was standing over Grigory's remains not five meters away, his muzzle and forepaws streaked cardinal red like the surrounding snow. He tipped his sleek head to one side and looked at Lazarev curiously.

Lazarev set the rifle to automatic, raised it to his shoulder and fired a long burst into the bear. Staring over the smoking barrel, he wondered if he had even hit anything. The bear had already been bloody, and he was never any good with a rifle. But the beast lay down on the ice like it was going to sleep after its meal. Lazarev crept over and emptied the rest of the magazine into the white bear from so close he was standing in Grigory's blood.

When he arrived back at the station dragging the seismometer the Pleskov team was laying siege to the radio tent, which perched on its pillar of ice like a mountain redoubt. Three of them carried rifles. Dead Pleskov was with them, still on his sled. No one asked about Grigory.

"Lipatov and his conspirators have barricaded themselves inside," said Ostrovsky. "We will overtake them by force. The Institute must be notified and Lipatov must be relieved of command and arrested."

Lazarev staggered off to the side and leaned against the cook-house, one hand up against the side, his head lowered, exhausted. If they were all going to kill each other, at least then he would be alone, he thought.

"Lipatov, show yourself!" bellowed Ostrovsky. "You can't hide out here."

Dear God, prayed Lazarev, tell me there is some purpose to all of this. Help me to understand.

In answer, the ice was yanked back out from under his feet, slamming his head against the canvas side of the cook tent and then bouncing him back out onto the ice and water, flat on his back. Over his head and from an upside-down perspective, and to the accompaniment of a tremendous cracking, Lazarev watched the floes rise up in a wide pressure ridge just beyond and already higher than the radio tent. The common foe had arrived. The cries went up.

"Ice emergency! Ice emergency!"

As Lazarev watched the radio shack rise in front of the giant pressure ridge, he saw Pleskov's sled start to slide back directly towards him, picking up speed all the way. Lazarev rolled aside just in time. Pleskov's sled shattered against the ice pillar under the cookhouse. The force of the impact threw Pleskov's body onto Lazarev. A strong smell of sulfur filled the air, and for a moment Lazarev was convinced that the foul spirit Pleskov was there to drag him directly to hell, just like his father. A terrified, screaming Lazarev pushed the stiff body away and scrambled to his feet.

Lazarev looked around and could see the feud had been suspended. Lipatov and his men poured out of the radio tent, and they and the Pleskov faction ran around like ants after someone had kicked their hill, randomly executing bits and pieces of the drills that were supposed to save them. The sulfur fumes were overpowering now, and some of the men dropped to the ice, unconscious. Sulfur from volcanic activity? Where were they, the Gakkel? Impossible.

Lazarev took out his facemask, soaked it in the water at his feet and pulled it over his head, covering his mouth. He climbed up the ice towards the radio tent, now teetering perilously on its pillar, and looked inside. Sidorov, the camp's radioman, was still at the controls, yelling into the microphone. "This is SP-19, we have an ice emergency, I repeat, ice emergency. Immediate assistance required, over." Then the tent lurched back, throwing Sidorov back onto the wooden floor and sending the table with the radio sliding all the way across the room until it slammed into a pole at the side of the door, knocking it down and collapsing that side of the tent. Sidorov must have hit his head because blood was pouring down the side of his face. He sat dumbly on the tilted floor and pressed his hand against his head to staunch the flow. The microphone lay right in front of him.

Lazarev scrambled under the collapsed wall of the tent up onto the floor, grabbed the microphone and pressed the switch. "This is SP-19, requesting emergency assistance. The ice has become unstable, we need immediate evacuation. Please respond. Over." Did it still work?

The radio crackled. "SP-19, this is L-9." Thank God, thought Lazarev. The Institute operations center in Leningrad. "Please identify yourself," said the voice on the radio.

"This is Oleg Maksimovich Lazarev, of the Ministry of Geology. I am sorry, but no one else can come to the radio. Many are injured, some may be dead, it's terrible. Please send a plane, a ship, anything, please just get us out of here."

Dead silence. Had it gone out? By instinct, he resorted to his contacts. "I have collected important data that I need to deliver to the Ministry of Geology, very important data. My experiment has been a wild success. Trust me, you must help us."

Lazarev waited, breathless, but there was no response. He could hear the men screaming outside. The wait seemed endless. Then the radio crackled again.

"SP-19, this is L-9. Assistance will be available with October relief flights. Until then, please fully utilize all onsite resources. Report status every twenty-four hours. Over."

"What?" yelled Lazarev, throttling the microphone. He couldn't believe what he was hearing. He could feel the ice continue to rise. In his mind's eye, the inside of the tent began to swirl in front of him, then dissolved in a brilliant bright light, and he was blind. He started screaming into the microphone. "You are insane. You are all insane, and you can go to hell every last one of you. You want a status report tomorrow? I'll give it to you now. 'Today's status is that we're all dead!' How's that? How's that?" He swung the microphone by the cord, smashing it down again and again on the wooden floor of the tent until it was destroyed.

Then the floor finally slid out from under him, pitching him forward. When it hit the ice next to the pillar it snapped him back again and threw the rest of the tent down on him. Lying under the collapsed tent he listened to the shouts, and the shots. After he collected his breath he crawled out from under the canvas and stood up. The old animosities had returned. There were groups of men hiding behind the tents that remained standing, yelling and firing at each other. Oblivious to the crossfire, Lazarev walked calmly to his sled, pulled the data tapes out of the seismometer and stuffed them inside his jacket. He picked up the seismometer and heaved it at Pleskov. He walked over and kicked the dead scientist, picked up the reins to his sled and pulled it over to the stores shack. Most of the food had already been moved out. All that was left was about two dozen cases of identical cans, all unlabeled. He took them all. Also a shovel, a stove, fuel and a tent. Outside he grabbed the wooden kayak and a paddle. Back at his tent he grabbed his small bag of personal effects, which included a compass and all the ammunition he had squirreled away for the Kalashnikov. Then he took a quick reading on the compass.

The shots and screams faded away only after he was far out across the white desert.

CHAPTER 2

GIANTS

North Atlantic Ocean
Early August, Monday night
Present Day

After thirty years in the oil business, Charlie Joiner knew all about demons. They had all the oil. It was his job to get it from them. And so the oak and marble and leather-trimmed cabin of his precious sportfisher resembled a Viking hall after a raid. Long-haired, well-armed men lay everywhere, banging down their glasses like hammers after each toast to their bravery and fellowship and the golden-haired girl twirling on the coffee table. Jagger howled from the stereo about St. Petersburg and the Tsar as the clan feasted on the spoils of Reykjavik. Pickled herring and smoked mutton, lamb sausages with melted cheese and a heavy dark mass called thunder bread. It was night and the cabin was lit but their hand-rolled cigarettes had reduced the visibility inside to something short of the opposite bulkhead. Charlie watched from the bench seat that wrapped around the main table. Immediately to his left, the famously-ascetic head of the Russian Natural Resources Ministry sawed furiously at the mutton with a combat knife.

"Of course they exist," said Oleg Lazarev. "The only question is whether you will recognize them. Their shapes, their schemes…" He poked the greasy knife at Charlie for emphasis. "Constantly changing.

This is why they so often appear as Americans." Lazarev speared several slices of meat and shoved them in his mouth with the blade. He
looked sideways at Charlie as he chewed, eyebrows raised as if inviting
comment, or confession. Charlie stared into his empty glass, considering the notion. Beneath the music, he could hear the twin turbodies-
els moaning as they drove the *Final Play* hard over the North Atlantic
swells. Too hard, his captain had said. One missed bergy bit and the
boat would look like a bug on a windshield. Charlie told him to keep
the throttle and his eyes wide open. They had ground to cover.

"Shows what I know," said Charlie, picking up a fork and stabbing
a sausage. "I thought it was for the schools."

Lazarev stared at him blankly. "Very good, Charlie. When the
West collapses, you can use your excellent humor to console all the
other Texas oilmen." He picked up his cigarette, sucked on it like he
was loading a weapon and blew the smoke back in Charlie's face.

They hadn't seen each other in over twenty years but were picking up about where they left off, with Lazarev screaming at Charlie's
back as he walked out on their negotiations in Baku. The Soviet empire had just died and Charlie figured he didn't need Lazarev's permission to drill in the Caspian anymore. Lazarev had felt differently.
Catching up for lost time, Lazarev had spent the last couple of hours
bringing Charlie up to speed on satanic spirits, the One True Church
and God's dim view of rootless, mercenary Western democrats. The
Russian had well-developed views on good and evil, and though he
was still building to the punch line it was clear he thought Charlie was
playing on the wrong side, right next to the Antichrist and fast food
franchisees.

Lazarev had never made much of an effort to disguise his con-
tempt for Charlie, but this religious aspect was new. They had met
after Texso sent Charlie to Arab nationalist North Yemen on his first
exploration project. Lazarev was working across the border in Marxist
South Yemen for the Soviet Ministry of Geology. Being open about
your beliefs wouldn't have done much for a rising energy bureaucrat
in early-80s Moscow, Charlie supposed. But the Russian Orthodox

Church was experiencing a strong revival in post-Soviet Russia, and Lazarev had been very public about his faith leading up to the elections last December. His Russian Path party had ridden that, their opposition to Texso and a witch's brew of other nationalist and religious sentiments to an impressive 38 percent of the popular vote. The actual tally was undoubtedly much higher, but only Putin's ruling United Russia party knew for sure. Even that was good enough to be begrudged sixty seats in the Duma, the head of the Natural Resources Ministry for Lazarev and two additional board seats on each of Rosneft and Gazprom, the country's oil and gas champions, respectively, together with the financial considerations these implied.

There was a chance it was all contrived, but then the strident orthodoxy was very Lazarev. There was also his well-publicized walk out of the Arctic which did at least suggest divine intervention. And then you just had to look at him. The Russian papers speculated that modesty prevented Lazarev from confirming rumors of his ascetic practices, but it seemed unnecessary. Old Lazarev, the awkwardly tall, lumbering geologist-turned-oil general had wasted away, leaving a towering, skeletal figure with white, closely cropped hair covering his oversized head like hoar frost. Charlie had meant to fluster Lazarev with all the food, but now it seemed an act of charity. He broke before the cheese had melted, attacking the buffet with a knife he took off a bodyguard. Unfortunately for Lazarev, even after the makeover his complexion still had that yellow, bad-teeth tinge and the small, random facial scars which might at one time have benefited from the attention of a good plastic surgeon. Overall he looked desperately deprived, but tough, too, like he had been frozen in a glacier for the last couple of decades but still managed to chip himself out in time for the meeting.

Despite Lazarev's suspicions of shapeshifting, Charlie's appearance had by comparison changed little over the years. In the late afternoon of his life he still had his sandy hair and the remnants of the build that had been just athletic enough to keep him playing a boy's game well past the time he should have known better. Charlie was not immune from life's decline, but the worst of it was so far apparent mostly to him. The dimming eyesight, the inability to sleep or drink properly, the deep fatigue after rough use. And the quiet panic of a man suddenly without enough time. His face was heavily lined around the eyes, but those who knew him could tell you he had picked up most of those years ago, after Yemen.

Lazarev leaned closer and assumed a conspiratorial tone. "You know, I watched you from when you first landed in Moscow. I think, here is Charlie again. We don't know what will happen, but we know it will not be good. And yes, you had a fantastic story. The *siloviki*, when they hear it, their stone hearts begin to beat, their greedy hands start to sweat. You get Chernov to whisper in the right ears, to buy the right people. And then they pass your PSA and it is done, a fifty-year plague for Russia. Tell me, Charlie, who does these things? Maybe we should throw you overboard and see if you make it back. Then I would know. What do you think?"

"Sounds fool-proof," said Charlie. He picked up their bottle and shook it, sending the dregs swirling. "But if I were the devil, would I be running out of vodka?" As he looked around for a bottle that had escaped the Russian onslaught, Charlie had to admit that Lazarev's threat was not entirely idle. Controlling territory always came down to who had boots on the ground, and all the boots he saw belonged to Lazarev's *Neftepolk*. You were no one in the New Russia without a private army. Every file clerk and corner grocer had his own special forces unit, and in the aggregate they outnumbered the Red Army. Lazarev had taken it to a new level. The infamous Neftepolk, or Oil Regiment, was the private security force for *Kulneft*, Lazarev's West Siberia-based oil company, and the rumor was he had over a hundred thousand men under arms.

The nine on board wore their hair long and most had beards, but their bearing and gear suggested ex-military, although not presently. Over on the couch three of the Neftepolk were trying to impress something very important upon Olivia, waving their arms and talking loudly all at once. Kirill, obviously the ladies' man, took lead and the prime seat next to Charlie's newest crew member while his wingmen Arkady and the bearded Aleksei hovered close by. Short, ugly Yakov sat at the small table with Jeff teaching him how to drink properly. Gaunt Vasiliy sat with them but not drinking, just staring out the dark windows at nothing at all. The handsome, long-haired Nikolai, their leader, was at the aft table on the other side of the sliding glass doors drinking with his second-in-command, Leonid, who sported a shaved head with his beard and appeared to be hewn out of stone. Beardless Aleksei stood in the corner and watched them all with a cold passivity, waiting until no one was watching so he could do God knows what with the silver spoon hung around his neck, thought Charlie. The bowl was long and pointed with serrated edges, like a silver shark's tooth. Rounding out the squad was the grimly serious Maksim, last seen up in the pilothouse spinning the dials on his radio as he muttered and cursed in Russian.

Before leaving Reykjavik, the Neftepolk had scoured the boat and the charts with flickering, anxious eyes. Charlie had greeted each of them personally and showed them Lazarev's picture on the wall in the master stateroom, in Charlie's hall of heroes. Boxes of equipment were hauled aboard and stored out of sight, except for the communications gear they set up in the pilothouse and a sidearm or automatic rifle for every man, just in case Charlie and his skeleton crew turned hostile. After they were safely at sea and the sun began its brief sojourn below the northern horizon, the Neftepolk seemed to conclude they would not die this day and so turned to the matter of living, beginning with a drink. Lazarev made the first toast, a long, dark, growling thing that built to a roar and sent his men into convulsions. Having no Russian, Charlie lifted his glass to the unknown and threw in a Gig 'em Aggies for good measure.

For Charlie, seeing Lazarev was always like looking at a warped reflection of himself in a carnival mirror. Both men had been trained and made their names as petroleum geologists. Oil finders. In hindsight, it was clear they also both had the misfortune of entering their chosen field just as the golden age of oil exploration ended in the early '70s with the last discovery of a major oil province, the North Sea fields. Since then, it has been a fact that although competent exploration geologists could usually find good work on existing petroleum plays, few of them would ever make any significant new discoveries. If they did, it was certainly nothing large. Oil finders that had discovered a giant, a field with over five hundred million barrels, were less common than lottery winners. So anyone in the field would tell you that it was quite astounding that two men on the *Final Play* that night had each hit the lottery more than once.

Five years Charlie's senior, Lazarev discovered three giants as a young geologist working in the West Siberian basin in the late '70s and early '80s. Sutorminskoye over three billion, Verkhne-Kolikyeganskoye, five billion, Priobskoye, four billion. Immediately, Lazarev became an oil world celebrity, and he was invited by the US to spend a few months in Alaska digging in on the new Prudhoe Bay development. All went well at first in the US Arctic, and Lazarev's English progressed from good to excellent. But then someone suggested an ill-advised weekend trip to Disneyland. Lazarev spent a shell-shocked morning in the park before locking himself in his hotel room until it was time to head to the airport. As soon as he returned to Prudhoe, he grabbed his parka and rosary and high-tailed it back to Siberia.

For his side, Charlie had two giants to his name by the time he was thirty-three, the billion-barrel *Alif* field in North Yemen and the nearly two billion barrel *Cusiana* field in Colombia. On the strength of these finds and a string of lesser triumphs, Charlie had risen to become Senior Vice President for Exploration & Production for Texso, for many years the largest independent energy company in the world. A supermajor.

Even in his present, elevated station, Charlie's task was the same one he had the first day he first set foot on the Arabian Peninsula back in 1981. Find oil. It was only the nature of his activities that had changed. Contrary to common perception, despite having discovered most of the world's petroleum the supermajors and other independents owned little of it, less than ten percent. After decades of oil nationalism, nearly all of the world's reserves were now owned by the state-owned oil companies, such as Saudi Aranaco and Nigeria's NNPC. As head of E&P for Texso, Charlie was first and foremost focused on access to these oil regions, a matter more of politics, money and men than geology. Men like Oleg Lazarev, the newly appointed Minister of Natural Resources for the Russian Federation, which today controlled the largest share of the world's proven oil & gas reserves and, more importantly, most of the few undeveloped prospective regions in the world. Including the 1.2 million square kilometers of the Russian Arctic covered by the Texso's new PSA, or production services agreement. Upon its approval last year, the PSA gave KarLap, a partnership between Texso and its politically convenient allies, the exclusive fifty-year right to explore, develop and produce hydrocarbons from an area of the Arctic Ocean twice the size of Texas. For which a new technology called *Zhar-Ptitsa*, or Firebird, had been developed and stood ready to launch, provided Charlie could keep the men side of the equation from unraveling.

Two weeks ago Charlie's man in Russia had tipped him off that Lazarev would be heading to Iceland. Like rutting reindeer, the five Arctic nations would gather regularly to strut and spar and make their claims on the virginal and hopefully fertile North. No one liked to strut and spar more than Lazarev so he quickly made these conferences part of his ministerial brief. Charlie had been putting off meeting with Lazarev, but time was no longer his ally. He sent a formal invitation to the Ministry of Natural Resources, into which the Ministry of Geology had been subsumed in the most recent bureaucratic reshuffle, part of the ongoing Kremlin clan wars. Would the Minister afford Texso and Mr. Joiner the privilege of being his guest on a short cruise out of Reykjavik at the conclusion of the conference? Overnight, chopper back the following afternoon for the flight back East. They would be testing a theory about a new structure. Mr. Joiner hoped to repeat the success of their last trip, of which he still has fond memories.

As Charlie expected, the invitation was accepted.

Rod Pearson appeared from below carrying a case. "Ta-da. Look what just appeared. The good stuff, too." He cracked the case and set the bottles out. "How are we on food?" He scanned the galley, now in complete shambles. "Guess everyone's helping themselves. Good."

"Captain, tell me, how have you endured these many years, working for this man?" said Lazarev. The three of them had been at sea once before, a week before they nearly came to blows in the Caspian, when they stole away from Baku for a weekend in the southwest Indian Ocean, looking for big billfish out of Mauritius. Charlie sized Lazarev up over a weekend while Rod hooked him up with an eleven hundred pound blue marlin. A grander. Charlie's man in Moscow told him that Lazarev gave the photo of himself with his catch wide play back home, with no credit to the host after their falling out. "There must be many other American oilmen with boats such as this," said the Russian. "The spoils of their trade."

Rod slid his long limbs in at the table, pushing Charlie around the bench towards Lazarev. "Well, I suppose I could do that," said Rod, opening and pouring for the other two, not drinking anymore himself. "Certainly get offers, since you ask. But it would put Charlie in a bad spot. We may not have talked about this last time but see, he owes me. Weren't for Charlie I'd have played professional ball. Baseball. Know the game?" He made short cuts with an imaginary bat. "Worth checking out. Well, I'd be retired right now, still drinking and chasing skirts in my golf cart, waiting on the Hall. But no, because we had a chance at the conference championship. So Charlie kept calling for my slider. Wicked movement, but rough on the arm. Started to get real sore. Don't worry about it, he says, take a couple aspirin. Just to win a game. You know how he is."

"Yes, I am familiar," said Lazarev.

"It was your chance for glory and you took it," said Charlie. "I don't remember a lot of arguing."

"I rest my case," said Rod. "Anyway, my wing was never the same. Years go by I'm out of ball with somewhat limited prospects and our paths cross. My old buddy has a new boat but no skipper. What could I do? I turn him down, his karma's shot to hell. In your business, you know that's no joke. And now I've made this a lucky boat, everyone knows the *Final Play* raises the big fish, so I can't mess about. Special thing, unexplainable. So I'm stuck. I just try and make the best of it. After a certain point in life there's no do over." There had been three lucky boats, each christened the *Final Play*. The current incarnation was a ninety-two foot Viking, three times the size of the boat they took out of Mauritius. A long-range war wagon for hunting big game. She loyally followed Charlie as he roamed the world, sucking four barrels an hour along the way.

"There is no fortune, only the Lord's or the devil's hand at work," said Lazarev. "Who is responsible for your success, Captain?"

"Maybe it's the captain himself," said Charlie. "Just a thought. If I was a marlin I wouldn't want him after me."

"Couldn't really tell you," said Rod. "But whoever it is has his work cut out for him tomorrow." He picked up a hard roll and broke it open, watching Lazarev out of the corner of his eye as he slathered it with soft cheese. "Too damn cold for blues up here. If we catch a marlin it'd have to be wearing a wet suit." He bit into the roll, continuing to talk with his mouth full. "You see, your marlin are nomads. Live everywhere and nowhere. But, they are fish and that means they are cold-blooded. So they like it warm, at least in the 70s. Most folks say you won't catch a blue in the Atlantic north of forty-five degrees. Think French Riviera. But Charlie, now sixty plus and showing the signs, he will point out that temps are rising and that a five-hundred pounder did wash up on a beach in Wales couple years back, first time anyone can remember. That's about fifty-two degrees north. Tomorrow morning, unless we hit ice first, we'll be at fifty-eight degrees north. Think southern tip of Greenland. Just another 360 miles north. Few days back and forth for a big blue. Too far for an all-you-can-eat mackerel buffet? Maybe not. But me, I would have stayed in the Azores. Prime time down there right now. Rumor was, that blue in Wales, its last request was to be cremated so it could be warm one last time."

Back in the day, Rod would have now launched into a boozy rendition of *The Cremation of Sam McGee*. Rod endured one winter in Alaska when his father went to work on the pipeline. When spring finally arrived Rod graduated high school and moved back to Texas to thaw. He sold all his winter clothes and vowed never again to live anywhere he needed more than two layers. He and Charlie met their freshman year at Texas A&M playing ball. Rod had two pitches, neither with much movement, and no nerves. It was all Charlie could do to keep him on the mound. After college and a couple of years in the minors Rod's arm and his life fell apart. Charlie found him in a dive bar down on the seawall in Galveston, drunk out of his mind and going after some bikers with a baseball bat. Charlie dried Rod out and installed him as captain of the first *Final Play*, a used thirty-foot Bertram. He drilled out the bat and filled it with lead and told Rod he would hit him with it if he ever took another drink. In the meantime they called it the priest and used it to deliver last rites to big fish at the back of the boat.

"So, Charlie," said Lazarev. "You are just wasting fuel, as usual."

Charlie shrugged. "It's further north than I would like, but the structure is perfect. And the easy areas are fished out. Time to get creative." He took the bottle and filled up their glasses. "These fish, they never stop. They swim to eat, they eat to swim. If there's a giant ball of biomass in the North Atlantic, why wouldn't they have found it? Surface temps there are warm enough to hold marlin three weeks out of the year, and this is one of them. Besides, marlins are not completely cold-blooded, they warm their brains. And large blues can withstand cooler temps, because they have a higher ratio of mass to surface area." Charlie picked up his glass and stared at Lazarev over the brim. "So, if we do find blues, they are guaranteed to be worth the trip." He raised his glass. "Can't find oil if you don't drill wells." Charlie knocked back his drink and banged his glass down on the table.

Lazarev clapped his hands sarcastically. "Bravo, Charlie. Who feeds you these schemes, I wonder?"

"I did have some help finding the structure," said Charlie, wiping the back of his hand across his mouth. "This guy at the Arctic & Antarctic Institute. Two horns, tail, nice suit. Alexandrov, I think it was."

Lazarev frowned. "What business would you have at the Institute?"

"Well, we're contracted for the biggest Arctic development project in history, so I thought I should brush up," said Charlie. "After my talk with Alexandrov the idea just came to me. When I heard you were coming here, it seemed like fate."

"So then, Charlie, I will expect another grander tomorrow," said Lazarev. "Anything else would surely be a failure."

"Ah, the days when a man could be happy with a grander," said Rod. "I remember those. Now Charlie thinks they just waste his time. Takes one look and cuts the line. He wants a tonner. Fish of legends. Maybe the bigger daughter of that twenty-five footer Bart Miller saw in the Pacific, they say she may have run three thousand pounds. But that's Charlie, been that way since I met 'em. A buck seventy-five and swinging for the fences on every pitch. Goddamned unnatural, it was."

That's exactly what his coach had told him, remembered Charlie, right before sticking him on the bench for a week to think about it. Sheila tried to console him, not contesting it exactly but telling him unnatural seemed a bit harsh. Some may call it that, she said, but on those rare occasions he connected it was improbably divine, in a giant meet stone kind of way, and it was the only reason she bothered with the game so he'd better not stop. He couldn't even if he had tried. He would get up to the plate on those soft spring nights and all he could think about was sending that ball off into the infinite darkness behind the fence, like he had launched them into orbit, to fly for all time. And then after their talk he did it just for her. His coach eventually gave up and just batted him ninth because he needed Charlie behind the plate.

"So he wants to be a legend?" said Lazarev. "Charlie, you're already famous. Every day I pick up a paper, I see another story about you. Investigations, accusations. You are such a smart guy, Charlie, why are you taking all this punishment? Just like when you were this catcher, no? The equipment, what do they call it, Charlie, the tools of ignorance? Is this true? Bell from UKP told me this. Corrupt as a commissar, but a very amusing man."

"Oh, he's a riot," said Rod. "We had him out one day and he spent the whole time with his head between his knees. Fact is one in a hundred guys can catch."

The sound system started pounding out a techno beat and Olivia was up dancing with the three Neftepolk again, waving her hands overhead as the men slide in close. Jeff watched and stewed as Yakov poured more drinks for the two of them and the brooding Vasiliy. Beardless Aleksei had disappeared.

Rod stood up. "Okay, Olivia's playing with the stereo again, time for dad to go up top. Call me if they get out of hand and I'll be happy to put them back to work."

Quiet Jeff had two days off in Faial and returned with the tall, fair-haired Olivia, thoroughly besotted. How he attracted this otherworldly being was a mystery to them all. Jeff was the same age that Charlie's son would have been, and he couldn't bring himself to say no outright so he had Rod check with her prior captain. They only exchanged messages before he left port, but the note said she was surprisingly strong on the wire and could be a fit for the right boat. Charlie called the number she gave for her permanent address and spoke with her father in Ohio. He said she was a headstrong girl that had been gone too long and if Charlie could convince her to come home he would be grateful. Charlie said he would try and told Rod to bring her aboard. "Just don't get her wet or feed her after midnight," said Ryan, as he was moving his things into Jeff's berth to make room.

Olivia was jumping up and down on the couch and swinging her hair around in a circle, to the shouts of Kirill and his posse. The Neftepolk were a world away from the reserved professionals of Texso's executive protection group, thought Charlie. But then Olivia wasn't his typical deckhand, either.

"Yes, I spoil them," said Lazarev. "But they are like my children. Russia's children. This is what remains of a *Spetsnaz* platoon that went to Chechnya many years ago. God brought these nine back out of a hundred. They are blessed."

Russian special forces, thought Charlie. Sent in 2000 by the new President of the Russian Federation, Vladimir Putin, into the Second Chechen War. Putin and his fellow *siloviki*, or hard men, were the elements of the KGB and other intelligence services that had eased themselves into positions of power around that time and put an end to the anarchy of the '90s. Distinguishing themselves from the bumbling, corrupt Yeltsin family, the siloviki set about pacifying the breakaway Muslim republic, even if they had to level it as a result. Which they nearly did, making their reputation in the process. Putin, Chernov and the rest of their inner circle stood astride the various warring siloviki clans and ruled Russia with a firm hand. Putin's photo-ops showing him shooting tigers and whales were as much for Lazarev and the clans as the Western world, though that point seemed to be missed outside Russia.

Lazarev slid around the table closer to Charlie. "Ninety-one of their brothers slain by those blackarses," he said. "The Muslims would scoop out their eyeballs with sharpened spoons. Sometimes after they were dead, sometimes not. Knee-deep in the blood of their brothers, these men learned the depravity of the enemy, and what is required to defend the Motherland, and their faith."

"Onward Christian soldiers," said Charlie.

Lazarev squinted at him. "Don't tell me you won't get dirty, Charlie. And yes, make no mistake, we will fight. We failed to defend our faith against the Bolshevik conspiracy." The Communists, thought Charlie. "Never again," said Lazarev. "Russia is reclaiming its soul. That is what this election was about. Why Russian Path was embraced with such passion."

"Good. I'm glad it wasn't the part where you kept telling them you were going to rip up our PSA," said Charlie. He was inviting the issue but then why else were they here?

"It is all connected," said Lazarev. "And so you know why I am here. Yes, the Ministry has completed its investigation. To no one's

surprise, we have found a number of very serious problems with
the KarLap PSA. Bidding process, accountability of funds, environmental, taxes, other contract compliance. Frankly, everywhere
we looked there was rot and corruption. We are suspending the
necessary permits, there is an announcement planned for Monday.
Perhaps at a later time you can continue in some other fashion, but
KarLap as you know it is finished. I am telling you this in advance as
a personal courtesy. In light of our long relationship." He failed to
suppress a smile.

After much debate at Texso, Charlie had received board approval
to push forward on Firebird. He had delivered assurances from the
Russian President that the PSA would be honored and Lazarev could
be satisfied in other ways.

Charlie had told the board when the agreement was signed, and
then again after the elections, that it should not be a surprise if the
Russians came back to challenge the agreement. If not Lazarev, it
would have been someone else. Sticking to an agreement as a matter of principle was foreign to them. You had to make the case that
continuing the agreement was of mutual interest, with the benefits
shared more or less equally. That didn't mean that you caved into
their demands. The best tactic was to appear strong. Unless you knew
exactly what they wanted, any offer to compromise would be per-
ceived simply as a sign of weakness.

And Charlie knew that there was something that Lazarev wanted.
Charlie did not overestimate the strength of their relationship. If
Lazarev hadn't wanted something, he would not have accepted
Charlie's invitation. Which was why Charlie and Texso had seen the
acceptance as an extremely positive sign.

The only question was what Lazarev wanted. Russians were particularly difficult to read. They tended to ask for the moon and the
stars and see what they could get. The fact is that Charlie had room
to move, but to where? The ascetic angle was an additional challenge.
What worldly counteroffer would suffice? Charlie had considerable

experience in negotiations, but not much with ascetics. As far as he knew, there was only one in the entire industry. Oil barons tended towards the other direction.

"Right," said Charlie. "Who wants what now?"

"No," said Lazarev, shaking his head. "This is not a negotiation."

"Negotiation isn't the word I was thinking of."

Lazarev smiled. "You are disappointed you can no longer take advantage of us. Well, much has changed."

Charlie leaned in. "What's changed is that I wired a two hundred million dollar signature bonus into a Russian Federation account and sunk $2.4 billion into single-purpose hardware which will be just expensive scrap unless I can quickly lease another unexplored continental shelf twice the size of Texas. Just two of our many obligations under an agreement we spent three years negotiating before it was approved by every Russian we could find that had any passable claim to authority, including the full Duma. Russia's only obligation was to not go back on our agreement."

If God forbid you ever had to resort to legal means to enforce a deal in the developing world, what you quickly learned is that not only was the contract itself important but also all of the host country's laws, regulations and written and unwritten rules that dictated how the contract would be interpreted, enforced or ignored. Unfortunately, in many of these countries, including Russia, legal regimes changed like the weather. So for high-stakes projects in these jurisdictions, where the cost of uncertainty was prohibitively expensive, the production services agreement, or PSA, had been developed. The PSA was a business contract like any other, but it was also approved by whatever legislative and executive bodies were at hand and thus was elevated to the status of law itself, complete with its own self-contained schemes of interpretation and enforcement and taxation and theoretically impervious to the whims of corrupt judges, creative tax authorities, or the shifting sands of coalition politics. But PSAs were still no guarantee. In the international arena, you didn't so much have agreements as relationships. Dysfunctional ones. Just ask UKP, Exxon or Shell. In the end, the law came down to who had boots on the ground.

Lazarev jabbed a finger at Charlie. "You are the one who wasted your money. You knew this was coming, but still you went ahead and built all those seismometers. Even so, I am willing to see that you are paid for your trouble."

"Sure," said Charlie. "You'll mark down the value of my KarLap shares to some firesale price, pay in oil valued at some inflated amount and then deliver it when inventories are high and you can't sell it somewhere else." He locked eyes on Lazarev and knocked back the vodka. Lazarev reluctantly did the same.

"No thanks. We don't want our money back," said Charlie, slapping his glass back on the table. "We spend money to find oil, that's what we do. If I get money back, that's like anti-work."

"We are perfectly capable of finding our own oil," said Lazarev. "There was never any reason for Texso to be involved. If we need capital, we can go to the Chinese, who now have most of yours. The Firebird technology is ours, but for the fact that you have stolen it. And what technology we don't have, we can buy from the Norwegians, cheap. You knew this three years ago but you couldn't help yourself, you forced your way in. I am here to say, enough. No more."

"We developed Firebird," said Charlie. "You couldn't make it work and threw it in the trash. And with Firebird we can get you in the Arctic cheaper and faster. This is in our mutual interests."

"Russia is in the Arctic, we have been longer than anyone. What we don't need is oil out of the Arctic tomorrow. America may need the oil now. But that is not our concern."

"You do need that oil in the market. The siloviki know, they want as much pumped as soon as possible. Who knows how long these prices will last? Just last year over three hundred billion dollars was invested in alternative energy technology. Ask Putin, he'll tell you. It's now or never for the Arctic."

"How can you say that to my face? You know prices are only going one way, up. Putin, that sooka. He was in Dresden tapping German

housewives while I was in Siberia, up to my neck in mud and building the world's greatest oil province. What does he know about oil?
He wants you to hold our hand in the Arctic because domestic production is declining. How will he keep the clan wars in check if the
money starts to dry up? He is not concerned about the long view. He
wants to know how much money he will get next year. He will take
whatever he can get."

"So what, you are going to rip up another PSA? Do you still want
to do business with the rest of the world?"

"An agreement extorted from us in a moment of weakness, with
the assistance of criminals," said Lazarev. "If that is doing business,
then I will say to the whole world we are not businessmen."

"We deal with the government we find," said Charlie. "I'm busy
enough finding oil, I can't perfect your politics, too."

Lazarev stared at the food on the table, as if seeing it for the first
time. "Your arrogance is breath-taking, as always," he said. Lazarev
closed his eyes. When he opened them again, he seemed composed.
He considered Charlie, closely.

"Tell me, what do you expect to find up there?" said Lazarev. "All
this scheming. For what? A few gas fields? Another Shtokman? Is this
what the great Charlie Joiner is reduced to?" He laughed.

"No, that wouldn't do it," said Charlie, staring into his empty glass.
"Texso is still a big company, we need opportunities that move the
needle. That means oil. At scale. And there are only so many places
we haven't looked." Very few, he thought. Pull together any three
petroleum geologists and the odds were that between them they had
personally walked, shot or drilled every non-polar petroleum basin in
the world.

"Charlie, Charlie." Lazarev shook his head. "Everyone knows the
Arctic is gassy. Unfortunately for Gazprom, you can go frack shale in
your backyard if you want that. But there are no big oil plays." He was
enjoying himself. "Do you talk about this in public? And still keep
your job? Don't tell me you believe this Azolla nonsense." Azolla were
freshwater ferns that grew in the Arctic Ocean fifty million years ago

when the polar sea was hot and landlocked. Some less-than-reputable individuals speculated that leftover layers of ocean-bottom Azolla could possibly have turned into pockets of undiscovered oil.

Charlie stared at his empty glass. "Then where are they?"

"Where are what?"

He looked up at Lazarev. "The missing giants. The two at the top."

Lazarev pounded the table with his bony fist. He laughed so hard the Neftepolk stopped their loud conversation and looked at them. "Oh, Charlie," said Lazarev, wiping the corners of his eyes. "Are you still thinking about that? All this time? Is this how you keep going? This nonsense you embarrassed yourself with in Mauritius? Oh, this alone was worth the trip. Come, we must have another drink." He grabbed the bottle and filled their glasses until they overflowed. Lazarev lifted a dripping glass, his eyes gleaming with self-satisfaction. "To Charlie, who only sees what he wants, which is always more, more, more." Lazarev knocked back his glass. The spirits burned at the back of his eyes. Charlie left his glass on the table. "The curve you must navigate now is your Hubbert's, not Zipf's."

Hubbert. Full name Marion King Hubbert, but he preferred 'King.' A scientist in Shell's Houston labs after the War. In 1956 he published a disturbing prediction. US oil production, for decades so prolific it had to be controlled by the Texas Railroad Commission, the spiritual ancestor to OPEC, would start to fall in 1965. This was a somewhat controversial stand in the oil patch, and only someone as contrary as Hubbert would have advanced it. Shell was still trying to talk him out of it as he was walking out on the stage to present his paper.

The gist of his idea was simple. US oil production was still rising, in fact it was doubling every ten years. But oil was finite. That was a hard, physical fact. The fact that the earth itself was finite was your first clue. And so production couldn't keep doubling forever.

In fact, crowed Hubbert, it had to start falling, and sooner than you think. Two years prior the *rate* of increase in US production had started to decrease. A point of inflection had been reached. Graph the annual production over time and you would see your line, which had been rising and curving up, was still rising but now starting to curve back the other way, ever so slightly. Squint your eyes and you could envision, as Hubbert had, the point where the line would reach maximum height. Later you would find that inflection point was the peak of new discoveries. So with new wells coming on line at a diminishing rate, once peak production was achieved it couldn't just plateau while you had a chance to get used to it. It would plummet! Production disappeared just as fast as it had been rapidly built up. The vast majority of the oil would be chugged down in an orgy of consumption in those middle years. Just look at what happened to coal, or oil in Ohio. Resource extraction always followed the same pattern. Hubbert just extrapolated it to the seemingly endless supply of US oil.

Hubbert was a little vague on how he drew his curve, and he was so prickly his colleagues were afraid to ask. Later on he made some reference to having had in mind the logistics curve. It was a common scientific paradigm for understanding growth, of everything from predators and their prey to computer networks to tumors. In the early years, when the remaining oil in comparison to production was essentially infinite, production growth depended only on the amount of resources you threw at it. Imagine a lake in farm country that's full of fish, but no one's ever fished it because they're all too busy farming. Finally, one beautiful day a farmer takes an afternoon off and tries his luck. It's like shooting fish in the proverbial barrel. Seeing their friend grow fat while sitting in a boat all day, a few of his more enterprising buddies trade in their plows for boats. The fishing is easy, and life is good for all. But eventually, growth in the overall catch depends not on the number of fisherman, but on the number of fish left in the lake. And as the number of fisherman exceeds a certain level, that growth stops. And then it turns negative. Look out below. Now imagine those fish don't reproduce. Or they do, but it takes five hundred million years. No hunkering down for seven lean years until the fish bounce back. Those fisherman better remember how to farm.

So that was the cheery scenario Hubbert presented. If you're an oil professional, you better get ready to sell your Houston rambler and move to the Middle East before 1965, because the US was toast. Or 1970 at the very latest. The precise date depended on exactly how much oil was in the ground, both produced and yet to be produced. That finite number. You could come up with a reasonable estimate without too much effort, by looking at the results in well-explored areas and extrapolating to geologically similar but less-explored territories. If it was 150 billion barrels in the US, Hubbert showed them a curve with a peak in 1965. Another fifty billion barrels, like what we might now squeeze out of the Permian Basin in Texas with advanced fracking technology, would only move the date of peak production by five years. It was that orgy in the middle that got you. The peak was coming, it should be obvious to anyone. If you could stomach doing the math. Hubbert could. They started calling it Hubbert's Peak.

When they would talk about it at all. The oil and gas community was not inclined to believe Hubbert. It was not an environment that bred pessimism. They didn't last long. Not when one in a hundred holes yielded a producing well. If you weren't a die-hard optimist you couldn't get out of bed in the morning. Besides, they were used to false prophets. For the last fifty years, someone had always been saying that oil would last another ten, and the oil finders kept proving them wrong. And truth be told, Hubbert seemed to relish the role too much. Always quick to tell people he knew better. In the '30s he co-founded a group called Technocracy, Inc., to educate the world about the advantages of turning over the country's management to a team of elite scientists and engineers. They wore natty double-breasted suits with gray shirts and blue ties and saluted each other. Hubbert seemed surprised when his position on the Economic Warfare Board was questioned in '43 for suspicion of Fascist sympathies. Charlie didn't understand men like these. In his experience, things rarely went according to plan. He didn't see the sense of building your world around them.

But then it happened. US oil production peaked in 1970, a fact that became undeniable right about the time of the Arab oil embargo in 1973. As oil prices tripled, Hubbert went from pariah to industry oracle. Disciples started laying a logistics curve on world oil production data. The inflection point was reached soon after, right around the time Charlie was shipped off to Yemen. At the time of peak discovery. The curve they drew showed peak global production would hit right about....Well, right about any day now.

"I could never hear of Hubbert's theory without thinking of you, Charlie," said Lazarev. "The logistics curve. The path of the predator. Feasting blindly on dwindling prey, a slave to his desires, the instrument of his own destruction. Oblivious the whole time. Remind you of anyone?" His laugh was starting to grate.

Over Lazarev's shoulder Charlie could see Olivia dancing with her arms around two of the soldiers, and the others were trying to get their turn. He was worried the good Christian boys were about to turn into wolves. Jeff was standing and muttering to himself. Rod was nowhere to be seen. Charlie was going to have to draw this to a close. Now.

"I don't follow curves, Oleg Maksimovich," said Charlie. He grabbed a new bottle, screwed off the top and started filling their glasses. And kept pouring. "I bend them." The vodka ran onto the table, around the cheese and fish and lamb and finally off the side.

Lazarev jerked around in his seat, but the vodka ran into his lap. "Is that what you did in the Caspian?" he said, flicking vodka off his fingertips, angry and red-faced. "Bend the curve? Your own government doesn't think so, they want you in jail, from what I hear. I knew you were corrupt, but you were so good at hiding it. What else is someone like Sanders good for? Now even the siloviki are uncomfortable doing business with you. You make them look bad, which I never thought possible. You should have taken another wife, Charlie, had another family. Maybe things would have been different. Instead, you took this dark path. Madness. You have no responsibilities. It makes you reckless. You are a burden and a danger to everyone."

To Lazarev's credit, that also seemed to be the current view at Texso. Charlie grabbed Lazarev's pack off the table and lit a cigarette. He drew deeply and blew the smoke up into the cabin.

"Oleg Maksimovich, I appreciate the courtesy of a personal appeal. But Texso has no intention of withdrawing from KarLap or in any way slowing Firebird. We will expect the Russian Federation to abide by the terms of the PSA or we will seek full remedies. But I do not expect that to be necessary because the President is firmly behind the project. So, what do you say? Enough business for one night?"

"Fuck you and fuck your PSA and fuck your food," yelled Lazarev. He swept the table with his arm sending dishes and bottles crashing into the marbled kitchen. At the same time, a crack of fist against jaw announced that Olivia had finally caused the Spetsnaz to forget all brotherly bonds. Quiet Jeff also set off across his personal Rubicon and dove in to save her, throwing Russians to and fro as he went.

What Olivia had torn asunder, Jeff quickly mended. Leonid jabbed his hand into the bridge of Jeff's nose. Jeff let out a sharp moan and grabbed his face as Bearded Aleksei swept Jeff's legs, dropping him to the floor. Kirill drove his knee into the back of Jeff's neck and then twisted his arm behind his back as he screamed. Charlie scrambled around the table to intervene, but Nikolai caught him by the throat and pushed him back up against the wall, gripping him so tight he couldn't even turn his head. But he could see Rod at the aft sliding glass doors, the priest over his shoulder. And so it ends, thought Charlie.

But not everyone was finished, and the cabin exploded with an ear-shattering burst from an automatic weapon. The hard safety glass in the starboard cabin window ripped open and fell into the sea. The roar of the wind and sea filled the cabin.

Nikolai still had Charlie pinned against the wall, but now the Russian had the razor-sharp tip of a gaff at his neck. A gaff wielded by Olivia, who was also pointing a smoking rifle barrel at Lazarev. "Let go of my boyfriend," she said.

"Okay, okay," shouted Nikolai over the wind. "Easy does it. We are just having fun, girl. Just having fun." He let go of Charlie. Olivia withdrew the gaff, then reached out into the crowd and slipped the hook deftly into Jeff's belt. As she covered Lazarev with the gun, she pulled Jeff in, back down the corridor into Charlie's cabin to which she closed the door and locked it with a snap.

Lazarev walked up to Charlie, so close their noses were nearly touching. His skin was flushed with pale fire, and his breath was hot on Charlie's neck.

"Go home, Charlie. You are not welcome in Russia. Not anymore. Unless you want to stay forever."

He took one of Charlie's hands and held it up. "So smooth, Charlie. If my wife and child had burned to death in front of my very eyes, my hands would bear some scar. Some trace." He dropped the hand and retired to his cabin.

With Lazarev's departure, the situation resolved itself fairly amicably. Charlie had the impression these scenes were not uncommon for the Neftepolk. Nikolai apologized to Charlie and Leonid helped Jeff to his feet. Rod re-stowed the priest in the cockpit and got Arkady started taping up plastic over the gaping hole in his cabin. Jeff would have a nasty bruise, but Yakov helped him get cleaned up and bandaged. Charlie helped Ryan clean up in the galley. When they finished, Ryan and Jeff went to the aft crew berth to catch an hour's sleep and Charlie went up to the bridge.

Maksim was over in the corner, wearing headphones and carrying on an intense conversation in Russian with some distant party. Charlie sat in the second captain's chair next to Rod and looked out. The night sky was clear and lit only by the stars, and they were racing ahead into nothingness. Rod monitored the navigation equipment, piloting by the instruments. Radar, infrared, and satellite. Maksim banged his headphones down on the table and went below.

"After this trip I might be spending more time on the boat," said Charlie.

"Good. I don't think Olivia is a long term solution, so we have an opening."

"They want me to resign."

"What? That's crazy talk. And who's they? Wait, don't tell me. Crawford." Roger Crawford, Texso's general counsel, had once been a regular on the *Final Play*. But that was years ago. There had been a falling out sometime after, and then Charlie made Rod spend two months poking around the Tahitians looking for Crawford's college drop-out son gone missing on a drug bender. Rod found him, of course, but the whole experience did nothing to endear Roger to Rod, or vice versa. "Don't listen to him, he's poison. Go talk to Wayne."

"Roger was the messenger, but he had a package for me and everything, which means the board was involved. And Wayne." The sealed envelope was tucked into his bag, unopened, like death lurking. "He said they want it to be voluntary, that I'm just supposed to think it over, but they're just waiting for it to sink in." He rubbed his face. "Not exactly on a winning streak."

Rod looked at Charlie's with mock horror. "A third-world dictator has stolen money stashed in a Swiss bank account? Stop the presses. And they assume this is your doing? After thirty years they suddenly don't know you? There's your thanks. You out in the bush all those years, finding oil like you can see through rocks, Roger sitting nice and safe behind a desk. Not to mention all the abuse I take, where's my thanks?"

"They want me to transition KarLap to Bob Peterson. The change-the-negotiator routine. They think it's the best way to handle this Lazarev issue."

"Look, who understands your methods? But they've worked in the past, right? They're nuts to pull you out, that's what I say." Rod shook his head while zoomed the infrared scanner in on a suspicious shape. "Hell with 'em, then. They can do it themselves. We'll go fishing." He looked at his watch. "Jesus H. Christ. Sun's up in three hours and I've gotta get breakfast together for a dozen hung-over Russians.

Go do your Carl Sagan routine and then get some sleep. And if you go up there without a safety line I'll tell Nikolai you said he got beat by a girl."

Charlie went out the sliding glass doors at the back of the pilothouse, climbed the tower and sat in the helm chair. Thirty feet above the water, he scanned the horizon. They were cruising flat out at thirty-five knots, and already over a hundred miles out. The night was cool and clear, and there were no vessels in any direction. He leaned back and looked up at the sky.

Rod objected to introspection as a matter of principle, so he didn't care for Charlie's ritual stargazing. He picked up the habit back in the summer of '76. Toward the end of his first year of college Charlie busted his shoulder protecting home against some Texas kid who thought he could beat Mason's throw from deep center. Charlie woke up still clutching the ball but with his clavicle in pieces and the doctor said he couldn't play for two months. Never one to sit still, he tagged along with a group of grad students from the geology department headed out to the Green River Formation in Wyoming and picked rocks for the rest of the summer with one arm. That's pretty much the way it had always been for him. Growing up in East Texas in the 60s Charlie's hands always held either a rock or a baseball. His father Stan was a driller. All the action then was out in the Gulf so his father would be offshore for weeks at a time. On the rare weekends when he was home and there were no games he would take the boys up to hunt or fish around Sam Rayburn Lake. When the fish weren't biting they would drive up and down dusty back roads with the boys in the bed of the pickup and play rockhound. Charlie would fill up old cement sacks with so many fossils he could barely carry them.

When Charlie turned twelve he got his hunting license. The first morning at the lake before anyone was up he took the truck with the 30/06 and headed out to find that big hog he had been tracking since he was eight. At daybreak he surprised the old boar coming out of one of its favorite lairs. Charlie dropped him in the one spot he had found where he could drive the truck under a heavy overhanging branch. With the truck and a pulley system he had built over the summer he lifted the eight-hundred pound hog up and dropped it into the bed. When he got back to camp they were all still sleeping so he woke his dad to ask for help dressing it out.

In the evening, Stan would cook up steaks and beans while he talked about whatever play he was working. The four older brothers would half-listen as they wrestled and scrapped like roughnecks coming off a double shift. But the smallest would sit near the fire, close to his father, rapt, while the older man pirouetted on his plastic leg and taught him how to hunt for oil.

Every play has gotta have a story, Charlie. That's what our rock docs do. They come up with these stories. Like any story, you have to have all the parts, or it doesn't work. A beginning, a middle and an end, sorta like that. The story has to start with a good source rock. That's where the oil started out. Remember, oil didn't come from dinosaur jungles. That's coal. No, oil's special. Rare. Comes from tiny little sea critters that died and settled to the bottom of old shallow seas. Basins, we call 'em. Next, you cover them up with sand and mud washed down the rivers. Real quick, with no oxygen so they can't rot. That thin layer of muck becomes your source rock. Next, you have to bury it. Real deep, so the pressure warms it up, something like a hot bath. Not boiling hot, or the oil cracks to gas. Get 'er in the oil kitchen, we call it. Couple of miles deep is perfect. Cook it for a while. Fifty million years is good. And there's your oil. But hold on, that's just the beginning. Now it gets interesting. As that oil cooks, it expands. It cracks the source rock and starts to flow, like it wants to escape. Through the tiny holes between the rocks. You think rock is solid but it's not, see, it has tiny pores. Inside of which battle two mortal enemies, Charlie. Water and Oil. They won't mix. And oil is lighter, Charlie, so it climbs up over the water. Through the rocks with holes, around the rocks without. All the way to the top if it can. Where it leaks out on the ground, in a tar pit or an oil seep. Where it degrades and washes away, forgotten for all time. But, sometimes on its way up that oil hits a dead end. What we call a trap, a spot where the earth has folded and faulted just right so the oil can't flow up anymore, like if you were sitting in that tent and it just collapsed on you. That would be an anticline, Charlie. A big tent of solid cap rock on top of you. Those are easy, you can spot 'em from the surface, these hills. The old man, he used to say, 'You just find me the anticlines and drill 'em, you let God worry about putting the oil there.' Some traps are more complicated than that, but we'll leave that for when you're older. Trap, reservoir, cap. That's what we call a play, Charlie. So our rock docs have to make up stories that fit what we know about a basin. Take the facts and let your imagination go. But don't forget. Until I make hole with my good personal friend Dr. Drill, that's all it is. A story. Because there's so many things that could have gone wrong with a play, Charlie. Not enough beasties. Not hot enough. Too hot. Trap formed to late. And so on and so on. But don't get all hung up on that. You just drill. And if it's a dry hole you just drill another one. Got it? 'Course you do. You gotta good head on your shoulders, Charlie. You could be a rock doc, you know that? Hey, you other knuckleheads catch any of that? How the hell you get that hog in the truck, anyway? He'd laugh and ruffle Charlie's hair and serve up the steaks to his ravenous brothers, trying not to lose a finger in the process.

So Charlie would lie out under the Wyoming skies and stare into the bottomless well of stars, trying to wrap his mind around several hundred million years of geology. He'd see if he could imagine the formation of all the famous basins and the eons of folding and rifting and erosion. He memorized and replayed the history of famous plays, seeing it all in his mind.

When he was younger, the limitless heavens and the great expanses of time had never made him feel small, not when he could stretch his mind to swallow it all. In Yemen, Sheila would join him outside at night and they would look up into the shimmering desert skies and make secret plans. Most of Sheila's involved getting back to Houston.

But now, running through the North Atlantic at the end of his life, all he could see were lost loved ones, landlocked seas and oceans of ice, and the cold, impersonal vastness threatened to roll over him and wash him away. Life's misfortunes had stripped him of everything that made him want to keep living. His wife, his son, his reputation and success.

But still he could not stop. Each night he lay awake and exhausted, in hotel beds in Moscow and offshore bunks in the North Sea, turning, flipping, helpless, as Nature beat out a rhythm on his head like it was a drum. It was in the shape of the Niger delta he saw flying out of Port Harcourt. In the pattern of city lights across Europe. In the sizes of moon craters on clear nights. In records of earthquake activity in the North Atlantic. And in the size of oil fields in any basin around the world. The same pattern. The tracks of a beast. Somewhere out there in the dark. Hidden. And he was the hunter. That's all he was now. Not husband, not father, and soon not even colleague. There was nothing left for him but this hunt.

On the outside men appear mostly average. Measure their various heights and weights, the length of their index fingers or their hundred-yard dash times, and the results huddle about the mean. The distribution mirrors that observed whenever several randomly distributed factors are added together. Three plus three plus three equals nine. Then two plus four plus zero equals six. Repeat it enough times and you will see the familiar bell curve.

But measure their incomes and an entirely different pattern emerges. The distribution is shifted. Towards the high end. Twenty percent of the people made eighty percent of the money. Because it is easier to make a million dollars if you start with a million dollars. This is the world of proportionate effects. Where it takes money to make money. Where the young are drawn to large cities not small ones. Where three times three times three is not nine but twenty-seven. And two times four times zero is not six but zero. Man might rise by hard work or even luck, but whether it was one or the other it didn't really matter, he had a much better chance of continuing to rise than someone who hadn't quite made it to his level yet. This is the world where success begets greater success and any failure is punished mercilessly. This is the world of giants.

The Italian economist Pareto saw the pattern first, in historical data on income distribution, everything from rents in Paris to income taxes in London. He attributed the extremes to a special class of man, providing the philosophical underpinnings for Mussolini's Fascism. The American linguist George Zipf observed the pattern in the frequency with which each word is used in the English language. Playing with this data, he observed an elegant pattern. Take any reasonably sized book and use it to make a chart. Count how many times each word in the book is used. Draw a bar of a height that shows the number of times the most frequently used word appears in the book. Just to the right of that bar draw another that shows how often the second most frequently used word appears. Do this for about the top ten or so. Now, compare the heights of the bars. What Zipf noticed, and so the observation is now called Zipf's law, is that the second bar, for the second 'ranked' word, is half the height of the first. And the bar for the third-ranked bar is one-third the height of the first. And the fourth is one-fourth the height of the first. And so on. You could try it for any book, the result is the same. Another way to show this relationship is to divide the height of each bar by its 'rank.' The new bars should all be the same height.

Pareto and Zipf failed to make the broader connection, and so their explanations for a time remained unique to their realms. But then it was observed in the size of moon craters, and forest fires, and cities, and river tributaries. And the size of oil fields. In fact, the pattern would emerge any time factors combine in a multiplicative way, even if completely random factors were added in. With a pencil and paper and a little knowledge of calculus you could prove it yourself, for large enough numbers. The patterns are quite prevalent in nature, particularly geological features. Chemical systems are well-known to exhibit proportionate effects. Double the heat and a chemical reaction runs four times as fast, not two. And Nature, with her chemistry, produced oil.

And the world of oil was indeed dominated by giants. Fifty fields, out of fifty thousand, held nearly half the oil ever discovered. With over five billion barrels each, they were referred to as the supergiants. If you wanted to satisfy the world's oil needs, small fields weren't the answer. Too little, too late. You needed giants.

Funny thing is, make a bar chart showing the sizes of the biggest oil fields in the world. Start with the biggest, Ghawar at 82 billion barrels. Then add Burgan at 50 billion barrels. Safaniya at 36 billion barrels. Then Cantarell. Bolivar. Samotlor. Do the top twenty or so, all the way through Ahwaz at 10 billion barrels. It looks like the right curve. But then divide the height of each bar by its rank. The curve is not flat. It curves down on the left. If I were Zipf, I'd say the largest fields are too small. What if we add two large fields at the top? Say Texso #1 at 200 billion barrels and Texso #2 at 100 billion barrels.

Flat.

This was the thought exercise that Charlie had shared with Lazarev in Mauritius. This was the dream that had haunted him for over twenty years. To the Fascists, Zipf's law sanctioned the exercise of power by the privileged few over the wretched masses. To Charlie, it meant that if by virtue of hard work and good fortune you were in the position to do something special you owed it to everyone to take your best shot.

And if he didn't do it, he had a bad feeling no one ever would.

The end of oil was near, no one had to tell Charlie that. He lived it every day. Alternatives were coming, thank God, but they were nowhere near ready. They couldn't replace oil. Expecting solar or wind to take over now would be like expecting your one-year old to ride a two-wheeler. There you go, just pedal! Harder! You know how that would end. The world needed more time. It needed more oil.

So for years, Charlie continued his hunt. A hard slog through lands torn by cruelty, war and suffering. But now in his darker moments he heard whispers of despair. That it was over. That everyone knew it but him. That although the math showed the odds of going

completely to zero were infinitesimal, you would might get so close
that the chance of recovering was infinitesimal, too. Some mistake,
some shortcoming, some terrible tragedy that took you so close to
zero that you never came back. Not enough to matter, anyhow. You
just limped along. A shell of your former self. Thinking you were
alive, but really just a ghost. Like he had died back in Yemen and this
was all just a dream.

He glimpsed flashes over his head, so he spun around. High
in the north were shimmering curtains of light. Strong solar winds
breaking in brilliant splashes on high magnetic beaches. At the little
shop in the Arctic and Antarctic Institute, he had picked up a small
volume of works by Mikhail Vasilyevich Lomonosov. He enjoyed it so
much he had his assistant Vicki buy their entire stock so he could give
them away. Born in the far north, with singular talents and desire, in a
land being left behind by the Enlightenment, Lomonosov had willed
himself to become one of the intellectual giants of his age. He had
predicted the discovery of the Antarctic land mass by merely observ-
ing the form of southern icebergs, to his eye formed on land not sea,
but the insoluble mystery of the auroras had compelled him to contemplate the limits of man and even his God. *A tiny glint in endless ice,
so I am lost in this abyss, oppressed by thoughts profound. How can it be, fire
from winter's depths, where oily darkness battles water? Tell us, how enormous
is the world? Are thou aware of all creation's end?*

From beneath the aurora came the sound of voices, sharp and Russian.
Helen of Troy had nothing on Olivia, thought Charlie. Leaning over,
he could see Neftepolk on the aft deck. The only face he could see
clearly was Vasiliy's, because he was being held back against the transom, his terrified features appearing as some ghastly image projected
by the cabin light. Vasiliy was pleading hysterically, first to one, then
the other, in a wild torrent of different tactics and tones. His pleas
brought only shouts and shoves, and with a final, angry push he was
flung off the back of the speeding boat. After a brief flash of arms and
legs against the white wake, he was lost in the darkness.

Charlie flew down the ladder, yelling man overboard into the pilothouse. Then he dropped down the second ladder into the middle of the Russians. Rod had cut the throttles and they were slowing to a stop, pitching fore and aft as the boat fell off its plane, the engines idling. Nikolai was facing the stern, head down and arms splayed out on the transom. "Not on my boat, not on this boat," Charlie yelled. Nikolai whipped around and pulled a pistol from his waistband and pointed it at Charlie. "Who are you to make our decisions? You know nothing. You understand nothing." Charlie could hear Vasiliy begging for his life far across the water, screaming desperate acts of contrition. Charlie called up to the pilothouse. "Back it down!"

With a low roar the *Final Play* charged backwards and they were all thrown forward and the cold sea came crashing over the stern. On his knees, one arm clutching the back of the transom, Nikolai pointed the gun at Charlie and tried to scream over the engines. Charlie understood everything but the words.

The engines cut out and Rod had the spotlight up, no doubt looking for something he had spotted on the infrared. Instinctively the men in the cockpit followed its beam. But they heard his cries again before they saw him.

A gun blasted in Charlie's ear. He covered it too late as he spun around towards the source. Beardless Aleksei stood on deck with his eyes closed, gripping the pistol with two hands. He fired twice more.

The beam finally found its target. Thirty meters or so off to starboard. Something in the water. No more cries.

Charlie climbed up to the pilothouse. Rod had one hand on the wheel and in the other held the radio handset, but it just hung at his side. Charlie took the handset and put it back in its bracket. Then he leaned in and spoke quietly into Rod's ear, and for several long minutes they huddled together, the *Final Play* holding still in the water. Then they resumed their original course heading south.

Charlie peered deep underground into layers of multi-colored rock. A series of crazy rainbow cakes with faults and arches and domes and reefs that spun and twirled and exploded into pieces that spun and twirled again. Gabon, Malaysia, Paraguay, Burma, Sri Lanka, Uganda, Greenland. Play after play after play. Searching for a giant.

Nothing.

He woke with a start and ripped off the goggles. He was on the couch in the pilothouse. The boat was stopped. He was cold and drenched in sweat. The skies were light and he could hear activity below. He went down to the cabin and found Ryan restoring order in the galley. "Still some coffee, but they ate everything else. Let me see if I can find something for you."

"Olivia?" Ryan didn't look at Charlie, just jerked a thumb towards the bow. Rod and Jeff were eating at the table on the aft deck, and Charlie took his coffee out to join them. The morning was mild but cool and they were enshrouded in fog. They appeared to be nowhere at all. Four of the soldiers had light rods and reels and were fishing over the side.

"This must be the right place, found a school of skipjack bigger than one of Wayne's ranches," said Rod. "I've got them fishing for bait. Thought it was best to keep your little jackals busy."

Charlie frowned and took a sip of his coffee. "Nice visibility, Skipper."

"Water is warm, as you ordered, but the air is cool so we're getting this steam-pot fog. It'll burn off by mid-morning. We'll get us underway and start running the bathy." The *Final Play* had high definition sonar that could generate a three-dimensional digital model of the seafloor with enough passes.

Nikolai was in the fighting chair, staring into the fog. Charlie walked down and stood behind him. Nikolai turned to look at Charlie.

"You want to know. You wonder, how can they do this?"

"No, not really. You overestimate yourself. It's not that complicated." Charlie tossed the rest of his coffee over the side and turned to the tackle center at the back of the cockpit.

As Charlie started to pull tackle out of the lockers, Rod yelled down to stow the rods and they started to make their survey at ten knots. Charlie felt eyes on the back of his head. When he turned the Spetsnaz were watching him, so he put them to work checking the terminal tackle.

Nearly any billfish you are likely to find can be boated with medium-weight tackle grabbed right out of the locker. But a marlin that can rip five hundred yards of 130 pound mono through the water at twenty-five knots like it wasn't even hooked, stripping line so fast the deckhand has to douse you and your smoking reel with water, this marlin will find that nearly invisible nick where your line got caught on the stern cleat last week and snap it, right there. Given the improbable combination of skill and luck required to raise such a fish, and their modest expectations of success if they did, most anglers don't bother preparing for the possibility. But that was not Charlie's nature. And today he was hunting a giant.

The Russians were quick learners. Arkady found a leader worn at one end so Charlie showed him how to cut it down and recrimp it. They looked over the last thirty feet of line on each reel. Bearded Aleksei found one that was quite worn, so Charlie had him strip off fifty feet and then showed him how to retie it. They made sure of the gaffs, one flying, two straight and one hand, taking off the tennis balls on the tips and making sure the points were sharp. The regular gaffs had six-inch hooks on six-foot poles. The flying gaff had an eight-inch hook that would detach from the pole and remain connected to the boat with a strong, thirty-foot line that they tied to the pedestal of the fighting chair. Charlie took a small folding knife with a plastic handle from the locker and tied it around his neck with eight-pound mono, so it hung where he could reach it quickly and slid a pair of wire cutters into a leather sheath onto his belt. They laughed at the size of his knife and at Kirill's comments which Charlie couldn't understand but could guess.

Finally, he picked the starting lure spread and laid them out. An Azores-type group, for big marlin. Four sliced face lures, one concave. Good mix of bubble trails. Yakov picked up each of the lures and examined them closely, flicking them back and forth in his hand. Charlie would have been challenged to explain the whimsical paint schemes. Marlins were aggressive fish that responded to the bubble trail, but no one knew whether they could even identify color.

Olivia came out on to the deck, looking fresh and ready for battle. She had her hair back in a ponytail under a ballcap and wore dark sunglasses, a black neoprene vest, tight shorts and leather fingerless gloves. She smiled good morning to Charlie and rechecked the gaffs, drawing blood on a finger which she sucked on as she smiled at the men, who appeared well on their way to more foolishness.

"I expect you to surprise me, Charlie, but then I am still always surprised." Lazarev stood at the top of the stairs, his hands in the pockets of the foul weather jacket from the locker in the master state-room. He nodded over Charlie's head into the distance.

"If I bored you, then where would I be?" said Charlie.

As Lazarev lit a cigarette, Charlie turned around. Visibility had improved and through a break in the fog they could see the heavy lift ship *Blue Marlin*, carrying on its low, submersible decks the Arctic drillship, *Texso Arktika*. The massive ship and its cargo, nearly a quarter-mile stem to stern and displacing over three million tons, sat in the water a thousand yards away, not making a sound.

"So Texso can build an ice-class rig in fourteen months, while ours is still in dry dock after five years, is that the message? Expensive to stop a ship like that, Charlie, what's the day rate?" asked Lazarev.

"Officially it hasn't stopped, just slowed way down, but you don't have to mention it to anyone. But no business today, Oleg Maksimovich, just fishing. And this morning its only purpose in life is to help us fish."

"What would the devil be without his schemes?" said Lazarev. "Okay, tempt me with the kingdoms of the world, Charlie, and let's see how you do."

"I do have something to show you," said Charlie, as he led the way up to the pilothouse.

"We've been building a bathymetric chart with the sonar. Take a look." On one of the screens was a fine, full-color 3-D image of the seafloor, showing a flat plain rising into a rounded peak, with one slumping shoulder. A stylistic image of a boat marked the spot of the *Final Play*, as well as the *Blue Marlin*, directly above the peak.

"This," said Charlie, pointing at the peak, "is the Shtokman Seamount. It rises three thousand meters above the abyssal plain, peaking just three hundred meters below the surface, right beneath the *Blue Marlin*. The North Atlantic Drift, trending northwesterly here, hits the seamount and forces the deep waters, which are cool but rich in nutrients, up into the warm surface waters. This supercharges the growth of sea life, starting with plankton and going right up to the top of the food chain to the pelagics—tuna, dolphin fish and the big billfish. Sailfish, swordfish and marlin. A good place to hunt."

"A Russian hunting ground," said Lazarev smugly. "That is one of the seamounts surveyed by the Pleskov Marine Expedition. With submersibles from the Arctic and Antarctic Institute. Alexandrov told you about this?" He frowned. "And the drillship? So we are drilling for marlin?"

"Fish gather around floating objects in the open ocean, even a palm frond or a coconut. In Hawaii they anchor steel buoys offshore to gather marlin. A fish aggregation device, or FAD, to be technical. Like a coffee shop for fish. We heard about a boat fishing around a drillship off Ghana that hooked up eight marlin in six hours. This is our super-FAD. It's also the helipad for your trip back and a fueling station for the *Final Play*."

"Okay, okay, Charlie," said Lazarev. "Lot of work. Let's see if it was worth it."

"Well then," said Rod. "Let's get some lines wet."

They got underway. The crew set a five lure pattern with a stinger off the bridge deep, lures on the corners on the face of the second and third waves, and off the riggers on the fifth and seventh waves.

And then nothing. Mildly hungover, tired and trolling back and forth on the rolling seas, in warming weather, nearly everyone struggled to stay awake. Lazarev huddled up on the second deck alone, poring over the courtesy copy of Lomonosov Charlie left in his cabin. But up in the sky bridge Rod, as always on a hunt, was consumed. He monitored the sea, the fish finders, the surface temperatures and the positioning system, cross-referencing it against the digital bathy to set their course and speed. He blasted the sonar on the sound system, scrutinizing every ping like a demanding, maniacal conductor. Charlie felt he was on a WWII submarine, hunted by destroyers, their sonar relentlessly pinging him, waiting for the depth charge to explode in his ear. Charlie would have asked Rod to turn it down but he knew the answer. For over two hours they crisscrossed the seas.

On the down current side from the *Blue Marlin* they had a very large return off the sonar, but they traversed the area several times with no success. "Sunken debris or a whale or a big frozen marlin" was Rod's final analysis.

Charlie sat in the fighting chair with his eyes fixed on the water as he tried to guess what Lazarev was thinking. He had likely delivered his message and was ready to go. Watching Charlie fail was enjoyable, but how long was needed to prove the point? Apparently about two hours, as Lazarev walked into the cockpit.

"Sometimes schemes are only that," said Lazarev. "You are not so lucky anymore, Charlie. All used up?"

"Some time ago, I think."

"Vasiliy's sister has been missing two weeks. He does not tell us, we must find this out ourselves. He says he does not know what happened to her. If he had told us then, we might believe. But he does not, so there is only one explanation. He was forced into a great betrayal. We will find the FSB svolochi that are holding her and avenge both Vasiliy and his sister."

"I'm sure he'll appreciate that," said Charlie.

Lazarev was polite when he held the winning hand. "Now we should return. Thank you for the invitation, Charlie. It was good for us to meet. Perhaps we will see you later this week?"

"Sure. Let me get on the radio, get you home."

Charlie climbed the ladder to the pilothouse.

"Okay, Skip, what's Plan B?" said Charlie.

"I would say the Antarctic. Could just be the wrong pole."

"How about slow-trolling bait? Maybe they just aren't as aggressive in northern waters. Adaptation to the cold? Let's put those skipjack out."

"Oh sure, why not? I hear walrus will hit on skipjack," said Rod.

Charlie went back down to the deck. "They're swapping out a part on the helo. They need a couple more hours. Why don't we try something different? Just to pass the time." Lazarev scowled.

Charlie put the Neftepolk to work switching out the lures for the bait. With the overwhelming success of artificial lures, fishing for marlin with live bait was becoming a lost art. You could troll faster and cover more ground with artificial. Using live bait was expressing great confidence in your target area. It was not straightforward to rig the bait, but the Russians mastered it quickly and they had their spread in the water in twenty minutes. Three lines this time. Two on the outriggers, one at fifty meters and the other at a hundred meters. Then one down deep off the transom with a downrigger. By the time they had the pattern set, Lazarev was gone.

They got underway again, trolling slower at only four to six knots. Rod had given up on his sonar and the pinging had blessedly stopped. With the silence and the slow speeds and returning warmth the Russians and the crew were dropping like flies and lay sleeping everywhere. Charlie watched the lines.

The transom reel started to scream and suddenly they were all on fast forward. From the sky bridge Rod was yelling hook up, hook up, hook up. Ryan, Jeff and Olivia jumped to their feet and started to clear the other lines. Arkady leaped into the fighting chair and buckled in.

How the rod is to be handled is always discussed beforehand, because to qualify for an international record only one angler can touch the equipment. Earlier, Charlie felt obligated to raise it with Arkady

and Yakov and they had laughed. Apparently the strict individual-
ism of the IGFA was a distinctly non-Russian concept. They discussed
it with Lazarev and returned with the decision that this would be a
Russian team effort resulting in a Russian record. Arkady and then
Yakov would tire the fish for Lazarev to land.

Yakov lifted the rod, set it in the chair's butt holder. The line
was ripping off the reel with the high pitched whine of a motorbike.
Charlie heard the engines throttle up as Rod set the hook. There
was no jump. If it were a marlin, often as not it would jump and tail
dance, trying to shake the hook. But nothing.

The fish made a huge arc around to the port side of the boat.
It was very fast. If not a marlin, a large mako? They were already in
danger of getting spooled. Rod accelerated and tried to get out front
of the fish. The line started to peel off more slowly. Then it stopped
and Charlie coached Arkady to take in line. He furiously worked the
reel and started to bring it in. Arkady had made a few dozen turns
when the fish started to arc to the starboard side of the boat and
again the reel started to scream. Out of the corner of his eye, Charlie
could see that Lazarev had come out of his cabin and was standing
on the steps.

On the fish finder Rod noticed a school of bait coming in and the
line started to dash back and forth. "Gentlemen, I don't think she
even knows she's been hooked," yelled Rod. "She's feeding."

And so it went for thirty minutes, until Arkady and Yakov switched
places.

Showing his inexperience, Yakov apparently decided he was going
to make a bit more progress on the fish. He started reeling in on the
fish aggressively, jerking the line. This got a response, as the fish ripped
off twice the amount of line again and Rod had to play catch up.

After another thirty minutes, they had made no progress and
Lazarev tapped Yakov's shoulder and spoke to him in Russian. With
great deference, Yakov swept out of the chair and helped Lazarev in,
as Arkady held the rod. Lazarev settled into the chair as two more
soldiers came forward to strap him in.

As Lazarev sat in the chair, the line stopped running. He spoke again in Russian, in low, soothing tones. Praying. An incantation. To the fish? In any event, it kept coming back in and Lazarev was winding up many turns with less effort. He was visibly pleased with himself and not even breathing hard.

"Charlie, why am I not surprised you were able to turn up something?"

"We don't have anything yet," said Charlie.

"If Firebird is important to the US government, Charlie, have them come and tell me why we should reconsider. Otherwise, you can just go home. If they do come, don't waste my time. Bring Dickinson. He understands what happened in the elections." Tom Dickinson, the US Vice President. His office was very hawkish on the siloviki. Lazarev continued to reel in line, much too easily. "One question, Charlie. It occurred to me this morning, when we had all that time. Why all the way to this seamount? We must have passed dozens during the night."

"It's not just the seamount, it's the iron. That's what really catalyzes the plankton growth. They found a deposit of magnetite-apatite ore on the seafloor, at the southeast base."

"Here? That ore is only found in Kola."

"It's not a natural deposit. It's from a wreck."

"A wreck? A Russian wreck?"

"American. WWII. Coming back from the Murmansk run. She was carrying the ore for ballast."

"Where? Down there? Dead Americans?"

"Right down there. The *Tesso Port Arthur*. Sunk by U-125, September 1942. Sixty-five perished, three survivors."

Lazarev turned and stared at Charlie in horror. "You bring me to fish in a graveyard? A graveyard with unclean souls?"

Charlie shook his head. "Americans that died hauling aviation fuel to Russia. Pretty clean, I'd say."

"No, no, we should not be here. You are the worst kind of devil, Charlie. Marshall every demon you can find, Charlie, you shall still not have it. I will make sure of that."

The fish was coming in fast. The crew started preparing to boat it. The quick turn of events had caught everyone by surprise. Ryan stood with a straight gaff off the port corner of the chair, low. Olivia and Jeff both wore gloves and stood ready to grab the wire leader when it got close, Olivia in the starboard corner of the stern and Jeff in the port.

Lazarev was still winding up the line, but he had clearly lost his enthusiasm and was muttering to himself in Russian. "Just keep reeling, Oleg Maksimovich," said Charlie. They were using wind-on leaders, with no swivel, so Lazarev wouldn't have to stop when he went from mono to the last thirty feet of wire, he could just keep reeling. Safer, as it prevented loose leader from collecting in the cockpit and tangling. "Just keep reeling, even after you hit wire, and Jeff or Olivia will grab the wire when we get close."

The fish was going to be too green. It was safer to gaff a tired fish. The last thing Charlie wanted was a fresh thousand-pound marlin or mako thrashing at the stern. Suddenly Lazarev hit wire. In a flash Olivia had the leader in her hands and started pulling it in hand over hand.

"Bring hell itself to your side, and I will stop you. You will never have it. The Arctic belongs to Russia. Everything you find, you understand? It belongs to us. There is no other way. You will not have it." He stopped winding and stared into the water. "Bring on your demons, Charlie. Paashol v'chorte!" He threw the rod down and started to unbuckle himself.

From the deeps below came a very large, dark shape, following Olivia's lead and slowly undulating up to the boat. Not being dragged, but swimming up. Olivia worked as fast as she could and loose leader spooled haphazardly into the cockpit. Though Charlie knew you couldn't be certain of estimating lengths underwater, he could only think that the shape was nearly twice as long as the cockpit was wide. Over thirty feet. The size of a small submarine.

As it came up to the surface it began to slowly roll over away from the boat. It was shaped like a tuna, with a rounded body, a massive oval. But as its sides caught the morning sun, the long shimmers of blue and yellow and pink, and the large sail and pectoral and anal fins were unmistakable. This was a blue marlin. A big, fat blue, with a belly so large it had the rounded look of a tuna rather than the torpedo shape of a marlin. It looked big, fat and languorous. Closer to two tons than one. And old. As old as Charlie, most likely. Its bill was longer than a man and notched and twisted like a walking stick. And one dark, unblinking eye, as large as a dinner plate, staring at them. An eye full of silent awe and terror, from years of staring down into the abyss.

Charlie stared right back. Giant, meet stone.

"Vodyanoy!" Lazarev ran screaming towards the fish with the priest held high. His men fell to the either side until he was blocked only by Olivia. Casting her aside, he reached far over the boat and swung down hard with the leaded bat. Charlie managed to grab Lazarev's belt as the priest hit home with a dull thud.

The water exploded with tons of enraged marlin thrashing back and forth at the stern as Charlie yanked Lazarev back into the cockpit. The fish was up high, blocking out the sun. Charlie saw golden hair whipped around in a fury as Olivia swung the flying gaff into the dark shape. Followed by a booming plunge into the water, a jerk that shook the whole boat, and a scream.

Olivia had hit home with the gaff and the fish was now at the other end of the line, pulling the *Final Play* backward. But pinned under the rope, against the stern and shrieking, was Yakov. The line was across his midsection and he was being severed in two.

"Man overboard!" Ryan was pointing into the water. Charlie was up and leaning over the transom. Jeff had gotten tangled in the loose leader and had been dragged over by the marlin, temporarily stopped only by the gaff line.

"Give me your knife!" Lazarev yelled at Charlie. Far under the water Charlie saw the wavy image of a young man, his arms reaching up. Lazarev reached over and ripped the knife off Charlie's neck. He opened it and started sawing the gaff line.

As Yakov howled, Charlie grabbed the mono and worked hand over hand to the leader which he yanked up under his belt. He took two quick wraps around his hand then heard the last threads of the gaff line shred and snap and Charlie was yanked off the boat and slammed into the water and blasted off across the void.

He felt the impact, then the cold, then the taste of salt, then with his whole body the deep sounds of the engines and the water rushing past him as he was dragged hard and fast. The power of the fish was beyond his imagination, like he was tied to the bumper of a rolling semi. The water became colder and darker as the fish dragged them both rapidly down to hell. He prayed, not for himself but for the boy, hoping that he had been right, that dragging four hundred pounds through the water would break the tackle or force the fish to stop.

And he was right. Deep into the numbing cold, where light gave way to darkness, Charlie climbed hand over hand up the leader, to a foot. He grabbed his wire cutters and cut the foot free. Then he grabbed the boy by the collar and kicked up, dragging him towards the light.

CHAPTER 3

SNOW MAIDEN

Sredny Island
Thursday morning

As the Antonov An-74 descended to the melting ice runway through a fifteen-knot crosswind, Avinashi Sharma shut her eyes and listened dutifully to Maggie Thatcher on her headphones, her small gloved hands locked onto the seat rests. She wore the gloves, along with two insulating layers under her KarLap parka and wind pants, because she was always cold at Sredny, even in August. Avinashi was embarrassed by this, but not surprised. After all, she weighed one hundred pounds with her gear on and prior to joining Texso had never been further north than London.

From her last peek out the window, it appeared that they would be landing sideways, nose up into the wind. But with a quick, gut-wrenching turn back to the runway and an assist from the forgivingly slick surface, the Russian pilot skillfully slid the small jet home. But the knot in Avinashi's stomach only twisted tighter as her phone immediately began vibrating, repeatedly. Two thousand miles from Moscow, a thousand miles beyond the inescapably remote labor camps of the Gulag, Avinashi was easier to track down at the airfield with its satellite-linked cell site than she was back in Houston.

Stiffened by the Iron Lady's insistence that Avinashi not go wobbly, she forced her eyes to open and scrolled stoically through the messages streaming in. Multiple emails from Sredny base detailing the continuing, endlessly varying aircraft issues. Something from her aunt about a bear. And dozens of others, the only consistent theme being cock-ups for which everyone assumed she was somehow responsible. *Can you do your job Ms. Sharma? Let's discuss. Rupert.*

Charlie had woken her in one of the few dark hours of her Tuesday night to tell her of his decision to begin the final phase of KarLap's Project Firebird, immediately. She was in Yakutsk, recently but already deeply asleep at the modern Polar Star Hotel, in one of its new, armored rooms. The safest, most peaceful room in the city she had been informed by the proud desk clerk. She was fully dressed, having collapsed onto her bed minutes earlier after a late dinner of baked foal ribs and as little vodka as she could manage with aides to the President of the Sakha Republic, to commemorate their agreement in principle regarding appropriate taxes, fees and KarLap-funded capital improvements arising from KarLap's nominal but politically required use of the airport in Tiksi.

Working in over half of the world's time zones concurrently, Avinashi's sleep since the launch of Firebird in April consisted mostly of those rare and brief moments between conference calls and meetings, whether that was sitting on an airplane, face down on a desk, or lying down in an armored room. The decreasing sleep quality seemed to coincide with the increasingly vivid visits from her mother and the former British Prime Minister. But when Charlie rang from his boat in Reykjavik, she dutifully and groggily grabbed her notebook from her mother's soft leather case, which together with the dog-eared, marked up biography of Dame Thatcher were the only items she had to remember her by, and made a list with him of the urgent action items. All manageable. With one exception.

"Well, we'll have to skip the stakeholder visit," she said. "Unfortunate."

"We can't skip it. Part of the PSA."

"Charlie, there won't be time."

"You'll get it done. I have complete faith in you."

The latest in her series of assigned Herculean tasks, the stakeholder visit would involve collecting a representative from each major critic of the Firebird Project, together with a friendly or two for optics, and providing them with a tour of the operations and thereby gain their implied consent. Oh, and because the clear intention was to allow them to see the actual deployment, she should really do it by Thursday. Theoretically they could be finished by then, if all went according to plan. Charlie assured her that there were no style points available for this one, they just needed to tick the box. Get the word out, collect as many as you can, get them up to Sredny and give them the cook's tour, answer their questions politely and return them with home with no major incident. If they couldn't make it, well then fine, they had asked and they would get them up there later after the big show. Fortunately, she could do it in her sleep, he laughed, before he thanked her and hung up.

Furious, she whipped the phone across the room. It penetrated the cheap drywall and would have gone into the next room if not for the steel. She watched the handset bounce on the cord which hung out of the hole. Her explosive anger surprised her. She wasn't like this before Russia. So tired, she thought, as she tipped over and fell asleep before her head hit the bed.

Over the course of an exceptionally long Wednesday, Avinashi had managed to gather at Khatanga for the early Thursday flight to Sredny one senior Russian oil bureaucrat, one German lobbyist, two environmentalists, two journalists, one representative of the indigenous peoples and one very junior member of the US embassy in Moscow who had somehow gotten wind of the trip, together with their collective attendants and staff, fifteen in total. Invariably Avinashi met with withering but justifiable criticism for the ridiculously short notice, but Firebird was the most significant event in the petroleum industry since Iraq invaded Kuwait, so for the most part her guests just grumbled and rushed out the door to catch their flights. The only ones unable to join were a Russian legislator gone missing in the wake of an agency reshuffle and a junior minister from the Russian

Ministry of Energy who laughed coldly at the invitation and wished her a good trip.

"What an incredible landing, and you do this all the time," said Flannery Ayers, the fresh-faced, eager young woman from the consulate. "You're amazing." Since arriving in Khatanga, Flannery had seized upon Avinashi as a kindred spirit, another young woman making her name in global affairs, albeit with a mercenary multinational rather than Flannery's high-minded State Department, but still. Sisters, practically. She had grabbed the seat across the aisle from Avinashi at the rear of the cabin and chattered nonstop from Khatanga, causing the Norwegians in front of her to periodically interrupt their healthy snacking to turn and glare, to no avail.

"It's not always quite so exciting," said Avinashi, forcing a smile. "Excuse me, time to play tour guide."

As the plane taxied, Avinashi unbuckled and made her way to the front of the cabin. As she passed the Norwegians, she nodded with a smile and a quiet but suitably jubilant '*we're here.*' Finn Jensen, the older but extremely fit founder of the environmental group Terra Mater, and Marcus, his tall, fashionably messy-haired intern, nodded back grimly, maintaining the strict tone of disapproval they had displayed since arriving in Khatanga in their well-worn, high-end polar expedition gear. They had declined the complimentary KarLap parkas.

In front of the Norwegians sat a young, dark-haired man reorganizing his carry-on. Denis Federov, head of Taymyr Environment Watch based in Dudinka. Federov's group was one of those that spontaneously launched upon the announcement of any major foreign energy project in Russia, a homegrown, grassroots watchdog that tirelessly represented local workers and residents. It was widely accepted that the real reason behind the group's founding, and the reason for its alleged financial support from the Kremlin, was to bring information to light that could provide leverage to the Russian authorities whenever they needed to make a point with their foreign partners. Among the various items on his tray was an open jar filled to the brim with a dark liquid.

"How about I dispose of that for you Mr. Federov?" asked Avinashi, as she deftly swept up the container. A quick sniff revealed it to be West Siberian crude, a favorite photo prop for the environmentalists. A splash here and there always added just the right element of corporate greed to your nature photos.

"Hey, I need that," said Federov.

"We'll keep it safe," said Avinashi, continuing down the aisle. "Was there a lid? Never mind, I'll have it for you when we get back."

"Safely in, Chancellor," said Avinashi, smiling to her next guest, her only friendly after the two no-shows, and the only one to accept a KarLap parka, which he now wore over his suit jacket and pants, sans tie. Ex-Chancellor of Germany Claus Huber and his group had staked out the seats ahead of Avinashi, including a buffer row behind the Chancellor where his two assistants had laid their coats. Eight years out of office, Huber was putting his name and considerable influence to work on behalf of KarLap, in exchange for very substantial compensation, to persuade his former constituents and their EU brothers and sisters to fund and commit their energy futures to new natural gas pipelines stretching even further into the Russian Arctic. In addition to his assistants, a handsome and serious young man and woman, Huber had also brought his own photographer, when Avinashi to his surprise had informed him that KarLap did not intend to provide one.

"Excellent, Ms. Sharma, very good," said Huber, raising his head briefly from his papers and peering at her over his reading glasses before going back to his work.

Tubyaku Porbin, a quiet Nganasan and the representative of the Association of the Native Peoples of the Taymyr Peninsula, meaning the Dolgans, the Nenets, the Enets, the Nganasans of course and some scattered Evenks, sat with his usual air of resignation. He blinked and twitched at Avinashi as she went by offering a quick smile, which may have been connected to the open plastic bag on his tray which contained a knotty, root-like substance.

Sprawled out in the seat in front of the Huber crew, sleeping with one hand on a large canvas bag with leather straps, his head tipped back and mouth open as if at a badly needed dental visit, was Ivan Petrov, a standoffish reporter for a small Russian language trade journal, *Rodina Neftegaz*. Motherland Oil & Gas. The worst journalist she could imagine, he asked no questions, took no notes and had the deadest eyes she had ever seen, like two small forms of poured concrete.

Across the aisle from Petrov, occupying most of two seats, was the astonishingly large bodyguard for one of her guests, who had introduced him only as Duman. Turkish, Avinashi believed. She smiled at him as she went past and he nodded back without expression from behind dark glasses. Several sizes too large for any of her KarLap parkas, he wore just the leather jacket he had brought with him.

Reaching the end of the aisle, with the brightest smile she could muster, she turned to face her guests. To her dismay, she found that between her modest height and the high seatbacks she could not see past the first row. On her right sat an elderly, weathered man with a small, pointed face, her guest of honor, First Deputy Minister Yuri Telnov of the Russian Ministry of Natural Resources. His two sullen staff members sat across from him on the left.

Sitting next to Telnov on the window, in her usual seat next to an influential oilman, leaning in close on his shoulder and whispering, was Shirin Yazdani, a tall, imperious beauty and the publisher of the National Petroleum Report, the most influential, high-priced newsletter in the global oil & gas industry. Seeing Avinashi, they abruptly stopped their hushed conversation to stare at her.

With her one free hand, Avinashi snatched the microphone off of the bulkhead. "Welcome to Sredny Island, part of the last archipelago discovered on Earth and the aviation hub for KarLap's Project Firebird. For your own safety…"

Sredny Island was covered year-round by ice, and so its airstrip was also ice. But when properly prepared and reasonably dry, an ice runway can offer traction comparable to concrete. Which is how the pilot turned the plane abruptly right towards the fueling station, tossing Avinashi over into Telnov's seat, and in turn tossing Federov's crude all over Shirin's brilliant white parka. Caught in Telnov's bony arms, Avinashi stared aghast at her Pollock-like masterpiece. Behind her a camera shutter clicked repeatedly.

"Zhizn' ebet meya!" shouted Avinashi, channeling her mother, or at least that privately profane side of her, who would sharply spit out this Russianized Indian phrase when she felt, truly, that 'life is fucking me.' Still processing the twin shocks her of spill and her profanity, Avinashi was picked up by a pair of incredibly strong hands and propped back upright in the aisle like an errant chess piece.

"Duman, thank you," said Shirin, as the large Turk sat back in his seats.

"I am so sorry, Ms. Yazdani, let me try to clean your jacket," said Avinashi.

"Don't bother, it is ruined. Just a towel, please. But you work for Charlie, don't you? Just tell Mr. Joiner he owes me dinner then, will you, someplace nice? Yuri Markovich, are you quite alright?"

"That would have earned you a bullet when I was your age, Ms. Sharma," said Telnov, in deep, gravelly Russian. He accosted her with small, pitiless eyes. "Or something worse. There is always something worse."

"Apologies, Deputy Minister, usually a bit more steady, I assure you."

"Your Russian seems quite authentic, Ms. Sharma, where did you learn?" said Shirin, as she carefully peeled off her oily parka.

"Thank you, from my mother," said Avinashi. "But no, I mean, not that of course." Change tack. "She was in the Indian foreign service, a Russian speaker, before she married. She taught me at home." And then in West Siberia. For a too-brief time in Nizhnevartovsk, until she passed away.

"Where in India are you from?"

"Houston, actually. My father came over to work for an independent before I was born."

"I see. Well, good for you. Charlie is lucky to have you. And yes, I will take one of your complimentary parkas now, thank you."

And then Yazdani closed the matter by murmuring again into Telnov's ear.

Avinashi retrieved the microphone from where she had left it dangling at the end of its cord. "Our CEO Rupert Green is on hand to welcome you personally, and we also have refreshments for you after your flight. Then we will head directly to the cargo jets so that you can witness the exciting deployment of our Firebird technology."

As usual, the pilots stayed unhelpfully in the cockpit, so Avinashi wrestled with the door herself until Duman stepped in and opened it for her. She pulled on her hood, zipped up her parka and stepped down onto the slick ice. The skies were overcast and the air felt very cold, although it was only two degrees Celsius according to the large display on the hangar.

Sredny was a small, narrow island in the western part of Severnaya Zemlya, or *Northern Land,* a large archipelago off the northernmost tip of the Russian mainland, in the rough center of the country, east to west. The Russians built an ice airfield on Sredny in the 1950s from which strategic bombers, the venerable TU-95 Bears, could threaten the United States. It was quite far north, nearly two hundred miles further north than the US's cold war airbase at Thule, in northern Greenland.

When KarLap arrived, Sredny was still maintained to service An-26's and An-72's ferrying passengers from Khatanga on their way to the Pole. Since then KarLap had funded a significant expansion of the airfield, lengthening the runway, adding state of the art communication and navigational equipment and building hangars, garages for the heavy equipment, a larger power station, a large administrative, dining and recreational center and residential facilities.

The first thing she noticed is that there were far too many of the large, droop-winged Ilyushin IL-76 cargo jets on the ground, all of which should have been in the air scattering Golden Feathers.

"It appears you did not get KAL squared away, Ms. Sharma," said Rupert Green. "Although it is difficult in this part of the world to distinguish between incompetence and malice, I would wager on the latter."

Avinashi had deposited their guests in the mess hall for a late breakfast and found Green holed up with the base manager, Ed Maxwell, in his office. Green was seated at Maxwell's desk, bumping him to one of two folding chairs in front. Green looked every inch the patrician executive, with his salt and pepper hair, expensive, sturdy pinstripes and regimental tie. The visitors would think that he had dressed for them, but in fact this was his everyday outfit, even in the field. The rare UKP man who survived a move to Texso, he was more useful than admired. Charlie had positioned him with shareholders as the ideal KarLap CEO, an independent mind, from but not of Texso, able to hear out diverse viewpoints and bridge cultures. Privately, he led them to believe he was a weak, feckless executive susceptible to influence by all shareholders, large and small. Green became the consensus choice of the board and so, with Charlie as Chairman, Texso controlled the top two positions at KarLap and the company.

"I did a face-to-face with Egorov last week in Moscow," said Avinashi, as she sat down in the other folding chair. "I met with all our partners, just as we planned." The KarLap PSA had extensive local sourcing requirements, including aviation services. In addition to being a requirement of politics and the PSA, outsourcing work allowed them to keep their fixed costs low until they knew how and when they would be going into production.

In fact, because Charlie held most of the key government and other relationships himself, he had just seconded Avinashi from Texso over to KarLap as its in-house government relations head. Because as a practical matter Avinashi worked first for Charlie, Green did not consider her part of his team and did everything he could to put her on the defensive, so it seemed. Which was why Avinashi would regularly have to explain that there was in fact no Director of Government Relations, and that as Assistant Director they could be assured that they were speaking to the appropriate person.

Over the past two months she had met vendors for everything from milk to concrete to icebreakers to IL-76's. The game was to utilize the locals where they were likely to do you the least amount of damage. Russian aircraft and pilots, provided you could get them in the air, were highly capable at operating in the Arctic environment and very cost-effective. Russia had been flying extensively in the Arctic for decades, and generations of Russian boys dreamed of becoming heroic Arctic aviators the way American boys dreamed of a playing professional sports.

"Well," said Green, "let's review the progress made while you have been off playing travel agent and you tell me if you spot any issues. Ed?"

"Well, okay, but I think Avinashi knows most of this already," said Maxwell. "We have chartered six IL-76's from Khatanga Avia Leasing for the geophone deployment."

"Twenty-nine thousand and some odd geophones, across 1.2 million square kilometers of ice and water," said Green. "By tomorrow morning, thank you very much Charlie."

"Right," said Maxwell. "First up, none of the planes would take off yesterday at initiation because they hadn't been paid."

"Not just for this job," said Green. "Any work. For the past six months."

"We paid an agreed-upon amount into an account of the lead pilot, including amounts not owed for this project," said Avinashi.

"Which excess you will of course recover, Ms. Sharma," said Green. "Please don't neglect to add that to your list."

Maxwell continued. "Subsequently, two aircraft were still unable to depart because of unspecified mechanical issues. Of those that took off, one returned to base with its full load because its cargo door refused to open. Two of the others laid their geophones in the exact same sector. And the last plane developed mechanicals while airborne and was forced to divert to Tiksi, where it is still impounded for improper permits. We also had information that one of our geophones was disassembled to determine what they might bring at salvage."

"And that was just before noon, right Ed?" said Green.

"Right, the afternoon picked up somewhat but honestly it seems more of the same. I think they're slow-rolling us."

"Rupert, I don't understand," said Avinashi. "Egorov asked for the meeting, but everything was fine. He didn't raise any issues."

"Ms. Sharma, he wouldn't have called for a meeting if there weren't issues. If you didn't offer something, he likely decided that you just weren't ripe for picking. We are now overripe and bursting. Call him and make this stop. Do you need me to write out step by step instructions?"

Maxwell didn't lift his head from the close study he was making of the notebook in his lap.

"No, Rupert, I'll get on him straight away."

"Next. One of the few geophones successfully dropped yesterday landed on a bear. Federov's little group is featuring the bloody remains on its web site. It was picked up in the evening US time last night and in Asia this morning."

"Oh, Rupert, that is so unfortunate. We knew it was a possibility but the odds were infinitesimally low."

"Oh, I'm sure it wasn't us. Multiply the odds of us hitting something with those of Federov being on-site with a camera crew. I'm not a mathematician but I believe they are zero. They probably hunted the thing down in a helicopter and blasted it with an RPG. Christ, the bloody thing was obliterated. Great story and visuals for them, I must say. Steel death raining down on the pristine Arctic, motherless cubs handfed by a darling Russian girl. All they need is a picture of Charlie with the blood on his hands. In any event, I need you to come up with an appropriate response. Up to it?" He gave her a look that suggested he wasn't sure.

"Of course, Rupert."

"Well, then, let's meet our guests. I'll take a couple of questions, but I want you to cut it off after fifteen minutes, got that? How do I look?" There being no mirror, Green checked himself in the reflection of the glass in the frame for a Texso poster on the wall, a picture of happy, healthy children of mixed ethnicities, standing under the

Texso logo, the red Circle T, and over it the Texso slogan "We're Your Future."

"Welcome, welcome. Everyone had a chance to enjoy some refreshments?" said Green, as he briskly led Avinashi into the mess hall, a long, utilitarian room of Formica and wood paneling, but with the summertime bonus of a large, insulated glass window with a view of the white airstrip and the gray Kara Sea beyond. The only one to have availed himself of the hearty workman's buffet was Petrov, who sat at one end of the table in front of three dirty plates, still as a potted plant. Flannery was trying to engage him in conversation but it appeared one-sided. The others had split into their respective camps along the table with cups of hot drinks and peeved expressions, as if someone had flown them to the end of the earth and then forgotten about them. Except for Porbin, whose expression was as blank as Petrov's, and Federov, who was taking pictures through the window.

"Fantastic. I'm Rupert Green, CEO of KarLap, and I'm so glad to have you all with us today. Avinashi, I'll have just a little fruit, please, thank you. Ah, Deputy Minister, so good of you to make the long, long journey."

As Green pressed the flesh, Avinashi wandered over to the buffet. Fruit? Sure enough, one of the cooks had been good enough to thaw some pineapple and soft but serviceable strawberries. She loaded a plate with some of each and left it at the head of the table where she was sure Green would ignore it, then she walked back to the hallway leading to the kitchen.

First, she would call Moscow. Most senior Russians weren't big on doing business by on the phone, but she was put right through.

"Colonel Egorov, this is Avinashi Sharma. Colonel, it is good to speak with you. I very much enjoyed meeting with you last week. Yes, in fact I am at the Sredny Island airfield right now. Impressive aircraft, Colonel, massive. Well, things are going well enough. I am calling because I feel I was remiss in not expressing greater appreciation for your attention to our schedule. If there is ever a situation where we could be of help to you or KLA, please do not hesitate to contact me. We value your relationship. Texso wants to work with the best. Do you have my cell phone number? Do you have Mr. Green's cell phone number? I am sure he would want to hear from you at any time. No I don't believe we have selected a contractor for that. Yes, just the sort of expertise we should be aware of. Ah, it sounds like a wonderful firm. Your brother, even better. How could we could go wrong?"

Next she ran down to Maxwell's office and jumped on his computer. She opened a browser and typed in the address for Federov's site. The photo of the bear was gruesome, but the little girl with the cub was adorable. Well played, Denis. She read their release and some of the other mainstream outlets that had picked up the story. The bear and its orphan had been discovered by a helicopter on a flight between Sredny and Arkticheskiy. She emailed Maxwell to have the radio tower find the pilot and the exact location. Most likely she could prove they hadn't even had a flight over the area within the possible window. In the meantime, she started typing up a press release restating the conclusions of their multiple studies regarding the negligible impact of the project on wildlife populations and the fact that they had launched an investigation.

As she typed, she started walking back to the mess hall. Green had already been talking for five minutes, and Avinashi needed to get back in there to limit the damage.

"And so you see, KarLap is a world-class Russian enterprise that has, in the spirit of true partnership, joined with the leading independent energy companies of the world as junior partners, to open, with Firebird, for the peoples of the Russian Federation, what we believe will be the next great oil region in the world. Unless there any questions, Ms. Sharma will escort you on to witness the very exciting deployment process. The aircraft awaits you as we speak."

Shirin raised one elegant gloved hand. "Rupert, how can you call KarLap Russian, exactly?"

Avinashi expected that it was difficult for the average oilman not to dismiss a question from Shirin Yazdani. Avinashi had never seen a woman quite so striking, and neither had any of the men, most likely. Certainly no such woman had ever shown an interest in speaking to them. Shirin was tall and shapely in every way that Avinashi was not. She had long, dark hair with that rich luster Avinashi's mother couldn't bring out in her daughter's however long she brushed and arresting eyes which the poor, besotted geologists probably remembered as having been just like volcanic glass. When she passed by, her barely detectable scent reminded Avinashi of the Damask roses her mother had grown back in Houston under the kitchen window. From a wealthy British Iranian family that traced back to the seventeenth century Zand Dynasty, Shirin was also brilliant, well educated and exceptionally cultured. She did not lack for self-confidence, and she interrogated her sources in commanding, incontestable tones.

From what Avinashi had seen, the oilmen spilled so much secret information to Shirin that the hardest part of her job must have been deciding what to print. For a few minutes of her attention, they would breach any written or unwritten obligation of confidentiality or loyalty or trust and not think twice about it, until they panicked when their unattributed but perhaps traceable comments ended up in the next issue. And for executives of the national oil companies, the NIOCs, she was one of the good guys, given the National's clear pro-country editorial bias. They didn't stand a chance. Avinashi wasn't expecting much better from Green, now sweating and stammering at the front of the room. Shirin was seated directly in front of him wearing an immaculate white ribbed turtleneck, having tossed her KarLap parka onto the seat beside her.

"Shirin, I don't quite know what you mean. We've been very transparent about our ownership. Gazprom holds 40 percent plus 1 of our shares, Rosneft 10 percent plus 1, and they appoint a majority of our board, all Russian nationals. Wouldn't that be Russian?"

Gazprom and Rosneft were the two large energy champions for

Russia. For the most part, Gazprom had the exclusive rights to gas, Rosneft was the king of oil. But Rosneft owned part of Gazprom, and Gazprom also produced oil, so it was complicated. Unlike the other energy states, Russia permitted limited foreign ownership of its energy titans, and each had raised capital from foreign investors, but in each case selling less than half of the company.

"So they own half of KarLap, and the Russian Federation owns half of them. So Russia owns a quarter of KarLap. You don't think we can multiply, Rupert?"

"Shirin, yes. I mean no. But you're forgetting holdings in the two companies of private Russian investors, aren't you?"

"Rupert." Avinashi could not see Shirin's face, but from Green's reaction it was clear he was falling out of favor. He became very still. His glistening brow began to wrinkle.

"Yes?"

"Nothing. I have no further questions. You clearly refuse to take them seriously." She flipped her notebook closed and started to wriggle back into her parka.

"No, no, that's not true."

"You are trying to tell me that all Gazprom and Rosneft shares listed in Russia are held by Russians."

"No, no, but it is very significant. I know it's not public information, but I have the data. I'll show it to you. Russian ownership is very substantial."

Avinashi reminded herself to hide Green's laptop when they were finished, before he just handed it over to Shirin.

"In any event," said Shirin, "we can be sure Russian ownership of KarLap is less than 50 percent, do you dispute this?"

"No."

"I see. So less than 50 percent Russian ownership. With Texso having day-to-day control. Or really Charlie Joiner. How is this Russian, Rupert?"

Avinashi thought she had better call the fight. "Rupert, the next flight is leaving very shortly. Shall we all button up and head outside?"

"Avinashi, please, this is important." Green waved her away with great irritation.

"Now Shirin, I'll try not to take that personally," said Green, tucking in his chin and looking down at the floor. Oh no, he's actually hurt, thought Avinashi. "I am the CEO of KarLap, not Mr. Joiner. And I report directly to the board as a whole, of which he is one member. I assure you, there is no mysterious Grey Cardinal behind the scenes, pulling my strings."

"Then who decided to begin the deployment?"

"Well, it would have been up to me, wouldn't it?"

"Was it? Why decide suddenly on Tuesday night?"

"Yes, well. I thought we were ready." Then he frowned. "Wait, why on earth do you think it was Tuesday night?"

"Because on Wednesday morning Ms. Sharma got me out of bed and told me I had an hour to get to the airport. Out of curiosity, where were you on Tuesday night, Rupert?"

"The London Philharmonic was in town, my wife insisted, you know how it is, taste of home."

"So Rupert, sitting with his wife late Tuesday evening in the Grand Hall in Moscow, listening to, what?"

"Rachmaninoff, I believe."

"Listening to Rachmaninoff, decides suddenly that it was time to begin."

"Yes. Something like that."

"It had nothing to do with the fact that Charlie Joiner was with Minister Lazarev on Tuesday, in his boat on some dreadful fishing trip? Charlie didn't decide, based on his trip with Lazarev, that for some reason it was now or never?"

"I know nothing about that."

"So he didn't even tell you why he had reached this decision?"

"What?"

"He just called you and told you to go ahead, immediately. Or maybe Ms. Sharma called you, she tells me that she works for Charlie. Did she call you with the news? Do you work for Ms. Sharma?"

"That's preposterous, of course Charlie called me, right during the second movement, bloody inconvenient." His voice trailed off at the end before he stopped himself.

"I see. So we have a mostly foreign-owned enterprise, controlled by Mr. Joiner, rushing to extract Russian oil and gas for the benefit of the EU, or perhaps to their detriment if Chancellor is successful on your behalf. Help me, Rupert, I'm just trying to write the lead for my story in my head."

The Chancellor had been listening quietly from his chair, with his head held high and tilted slightly back, his eyes squinting, as if he wanted to remain attentive but also aloof.

"Ms. Yazdani," said the Chancellor. "Given the close proximity, and its energy needs, a long-term supply relationship with Russia is most certainly in the interests of other Europeans, as well as Russia. The Russian Arctic could supply Europe's oil needs for the next seventy-five years."

"Seventy-five years?" said Telnov. Telnov and his aides sat far at the other end of the table, next to Petrov. "I wonder, how much oil would KarLap have to find for that to be true, Chancellor?"

"Deputy Minister, off the top of my head, I surely don't know. But at least seventy-five years, I assure you," said Huber, with a sweep of his hand and a politician's calm reassurance and magnanimous smile.

"Over six billion barrels a year, currently," said Jensen.

"Let us for a moment put aside whether poor Russia keeps any of this oil for herself," said Telnov. "With some growth, say 450 billion." He rubbed his chin. "Only eight times all the oil in the North Sea. You have high hopes for the Russian Arctic, Chancellor."

"Utterly preposterous," said Jensen. "None of the analysts have projected that much. The USGS is estimating only ninety billion in the entire Arctic. You will destroy the Arctic and the planet for stopgap measures."

"Myself, I very much appreciate stopgaps, particularly when they heat my home and cook my food," said Huber. "Imagine the two of us stranded together on a desert island. We are down to our last bit of food, a rich, decadent chocolate cake. But you will not eat the cake, because you are worried you might get fat, and so you starve to death. I don't care, I like chocolate cake. And then the day after I finish the cake, I am rescued. After which, I may or may not go on a diet."

"Speaking of starving," said Avinashi. "We will miss lunch if we don't catch this next flight out. Anyone ever ridden on an IL-76?"

The Ilyushin IL-76 jet cargo plane was designed for the unique challenges of operating in Russia. From Moscow, it could reach the farthest outreaches of the empire in under seven hours carrying fifty tons of men, weaponry and machines. It could operate from short, unimproved runways. With the parts it carried on board, two mechanics could perform all routine maintenance with no further support. And it was capable of flying in the worst weather the Soviet Arctic could provide. Introduced in the 1970s, it had become the most popular cargo jet in the world, with over eight hundred operating in over thirty-eight countries around the globe.

But it was a working aircraft, and Russian, so it did lack for conveniences. The ground crew at Sredny had done its best to prepare a VIP berth in the forward section of the cargo hold, just behind the cockpit, but it was still rough. Three rows of seats, eight across fastened to two pallets secured to the bottom of the hold, facing backward. Avinashi handed out noise-canceling headphones. The cargo hold was not insulated for sound.

Occupying the rest of the cargo hold was a large rack, eight feet high, ten wide and thirty long, with a latticework that contained hundreds of silver javelins, each about two meters long. As Avinashi had to continually remind everyone, yes we can still call them Golden Feathers even though they are silver. It's ridiculous to paint them gold, and the poem is about Golden Feathers not Silver Feathers. Use your imagination and get over it.

The Golden Feather was a seismic recording device, a geophone. With one end of the javelin stuck firmly in the ground, the geophone's sensors were designed to record vibrations occurring along three orthogonal axes. It was referred to as a 3C, or three-component, geophone. It also recorded time, with a highly accurate internal clock.

The oil industry had used geophones for decades to record seismic waves reflected or refracted off underground structures in its search for hydrocarbons. In the water, the device that recorded the waves was called a hydrophone. But the geophones used in the oil industry were all set up on the ground by technicians. Exploration geologists needed to place their geophones with some care. Location was important in reconstructing the underground structures.

"We have to place thirty-thousand geophones?" She remembered asking Charlie, dismayed.

"Not placed," Charlie had said. "More like scattered. Exact location doesn't matter for Firebird. Maybe you can use a plane. You'll figure something out."

It took a couple of weeks with Texso engineering and then she did. In the early '70s, America was bogged down in Vietnam. The North Vietnamese were withstanding withering US bombing and ground attacks with the help of supplies sent by China via the Ho Chi Minh trail. It was very difficult for the US to spot the convoys under jungle canopies and Viet Cong camouflage. An industrious US defense contractor came up with the idea of dropping geophones along the trail to listen for trucks. Looking like a child's model rocket except that it had a fake plant attached to its tail, thousands of the green-painted Steel Eagles were dropped along the trail. They had a very short range and relayed their recordings by radio to airplanes flying overhead. Problem solved.

But the Golden Feathers collected data underwater. Radio signals will not travel underwater, at least for more than ten meters. So after recording its data, the top portion of the Golden Feather had to be lifted to the surface to transmit. Sometimes through ice. Luckily the US military had also developed technology that would be useful to address that issue as well.

The US Navy dropped sonobuoys in the oceans to listen for submarines. The large Soviet ballistic missile subs hung out mostly under the ice, so the Navy developed sonobuoys with shaped charges that could be dropped onto the ice and blast a hole through with they could listen. Texso designers had turned this on its head. After recording its data, the top portion of the Golden Feather detached itself, was carried to the surface with a self-inflating lift and, if it encountered ice there, blasted through. Where the data was transmitted to one of the six IL-76's traveling overhead. The only satellites with polar coverage were Motorola's Iridium satellites, but they didn't offer the necessary bandwidth. Six IL-76's at forty thousand feet could do the job nicely.

Avinashi watched as the crew checked the straps that fastened the rack to the cargo floor. There were six hundred and six geophones in their load, plus or minus fifty or so depending on the exact sector. Each geophone was approximately two meters long and seventy-five kilos in weight and either silver or dull gray in appearance. The tips of the geophones were pointed towards the rear of the aircraft, ready to be launched. The tubes flared front to back, in a graceful curve, not straight. Precisely engineered to provide the right amount of deceleration as they hit rock or sediment. The rack was equipped with spring mechanisms that would launch the rockets into clear air, after which gravity drew the slender tubes down to the sea and the earth. Seventy-five kilos of aerodynamic steel would be traveling at five hundred miles per hour when it hit the sea. If there were ice, so much the better. The ice would be vaporized, providing the first deceleration for the geophone. Then the sea itself would provide further deceleration. The surface of the geophone was painted with a special material designed to induce friction with the water, slowing it further.

The Russian continental shelf was quite shallow in spots. But they were also dropping geophones off the continental shelf in fifteen hundred meters of water, just east of the Gakkel Ridge. There they would use slender, Teflon-coated geophones dropped from forty thousand feet. They still needed to impact the bottom at sufficient speed to plant to geophone securely in the crust. In their tests, they had achieved a 90 percent survival ratio. For safety, they still launched three geophones at each location. The more that survived, the better. Each one was designed with slight variations from the ideal. Even if they made a miscalculation on the location, one of them still should survive.

After they were all buckled in, Avinashi asked the pilots if they would like to say anything before they took off, but they shook their heads no. She tried to make an announcement to her group but they all stared at her with their headphones on. Green, sitting next to Huber in the front row of seats on her right, drew his hand across his throat so she gave a thumbs up and sat back into her seat.

The huge jet engines began to roar. Then stopped.

She got up out of her seat and went to the cockpit. The pilots pointed through the windshield to the runway. She bent all the way over and looked out. Dozens of people, all dressed in brightly colored polar gear, were seated on the runway, arms linked, and three rows each stretching from one side to the other. The nearest row held part of a long banner, which was flapping wildly in the wind. It was in English, but Avinashi could make out a few familiar words—KarLap, Texso, death, oil, blood.

"Damn polar trekkers," said Green from over her shoulder. "Avinashi, why don't you go straighten this out?"

The Russian Arctic had become a busy place over the past couple of decades. With the warming weather, receding ice and greater numbers of ice-class ships, traffic through the Northern passage was booming. Ice breakers were in heavy demand. When they weren't escorting shipping or providing ice management for drilling operations, they were carrying tourists to the Pole.

And in the age of GPS, satellite phones and Russia aviators eager for foreign currency, access to the Pole for the casual adventure traveler was wide open. Russia had been gaining on Canada as the most desired "jumping off" spot for the Pole. Costs were lower here, but the myth of Siberian also provided an advantage. How exotic or dangerous was it to travel anywhere in Canada, regardless of how far north? Canada's image was embarrassingly benign to the serious adventure traveler.

And so the Russian route was booming. From Moscow to Khatanga, Khatanga to Sredny, then either from Sredny to Cape Arkticheskiy at the northern tip of Severnaya Zemlya and on to the Pole by sea and ice, or from Sredny by air or sea via the nuclear icebreaker *Yamal* to Borneo Ice Camp, established every spring on the pack ice within striking distance of the Pole. A camp was not established directly at the Pole because ice conditions did not always allow and besides, the ice at the Pole was always moving. During the peak months, from March to May, the air traffic at Borneo was equivalent to a small executive airport near a major city.

And once at the Pole, the recreational opportunities were endless. Not only could you ski, kayak, snowshoe, dogsled or ride snow machines, but you could also parachute, paraglide, balloon, scuba dive, swim or just have brunch. A North Pole marathon race was held every year in March. Prince Albert of Monaco had been up to make the trip by dogsled. That is not to say the spirit need be neglected. The Russian Orthodox Archbishop from Kamchatka had celebrated the Divine Liturgy inside a temporary tent chapel erected on the ice atop the Pole. The ceremony was not abbreviated for the extreme locale or conditions, but lasted for the traditional three hours. As busy as she was, even Avinashi partook, but only after relentless pressure from one of her colleagues. The lead scientist on Firebird had been pushing for the skydiving, but she had insisted on sticking to the hot air balloon, and they had a memorable ride across the top of the world before she had to hurry back to work. It was in truth the most fun she had had in ten years.

And so it was not that unusual to have two dozen trekkers passing through Sredny on their way to Borneo. Nor in hindsight would it have been surprising that such a group would have a different perspective on oil exploration in the Arctic, perhaps protest, even. Although Avinashi was convinced that none of this would have occurred were it not for the machinations of Denis Federov, now out on the ice snapping photos of the continuing protest.

Avinashi was donning her KarLap parka at the open door when Petrov, the journalist, pushed through carrying a large, black handgun. He climbed quickly out onto the ice, and started firing.

Chaos ensued. Some of the protestors ran, some curled up in a ball on the ice, others just fell over each other. The banner flew out of their hands and out of sight down the runway. Petrov kept firing.

Avinashi yelled at Petrov and ran out to the protesters, a small, fast blur. Too fast to be hit, she hoped, having been nationally ranked in cross-country at the University of Houston. She was also trained in first aid, and she was repeating *ABC, ABC* over and over as she ran onto the airfield, expecting blood. But when she reached the protesters, there was none. Just Avinashi, in her parka with the big KarLap logo, and the protesters.

"How many lives per gallon?" yelled a burly trekker in a red suit, as he grabbed the front of her jacket and lifted her off the ground. "If the earth dies, we all die!" Avinashi pulled her face away from his as best she could, her arms and legs flailing as she dangled in his grasp. Not helping her at all, Federov stood to one side snapping photographs. "Pozvonite v militsiju! Pozvonite v militsiju!" she screamed back at him, calling for the police, but really wanting just to shout loudly in Russian. The trekker dropped her down on the ice, terrified that he had grabbed a Russian national. Whereupon she ran quickly over to Petrov.

He stood absolutely still and calm, the gun down at his side. It dawned on Avinashi that he had been firing over their heads when he raised his gun again.

"They are starting again," he said, lifting the gun. "We must not let this delay our flight."

"Mr. Petrov, stop! I must insist."

"We must get on board the aircraft," said Petrov. "We must see the deployment."

"I will handle this. Why do you have a weapon with you, Mr. Petrov?"

He shrugged. "I am in a dangerous profession. Are we going on the plane now?"

She assessed the situation. No one appeared hurt. In fact, to their credit, they were regrouping.

"Mr. Petrov, I can assure you that you will be perfectly safe on the remainder of our tour. I'm afraid I'll have to ask you to check your gun until we return. Just to avoid the potential for any accidents. Please."

He shrugged again, deftly emptied the chamber and ejected the magazine and handed her the weapon butt first. Given the lack of resistance, she knew he had another, but she didn't want to push her luck. She took the gun and walked back into the plane.

They all stared at her in shock, except for Telnov who was on the phone and Federov who was reviewing pictures with a big smile on his face. Green pulled her aside.

"Where did you get him? This is outrageous," said Green.

"The Ministry of Natural Resources, they were allowed to designate one journalist. It wasn't someone I selected, Rupert."

"Well, they're not giving up. Maybe we should let him have another go at it?"

"Let's come back to the feathers, and go see Firebird first. Once Federov is gone, they'll move on. Hopefully no one presses charges. Can you do that here?"

Within twenty minutes they were rising up over the runway in the helo, from where they could see the protesters still squatting on the ice and waving their banner. It would have been sooner, but Avinashi held them up while she heaved on her baggy, bright orange survival suit. Texso employees had to strictly observe all Health, Safety and Environment, or HSE, standards, which required her to wear the suit on all offshore helicopter flights from Sredny. Green wouldn't be joining her because as usual he was heading back for Moscow as quickly as he could arrange.

For non-employee visitors, particularly VIPs, the suits were offered but not required. Telnov reacted with great amusement when he saw her come out of the flight-ready room. She wore the smallest size available, but to walk she still had to bind the loose folds up at her waist with a strap. She looked like her Uncle Parvesh with his runaway potbelly. The Norwegians, fascinated by any outdoor gear, were the only others to put on the suits and Birget shot photos of Jensen climbing into the helicopter.

This time they flew in an American aircraft, though the manufacturer had been founded by the Russian émigré Igor Sikorsky. A large helicopter services company, trying to position itself for the profitable, long-term contracts that would be sure to let once KarLap started production, had offered to lease them a Sikorsky S-92 on very favorable terms for the duration of Firebird. It was state-of-the-art transportation for the offshore oil industry, with room for nineteen passengers, a range of nearly nine hundred kilometers and full de-icing capabilities. Charlie agreed, provided he could choose the pilot. And so Roy Cook, a Texan who had flown Blackhawks for the US Army, was at the controls of the S-92 as they climbed to make the jump over the archipelago.

The peaks of Severnaya Zemlya were ice domes nearly a thousand meters high, and the shortest route to Firebird was right over the top. They would head northeast from Sredny and then cross over two of the four main islands, Pioneer and then Komsomolets. Firebird was thirty kilometers offshore and to the northeast of Cape Arkticheskiy, a total distance of 230 kilometers and reachable in about fifty minutes in the S-92.

Configured for commercial passengers, the helicopter had airline type seating and windows at every row. Telnov and Huber had boarded first and selected opposite window seats in the first row. Avinashi had boarded next but stood at the front, politely allowing her guests to choose their seats first. Mortified that she was too flabby for Duman to pass, Avinashi made room by stepping in front of the empty seat next to Telnov, just as Shirin ascended the stairs. To Huber's great delight, this directed Shirin into the seat beside him, and left Avinashi, after Duman took his two seats, to squeeze into the last open seat next to the incessantly brooding and malevolent Telnov.

"Did you know, my dear," said Huber, as they climbed up over Pioneer Island, "that that this was all thought to be one island until the Graf Zeppelin flew over in 1931?" The passengers all wore headphones with mikes connected on the same audio line. Great, thought Avinashi, I get to hear all of Huber's pillow talk.

"Can you imagine?" continued Huber, "sipping cocktails in the lounge, floating over these islands for the first time? No heat in those airships, though, how do you suppose they kept warm?" He laughed like he had some idea, an idea that made his cheeks flush and eyes pop. Shirin zipped her parka up to her neck.

"Curious," chipped in Telnov. "How the meticulous Germans managed to accidentally expose all the aerial photographs they took on that flight with their wonderful large-format Zeiss. Ruined, everything. Nothing to share with us, as we had agreed, they said. Undoubtedly the fault of those clumsy Kriegsmarine intelligence officers trying to pose as scientists."

Huber ignored him. "Did you also know, Shirin, that the first leader of the great Soviet polar expeditions was a German? Oh yes, Herr Doktor Otto Schmidt. The 'Polar Professor,' that's what they called him. That's Schmidt Island up off to the left, I believe. Here, if you lean over towards me you can just see it."

Telnov turned away from his window, towards Huber. "Do you think, Chancellor, the Soviets would name Russian land after a German? This one October, that one Bolshevik, and then this one after that German? No, Schmidt was born in Belarus, a Latvian. And a Hero of the Soviet Union." Latvian mother, thought Avinashi. Otherwise, quite German.

"Well, I am sure you are correct, forgive me. I understand that there is an effort to rename the islands after the martyred Imperial Family," said Huber, smiling obsequiously.

"The politicians, they still argue this," said Telnov, shrugging. "As long as it is a Russian, I have no quarrel."

"Perhaps we should be focused on the future, not the past," said Jensen, from somewhere in back. "Ten years ago, the Kara Sea would have three to five-tenths ice concentration at this time of year. Now look at what we have."

Severnaya Zemlya separated the two marginal Arctic seas, the Kara and the Laptev, from which KarLap derived its name. The Kara Sea was visible off to their left, dull gray waters interrupted by occasional lighter ice, stretching as far as they could see.

"Thanks to Texso we'll see cruise ships in here before long," said Jensen, mostly to himself. "Won't that be special."

Then they were out over the Laptev Sea and approaching Firebird.

Northern Ranger
Laptev Sea
Thursday morning

"Where? There? Is that it?" said Huber. He struck a theatrical pose. "*A tiny glint in endless ice.*"

Someone has been reading his Lomonosov, thought Avinashi. Charlie had given her a volume he had picked up somewhere, which she had dutifully speed read.

"Just like Chernobyl," said Jensen.

Avinashi had asked Roy to circle the site a few times to give everyone the lay of the land. The skies had cleared temporarily, and the sun was brilliant. Down below, surrounded by loose pack ice, was Texso's drillship the *Northern Ranger,* currently serving as the Firebird.

She was 169 meters in length, with a beam of 19 meters, which included Arctic sponsons to provide more lateral stability. Her profile was dominated by forty-five-meter drilling derrick amidships and a large heli deck on top of and projecting forward from the bridge, looking like the brim of a baseball cap. Two large satellite dishes were mounted on top of the rear superstructure. On either side of the forward superstructure, back of the bridge, were two bright orange, covered lifeboats, looking like thick mini-submarines and suspended on davits ready to swing out and lower them to the ice and water.

Formerly an agricultural produce carrier operating between Chile, Argentina and the US, the *Northern Ranger* had been upgraded and retrofitted in Korea as an ice-class drillship. Texso planned to use it to prospect sites leased in the Beaufort Sea off Northern Alaska. But the Beaufort drilling operations were halted by litigation in US courts, so the *Northern Ranger* was diverted to drill exploratory wells in Malaysia until April when Avinashi laid claim to her for Firebird. After another upgrade in Korea to add special equipment for Firebird, she was on her way to Severnaya Zemlya via the Northern Sea Route from East to West. By late July she was on-site off Komsomolets.

"As you can see, there are significantly greater ice concentrations in the Laptev," said Avinashi. "Over the last week we have been seeing eight-tenths coverage, mostly first year, with the occasional multi-year floes coming through. The *Ranger* is made fast to the seafloor with an eight-point turret mooring system. That means it can swing 360 degrees around its 'turret' on the bow where the eight lines are bent on. To help keep it on position, we have leased two ice management vessels. A nuclear-powered icebreaker the *Papanin* to break up the larger, multiyear floes, and the diesel-powered *Hnoss* positioned closer to the *Ranger* to run interference on the remainder. The *Papanin* also has a helicopter it can launch to be its eyes in the sky. Since the *Ranger* began drilling last week, the coordination has been fantastic. The crews are really first rate and work well together."

"I only see one ship," said Flannery. Avinashi strained her neck to look as far around as she could through the small window. She saw the *Papanin* at least two kilometers east and a bit north. She didn't see the *Hnoss*, either.

"Trust me, it's out there," said Avinashi. How can we possibly lose an icebreaker out here, she thought.

Roy had finished the tour and was descending towards the *Ranger*. Telnov took off his headphones, and Avinashi followed suit.

"Ms. Sharma," said Telnov. "Are you familiar then with our legend of the Firebird?"

"Oh, yes. Marvelous story. Magical bird, feathers of gold, each bright enough to light a room. Keeps breaking into the Tsar's garden and stealing his golden apples, so he sends his son out to catch him. Lots of gold in the story."

"Yes, there are several versions, that is one of them. But in each the feather initiates a destructive quest, and the hero later blames the bird for all many his troubles. Old stories, simple truths?" He paused. "You were informed the Ministry is not in favor of this project and we are participating today under protest, yes?"

"Please just give us a chance, Deputy Minister. Perhaps we can change your mind."

"That is for the young, Ms. Sharma." He looked out the window. "Is this the Tsarevitch now? Not very promising."

"Is he wearing a top hat and cane?" said Flannery from behind them. "How darling, it's Willy Wonka. Oooo, I want a Gobstopper."

Avinashi thought the odds of Ted Crawford wearing formal attire were very low.

Roy set the Sikorsky down, and they stepped out onto the sun-drenched deck as the engines spun down. A flat slurry of white pancake ice and dark seas extended out under a bright blue sky to a distant, misty horizon.

At the front of the deck by the stairs, a young man leaned on a golf club. His long, sandy brown hair trailed out the back of a bush hat and flipped around in the light, southerly wind. He wore cargo shorts and flip flops with a sleeveless fleece vest, and his lean, well-muscled arms and calves were bare except for dark Polynesian tattoos. As Avinashi hurried over, she saw next to him a small green mat, a bucket of orange balls and a dark metal, conical object about the size of a paint can. His smile was white and guiltless.

"Hey, super girl." He looked her up and down. "Okay, this is the final straw. I'm having you fitted for a custom survival suit. All the up and comers at Texso have them."

"Ted, you're not even trying."

"Trying to remember how to swing a long iron. Besides, I needed some sun. Got the Arctic blues."

"You can't get them in the summer, Einstein."

"Is that so? Well, I nearly killed Brandon last night just because he was spinning the ball on his toss. Wakeup call, I'll tell you."

With several fused bones in his right ankle and a competitive streak that made Avinashi feel reassuringly well-balanced, Ted Crawford was a devout practitioner of what he claimed the Germans called *Stellung*, or position, sports. As Avinashi saw it, this suspect classification referred to any competitive activity which didn't require the participant to run very far and had a close association with drinking or recreational drugs. This included golf, ping pong, billiards, darts and, his chief passion, surfing. A serious student, Avinashi had been unaware the innocent game of ping pong was so associated until she was held over on the *Ranger* one night due to weather. As for the tattoos, Ted swore they were the result of a mysterious skin infection he picked up while doing experimental drug research in Tahiti.

"Please be serious for one second," said Avinashi. "You never got back to me on the agenda I put together."

"Right, didn't quite get to it. Just wasting my time on this recurring system crash in our mission critical software. My bad. Oh, we did figure it out an hour ago, you're welcome. And you're early, so also not really my fault. But don't worry, I've totally got you covered. Now can you give me one of those sweet intros? It's the only time I get to hear you say nice things about me."

Ted shook hands all around as Avinashi cringed and introduced him as the brilliant young geophysicist Dr. Ted Crawford of Stanford University, the lead technical consultant for Project Firebird.

Ted tipped his hat and kicked it off. "Okay everyone, before we get started I'd like you all to close your eyes. There's a tiny bit of swell today, so if you think you might fall over, you're welcome to sit down."

Flannery closed her eyes, started to tip over and then sat down. Avinashi could not tell if Duman closed his eyes, but she doubted it. The others simply stared.

"Okay, tough crowd," said Ted. "Ma'am, you can open your eyes, and I do appreciate your singular cooperation. Okay, how about if instead you all just stay right where you are? Don't move, keep looking straight ahead. Admire Avinashi's survival attire."

He picked up the metal object and limped around behind them.

"Okay, don't look. Just listen." He paused. They could hear low, droning machine noises coming from the derrick.

"So why are we littering two unspoiled Arctic Seas with over two thousand metric tons of steel?" he said. "Why do all these polar bears have to die?"

Avinashi turned and glared at him, and he winked back.

"So we can listen. We are going to ring those basins like a bell, and then listen. Listen for oil."

With the head of the iron, he struck the ship's bell. It rang steadily, rich and clear in the cool air. "Not to this." The tone tapered off gradually. "Not to this." Now barely discernible. "To that." Avinashi could still just hear the ring, or her memory of it.

"What we call the coda of the seismic signal. The final, forgotten sound of the bell after it's been rung, well after it's been heard, but before it's silent. Usually just an afterthought, ignored and thrown away.

"Traditional seismic exploration is analogous to sight. We blast the sound waves into the ground and look at the reflections, so we can form images, of traps and caps and pinch-outs and salt layers. But we never see the oil. You can't see the oil, at least not this way. So we look for structures where we've found it before, or where we think it might be and then we cross our fingers and drill.

"But what we've found is that the oil will tell you where it is if you just sit back and listen. You can't see it, but you can hear it. Listen carefully, to those soft, final tones. The sound waves that get scattered around and around inside the rock and then leak out, arriving at your ear later, nearly spent."

He walked around back in front of the group. Flannery, for one, appeared spellbound.

"But the continental crust of our survey area weighs three trillion kilograms. That's a big bell, we need to hit it hard. So we need someone stronger than me. Someone like Avinashi."

He stood holding the bell up with one hand, the other hand in his pocket, with an insufferable grin.

"Ted."

"Just a little pull, c'mon. Then we can go downstairs."

Resigned, she walked over and gave the rope attached to the clapper a sharp, sarcastic jerk.

A blast shook the deck, buckled her knees, and knocked the wind out of her all at once. She lost her balance, twisted around and fell. Ted caught her before she hit the deck.

Now he looked guilty. "Ohmigosh, you okay, Avi? Sorry, just a little joke. Ship's horn. I told Ricky to sound it when I blipped the radio." He waggled the handheld radio that had been in his pocket.

He helped her to her feet. The others were rubbing their ears, all except Porbin, who appeared unfazed.

"Sorry everyone, but I wanted to prove a point," said Ted. "That sounded loud to us, but on the *Papanin,* just five clicks away, we can only hope it gets their attention. On an oceanic scale, it's very, very quiet. So keep that in mind as I show you what we're going to do."

Ted led them down the stairs at the front of the deck and onto a series of iron catwalks and stairs, Avinashi apologizing profusely all the way. "Sorry, so sorry. Scientists, lacking the normal social graces I'm afraid. Get caught up in an idea, you know how it is. But brilliant, really, quite brilliant. You'll see."

The water in the moon pool was a brilliant pale blue. They had crossed back under the heli deck and made their way to the middle of the ship. Avinashi gathered the group on a catwalk just below the main deck, looking down into the middle of the ship where the hull had been cut away under the derrick to allow access to the sea. In the middle of the opening, called the moon pool, the casing extended down, out of sight. Into the casing went the turning, twisting drill pipe, which also extended halfway up the derrick.

Jensen tried to ask a question but it was too loud. Ted waved them on into the drilling room, a glassed-in enclosure with a view of the moon pool and all the drilling equipment. Three technicians sat in front of instrument panels that looked like airplane cockpits. They supervised and controlled the whole drilling operation from inside this room.

"We're not drilling for oil," yelled Ted. "Not yet. We're drilling a large diameter borehole down to a Devonian layer three thousand meters down. Where we'll place our downhole seismic source."

"A very benign description, I am sure," said Jensen. "Exactly what is this source?"

"Off the shelf chemical explosives. C-4, specifically."

"And? How much?"

"We figure eight kilotons should do it. Our geophones are pretty sensitive."

"Eight kilotons? That's like a small nuclear weapon."

Ted tilted his head before he answered. "Sure, but only if a stick of dynamite is like a really, really small nuclear weapon. Modern nukes are around a thousand kilotons. A megaton."

"Those are the big ones, though. What about something like Hiroshima?"

"Hiroshima was, I believe, thirteen kilotons."

"So half the size of the weapon that killed over one hundred thousand people and ended a World War."

"Just over half, yeah." Ted looked down into the pool. "Look, I know this is a sensitive issue, but please try to keep some perspective. This charge will be three thousand meters under the seafloor. And it needs to be felt up to right hundred kilometers away and generate the Firebird signal. So I calculate that we need a source that will generate something that registers here somewhere around a 4.75 on the Richter."

"4.75? That's a major earthquake!"

"Nah, this area has seismic activity all the time. We're only two hundred kilometers from the Gakkel Ridge, where there's lots of volcanic activity. A 4.75 will easily get lost in the shuffle by your average narwhale. C'mon, let's keep going. This is the blunt end of the project. The sharp end is up at the back."

Ted led them out of the drilling room and back to the rear of the ship. They entered the high rear superstructure underneath the large satellite dishes and began climbing stairs. When they reached the top of the stairs Ted used a keycard to open the door and they followed him inside.

They were in a long room with no windows. It was warm by comparison to the outside, but still probably around sixty degrees. One wall of the room was filled with banks of servers. The rest of the room was filled with over a dozen workstations, some of them occupied by young technicians.

"This is my domain, and these are my insanely loyal subjects. Meet Ahbi, Brendan, Chloe and Derek. Yes, the ABCD team. Any one of them would give their life for me." They looked up briefly with dark, weary eyes and gave weak waves. "They thought the Arctic sounded glamorous, but we found the one place duller than Palo Alto. Why are they still here? It wasn't just the hazard pay the extorted from me last week. It's because they know that this room is ground zero for the next quantum leap in the economics of the petroleum industry. This is where we listen for the oil. Right, Chloe? Derek?" He pumped his fist in the air. No one even looked up.

"Total concentration, what a team." He ruffled Brendan's hair then rubbed his hands together. "So, at T equals zero we detonate eight kilotons of high explosives three thousand meters below the seafloor, shaking the floor of the North Kara and Laptev Seas. The geophones record the signature at their respective locations and then are immediately released to the surface. They bob up on the surface or blast through the ice and then pulse their data to the IL-76's overhead, which relay the information to us. Then it's processed right there." He lunged at the servers with a pointed finger. "And in less than a couple minutes, we have a full analysis of the entire region." He sat on the corner of a desk, crossed his arms and smiled.

"So fast, how can that be possible?" asked Shirin.

"Like magic, right?" asked Charlie. "But no, just math. You're probably more familiar with the process of converting seismic reflection data back to an image of the reservoir. Then you're talking migration imaging, velocity estimation, dip moveout, slant stack, yada, yada, right? And you need to record hundreds of channels of information for every square meter of rock. Hugely computationally intensive.

"We have 28,800 geophones, but only 75 percent will likely survive to send a signal. The signal is just a four-channel record of a one minute, forty-seven second interval. Together with their position. Not large data set. We just screen this for the Firebird signature, and then compare the data from neighboring geophones to refine the location and size. We can get our results, and present in 2-D, 3-D images, with location and size estimates, in minutes. After the adoption of 3-D seismic in the '90s, the success rate on new wells went from 13 percent to 47 percent. The cost of finding oil went from eight dollars per barrel to one dollar. We won't see costs like that again, particularly in the Arctic. But with Firebird, we can take the success rate on wells to 100 percent. This would be a profound shift in the industry, obviously."

"Well, congratulations," said Telnov. "So tell us the whole story, tell me how you invented this technology, Dr. Crawford. Can you do that for me?"

Ted hesitated. "I suppose you're referring to the original idea part, not the part where I recognized that it might work and then made it work. Sure, yeah, we can go through that, happy to. C'mon, we can talk out here."

At the far end of the data room they went through a door into a large lounge area. It looked like the break room for the Silicon Valley startup. Funky soft chairs, ping pong and pool tables. A dartboard hung on the wall with a photo tacked to it, something ripped from a newspaper. It looked like Lazarev, but it was hard to tell with all the darts. Avinashi tore it down just in case, but not before Federov snapped a quick picture. There was a refrigerator in the corner from which Ted pulled cans of super-caffeinated beverages.

"As I believe Deputy Minister Telnov is aware, the Firebird technology is Russian," said Ted, setting the sodas on the large round table. "A bit of scientific debris caught up in the brain drain from Russia in the early '90s. At this time, Dr. Felix Rynin, of Tyumen State University, decides to see if his friend and sometime collaborator Dr. Anatole Friedel of the Stanford geology department can offer a way out of the chaos. Shortly thereafter he takes up residence at the Stanford Exploration Project, a special industry/academic partnership for geophysics research, bringing with him a dusty trove of research projects, mostly aborted for lack of funding.

"As the new guy, Dr. Rynin is assigned all the worst graduate students. One in particular lacks all initiative, so he shows this student the boxes with all the research and tells him that his thesis topic is somewhere in there and he needs to start looking. At the bottom of the last box, there is a paper with the title 'Abnormal Attenuation and Velocity Dispersion of Seismic Waves in Oil and Gas Fields.' The author was one V.A. Kolotkov. He died 1983, and that's about all we could find out about him. And that he had a literary bent. At the top of the paper there was a reference to the Russian folktale of the Firebird. In the paper he postulated the existence of a unique hydrocarbon signature, and what it might look like. All I had to do for my thesis was to develop a way to identify it."

"A signature. You mean a DHI," said Shirin. "A direct hydrocarbon indicator? That's the holy grail of geophysicists."

"And just as real," said Telnov. "The French developed 'sniffer' planes in the 1980s that they said could smell oil from the sky. Then the British had planes that could see where oil seeped out of the ground, where no one else could see it. Fantasies, all."

"This time it is real," said Ted.

"Oh, so you've tested it. Tell us."

"In a sense. We've seen the signature in field tests at small scale. Not on a large scale. You have to find the right place."

"I suppose it's hard to find countries that will let you detonate eight kilotons of explosives," said Jensen. "So tell me, Mr. Crawford, will this technology create new billion-barrel oilfields?"

"No, but if they're there it'll sure help us find them."

"Are you familiar with cargo cults, Mr. Crawford?"

"Weren't they a steampunk band from Chico?"

"Perhaps. But the cargo cults I have in mind are isolated tribes that were so overwhelmed by advanced technology that they took it for magic. Explorers flew in to study one such tribe and gave them the gift of Spam. After that, the tribe built airport terminals out of co-conuts and thatch to lure more shipments of canned food out of the sky. That's the way Americans are. They keep expecting some magic technology to come and solve all their problems. If they just keep acting like an energy-rich people, they will stay an energy-rich people. The fact is, the oil is gone. But you can't stop yourself. You just keep going, destroying the planet until it won't sustain anyone."

"Oh, my God. A doomer, right before my very eyes. Careful, let's not anyone make any sudden moves. Don't want to scare him off, this is a perfect specimen. Don't mention nuclear or orbital solar power or he'll run off and we won't see him again. Ah, the peaker mantra. 'Easy oil gone, it's all over, look out below.' C'mon, it's just getting interesting. Who wants to find the easy oil? Idiot Pa Joiner, sticking a drill in the ground on a tip from his vet. More fun to try to do it over a whole ocean, or under the ice. Look, even under your scenario, half of it is still left. Half of all the oil on earth that ever was."

"It's not the size of the cup, it's the size of the straw," said Jensen. "The remaining oil is hard to find, hard to produce, hard to process. It's thick with sulfur, its expensive to produce. And what matters for the world is the gap between supply and demand. And once the supply stops to drop down that slope, it's going to drag the world with it. The oil-based part of the economy, anyway."

"Okay, let's back up," said Ted. "So how do you know exactly what future oil production will be?"

"The basics of prediction of oil supply have been known since the '50s. Your Dr. Hubbert developed them and predicted the peaking of the US supply twenty years later."

"Highly scientific," said Ted. "He hand fit a logistics curve to some known data and extrapolated it. And his prediction was 1965. If he hadn't had 1970 as a fallback date we might not even be having this discussion. He also was off on total production by 20 percent and on gas production by well over 100 percent. Oh, the technique is great, though. It works everywhere except where it doesn't."

"So this is how it ends, with an immature boy and his computers, destroying the world," said Jensen. "Have you seen the gas bubbling off your ship, Mr. Crawford?"

"Brendan was supposed to look into that. Brendan, c'mon, man."

"Methane trapped in the seabed," continued Jensen. "It is melting. The unprecedented release of carbon into the atmosphere over the last hundred years has raised temperatures, in the Arctic and elsewhere. As you like to say, the world is complicated. So you probably will understand that many climate scientists do not expect the resulting changes to be linear. The warming we have seen to date has caused the Arctic to warm, and releasing, as we speak, more methane that is currently trapped in the Arctic seabed than is contained in all the hydrocarbon deposits in the world. As those leak into the atmosphere, you will see coconuts at the North Pole."

"So we better jump on that sequestration program, right?"

Porbin started coughing uncontrollably, like he aspirated one of his roots. He was on one of the soft bean bag chairs away from the rest of the group. Avinashi began pounding him on the back. The potential for complications between mushrooms and high doses of caffeine ran through her mind.

Porbin stopped coughing and stood up. He staggered over to the window and stared out. He bent his knees slightly and started to sway back and forth. He coughed again, then fell back on the bean bag chair, dazed and silent. Federov knelt down at his side and spoke softly to Porbin in Nganasan. Porbin whispered back.

"Poor bastard," said Federov, listening and shaking his head. "He's on a bad, bad trip." He leaned in again, more whispers. "Something about spirits in the water. A demon with eyes that never shut. Fire on the water, but great treasure below. Another demon come to kill us for being wicked. But a hero is coming, the two will battle. Something about a beast that escapes, pulled by his bears." More whispering. "Something, something, something. Okay, now he's not making any sense at all. Two futures? Could be something to it, though. Better put it out there." He took out his notebook and started jotting things down.

Porbin lunged at Avinashi and grabbed her head with both hands. His breath smelled of musty reindeer as he shouted at her in Russian. "You must drill! You must drill!" My God, she thought, did Charlie put him up to it? I get it, I get it.

The ship shook with a deep boom, as if rung like a gong. Then came the distant scream of twisting metal.

"Stay here. I'll check this out," said Ted as he disappeared through the door to the lounge.

Avinashi settled Porbin back in the chair and got him some water. She picked up the plastic bag that had fallen next to the chair and stuffed it in her pocket.

Ted popped back in.

"Just a little ice management issue. Nothing major. Captain thinks it's best to send you on your way, though."

Avinashi pulled Ted into the data room and shut the door.

"What happened?"

"Our friends on the *Papanin* decided to take a little siesta. They let a city-size block of multiyear ice hit us in the starboard bow. By the time they figured out the *Hnoss* couldn't handle it was too late to pull the drill string and disengage the turret mooring. The drill pipe shattered under the force of impact. But they can get it back online, we're good. But not until we get around the next piece."

"Another one?"

"Bigger. That's why the Cap thinks you should get out while you can."

"Oh, no. Alright, let's get the group together. Could you have someone call Roy?"

"Sure, sure. Say, Avi, I know this probably isn't the best time, but if you're going to be rushing off, I just wanted to follow up on what we were talking about last time. You told me you were going to give it some thought, right? So, I just wanted to see if you had. You know, thought about it."

"What are you talking about?" She knew what he was talking about.

"You know, about me asking you out. You said you wanted to check the company policy first."

"I said I would have to check the policy first, then I laughed. Big difference. And that was after three games of beer pong." She had in fact checked the policy, and her face flushed with her private embarrassment. "My God, Ted, I don't have time for this. We have a medical and ice emergency and we have to evacuate."

Ted would be the perfect boyfriend if she hated her parents. Which made it all the more troubling that last week she had a dream of the two of them looking at glassware together in the Stanford Mall Pottery Barn. And then later she cooked him dinner, and she didn't cook.

"Okay. But if I get things squared away here, I did get Charlie to agree that I get to go to the Ministry dinner in Pete on Friday. Maybe we could ride over together? You know these dinners are formal, right? You'll need a dress. No survival suits."

"End of conversation. Go."

The moon pool was filled with a dark cloud as they went past.

"Spill," said Jensen. "God damn it, you guys are just winging it out here. You don't know what you're doing."

"It's just some drilling mud," said Ted. "Technically it's a natural substance."

They arrived back at Sredny in time for a late lunch.

"We must see the geophone drops," said Petrov.

"Yes," agreed Jensen.

The protesters were gone. Hopefully, well on their way to Cape Arkticheskiy, snapping photos of walrus. Green had bolted for Moscow.

There was only one Il-76 at the airfield, and it looked to be refueling. That was good. Unless they were all impounded somewhere.

The skies were still clear, so it was time for their much-delayed flight.

They were buckled in with their headphones on. The huge jet engines began to roar. They pilots didn't waste any time. The plane whipped around and barreled its way over to the runway and launched into the air. The pilot took off at an insane angle and their heads hung over their straps like dolls.

She had arranged for a short run. But after they were in the air for fifteen minutes she unbuckled and went up to the cockpit and asked why they weren't there yet. They explained that it was over an hour to the site, just past the Gakkel Ridge, in the open ocean. Of course.

Finally they were over the drop site. The cargo door opened and the noise level increased. Out the huge doors they could see the brilliant white of the sea ice. They were high, over eight miles up. The geophones started to drop. Three at a time, once every three minutes. Every ten kilometers, at their air speed of three hundred kilometers per hour.

Finn was shaking his head. Birget appeared to be crying. Avinashi herself had mixed feelings. It wasn't the debris, the Russians had been littering the landscape for decades with far worse. It was a frontier they were killing. Forcing a huge section of the Arctic to yield its mystery. Pinning it down, like Lilliputians tying down Gulliver. Something deserved to be mourned.

Avinashi was pondering this as she watched the geophone rack start to roll away from her toward open space. Then, shockingly, right out the cargo bay doors. The safety strap for the rack drew taught with a snap and the plane pitched up sharply. Avinashi's world twisted violently as the view out the back changed from blue sky to white ice.

The engines thundered as the pilots tried to regain control of the aircraft. The stakeholders for Project Firebird screamed for their lives. Avinashi prayed the seats were bolted in tightly. Particularly when she saw that the safety strap led back across the cargo hold to the base of Huber's seat. Then one side of Huber's seat yanked free.

The Chancellor was yelling at the top of his lungs, ripping furiously at his seatbelt. Avinashi reached out and tried to help but she couldn't reach him. She unbuckled her seat belt. She climbed over to his row and holding onto the empty seat next to him she worked on the buckle to his seatbelt. It was jammed and wouldn't open. Completely frozen.

Huber's seat finally broke free, with him still safely buckled into it. Porbin grabbed Avinashi and held her as the Chancellor flew out the back of the hold, tracing the beginning of a graceful arc down to the ice before he disappeared from view. Free of the rack and the Chancellor, the plane leveled off.

Avinashi clutched the seat, hyperventilating. The air was so thin. She couldn't catch her breath. The cargo hold cranked shut. Finn Jensen ripped off his mask and was yelling at her. She lifted one side of her headphones. "What kind of operation do you run here Ms. Sharma? Get us back to the airfield immediately!"

She went to the cockpit. She got on the radio and called the Sredny tower. She asked to be connected to the base manager and gave him the brief details but she wasn't sure if he believed her. She went back to her seat and sat back in shock.

They hit the runway hard and started the quick taxi to the concourse. Her phone buzzed. One of the emails was from Vicki, Charlie's assistant in London. Would she be available for a breakfast meeting with Charlie at seven on Friday at the Hotel Europa? Since they were both in St. Petersburg Charlie wanted to do her six-month review. Please confirm.

CHAPTER 4

FIELD WORK

St. Petersburg
Thursday night

C harlie stared at Lazarev on the TV. The Karela One announcer intoned profoundly in Russian over black and white footage of Brezhnev shaking the young oil finder's hand in Siberia.

Charlie called his protection service on his cell phone. "Turning in early, so go ahead and take the night off." Charlie left the phone charging on his nightstand. He checked his cash. Then he put on his suit jacket and left his suite at the Grand Hotel Europa.

Around the corner from the Grand, two cabs waited outside the Hotel Primavera. He opened the back door of the second and climbed in. He paid the driver a thousand rubles and directed him randomly back and forth around the center of the darkening city for half an hour. The cab had no air conditioning and a foul smell, like the city, but the traffic was thinning out and mercifully they could move fast enough to have a breeze through the windows.

Amid the decaying Baroque and neoclassical facades and the trash-strewn streets and plazas, Peter's window on the civilized world was showing some signs of renewal. Here and there someone cared enough to try a new coat of paint or even restore a building. Small, high-priced shops with European and American brands catered to someone, and restaurant patrons overflowed onto the sidewalks.

He saw a crowd emptying out of the Alexandrinsky Theater and told the driver to pull over. Charlie paid the man another thousand rubles then walked against the crowd up into the lobby. He stopped inside, turned and watched. He walked out through a side entrance and down the side of Orlovsky Square. The theatergoers lingered in the late summer night, walking slowly in the square around the monument to Catherine the Great and crowding the small café. The tall trees hissed in the light breeze.

Two militia police came up to him and asked for his papers. Skinny teenagers from the provinces. He slipped them each two hundred rubles and kept on walking.

At the other side of the square he was back on Nevsky Prospekt, just a few blocks down from the Grand. He found an internet café and paid for an hour. He logged into a free email account and opened a draft email. He copied down an address then logged out and erased his tracks as best he could. Outside, he flagged down another taxi and gave the driver the address. The man nodded knowingly, crumpled the paper and tossed it out the window. None of this would shake the FSB, but Charlie wasn't worried about Chernov.

They continued on Nevsky Prospekt, heading away from the city center. At Vosstaniya Square across from the Moskovsky Rail Terminal, trains departing for Siberia daily, they turned left and headed up Ligovsky Prospekt. Shortly after they turned right and started to work their way through side streets.

On a wide, leafy avenue somewhere near the Neva the driver pulled sharply into a long half-circle driveway lined on both sides with expensive cars. At the top of the drive, behind a long row of concrete barriers and up two flights of broken stone steps was a large pink palace fronted by brightly lit, two-story columns and topped with a white dome. Three large men in blue camouflage fatigues and boots approached the cab as they pulled up. The driver quoted Charlie an outrageous fare which he paid. One of the men opened the door and Charlie got out of the car.

"Mr. Berra here to see Mr. Ford," said Charlie. The man spoke into his sleeve and then pointed up the steps.

At the top of the stairs another security guard opened one of the massive white doors. Charlie walked into a quiet entryway with heavy dark wood paneling and a thick gold rug. There were more men in blue camo, a small Mongolian in a cheap suit and an ethereal blond in heels and a see-through pink dress who was taller than Charlie by half a head.

"Mr. Berra, Polina will show you the way back," said the Mongolian in a lilting accent. He stood behind a golden podium shaped like a swan. "But first, please."

As Charlie was subjected to a rough and probing search, several Russian Army officers came in through the front door and walked right past. When the security guards were finished with him, Polina came over and slipped her hands under his jacket. She straightened out his shirt with a couple of quick tugs in the front and the back and smoothed out his jacket. She smiled at him, and the corners of her mouth turned up and around in perfect, graceful French curves. She invited him to follow her in heavily-accented English.

They passed through a short, wide hallway and entered an immense room with high ceilings. The far wall was entirely glass and looked out into dimming gardens. Several massive crystal chandeliers filled the room with a pink glow, as if the last light of the day had been caught and kept bottled up inside. Throughout the room, on plush couches and chairs, lay dozens of barely dressed women, still and silent as if reflecting on the dying light. Electronic music, something downtempo with sitars, played in the background.

Charlie followed Polina as she wound through the room. What there was of her dress disappeared in the rosy light. Pretty women stirred as he passed. Some turned to look, eyeing him with suspect desire. Some stood and stretched their slender limbs. Others managed to be just in the way and brushed their scented, naked bodies up against him as he squeezed by. As Charlie and Polina exited through a sliding glass window into the courtyard, he could see them slip back into their couches and chairs and resume their desperate vigils.

Outside, Polina took his hand to steady herself as she kicked off her shoes. The summer night was still warm in the garden. Fragrant flowers growing somewhere in the dark masked the smell of the city. Facing him now eye to eye, she slipped her hands under his jacket again and drew him close. She pressed her cheek to his and extended one long arm along their shared line of sight, pointing to a low wing of the palace that wrapped around the side of the courtyard. The wing also had floor-to-ceiling windows, and inside Charlie could see a party underway.

"Mr. Ford, he is there. You bring me? I was not chosen. I have been bad." She turned up her lower lip and touched the tip of her nose to his. "I could be bad for you. Very bad. Terrible."

"Thanks. But I have enough trouble. A holy man. Russian Orthodox. Help me with that?"

She made an annoyed face. "Pssht. Awful tippers. Never happy. You I could make happy." She took his hand and drew it up under her dress, across her stomach. As Sheila had done in Yemen.

Charlie felt her stomach carefully. Then he lifted his hand and cupped her left breast, squeezing gently. Polina winced and bit her lip. Charlie turned her to the light from the windows and dropped to his knees. He lifted her dress and traced his thumb on a faint line from her navel to the tip of her pubic bone.

He stood up. "How much for the whole night?"

"You like the pregnant ones? We are very expensive."

"How much to send you home?"

"Oh, my hero. Let me see." She took his wallet and fished out all the cash. "This much." She handed his wallet back. "I leave now. Mommy needs rest. Good night, hero man."

Expensively dressed men filled the long, low room. They sat in groups, laughing and eating and stroking the women who made it out of the rose room. At the far end were a dozen men in Russian military uniforms. A confident man, late 40s, sat in the middle smoking a cigar. Clearly the senior officer. And right at his side was Don Sanders, the pride of Orange County, California.

Sanders saw Charlie right away and came weaving through the crowd, calling his name and holding high above the fray a full glass of his ubiquitous Johnnie Walker Black. With his ruddy skin and blow-dried hair, his top-of-the-line camel hair sport coats and ties colored like LeRoy Neiman paintings, Don Sanders exuded the boozy good nature of a small-town American conventioneer set loose in the big city and in the mood for hijinks. Hopelessly out of place on the frontiers where they both worked, but definitely in his element.

"Joiner, Christ, get over here. I thought I was off-limits, but here you are. Hey, how'd you like my code names? That's us, one of the great duos. Matched set, yin and yang. Butch and Sundance, Martin and Lewis. True friends, through thick and thin. Loyal to the bitter end."

Sanders wrapped him in a bear hug and slapped him on the back like Charlie was choking on a dumpling. How Sanders could do this without spilling a drop was a continuing source of wonder to Charlie. Sanders would come stumbling toward you in a hopeless alcoholic stupor and just when you thought he was ready to fall into your lap or worse, his touch on your arm would be light, his stories would be short and have a point, and he would have the one key piece of information or contact that would make all your problems disappear.

"Good to see you, Don. I have been loyal. Have you?"

A short young woman with dark hair that fell in shiny waves down to her waist came up to Sanders and whispered in his ear.

"Oh, thank you, Ekaterina, but I must speak with my friend Charlie, here. But I promise I won't forget." He pointed to one of the small red leather booths against the wall. "Over here, Charlie, grab a seat. And let's get you a drink, you look parched."

He froze a passing waiter with a touch to his elbow. "Egor, two more scotches for the Americans, thank you. And quick as you can manage. You don't want to see me sober, believe me."

With the sweaty shine on his face and the unsteady tilt to his head, Charlie always expected Sanders to rip off his jacket or yank his tie loose, just to breathe, or to better settle in and drink, but he remained forever composed and properly attired. His blinding ties remained knotted, his cuffs stayed linked, his hair kept perfectly in place. Only his wide, manic eyes and devilish grin suggested a true deviant. As they slid into the booth, he leaned in on Charlie, reeking of scotch and secrets.

"So here he is, the biggest swinging petro dick this side of the Urals. I'll see your Russian Path nonsense, Lazarev, and I'll raise you this two billion dollars of Texso metal I'm throwing in the ocean. Take that, stick man! Hah! And to close the deal you tell the VP to clear his calendar and get over here to put the arm on him. Joiner talks, the US listens. They know who keeps the lights on at home and I'm damn sure glad they do. Dickinson, though, that vain prick. Good luck getting him to shut up."

"Lazarev asked for him. We were out this week on the boat."

"I know, I know. So, Charlie, what happened out there? A little birdie told me you sent a little message to Lazarev. Pushed one of his guys overboard and then left him for the man in the gray suit. Not a bad idea, really, and very Russian, but a lot of witnesses. Finally given up the old boy scout routine and gone native?"

"There was an accident. Or two. I wasn't responsible."

"Not responsible? Now you're sounding like me. A lot of accidents in your operations lately, Charlie. Sloppy, sloppy. Too many people falling out of your planes and boats. Hope you understand if we don't share a cab later." He laughed loudly at his own joke and slapped the table.

"It was a Lazarev family matter, let's leave it at that," said Charlie. "Otherwise it was a successful trip. I got what I wanted out of it, except for a big fish we left out there."

"Sure that was a fish? El Diablo himself from what I hear. This is really quite exciting, you're trying to scare Lazarev to death. I think we saw the same movie! Taking him out to a watery grave to hunt demon fish, Davey Jones locker and all that. You know that man went bonkers out in the bush, right? He sees the sign of the beast every day in his borsch. What's next, have you figured out a way to make blood spurt out of his gushers? And you know the man isn't well and all, fasting and whatnot, he's got one foot in the grave already. Keep it up, sure-fire coronary! Perfect!"

"That wasn't exactly the plan, but I was trying to knock him off his game a bit. Never know what you can pry loose. Don't worry, he's tougher than he looks."

"Oh, he is, he is. You know how he got so deep into all this Russian Orthodox crap, by the way, don't you? Paddled his way out of the fucking Arctic with only the clothes on his back and his trusty Kalashnikov. One shell for the bear and one for himself. When he broke that camp all he took were a few cases of cod liver oil. Hah! You ever smelled that stuff? Every time he opened one up every bear in a hundred miles came running. Took him two months to get to shore. Just in time, too. One more week and he would have been just another frozen caveman in a 25th-century museum. The public story was all about heroic Soviet man beating the Arctic at its game, but the secret is that it drove him completely batty. Now he's your Grade A Russian madman, Russian Orthodox edition. Explosive temper, violent mood swings, paranoid fantasies, the complete package. But five hundred kilometers across the ice will do that to you, I guess. Not only that, but then the Nganasans almost finished him off when he got to land! Oh yeah, one of them found Lazarev on the beach and took him for dead. He was helping himself to Lazarev's boots when Oleg Maksimovich up and shot him dead. That brought the whole clan running and the Nganansans took Lazarev back to their camp for a tent cleansing ritual, the human sacrifice version. True story! Like everyone else the Nganasans hate the fucking Russians, they really know how to bring it out in people. But Lazarev escaped and made it to an unmanned, nuke-powered weather station, which he jury-rigged to phone home like frickin' ET. Oh, god, I can't wait for the movie. I'm thinking Gary Busey for the lead, gotta be. Cut his hair real short, he does his crazy guy thing."

"How's it end, Don? Where is this going?"

"How should I know? But I got a bad feeling. This guy is seriously messed up. Too holy to eat. Prays all weekend in the woods with his Metropolitan Demidov, swapping conspiracy theories like baseball cards, filled with Muslims and Texans and the devil, scaring each other silly. Lost in the Arctic or not, how you let that happen to yourself is beyond me. But what do I know, the closest I ever got to being religious was dating a nun."

"Can we talk deal for a second?"

"You tell me. My lawyer tells me I should tape my mouth shut and call him the second you walk through the door. Thanks to you I've got a subpoena waiting for me back home that is sure is going to complicate my Christmas holiday plans."

"So what happened in Baku, Don? Where did all the money come from that you paid out? It better not have been my money."

"You think you're my only client? I've had my finger in every big deal in Eurasia for the last twenty years. But I can't go around spilling my guts every time someone gets curious or waves a subpoena. Would you like me calling Chevron every time you and I did business? And believe me, if I did not everyone would be so understanding as you. I can see it now—'I had to guys, it was the law.' They'd shoot me as soon as they could stop laughing.

"Look, I told them it didn't come from you. I can fake sincerity with the best of them, but they still don't believe me. They keep pressuring me to make a deal, roll over on you. They're threatening me with jail time, cracking open my Swiss accounts, and harassing my poor 80-year old mother in Irvine. In the plus column, they're also making my ex-wife miserable but that only goes so far.

"Look, just so we're clear, if they keep pulling my nails out on this I'm going to have to make something up. Because this isn't about me at all. They are dead set on making an example of you, Charlie, the golden boy who crossed the line. They don't care if you're guilty or not, that's almost beside the point. It's just the time-honored way to make everyone behave. Cost-effective, too.

"In fact, I think they want you more than Jamilov. Everyone expects him to be on the take, that's just part of the normal compensation package for the President of a lawless accident of geography like Azerbaijan. But taking you out allows for moral outrage, gets a bit of press, looks better on the website, maybe even a book deal for the top guy, certainly for the news hacks. Look at it this way, you'll be the cautionary tale for a whole new generation of kids. Doing some real good."

"You don't have to tell me anything," said Charlie. "Just tell them the truth, that's it. Whatever you can. I'm sorry they're coming after you, but I didn't do anything wrong. You're the one who knows that."

"Me? I don't know anything, Charlie. You're the only one who knows." He seemed to sense this was a little rough and backed off.

"God, I had high hopes for the Caspian, Charlie. Remember back then? Gorbachev threw open the cupboard and it was all there for the taking. I was an overnight success after ten years of walking the halls of every godforsaken communist bureaucracy this side of the Iron Curtain. And we did it, the 'Contract of the Century.' I thought that was it, the one that would let me retire, go back home, sit with my feet up in front of the fire, the dog sleeping on the rug. Didn't quite turn out the way we expected, did it?"

"Not yet. Maybe it was all for KarLap."

"We'll find out next week, won't we?"

"Maybe. But I'll need your help to make it happen."

"I can't help you. We're not even supposed to be talking. Didn't your side tell you that? If not, I gotta get me a new lawyer."

"You're still under contract with us."

"That's right, so tell Crawford to get up to fucking date on my KarLap fee. I've got two kids in college, for Christ's sake, or so they tell me."

"Well, he's not going to do that until we get this Caspian situation figured out. And his hands are tied with the subpoenas. What did you do with the first fifteen million we paid you?"

"You know how expensive it is to operate over here? To run with this crowd? C'mon, I barely break even. I practically run a charity."

He poured back the rest of his scotch and slammed the glass down on the table. "Egor, another round. Chop, chop."

"Lazarev is going to shut down KarLap. On Monday."

Sanders looked insulted. "Charlie, it's me. You think I don't know?"

"So, you want to get paid, you help me figure this out. I'm meeting with Chernov tomorrow morning. What's my play?"

Egor dropped two more full glasses on their table and swept away Sanders' empty glass. Sanders held still and stared at his fresh scotch as if it were speaking to him.

"Okay. Here's how I see it," said Sanders. "You want to take notes? No? Fine." He downed his drink and waggled the empty glass. "Egor! A man could die of thirst around here." He looked at Charlie. "What's wrong? You give up drinking?"

"Tell me how you see it," said Charlie. Another scotch appeared on the table and Sanders settled in.

"You have crossed over that line from being simply a money decision with certain policy implications to being a political decision. You are smack in the middle of the siloviki and Lazarev. You're a football, not the American kind, and you're about to get the crap kicked out of you in a game that you can't even see.

"You need to be sympathetic to the siloviki. They do want to keep KarLap on track. They want to show they can be a dependable energy partner for their customers and also, to a more limited extent, for the majors. The Saudis have proven that there can be real money in this. And they want to be just like the Arabs, except for the part about being a US vassal state.

"But they have a credibility problem, they know that, after shutting off gas to the Ukraine in the middle of the winter, throwing UKP out of Sakhalin, and stealing Yukos from Chevron, among other sins. This was all just the typical Russian way to do business, when they did any, from strength. You don't pay what we want, fuck the agreement, fuck what's fair, go freeze to death.

"But the siloviki need to get this figured out. They're just like you, they need to keep growing or they die. Your buddy Chernov needs an ever-increasing pie to divide up among the warring siloviki clans. So they're taking baby steps on the road to being a good partner. We're a ways off from siloviki retreats with trust falls and lectures on win-win negotiating, but they're starting. And it's this nascent goodwill that makes them want to fight their better instincts and stick to your PSA.

"But there are two complicating factors. First, with a little assistance from yours truly, you drove a fair deal, not a weak deal, which gives Lazarev all he needs to start criticizing the package. Recall my earlier comment about Russians valuing strength, and being new on the fairness concept. Lazarev's view resonates with the average Russian, as evidenced in the last election. It's going to cost real money for the siloviki to buy back those votes next time around.

"Second, being Russians, they do want to take advantage of the current situation. They feel the situation with Lazarev should not work wholly to their disadvantage, so they are going to come back at you on the terms. Tell you that Lazarev has turned up the heat, they need additional payoffs, balance of power, mouths to feed and all that. BS! They're just being good Russians, shaking you down.

"My recommendation? Two-fold. One, give back a little bit on the PSA to help them save face with the public, but not too much. Something pro-rata among all the partners, share the burden. Maybe a fifth of whatever they ask for. Keep the rest of your powder dry.

"Two, go on the offensive. Tell him you know that certain elements in the military have moved into the Lazarev camp and you're worried. It's Chernov's biggest fear right now, and he'll know that you don't think he's negotiating from a position of strength. It'll make him less aggressive, more defensive. Tell him you've spoken to the general with all those tanks in the Moscow suburbs and it sounds like he's a Lazarev fan. Why haven't they locked down a guy like that? He'll get the message."

"But I haven't spoken with him."

"Not yet. But he's right over there. Why do you think we're here tonight?"

"I'd be disappointed if you did this for fun, Don."

"Look at you, what are you saying? I'm always working, do you think I enjoy this? Egor!" He pounded his glass on the table. Egor appeared with a scowl and set a bottle of Johnny Walker Black on the table.

Sanders filled his own glass to the rim. "That's the problem here," he said. "No one wants to work." The young woman with the long hair came over to their table again.

"Donald," she said, letting the name roll slowly off her tongue. "How long?"

"Hold on, we're almost finished," said Sanders, as she wandered a short distance and then sat down in a chair to wait on him. "Sweet kid. I was helping her brother get a student visa to go to Boston College. But now." He raised his hands and shrugged his shoulders.

"We'll get this straightened out and then you can go back to your charity work," said Charlie. "Tell me about the guy with all the tanks."

"General Pavel Nestorovich Titov," said Sanders. He pointed to the cigar smoker. "Right there, the most powerful military man in Russia. Commander of the Tamanskaya Motor Rifle Division, stationed right outside Moscow. Control the Tamanskaya, control Moscow. Control Moscow, control Russia. This is the unit that decided both the '91 and the '93 putsches. The tank Yeltsin stood on? His. Although they were a bit late on the '93 deal, and it cost them.

"He's in town for Lazarev's dinner tomorrow night. Lazarev has been wooing him for some time now, and Lazarev wants to trot out the US VP and make him do little dances in front of Titov, just to show him who's a player. Lazarev's also been after the other generals, too, and they were ripe for pickin'. He's got nearly a hundred that are grand poobahs in his Orthodox Brotherhood, the storied Defenders of Karela. Think Knights of Columbus with beards and vodka. The Yeltsin and Putin reformers left the Army job for last, with good reason. The Army is the one institution that is still pure Red Star to its core—bloated, ineffective, inefficient, corrupt. There was only one way any reform could go, badly. And Putin's reform of the Army has made Hilary look like the maestro of health care. The generals despise Putin and all the good-for-nothing dilettante KGBers. Lazarev, on the other hand, sounds a little bit like the old Sovs, although he's vague on the specifics.

"Titov is a Defender, but he's wavering, because he's an ambitious guy and his childhood dream is to be head of the Moscow Military District. But his Defender status is a black mark on the resume in the eyes of the siloviki, to say the least, and they've been blocking it. Lazarev keeps saying he's going to deliver it for him, but so far no go. So he's in play. C'mon, let me introduce you to my good friend Pavel Nestorovich. Watch yourself, though, ok? He's a piece of work. Even for here."

Sanders leaned in and spoke into the general's ear. Titov bit on the cigar and extended his hand.

"So, Mr. Texso."

"Call me Charlie."

"Charlie Texso. Come, sit." One of the officers gave up his chair and Charlie sat.

"Oleg Maksimovich says that you have sold your soul to the devil," said Titov.

"Don't recall that. What did I get?"

"The power to see through rocks. To the oil. Is this true? You can get anything you wish, and this is what you ask for?" Titov smiled. "I find this very curious."

"I always thought that was a god-given talent. Maybe I'm just confused."

"Yes, who knows, really? Where our talents come from. My talent, for example. Would God really give one such a talent? Seems more like the devil's work. Have they told you what my special talent is?"

"Yeah. Tanks."

Titov laughed and relit his cigar. "Well, yes. But more importantly, I too see inside. But I see inside people, Charlie Texso, not rocks. I can see inside men's hearts. How? As I said, I do not know. In particular,

I see those with dark hearts. That is my special talent. Which I use to collect those people, and put them to use for others. That is a special talent for which others pay me handsomely. Because to control the people, you need to fire on the people. I find those people with dark hearts, who will fire on the others. Reliably. Effectively." He sat back, drew deeply, and blew smoke softly up into the room.

"Is it really that hard?" said Charlie. "No offense, just wondering."

"Hah! Of course you mean here in Russia, with madmen on every corner. Yes, Charlie Texso, even here in Russia you need a special talent to find those who are reliably bad. Someone who can find and bring out the worst in others. This will always be a valuable skill. Very soon as much as ever. Particularly as head of the Tamanskaya. Ah, Galina, what have you brought me?"

A strong, dark-haired woman that looked like she threw hammers on the weekend led five other prostitutes into the room. Polina was at the end of the line. She smirked at Charlie.

"Galina is helping me select a companion for our session tonight," said Titov. "Let's do a test." He snapped his fingers at one of his officers, who unholstered his sidearm and gave it to Titov. Titov turned off the safety and tossed the gun to Polina.

"You, shoot him," he said, indicating Charlie. "Now."

Titov stood up from his chair to enjoy the show. The other officers backed away from Charlie. No one wanted to get splattered, like last week.

Polina held the gun in both hands. Charlie could tell it was not the first time she had handled a weapon. But she raised it reluctantly, slowly. She stared at him with fire in her eyes and cursed him in Russian. For putting her in danger, no doubt. For putting her child in danger. She hated that she did not want to shoot.

Charlie saw Sheila risen from the sand, come to take her revenge for leaving her to burn in the desert. In his head, he begs her to shoot. To make it right. To punish him. To release him. To take away this task.

"Go ahead, Sheila" he said. "It's okay."

Polina drops the gun on the floor. "What are you saying? You are mad, both of you." She is visibly trembling.

Titov picks up the gun. "It was only a test," he said. "Don't worry. I knew she wouldn't fire. See, Charlie Texso, I can tell these things. She has a good heart, this one. Worthless to me." Titov hands the gun to Galina. "*Ubey yeye*," he tells her. Galina's lips curl into a cruel smile and she points the gun right at Polina's face.

Charlie explodes out of his crouch the way he was taught. But his legs are old and the gun explodes in his hand. He is pile-driven into the floor by Titov's men, his cheek nearly broken against the hard tile as one of them tries to insert a pistol barrel down his ear canal. Out of one eye he can see Polina holding the bloody side of her face. She is screaming. The tang of gunpowder hangs in the air. Titov crouched down next to Charlie.

"I see into you, too, Charlie Texso. And I see a very dark place. An obsession about something. I think it may be treasure you are after. A vast treasure. You are looking for it, but it eludes you. But you would do anything to find it. Am I right? Hah, I think I am, I am right. And you have done many things to find it. Bad things. And you will do more." He blew smoke down into Charlie's eyes.

"With my collection of dark hearts, Charlie Texso, it means that I don't have to listen to fucking American oilmen. Not unless they have something of value to offer me. Something more than what Lazarev is offering. You think about that. And tell Dickinson to think about that.

"Now, I am going to fuck this ugly, bloody whore one last time, as a favor to her. You know, you should have let Galina kill her. Do you know what the life of an ugly whore is like, Charlie Texso? She will be fucking in the alleys next week for a piece of bread. Anyway, I will see you at dinner tomorrow, Charlie Texso. Okay?"

Charlie watched the three of them disappear into an adjoining room, Polina holding her bloody face. He stared at the closed door for a few minutes then got up to go.

"Charlie, what are you doing?" asked Sanders. "Don't be a hero, buddy. The heroes in Russia are all dead, in case you haven't noticed. C'mon, let me find you a drink. Egor!"

"I have to go, Don. Breakfast meeting."

"Breakfast? Christ, gotta be Americans. Wish I could punch out, too, but another late night for me I'm afraid. Say, I tried to get a meeting with the VP's team tomorrow, but they turned me down. I know, shocker. When you see him tomorrow, put in a good word for ol' Don, will you? Stuck out here across enemy lines, out of uniform, but still carrying the flag. You know I am."

"I will, Don."

"Just one more for the road, Charlie? C'mon, stick around, it'll be just like the old days."

"There were no old days, Don. And get her a doctor. A real one. If you don't I'll find out and you'll never get another penny from Texso as long as I breathe."

"Hey, hey, of course, Charlie, it's me. What do you think?"

Charlie looked back before he ducked out through the door and saw Don slap the bare bottom of the long-haired woman who had slipped out of her skirt, making her shriek with laughter, before he offered another loud toast for the group.

CHAPTER 5

SHADES OF GRAY

Komsomolskoye Lake
Friday late morning

"The fish attacked him?" asked Konstantin Chernov, taking a sip of his beer.

"Something like that," said Charlie.

"Is that common? Maybe you could take him out again." Chernov smiled.

The day was sunny and warm so they were down at the lakeshore, watching Chernov's grandchildren play in the water. On a folding table covered with a bright red tablecloth, Chernov's wife had set out a picnic lunch of smoked fish with brown bread, sour cream, tomatoes, cucumbers and pickled vegetables. There were beers in a small cooler. She didn't eat but sat with her daughter on the dock. Chernov was dressed for the lake, in a white shirt with the top two buttons undone, light-colored slacks and sandals. Charlie wore a gray suit but had taken off his tie and jacket.

In the Russian popular imagination, there is always a power behind the throne, a Grey Cardinal, covertly advising Presidents or General Secretaries and directing the otherwise inexplicable course of events through guile and low cunning. By definition, the true Grey Cardinal could not be identified with complete certainty. Part of the fun, and part of the power of the legend, arose from the ongoing speculation as to who was really pulling the strings.

At this moment, the smart money was on the Chief of Staff to President Putin, Konstantin Chernov, the silver-haired, amiable man whose calm manner and sophistication appeared to make him better suited to soothing customers in a Swiss bank than baring knives in the back corridors of the Kremlin.

The archetypal Grey Cardinal was Mikhail Suslov, who first caught Stalin's eye with his rough stewardship of the Baltics, where he is said to have told his cabinet that soon "there will be no Lithuanians in Lithuania." A solid talent spotter, Stalin brought Suslov to Moscow and made him his Chief Ideologue, where he became the power behind the throne for nearly forty years. Suslov experienced a temporary setback after Stalin died, when his rival Khrushchev sent him into the proverbial wilderness. But Suslov returned by orchestrating a brilliant coup d'état that replaced Khrushchev with Brezhnev. When Brezhnev died, Suslov helped Andropov outmaneuver Chernenko. Then he groomed Gorbachev to replace Andropov. Suslov died peacefully in 1984 and was buried within hailing distance of his mentor Stalin in the Kremlin Necropolis.

Suslov was able to exhibit such remarkable survivability due no doubt to his superior political instincts but also by remembering the cardinal rule for Grey Cardinals, which is not to reach too far, to always advance the interests of others for the top job, supplicating oneself to the more powerful, the more ambitious. Rumor was that at anxious moments Stalin would relax by calling in Suslov and kicking his buttocks. Likely Suslov himself started the story, to eliminate himself as a rival. Although Cardinal Richelieu is said to have been truly distraught over the death of the original Grey Cardinal, his alter ego Father Joseph, crying "my support, I have lost my support," some did observe that the friar's untimely and unexplained death was suspiciously coincidental with his well-deserved nomination to the rank of Cardinal, where he would rival Richelieu in power, and that perhaps the tears Richelieu flamboyantly shed at his funeral were merely to maintain appearances in front of the imbecile French King Louis XIII, who was touched by the show of dear friendship.

Whether or not he was Suslov's true heir, Chernov was Charlie's point man for the KarLap PSA and the key to getting anything done in Moscow or the Arctic. Chernov had complete control over the day-to-day operations of the affairs of the President and was also one of Putin's long-time confidantes, a true Petersburger, going back to their days at Leningrad State when they were tooling around town in Putin's red convertible. And so Chernov was also the key to resolving his issue with Lazarev, whatever it was.

"So how big is my problem?" said Charlie.

"That is the trouble always with Olezka, what does he want, exactly? He is a difficult one."

"More TV time?"

"Hah! What else could they say? Until he performs additional miracles, that is. I am sure they will be forthcoming."

Over the last two weeks, Karela One had been broadcasting a series on the origins of the Russian oil & gas industry. The broadcast channel was owned by Lazarev's Orthodox Brotherhood, the Defenders of Karela. Eighteen hours a day it collected donations for the Brotherhood and pumped out religious and ultranationalist programming to a modest audience. This series was a marked change from their usual programming. Produced by the Natural Resources Ministry, the series chronicled the long and glorious history of Russian energy discoveries and production, from the first well in the world, drilled by a Russian in Iraq, to Baku, the first great world oil production center, to the Volga-Urals Region, Russia's second great oil region and finally the last great Russian oil frontier in Siberia. Last night's episode documented the opening of West Siberia in the 1970s. It featured prominently one young lion of the oil fields, Oleg Lazarev. Arriving in this barren, harsh landscape in the early '70s, Lazarev almost singlehandedly revitalized production in the existing fields, discovered great new fields, built pipelines, stamped out corruption—just a humble, god-fearing Russian doing his best to steward this vital national treasure.

"When we went off to university we all thought we had seen the last of him," said Chernov. "He was always the odd one. He's from a small town right up the road, you know. Priozersk. Logging town, and a little granite. More lakes. He and his mother moved to Peter when his drunken father fell into the river and drowned. After that we were all in third grade together. His mother's brother lived in the same apartment building as Volodnya." Volodnya, the diminutive for Vladimir Vladimirovich Putin.

"Olezka was always a clever one, even if he was odd, and it drove Volodnya crazy. Volodnya was a tough little prick, and he felt it his duty to beat the life out of Olezka in the common area when his drunken uncle was too tired to do it properly. Then Olezka tried to join Volodnya's judo club and it gave him a whole other excuse to beat him.

"Volodnya and I were going to Leningrad State. So to get back at us, Olezka always talked about how he was going to Moscow State, to study mathematics. He would have, too, he was that smart, if Volodnya hadn't sent that letter. It was the first letter I ever saw him write. I can still see the smirk on his face when he showed it to me. Somehow he had found out about a brother of Olezka's father, a priest, that had been out at the Konevsky Monastery in Lake Ladoga before he snuck over to Finland after the war." He smiled. "In those days, that's all it took.

"You could only apply to one university, that was the rule. If you didn't get in, your life was over. Very embarrassing. Later we heard that his uncle had a guy that owed him money and to make it up he got Olezka into a geology school out in Tyumen. Siberia. Studying rocks. Volodnya found it all very funny, although I don't think he still feels that way.

"Come to think of it, I don't know what was so awful about him. He was just the new boy. Different. If it hadn't been for Volodnya, he could have easily been one of us." He waved his hand around the compound.

Chernov's dacha was part of Ozero, *The Lake*. It was a co-op formed in the mid-'90s by several of the young, up-and-coming

Petersburgers to join together their dachas that neighbored each other on a small peninsula on Komsomolskoye Lake, a good-sized lake north of St. Petersburg, on the Karelian isthmus formed by the Gulf of Finland on the west and Lake Ladoga, the second largest lake in Europe, on the East.

The dachas were an hour outside the city, and the Ozero men sent their young families up for the summer and visited on the weekends. They watched sunsets on the beach together, they pooled their funds to put in a tennis court and they sat in the saunas and planned their rise to power. As they became more successful, they shared the cost of a high perimeter fence and guards with automatic weapons. Now they were heads of ministries, of banks, railroads and other businesses, they bought soccer clubs, and one became President of Russia. Putin rarely came any more. He had built a lavish new dacha outside Moscow more suitable for a head of state. But Chernov was more low-key, and sentimental perhaps, and he said he preferred the old, simple dacha that reminded he and his wife of happy times.

"So did Putin's dacha really catch fire from the sauna?" asked Charlie.

"I wasn't here that weekend. But with the crappy Polish wiring he was using, I have no reason to disbelieve it. It was so hard to get building materials back then it took him six years to build. He only finished after he had already moved to Moscow in the summer of '96. Six weeks later it burned to the ground. Firefighters arrived, but they didn't have enough water and their hoses wouldn't reach the lake. Volodnya had to run upstairs and throw his older daughter Masha out of a second-floor window.

"The people around here say it was because of a curse, a curse on us because we moved a few of them off the lake." He smiled and shrugged.

"Whatever the real story was, the story he told became more real and more powerful as part of his legend. The tough family man. Rescuing his daughter. Finding the cross his mother gave him in the

ashes, putting it on and reconnecting with the church. Reducing the
Soviet experience to a bad dream. Rebuilding the dacha, out of brick.
Punishing those worthless electricians. All very powerful. Better than
anything he can do today, like shooting tigers or gassing terrorists.
History has the illusion of being immutable, more genuine.

"That's why we need to be very cautious of Olezka and his stories.
In the Russian psyche Siberia has always been the true Russia, far
from the corrupting influences of Europe and the cities, particularly
from St. Petersburg. Lazarev, the TV star, he emerges from Siberia,
wealthy, humble, pious, to lead us on our special Russian path, to
fulfill our special destiny. He reinforces the Russian need, the desire,
to believe we are special, that all our suffering has been for a higher
purpose. He positions himself in direct contrast to Volodnya, whom
he paints as too European, selling our oil & gas to pad siloviki bank
accounts and heat German homes.

"Yazdani and her National Petroleum Report have been beating
this drum for Olezka as loudly as she can. You know of course she is
CIA? Yes. They think they are being clever by pumping him up, to
weaken us, but they are playing with fire. It is too risky, we may have
no choice but to deal with her. That said, I am looking forward to my
interview on Monday. She is a very charming woman, do you agree?"

"I have no idea whether she works for the CIA or not, but I think
the idea is ludicrous," said Charlie. "And if there's anything I've said
or done, Viktor Ilyich, that would suggest I'd welcome a casual reference to murdering a journalist then just so there is no confusion let
me tell you I don't."

"Charlie, Charlie, please forgive me. A figure of speech, I assure you. In Russia I can buy a front-page story above the fold saying
my enemy dines on small children for twenty-five thousand dollars.
There are many ways to deal with journalists here. Not all are violent,
so do not jump to conclusions. But I apologize, I know that she has
covered you for a long time and you are friends. Maybe you can talk
some sense to her, save us all a lot of trouble. But do be careful, she
is CIA."

"I appreciate your concern."

The children were running up the beach, wet, chilled and shrieking with delight in the glorious weather. The two women toweled the little ones down as they eyed the picnic lunch hungrily.

"*Yesh, yesh,*" said Chernov to the children. "Charlie, do you mind? We don't seem to be hungry. Two old men. Come, let's take a walk down the beach. Take off your shoes, relax."

Charlie took off his shoes and socks and rolled up his slacks. They grabbed two more beers and walked down the beach just above the gentle waves.

"Charlie, we are very concerned. Your operations seem out of control. Huber was very important to our efforts. Do you know how much we had paid him to shepherd our pipeline efforts?"

"Field work is dangerous. We never wanted them out there, that was forced on us. Accidents will happen. We're lucky no one else was killed. They almost lost the plane."

"Accident, pssht. Our pipelines are jeopardized and KarLap is embarrassed? No coincidence."

"A murder? Out at Sredny?"

"Your person should have cleared the invite list with us in advance. Very careless. This journalist from Rodina Neftegaz, there is no such person. A fake. Certainly he rigged it. Rupert is lucky he was not sitting next to Huber, I expect they wanted the both of them."

"Lazarev?"

"Who else? Almost as bad as losing Huber is the idea that Lazarev would be so bold. At one time he was this dangerous, but he had been quiet."

Chernov walked out onto a dock.

"Volodnya and I had an old motorboat that we bought in '92. We used to tie it up right here. We could water ski behind it, as long as we only had one person in the boat. He was good with engines, for a lawyer."

He stared out over the water. There were no boats at all that Charlie could see.

"At least this Huber mess is crowding out the fact that you allowed an iceberg to hit your drill station. Which caused an oil spill. Also the bit about the bears and wrestling with protesters. Who's running things up there?"

"Not oil, just drilling mud."

"Just don't let us lose confidence in you, Charlie. We picked you because we thought you could get this done. Don't disappoint us."

"No," said Charlie. "You didn't pick me. I picked you. I came to you with an idea and you signed on. I don't work for you. We're partners. Of necessity."

"Oh, right. A partnership. You sound like those pricks from McKinsey, coming over to lecture us on modern business practices, like we were a lost tribe of Old Believers. Wanted us to do this thing they called a 'trust fall.' They changed the subject when we told them they had to go first."

Chernov flung his empty bottle as far into the lake as he could. It skipped across the water a couple of times before it slowly started to sink into the water.

"You are a guest here, Charlie. And everyone is starting to wonder who invited you. I am one of your few friends left. You didn't make that any easier by bringing in Dickinson this week. People are very upset."

"We discussed that. And we agreed it was something that we could give on, and that it could help us, if we prepped Dickinson the right way, which I will do this afternoon. And you were going to tell me whether you were going to let Lazarev shut us down next week."

"Yes. I did. And the answer is no. If it comes to that, we have a judge that will stay his actions at the request of the Ministry of Energy, pending further investigation. But we don't want it to come to that, nor should you. It will cost us, financially and politically. And the resulting situation could be highly unstable, very uncertain. Not good for us, or our fifty-year energy project, yes? So my message to you is that you need to reach an accommodation with Lazarev. Find out what he wants and give it to him. We don't know. Short of Putin's balls on a tray, which is not an option."

"You've known him since grade school and you can't figure him out. How am I supposed to?"

"You are both oilmen. You understand each other. I think he even respects you, a little bit."

"He thinks I'm the spawn of Satan."

"He says that to everybody."

They walked back to the beach. The children were stretched out on towels, soaking up the sun after their lunch.

"There is another part of my message, Charlie. This whole affair has required us to make additional accommodations, to widen the circle. More mouths to feed. We'll need to adjust the terms of our deal. Everything has become more expensive."

Charlie let it drift away on the breeze, as if he hadn't even heard him.

"You will give us 10 percent back," said Chernov. "Split it up however you want."

Again, Charlie waited.

"And, Oleska is stuck on this question of territorial rights. He has discussed with you? He says Firebird will image parts of the Gakkel Ridge, which is currently disputed. If Firebird is to proceed, he wants the US to acknowledge our claims to the Gakkel. Seems reasonable."

Charlie waited to see if that was the last demand. He wasn't sure what was behind the territorial demand. That was new. The Russians had been coring out on the Gakkel. If they could prove that geologically the ridge was an extension of their continental shelf, they had rights to the ridge under UN treaties. But the process was taking decades and still unresolved.

That seemed to be it, so Charlie responded.

"You wouldn't just be taking advantage of the situation, would you?" said Charlie. "No, we'll stick to our bargain. If you need to re-cut things on your end, go ahead. We're not paying for your election losses. And there's no oil out on the Gakkel, so don't even waste our time on that."

"Does Texso want to become the next UKP, Charlie? Don't over-estimate our ability to be rational. You know deep down we want to throw you out."

"How do I know that's going to be the end of our problems? You can't even lock down Titov. The general that commands five hundred tanks twenty-five miles outside Moscow is meeting right now with Lazarev. When I talked to him last night he sounded very much like a free agent. Do you even have a handle on this situation? Where are we going to be six months from now?"

"Good for you, Charlie, so you know our weakness. We will be taking care of Titov. Volodnya wants to give him the Moscow Military District. Buy him off, so the Army knows we will keep them fed. I am opposed, I think he is underestimating the danger, but it is not my decision. You can tell Lazarev yourself, tonight." Charlie said nothing.

"So you think I'm bluffing, do you Charlie? You're the one that has two billion dollars bet on making this happen next week. I'm happy to wait."

"There is no second bite at the apple," said Charlie. "That was the whole point of going ahead this week. Now or never. You know that. I'll give you two percent, that's it. Let me know if we have a deal. Otherwise I'm going home and we're done. Seems to be what everyone wants."

As they reached Chernov's beach, his grandchildren came running up the sand calling *"Dedushka, Dedushka."* A little boy flies into his arms, and a little girl hugs his leg. Two older children shyly grab him around the waist.

"Da, da." With a wave of Chernov's hand it was settled. "Let us focus on what matters. Charlie, why did you not have more children? They are life's greatest joy. Eventually, our only joy. What else do we do this for?"

He handed the little boy off to Charlie and rushed off to help his wife with the folding table. Charlie stared into the little boy's blue eyes as he pulled at Charlie's ear.

CHAPTER 6

Smart Power

St. Petersburg
Friday mid-afternoon

Avinashi stood before the triptych mirrors of the Tchaikovsky suite, wrapped in gray-green chiffon. The shimmering silk gown and its sheer overlay floated around her, weightless. The gathered, one-shoulder neckline was pretty, yet modest. Her mother was pleased, though Dame Thatcher thought it a tad girlish. How Vicki had managed to find a dress and shoes in Avinashi's size was hard to imagine. She wanted Avinashi to have something for the Ministry dinner, her message had said, although she apologized that it couldn't be expensed. Did she still want it? As the gown was now the only nice thing in her entire wardrobe, Avinashi would not be returning it.

Avinashi was a familiar member of the Texso delegation, so the night manager of the Grand Hotel Europa had upgraded her to the historic suite when she had arrived in the middle of the night and he was short of rooms. As she contemplated the image in the mirror, with the elegant Imperial furnishings behind her, and the soft light from the samovar lamp illuminating the gown, memories of her rough life in the field and the ten-hour flight back to civilization melted away.

In desperate moments out east, when confronted again with the bleakness and sheer inhospitableness of Siberia, the local oil men would try to comfort themselves and her by trotting out their frontier

fables. Stuck in the mud on the way to inspect a factory in Novosibirsk
that turned out to manufacture only sub-standard drilling pipe, her
burly, rough-hewn host claimed to relish the challenges of the north.
Siberia was pure, authentic Russia, he boasted, where supermen such
as himself could flourish, in remote natural splendor and isolation,
free from the ink-soul bureaucrats in Moscow, far from the corrupting influence of Europe in St. Petersburg. Well, she thought, this superman was ready to hang up her cape for a couple of days.

But as she stood in the honeymoon suite of the tortured com-
poser, she mused that perhaps there was a factual basis for the Russian
suspicion of the city, some unexplainable but still measurable, corro-
sive effect it had on the Russian psyche. Last night, to ensure that she
appreciated his generosity, the night manager had regaled her with
the rich, sordid history of the suite. Now she couldn't stop imagining Tchaikovsky writhing in the bedroom's four-poster bed, agoniz-
ing over his marriage of convenience, his abandoned gay lover and
how to end his life, finally choosing door number three, the slow walk
into an icy river. And he was the stable one in the relationship, his
wife later dying in an asylum. Staring at the bed through the mirror,
Avinashi decided she would sleep on the couch.

Her cell phone rang. She grabbed it and looked at the number.
Charlie.

"Did I catch you in the middle of something?"

"No, not at all. I mean, I just ran back to the hotel to check email."

Pause. Something he didn't like but left it unsaid. Probably imagined she was off doing something more productive. "I'll be at the
Kazansky Bridge in five minutes, can you meet me there?"

"No problem."

Charlie had told her early on to assume that in Russia someone
was always watching. He probably had something else in mind, but
since then she had been changing, with some difficulty, under her
robe in the closet. But now she pulled her dress off as quickly as she
could without tearing it, scrambled into a suit and shoes, grabbed
her briefcase and ran out the door. Where was the Kazansky Bridge?

Since Charlie had pulled her into the Firebird project earlier that year, her work had seemed an unrelenting succession of missed deadlines, hasty workarounds and frantic improvisations, interrupted only by the occasional international incident, so the thought of having her review that morning had been making her nauseous.

She had hoped that Charlie would be too busy, and that it could be delayed until she had redeemed herself with some minor miracle. Instead, after a couple of hours of sleep, they had been the first ones in the restaurant that morning when it opened at seven.

To be frank, and in her defense, he was the worst manager she had ever had. He always dropped in unexpected—she would just turn around and he would be suddenly standing there. Then he would stick to her like a shadow for a day or two or three doing his alien mind meld thing, alternatively quizzing and lecturing her non-stop about rocks and plays and pumps and politicians, throw in a few baseball anecdotes and then disappear. Leaving her with more questions than answers, no direction and all the responsibility. How was this supposed to end any way but in her abject failure?

In the beginning the tap on the shoulder from Charlie had been thrilling. He was a god at the University of Houston Earth Sciences department. They only picked one graduating student a year to meet with him. It was considered a great honor to get the interview, which was good because she had never heard of anyone actually getting hired. When she arrived at the appointed time of six in the morning there was no great man, just a printed list of locations and questions. Be at the Dixie Chicken by six p.m. if you have all the answers. If not, no need to trouble yourself. Or him, it was implied.

So began a twelve-hour blitz of sedimentology, petrology, micropaleontology, tectonics, geochemistry, petroleum systems, seismology, hydrology and applied rock physics. She started in the micropaleontology lab with some rapid-fire lab exercises, then researched and wrote a short academic paper before debugging and rewriting some remote sensing code and blasting out the door for the trip up north to College Station. Into the mineralogy lab to identify 369 specimens and some geometrical analysis of mineral systems. Then she was to track down a Brunton compass if she committed the mortal sin of having left home without hers (she had—a kindly grad student lent hers) and head out to Whisky Bridge near Stone City. There she navigated the bluff up and down and around under specific directions that seemed to test her physical fitness more than anything. Then a near thesis level field study there of sedimentation from the Middle Eocene and its lessons for modern oil exploration and then ten minutes left to get to the Dixie Chicken.

Charlie was at the bar in dusty field clothes reading a paper and sipping on a beer. He looked up when she approached.

"Well, here she is, Charlie," said the old bartender, setting another beer out. "Finally."

"Sorry, I'm so embarrassed, I'm probably the slowest ever," said Avinashi. "I know it's too late, but I came anyway. Am I too late? I came as fast as I could. That was quite a list."

Charlie looked at her intently. He put down his beer and his paper. Picked up a different paper and read it.

"You're Ms. Sharma?"

"Avinashi. I mean, yes."

"You have all the answers?"

"I believe I do, Mr. Joiner."

"Very good. No, Avinashi, you are not the slowest ever. You are the only one that has ever shown up. Now let's see what you've got."

They met over a spare breakfast of toasted English muffins and black coffee. Charlie looked like hell. His right palm was red and oozing and he had an abrasion on his cheek. He must have raked the side of his face with his razor. And what was wrong with his ear? It was bruised dark purple. And of course he had the ridiculous goggle lines on his face. Every night she had to send him the day's seismic data. Everything Texso collected. Worldwide. Vicki told her he couldn't sleep without it. Sometimes he didn't sleep at all, she said, he just watched it all night.

A complete mess of a man.

"So, tell me how you think you've been doing," he said.

It seemed a cold and utterly cruel start, but she launched in on her disastrous spring and summer. She reviewed for him the few meager accomplishments for which, after painful hours of soul-searching on the flight in, she felt she could claim any personal credit, all the while expecting to be interrupted at any moment for her offensively self-serving analysis. After this summary, his silence was unrelenting so she was forced to move on to her shortcomings. She started to highlight a few situations where in retrospect she would have acted somewhat differently, and lessons learned, and suddenly recalled a few more, and then they just seemed to pour out, from stolen mud pumps to air-launched German Chancellors, one after another, in increasingly obvious disproportion to any value she brought to Texso. She finally slowed, exhausted and embarrassed, until the two of them sat silent, the fact of her complete inability to perform at her job finally and plainly revealed.

"There's only one thing I want to know," said Charlie. "How many feet have you drilled?"

"How many feet? None, but you know that. That's not my fault. I've got us this far."

"Just remember why we're out here," he said. "If we don't drill any wells, this was all wasted."

"Don't you mean if we don't find any oil?"

"No. You just drill wells. You let God worry about whether there's any oil there."

She paused to consider.

"That missing mud pump set us back a month," he said. "Does that bother you?"

That lit the fuse. Maggie was not taking this anymore. Weeks of fatigue and frustration and fear just burst out of her. She worked hard and she worked well and it was only a goddamned mud pump and anyway he couldn't fault her because the Russians were unrepentant thieves.

"Bother me? No, you know what, Charlie, it doesn't bother me. I have been out here doing my absolute best, performing daily miracles in impossible circumstances, where my only support comes from colleagues that don't want me here and actively plot my failure. And I'm expected to babysit a drug-addicted child scientist, who, oh by the way, the Russian nationalists want dead. In fact, I'm surprised every night when I go to sleep that I accomplished anything at all because everything about this job, this country, this project is utterly impossible. So no, the stolen, not missing, mud pump doesn't bother me at all. I got us another one. You want to send me back to Houston, be my guest. I should have gone to Exxon anyway, not this madhouse."

Oh my God, what had she done? Charlie shifted in his seat, reaching for his phone. One quick email to Vicki and she was gone. Who would touch her now after being tainted by these Texso cowboys? She could see herself at the door to her father's home in Houston with her small suitcase. Her dad's disappointed face, turning over the picture of her poor mother on the mantel so she need not witness this final disgrace. Wordlessly stumbling out to his pickup truck and driving out to their tiny ranch, alone. Her brother Ajay with his headphones on, smirking at her.

"Good," said Charlie. "Because it doesn't bother me, either. And if it bothered you then you shouldn't be out here. You have one goal. One. You are here to make hole in the Arctic. Right now, I don't think either one of us can know how that's going to happen. But it will. And you're going to figure that out. That's why I hired you. I saw that in you. You were someone that could make hole. Even out here. Avinashi, I don't want you to focus on failing less. You're right enough. I want you to fail faster. And no, you do not belong at Exxon sitting in front of a goddamned accounting ledger. You belong out here. With us."

He pulled out a book from his beaten leather bag and carefully cracked the spine and set it on the table. He pulled out a pen from his jacket pocket and carefully underlined a sentence. Then, of course, he closed up the book and slid it across the table.

"I'll call you when I get back. Gotta see the Grey Cardinal. Stay busy but be ready." He got up and left.

She picked up the book. Mandelbrot? The book flipped open to a page with an underlined passage. She read it and smiled.

She flew down the grand staircase as fast as skirt and low heels would allow, past the alarmed security staff, and out into the street. "Kazansky Bridge?" she asked the doorman. Anikushin's colossal Pushkin beckoned to her from a square down the street to her left. The doorman pointed to the right, so she turned her back on Pushkin and ran around the other end of the block.

Nevsky Prospect was the main boulevard in St. Petersburg, but the pavement was heavily littered and the elaborate facades were dirty and worn. It was another hot summer afternoon, and she was wet and sticky under her woolen suit. She ran down the block and out onto the broad bridge over the Griboedov Canal, startling more than a few with her speed, even though she ran slowly because of the shoes. Where would he be? On her left were the colonnades of the Kazan Cathedral, fronted by a filthy plaza, and to her right, down on the near side of the canal, was a set of steps leading down to a platform floating on the canal. Two tour boats were tied up, and a police launch.

A black sedan pulled up at the steps. Charlie stepped out of the back seat, phone to his ear, and he gave her a wave. She smiled back weakly and chased after him as he charged down the gangway to the launch. He showed his Texso ID to one of the two policemen on board and stepped into the launch and she did the same. After they were seated amidships on a bench seat, the officers accelerated quickly down the canal, veering back and forth around the prevailing traffic.

He ended his call and pointed ahead of them. "The Church on Spilt Blood," he yelled over the sound of the motor. "Have you been?"

Avinashi looked up at the richly textured façade and the onion domes covered in gold and swirls of yellow and blue. She shook her head.

"We need to get you out more. It's spectacular. Medieval Russia right in the heart of the city."

She had read that the shape of the iconic onion domes had no rational explanation. Like Russia itself, perhaps. Reaching for the heavens, they might symbolize the flames of icon lamps, or prayers and striving for heaven, or the growing flame of Russia fed by its martyrs, saints and ascetics and the occasional American.

"The blood was Alexander the Second's," shouted Charlie. "They got him on their third try. His assassins were very adaptive." He smiled. "Right there," he said, pointing to a small extension of the church extending out onto the embankment as they sped by.

"When Alexander took over the top job, he went to visit Poland, which his father had conquered. Gathered all the top people, told them 'above all things, let there be no dreams.' Of freedom. Not a great observer of human nature." He raised his eyebrows and started digging around in his briefcase. He pulled out a notebook and wrote something down.

"The traffic in this town has gotten insane," said Charlie. "It took me thirty minutes to go the last mile getting back and we're late as it is. I asked Vicki if she could get us a boat, it's way faster to Strelna. Turns out if you're meeting a visiting head of state the police will pick you up. Although I'll need you to cover the tip."

They turned left at the next canal and swept through the city, very fast. The canals were also very crowded but it didn't seem to matter to the pilot. Charlie pointed up to where the Hermitage and Winter Palace would be, barely visible through the buildings. He called out the bridges as they passed under, the Red, Blue and Green. She had read about all the bridges and so also noticed he was too proper to call out the Potseluev Bridge, the Bridge of Kisses, as they passed under.

When they broke out into the Gulf of Finland, Charlie motioned for them to move further back in the launch. There was no protection from the wind, and she sadly realized that she was going to meet the Vice President looking like she had been tumble dried.

He leaned over and spoke into her ear, but still had to raise his voice over the engine. "I know this is a little loud, but that's good. Private." He looked up and smiled at the second policeman who watched them impassively.

"I'm glad you're coming, I want you to have this in your toolkit. After the embargo in '74, the US government decided that oil was too important to be left to the oil companies, as they now continually remind us. So now they're always involved to some degree. Sometimes for better, sometimes for worse. Clinton and Gore were very involved with us in the Caspian. Your friend Maggie Thatcher got in the mix on behalf of UKP, so we needed to match that. Other governments have always been much more proactive."

She had talked about Dame Thatcher once with Charlie. He kept bringing it up.

"VPs are great," said Charlie. "Because they carry a big business card and you can get their time. They're always looking for something to do. Gore was a bit of the bull in a china shop, but what he lacked in subtlety he made up for in enthusiasm."

"So what are you expecting here?" said Avinashi.

"Well, the good news is that our guy on the NSC, Jacob Stoyan, will be there. He's well-informed on energy and he gets the Russians. His father was Bulgarian, fought with and against them in the war. The bad news is that the VP and his staff are here because they are very hawkish on the current Russian administration and very pro-Lazarev. That's why Lazarev wanted the VP. I'm going to try to get the VP on the same page with us, but our agendas don't match up perfectly.

"Our official role this afternoon is to round out his staff's briefing on the dinner tonight. We're a little bit late but we should have plenty of time. Lazarev and Dickinson are doing a short session before the dinner, then they'll share the head table, then Dickinson's on to Moscow. The VP can't come to Russia and meet just with Lazarev, so officially it's a side trip on the way to the Kremlin. Parking Dickinson at the Constantine Palace, right in Putin's favorite cottage, is pushing it far enough. Now, I want you to have a speaking role, so let's have you update him on Firebird. I'll cover additional background as necessary and deliver the key message. Now, in a setting like this they can't absorb more than two or three key ideas, so let's decide what those are. Then if you still have their attention have another three or four points in your back pocket. Does that sound good? Okay, let's go through it."

Constantine Palace
Strelna
Friday late-afternoon

Thirty minutes after boarding, they were on the pier at Strelna, and the grounds of the Constantine Palace. They were escorted onto an electric cart and tore off across the grounds, as fast as the little machine could go. The palace was to the south beyond the gardens. They headed east into an area that looked like a bad condo development.

"The palace was renovated to host heads of state," said Charlie. "That's when they built these residential buildings. Eighteen of 'em. Each large enough to house a visiting dignitary and all their staff. They call 'em cottages."

They were plain little flat-topped towers with pale walls and green pitched roofs around the edges on top, set on wide-open grounds in what appeared to be a very regular grid pattern.

"No trees. Takes away cover for the bad guys, opens up the sniper sightlines for the good guys. They have helipads over there."

They arrived at the cottage closest to the shore, on the far side. Inside, they passed through security, checked in all briefcases and electronics, and were led to a small conference room. The door opened minutes later and an older man with a quiet smile and a dark suit and tie hurried into the room. He reminded Avinashi of her Czech petrology instructor, Dr. Vanek, had he instead been an undertaker.

"Charlie, I'm so glad you're here." He grabbed Charlie's hand in both of his and gave it a firm, long shake. He did the same with Avinashi.

"Ms. Sharma, I am Jacob Stoyan. Thank you for helping us today. Come, we should hurry."

They went around a corner and entered a large conference room. The main table had been disassembled and stacked in pieces against the wall, together with the chairs, presumably to make space for what appeared to be a small trailer home in the center of the room. A roughly finished box of plywood, sheet metal, insulation and wires, all up on foam blocks. Jacob held the door for them and Avinashi followed Charlie inside. While Jacob squeezed around the far side of the long, rectangular conference table, Charlie stepped back to let Avinashi squeeze in on the near side and then he slid in next to her.

"It's a quick and dirty SCIF," Charlie said to her. "These cottages are basically big listening devices. Like being on an FSB reality TV show. The SCIF has electronic and acoustic shielding."

"Phelps is apoplectic," said Stoyan. "He didn't like you pushing back the briefing. The VP was going to go for a run before the meeting. Now Phelps is saying you've disrespected the office, embarrassed yourself, et cetera. On top of everything else this week. But they're still going to make us wait a respectable interval." There was no ventilation in the room and Avinashi was already very warm.

"I was lucky to get the meeting, I had to go," said Charlie. "What, he wants me to skip Chernov so Dickinson can get his run in? Good to see this isn't going to their heads. Would hate to see the two of them with any real power."

Brad Phelps was the Vice President's Chief of Staff. Phelps was the founder of a cyber security software company that he had built in three years with sixty people and twenty-five million of other people's money and then sold for three billion. He donated a significant portion to the Vice President and other groups helpful to him in the last election cycle. Forty-two and still running at a startup pace, he had asked for a staff position, not the usual ambassadorship or undersecretary slot, considering himself too valuable not to be in a role that felt operational, rather than policy. Disappointed

that his horse ended up in the number two spot, he was still determined to make an impact.

"Well, it's a good thing then I'm not here to make Brad Phelps
happy."

The door opened and Charlie and Jacob stood, so Avinashi followed. She recognized the first man to enter as Vice President Tom
Dickinson. She should, she had been seeing the former Senator from
Maryland on TV for most of her life. Her first thought, which arrived
in the form of a mildly shocking revelation, is that a politician like
Dickinson must be the result of some mass media natural selection
process. His face seemed evolved for television, with large, distinctive
features that seemed cartoonish in person, but probably projected
well on the small screen. He was older than you would know from
TV, heavily lined, but with hair that was eerily full and still, like a furry
animal in a diorama, and teeth and a shirt so white under the incan-
descent lights of the SCIF that they seemed to be generating their
own power, all set off by a sleek red tie.

Too close behind him was a doughy-faced man in khakis and a
blue oxford shirt with the sleeves rolled up. His hair was full, dark
and messy, and he was short and had a hint of paunch. Must be
Phelps.

Dickinson ascended to the head of the table as Phelps stood at
the open door. There seemed to be a lineup of others behind him,
outside the door to the SCIF. Phelps stared at Avinashi like she was a
piece of malware.

"Stoyan, this briefing is principals only," said Phelps.

"Mr. Vice President, Mr. Phelps, this is my colleague Avinashi
Sharma," said Charlie. "She's running Project Firebird for Texso. I'm
the one that's extra baggage here, so I can step outside if you need
me to."

Not again, don't you dare pull one of your disappearing acts on
me, thought Avinashi. She looked for a path to the door.

"That's fine, Brad," said Dickinson. "If Mr. Joiner wants to shift
some responsibility here, so be it. Let's get started."

Dickinson sat down, and the others followed. Brad bumped Charlie down a spot on his side, bumping Avinashi around to the end of the table, directly across from the Vice President. She sat in the chair but it was too low. She fiddled with the handle but nothing would make it stay up. The top of the table came nearly up to her shoulders. She put her elbows up on the table to give her extra height but she felt even more like a little kid.

The rest of the retinue piled into the room, and Avinashi didn't feel so badly about her promotion to principal. Middle-aged experts in bland jackets and dress suits and privileged young aides with ruthless eyes. All tight-lipped, clutching portfolios to their chests, and now engaged in a furious, silent battle for seating. Three of the senior set and one particularly aggressive junior member grabbed the remaining chairs squeezed into the corners, while the other staff members stood or, in one case, crouched on one knee at the corner of the table, like an eager ball boy ready to track down stray shots. Avinashi looked over at him and smiled, apologetically, which he returned with a challenging stare.

Barely reaching the table, on a tiny chair, in a soundproof box, in a tower, on the castle grounds, Avinashi felt like a Russian nesting doll. The tiniest doll of all.

Phelps securely fastened the door and, with his audience assembled and hushed, the Vice President began with his prepared remarks.

"Mr. Joiner, and I am afraid I must direct these remarks to you as well Ms. Sharma, given the short time you have left us with this afternoon, I have no alternative but to be blunt. So, for the record, I must say that in the pursuit of your narrow interests you are have made yourself a royal pain in the ass for those of us serving the American public."

He looked at Avinashi with wide eyes and jutting jaw, as if expecting some disagreement, and to her horror the aides all turned in her direction as well.

He continued, in measured, resonant tones, fiddling with the papers in front of him, as if repeating a very simple and familiar lesson yet again for a disappointing student, or playing to a camera. "I am here today because the US has vital interests at stake. Vital interests. These interests are, one, to support vigorous and open democratic processes in the Russian Federation by maintaining a respectful dialogue with all significant political participants and, two, to ensure fair access by US companies to a vital energy-producing region. I am not here, and this is important, as a bit player in a Texso-produced Broadway show, to be told what I need to know, to do whatever you say to maximize your return, to take your stage direction, hit my marks and head home."

"Mr. Vice President, we would expect nothing else," said Charlie. "Completely understood, no question."

"I'm sorry, did I sound like I was finished?" His pained smile and ironic look around the room displayed to all the depths, and great burden, of his exceptional patience.

"But I'm glad you agree, that's encouraging, Mr. Joiner. The Minister of Natural Resources of the Russian Federation, who, in addition to controlling a very significant portion of the world's oil and gas reserves, also heads the leading opposition party to United Russia, has requested the courtesy of a close consultation with this Administration, a consultation in which the number one issue is certain to be KarLap, and his strong desire to reexamine, given the new responsibilities he has assumed, the terms and process of awarding your very favorable PSA. So imagine my consternation when I no sooner get off Air Force One to try to salvage your project but I find that you and Ms. Sharma have gone ahead and dumped two billion dollars worth of equipment in the Arctic Ocean, together with one German Chancellor. Equipment which I understand will be expensive junk in one weeks time unless used. All with the sole intention of boxing him, and thus me, in."

"Mr. Vice President," said Charlie, "I should point out that this was a scheduled part of our operations on Project Firebird."

"Oh, really. Ms. Sharma is on-site, maybe she could tell us whether the timing was accelerated this week. Ms. Sharma?"

With the questions wrapped in speeches, the feigned solicitousness softening a sarcastic tone looking to score points, and the stonefaced aides standing in the background, Avinashi felt like a witness at a congressional hearing. Devoid of counsel's whispered guidance, she answered carefully.

"Our schedule has always called for immediate deployment of the geophones once they were available and weather conditions permitted. These conditions were first satisfied on Wednesday."

"Thank you, Ms. Sharma, I'm sure it fell to you to make sure they were." Point scored and pause. Cue sarcasm. "Congratulations on the success of your efforts." And two.

Less patient with the game, Phelps cut in. "Joiner, for a guy that has a draft subpoena somewhere with his name on it, you've got some balls coming in here and trying this line of bullshit. Mr. Vice President, if I may?"

"Fire away, Mr. Phelps," said Dickinson.

"We want to keep Putin off balance by promoting his only viable rival and we want Russian hydrocarbons flowing West not East. That clear enough for you, Joiner?"

"Got it."

"Good. Now, thanks to Ms. Sharma's little commando operation this week, you have now eliminated the only option that satisfies these competing interests. Which is, or was, to allow Lazarev to suspend the project, give him a few cycles to play to the crowd, tweak it, then go forward. Instead, in the interest of keeping your fifty-year project on schedule, you have thrown two billion dollars of KarLap's money on the table, on behalf of Texso and your little gangster friends. Why you have done this I don't understand. Your project won't turn on for fifteen years. You won't return a profit for twenty-five. Return of capital in year thirty-five, but who knows? I thought biotech was bad until I learned about Arctic oil & gas."

"Mr. Vice President, Lazarev wants this deal stopped," said Charlie. "He wants a delay, but he has no intention of ever letting this go forward."

"He can slow it, if we let him," said Phelps. "But there's no chance he can shelve it. We should only be so lucky if there were someone that could stand up to United Russia. Try to keep up, Joiner, we're trying to establish a counterbalancing force in Russia. Big difference between a one-party and two-party state. Maybe that's a little subtle for you."

"I think I understand. I just think it's a dangerous strategy. Lazarev is dangerous."

"Joiner, do you want me to tell you what dangerous is?" said Phelps. "Putin is doubling his military budget with the oil revenues you help him generate. He's sending bombers into Canadian airspace and scouting Venezuelan for airstrips. He rolls his tanks into independent allies in the Caucuses every time someone with a drop of Russian blood gets a parking ticket. Ukraine is late on their gas bill, so he lets their grandmothers freeze to death in their beds. And if anybody in the press raises a hey now, they end up taking their tea with a radioactive isotope."

"Look, it's easy to get trapped in your own little world," said Dickinson. "I know you're an oilman, Mr. Joiner. But try to step back and look at the big picture."

"Where we are today," said Charlie, "with estimates of undiscovered oil, and future energy needs, Lazarev is more dangerous. Autocrats that won't sell us their oil are more dangerous than those that will."

"Mr. Joiner," said Dickinson. "I believe that is one of the most cynical, frightening statements I have heard in my lifetime. Unfortunately, however, we don't have the time to further deconstruct your worldview." He paused, and settled back into full committee mode.

"Now that you've gotten the siloviki to draw a little line in the sand, where are we? I know in the usual course you'd just bribe him, or sweeten the deal for his side, but I think you've run into the one man that you can't buy. Damn it Joiner, we needed a concession to offer him. We help his standing, he looks like a winner, we just have a slight delay, stay on the good side of a power player that will be around a while."

The trailer is a sweatbox. Is she the only one that feels it, thought Avinashi? A bead of sweat rolls off her nose and loudly plops on the table. She has no handkerchief, should she wipe her forehead with her sleeve? What is it, is it from being out in the Arctic so long? God, she's an Indian, she should be impervious to heat. She glances beside her and she is relieved to see the ball boy's forehead is also dripping, but he seems determined to ignore it. He's been through this drill in the SCIF before.

"At this point," said Phelps, "we just need to take our best and only option which is to do the public meet and greet with the Minister, get on the plane and go home."

"So you have stolen some of the excitement from the weekend, Mr. Joiner," said Dickinson. "Not what I would have done, but your call. If you worked for me, frankly, I'd have canned you. Colossal error in judgment." Avinashi had a difficult time imagining Charlie working for Dickinson, or Dickinson running anything. "Ms. Avinashi, you would be on immediate leave, until I better understood your role. Brad, we finished? Maybe our side should stick around and circle up. Thank you, Mr. Joiner and Ms. Sharma."

They apparently want to do nothing. No action. Charlie won't like this, thought Avinashi. She could see Charlie slowly gather his legs under him beneath the table, on the balls of his feet, hunch slowly over the table, bring his hands together. He wasn't getting up from the table.

"Thank you, Mr. Vice President, sir, and Brad, I do understand. I do apologize, none of these projects unfolds exactly as we expect or would desire. I do agree with you that if we go into next week with this situation unresolved, the outcome is very uncertain. Putin's office would like to avoid such a confrontation. That's why they have informed me they would like us to broker a deal with Lazarev."

"Broker a deal for them!" cried Dickinson. "You've got to be joking. The only thing worse than doing Texso's work would be doing Putin's."

"Working in these parts often forces us to make tough choices. What you should be aware of is that if there is a confrontation next week, Lazarev would certainly lose, initially. Longer term, who knows? It could force the siloviki to take action against him. As I understand them, if Lazarev ends up in Khodorkovsky's old Mongolian jail cell on trumped-up charges this would not advance US interests."

"You want to play politics in Russia, Mr. Joiner," said Dickinson. "Manipulating them to their ends."

"With respect, sir, I am the one dealing with the duly-elected representatives of the Russian people. You are the one seeking to promote an opposition party."

"Well, I think they're fascist thugs. Why in the world would they want my help?"

"Lazarev wants you to shut us down. He'll say it'll just be a delay. He thinks you can do it, he thinks you'll be a sympathetic ear and that he can convince you. He knows you want him to succeed. If you disabuse him of this, it will cause him to reassess his position."

"You want me to threaten him?" said Dickinson. "Got it. Nice guy."

"To let him know where he really stands. To let him know where you stand. To offer him a good deal. It is a good deal for him. If it's not, all he has to do is turn it down. I think he'll take it. Also, the one thing we believe he wants is something only you can offer. We believe the critical issue for him is US support at the UN for Russia's claims to the Gakkel Ridge, as part of their continental shelf. Part of the ridge will be scanned in Firebird, and the territory is disputed. He wants a memorandum of understanding from KarLap to this effect, a personal assurance and public statement from you."

"Oh, Christ, Joiner, that's impossible," said Dickinson.

"Why? Your administration is on record as endorsing Senate confirmation of the Law of the Sea Treaty. The US can continue any challenge the economics around deep sea mining, which is the only thing holding up confirmation. This is just the territorial issue. What are you giving up? There's no oil out there. And if there is, this way it will be developed by KarLap. What are the odds that the US is going to get any greater interest in this sliver of international waters in the middle of the Russian Arctic than Texso's interest?"

"Easy for you to say, Mr. Joiner, all good for Texso."

"Here's what I would suggest. When you meet, you need to tell him that you would like to be his friend. The decision is his. You have decided that, if Firebird goes forward next week, the economic terms should be more favorable for Russia. You have directed me to find ways to improve the take for Russia."

"Increase the take?"

"The siloviki want their end improved. Complications, et cetera. The costs of instability. But it would flow to Lazarev as well, good optics for him. It's complicated."

"Complicated, like the Caspian? Ah, Christ, Mr. Joiner, you're killing me."

"You would also tell him that you would support KarLap's claims to the Gakkel. Tell him these are things that you can do for him. If not, you'll be on your way. You look forward to hearing of the Firebird results. Leave the rest to me."

"Ah, the rest. Do tell."

"That if he refuses, he gets nothing. Firebird is going ahead. They have a judge standing by to invalidate any permit revocation he tries. Also, there is another bit in it for him. I don't think it would be appropriate coming from you. But for your information, I can confirm that his ally, General Titov will be promoted on Monday morning to the head of the Moscow Military District. This would be communicated to Titov as an olive branch from Putin, not as a result of a deal worked for him by Lazarev. To Lazarev, it would be communicated as a concession deserving value in return."

Charlie sat back.

"Ah, Joiner, where do I begin?" said Phelps. "Is this how you spend your life, getting shaken down by gangsters, selling out your country's territorial interests? First of all, don't even think about sweetening the pot for your KGB pals. You drag the VP over here to embarrass him by ending up with a better deal for the siloviki and I will have you renditioned to Morocco. Second, the Vice President of the United States does not carry water for the Russian President. We are here to extend support to Lazarev, not shake him down. And what's with moving generals around, you starting a coup? Non-starter, all around."

Stoyan stirred in his seat, breaking his silence. To Avinashi, he looked like a stone statue come to life, a curse broken.

"Mr. Vice President, the success of KarLap is absolutely vital to US national security," said Stoyan. "The Arctic, together with perhaps ultra-deepwater, is the last frontier for new energy exploration. The KarLap PSA covers a vast region with tremendous opportunity. We need to be in there. We cannot give this up. Charlie has gotten our foot in the door with Texso, we cannot let this opportunity slip away. This is a major, major project that will give us the exclusive rights over the next fifty years to develop fifteen prospective basins in the Arctic. The West needs this project. We need these basins developed, we need to participate in the development, and we need to have a seat at the table to direct where those hydrocarbons flow. KarLap accomplishes all of that. The success of this project is vitally important. In my opinion, it far outweighs the advantage of balancing the power of the siloviki."

"What if you're looking at this all wrong, Jake," said Phelps. "Maybe we need you to fail, Joiner. A dirty, dinosaur business with hideous externalities, propping up autocratic regimes, destroying the climate. If there's a God we won't even have an oil business in twenty-five years. Wind, solar, biofuels, geothermal. I feel like we're going to war to bailout a buggy-whip factory. You're overplaying your hand with us, Joiner."

"Look," said Dickinson. "For several reasons, I'm the only one that's going to be able to connect with this Lazarev character. He knows that, he invited me for a reason, even though Mr. Joiner thinks it's because he thinks I'm an easy mark. He's a politician, with all the headaches and concerns that comes with that responsibility. He's also a man of faith, and so also answers to a higher calling, like myself. He's an oilman, Mr. Joiner, but he's not a businessman, at least as we recognize it. You two are going to be oil and water, pardon the expression. I can talk to him. Let me get in there, feel him out. We'll find some common ground. Offering support for his Arctic land grab is a good idea. Perhaps we can offer that, see where we go."

"Again, with all due respect, sir," said Charlie.

Dickinson interrupted. "Joiner, when someone starts that way, I always know they're going to tell me I'm an idiot. But please, go on."

"Mr. Vice President, they're not looking for common ground," said Charlie. "Or compromise, or win-win solutions. That isn't the way they think. They don't have a lot of historical experience with good intentions. For them, life is more of a zero-sum game. You win, I lose. The only way to deal is that is from a position of strength. Make your proposal, stick to it."

"So go in like cowboys, Mr. Joiner, guns blazing? Take it or leave it, Hobson's Choice, all that? No wonder we have the reputation we do. Look, with all due respect to you, Mr. Joiner, this is a bit above your pay grade. At least while this business is still relevant, to Brad's point, the oil business is too important to be left to the oilmen. Didn't anyone ever tell you that? Now, we appreciate your counsel, please allow us to adjourn while we develop our final strategy."

Charlie nodded to Avinashi and started to stand up. She had barely lifted off her chair before the ball boy had pulled her chair away and slid into it, a look of sweaty satisfaction on his face. She bumped and stumbled her way around the table to the door.

They exited the SCIF into the cool air. Stoyan stepped out with them and he closed the door behind him. Charlie walked over and spoke to him quietly.

"I tried not to soft-pedal it too much."

"It was fine," said Stoyan.

"He should be getting the call in half an hour," said Charlie. "We should both be scarce." Stoyan nodded.

"Call?" asked Avinashi.

"The President is calling him," said Charlie. "Directing him to provide all possible assistance. He and Wayne are close. They have an understanding on KarLap."

A Secret Service man slipped by them into the SCIF, then exited and closed the door again. Even through the acoustic shielding, Avinashi could hear the Vice President shouting, like a muffled voice in a dream. The door opened and Brad Phelps came out.

"The prick isn't even in town. He's not going to be at the dinner."

"The meeting's off?" said Charlie. "He requested it."

"He still wants to meet. But at something called the Karela Fortress. In Priozersk, wherever the fuck that is. Somewhere up north, forty-five minutes by chopper. And he specifically wants you there, too, Joiner. We're told he wants to meet you on hallowed ground. What the hell does that mean?"

"You wouldn't believe me if I told you."

"Try me."

"He thinks I'm a demon. It's a test. Better than some of the alternatives he's suggested."

"You know, he's not completely crazy."

"Okay, I'm ready to go anytime. Avinashi can cover the dinner. Right?"

"Okay, sure," said Avinashi. "I'll just need to go back to the hotel first."

"Could be tight," said Charlie. "Why do you need to go back?"

She searched for an acceptable answer. For a beautiful dress that made her feel like a countess, not a junior vice president? To meet our chief scientist in the lobby, so that someone might mistake us for a couple? She was stumped.

"I'll let you work it out," said Charlie. "This fine gentlemen could probably help you." He lightly touched the back of the shoulder of the nearest Secret Service agent. "Call me if you need anything. And have fun. This is one of the few perks I can offer you. Oh, and please keep an eye on Ted. He's got some rough edges. Do you what you can to keep him in line, okay?"

"Okay, sure. Thanks, Charlie."

He gave her another big smile and disappeared down the hallway with Stoyan. She turned to the agent.

"How can I help you ma'am?" he said.

"I need to change."

The agent stared at her blankly. "Ma'am, we can procure a change of clothing. Could you give me your sizes?"

"Actually, I was hoping to get some things from my hotel. A dress. And some shoes."

"A dress? What color dress, ma'am? And any other items? Toiletries, accessories?" He was pulling out a small notebook. Oh, God, she thought.

"You know what? I travel light. Could they just pack up everything and bring it here?"

"Affirmative, ma'am. We will need you to call the hotel to authorize the retrieval."

"Sure." She felt very silly saying this. "And could you tell them to be really, really careful with the dress?" He wrote it down.

Now if she could just find a closet.

CHAPTER 7

A MISTAKE, WRAPPED IN A PLAN, INSIDE AN IRON FIST

The Grand Palace
Peterhof
Friday evening

From the black and white tiled plaza above the golden fountains of the Grand Cascade, Avinashi gazed over the Lower Gardens, down the Sea Channel and out through the trees to the tranquil Gulf of Finland. As the setting sun turned the gardens gold to match the gushing Baroque statuary, Avinashi wished she were someone who could enjoy a quiet drink and a fairy-tale summer evening.

But instead she was someone so tired she could have laid down on the tile and been asleep before anyone noticed her, who was so continually stressed she had dropped five precious pounds but still couldn't keep food down. Someone responsible, as her CEO had suddenly announced before he headed off for the Throne Room with the rest of the guests, for the disappearance of the company's lead scientist and evening's featured speaker. Standing alone on the plaza, she had no idea even where to look. He had been missing ever since she arrived, conspicuously solo.

"Looking for your young man?" Charlie's odious middle-man Don Sanders appeared out of nowhere, reeking of alcohol and putting a light, creepy hand on her bare back. "Last I heard he was going to down to play in the grotto. Good lord knows what he's up to down there." He chortled like a third-grader at an underwear joke. "It's right below us. Down those steps over there, loop back around, right through the Grand Cascade. Would you like me to escort you?"

Avinashi had seen enough movies to know not to enter a damp cellar with the likes of Sanders. "Oh, no, I wouldn't want to make you late. I'll track him down, I know his habits. See you inside."

Carefully lifting the front of her gown, Avinashi hurried to the staircase on the right and tip-toed down the steps in her heels. At the bottom of the staircase, a narrow, wet ramp ran over the water into the middle of the fountains, then cut left and disappeared from view. This couldn't be right. There had been tour guides wandering around earlier, but they and the other guests had all vanished. All except Petrov, the worst journalist in the world and the pride of *Rodina Neftegaz*. He was looking over the stone railing at the edge of the plaza above. Even up close it was difficult to see any life in his eyes. At this distance, she had no idea if he was watching her. But he had been stalking her all evening, so it was a good bet.

She looked down the ramp. It was wet and slick and occasionally lashed with spray from the towering jet of water spewed from the jaws of the lion being throttled by Daniel in the center of the Grand Cascade. Or, Russia defeating Sweden in the Great Northern War. She waited for another blast of water, then ran forward in its wake, down the ramp and around the corner, scurrying out of Petrov's sight.

Avinashi would not recommend silk and chiffon for exploring fountains. The hem of her gown was marked with water stains, and the chiffon was losing its lift in the damp. In front of her, the façade of the palace just underneath the plaza was a stone wall, marked by six arches and decorated with the same gaudy gold statuary as the rest of the Grand Cascade. Beneath each of the arches was a dark, wet gloom. With all the water she would never hear Petrov coming down the stairs, but she didn't want to wait and find out. She had no better lead on Ted. It looked dryer. She skipped down the wet ramp and through the center arch.

Ted was inside, leaning over an oval stone table next to a couple dressed in period costume. On the table was a large bowl of stone fruit, in brightly colored yellows and reds and orange. In his tuxedo, with his long, blond hair parted in the middle and swept back over his ears, Ted looked to be taking time out for an Italian fashion shoot. Except that his sleeves were rolled up past his elbows, showing his tattoos.

"Avinashi, look at you," said Ted, whistling. "A vision. But a little damp. Did you walk through the fountains in that dress?"

"Ted, are you insane?" she hissed. "Everyone's expecting you upstairs right now. Let's go."

"Okay, sure. Just finishing my tour. But first, check out these fruit. So real. They even feel real. Touch them and see."

The male guide wore a ruffled shirt under a long maroon jacket with tails and a tricorn hat. The woman wore a blue hooped skirt with an impossibly cinched waist. They both wore impish grins and clutched each other while they stared at her, frozen.

"Ted, if you don't sprint right up those stairs afterward, so help me."

"Oh, I will, I promise you. But you have to check out these fruit, c'mon."

"Fine." She poked at an orange with her finger, causing an explosion of water. Water from the center of the bowl, water from the fruit, water from the middle of the table, the edges.

The couple launched into spasms of sputtering, barely-contained laughter, as if they had just enlivened another dull day of being royal with a cruel trick on the staff. Ted had a sad look on his face.

"Oh, Avi, I'm sorry, bad call. Why did I think that would be funny? You know, you're not that wet. Do I get credit for not running?"

The stains along her hem were hidden now among multiple dark, wet blotches that covered the front of her dress, and the chiffon on the front of her dress hung on her like wet seaweed. Her arms and face were wet, each too wet to dry the other.

Ted whipped the silk out of the pocket of the giggling nobleman and tried to dab her arms and face. "You know, you've had a classic 18th-century garden experience. Peterhof is famous for its trick fountains. When they perfected the formal garden in the late renaissance period, they got bored and felt the need to bring back a little whimsy. I think it speaks to the inherent instability of the human condition, wouldn't you?"

"It's a classic Ted experience, and it's getting a little old." She grabbed the silk from his hand. She was going to dab her face when she noticed it was already black.

"I'm sorry," said Ted. "I just really don't want to do this talk. Let's get out of here. I want to go to the Cynic Bar. Sounds fun, Russian. In a good, ex-pat kind of way."

"No, you are doing this talk. Now." She grabbed him by his bare arm and started pulling, then stopped. "Oh god, it's Petrov. He's been following me all night."

"No problem," said Ted. "I wouldn't go that way anyway. Too wet. C'mon."

He turned to the couple and put his fingers to his lips. The young aristocrats gave him a big grin and nodded, eager for their next prank. He held Avinashi by the arm and led her back into the grotto and around a corner. They ducked through a small cutout section of the stone wall into a narrow, dark hallway, lit only by a high skylight, covered in an iron grate.

"Secret tunnel to the palace," said Ted. "I bribed our friends with a flask of Jagermeister to show me the way. I wanted to see the pipes."

Down the hallway, another opening on the right exposed a large green metal pipe, nearly two feet in diameter, running through another brick-walled hallway.

"There are no pumps," said Ted. "All the fountains are powered by natural water pressure, from a higher source four kilometers away, near Strelna. It was almost part of the fun for it to be difficult, expensive."

After a hundred meters or so of snagging her dress and bumping her elbows through dark narrow hallways and up old stone staircases, they were back in the Palace, in a hallway that led to a hallway leading to the Throne Room. In which hallway Green and Telnov were sharing a tense conversation. Telnov looked at her, then went into the Throne Room. Green came over to Avinashi and Ted.

"My god, Avinashi, what have you been doing?" said Green. "You look frightful, I'm sorry to inform you. This was not the time to run off exploring, this is a working function."

Avinashi could never remember being sick a day in her life before Texso, but suddenly she under attack from her body. Tired and abused, it was in full revolt. Her head pounded, her stomach was cramping, and she was losing her sense of balance. She was wet, wearing only about fourteen ounces of fabric, and felt chilled and feverish simultaneously. All she had to do was get through four more hours of this, and she could rest.

Green furrowed his brow and looked at Ted, as if wondering whether to say something in front of him. Ted seemed sufficiently distracted as he tried to roll down his sleeves and reattach his cufflinks.

Green spoke to Avinashi in a lowered voice. "What exactly did you tell Egorov on Wednesday? Wait, never mind. I don't think I want to know. You realize he's a government official, don't you? You can't treat him just like some cement maker in Saami. Egorov has approached the Ministry, saying that you attempted to bribe him. Telnov is telling me they're considering bringing charges. I have no choice but to notify legal. I advise you to do the same at Texso."

She was rocked by a slow, cold wave, as blinders born of fatigue and urgency fell away, and a terrifying knowledge of consequences was born, screaming. From down the hall, Shirin Yazdani had the two of them locked in with her best peeved empress gaze and was approaching fast, trailing her oversized manservant.

"Rupert, very curious that Charlie hasn't arrived, don't you think?" said Yazdani. "And I'm hearing that Lazarev may not show either. What is going on here? Don't play me for a fool."

"Of course not, never, never" said Green. He had the look, which said that if he just had a few more minutes Yazdani would end up knowing more about the situation than Avinashi. "Let me tell you what little I can at dinner, I've had them seat us together. But right now I must introduce Ted, everyone's waiting. They've been kept waiting, thanks to Ms. Sharma."

"Fine. Go. Take the boy and do your little speech," said Yazdani. Ted looked hurt by the comment as Green dragged him away by the elbow.

Shirin peered down at Avinashi with a concerned expression. "Duman, please fetch my bag, will you? Ms. Sharma, I need to freshen up, will you join me?"

Avinashi looked at herself in the ladies' room mirror, horrified. Her eyes were ringed by dark whorls of makeup. Her hair looked like she had run ten miles. She could hardly recognize her beautiful dress.

"Let's just dry this up, shall we?" said Yazdani.

She pulled some tissues from her bag and offered them to Avinashi, who began dabbing away the stray makeup. Yazdani pulled out a small towel and pressed it to Avinashi's hair, then blotted down her arms and shoulders. There was not outlet, so Shirin unscrewed a light bulb. She pulled the perfect adapter from her bag and a small blow dryer, and started to lightly dry her.

"Ms. Sharma, you must tell me how to pack for the ice dome and the palace. You look lovely."

"Please call me Avinashi." And then uncontrollable spasms heaved her chest, and her eyes launched tiny torrents down her cheeks. She sobbed and sobbed.

Yazdani placed a hand on the back of her neck. "Avinashi, don't lose heart. You are doing exceptionally well. To survive here is to succeed."

Avinashi lost track of time as Yazdani calmly blew on the dress. The low hum and warmth of the dryer was comforting. After Avinashi managed to wipe her eyes she could see that the dress was starting to dry. Maybe the iridescent look would appear intentional.

"Charlie is with Lazarev," said Avinashi. "Up in Priozersk, at something called the Karela Fortress. Lazarev asked to meet Dickinson and Charlie up there. It was last minute. A surprise."

"Well, he must have a great deal of confidence in you to leave you to supervise those two. I am sure it is well placed."

Once Shirin had restored Avinashi to some sense of order, the two of them went down to the Throne Room. Flannery Ayers was coming out the doors, wide-eyed and ashen-faced.

"Firebird was developed in a concentration camp?" said Ayers. "How horrid. At least all that suffering had a positive outcome, I suppose. Have you found the ladies' room?" Avinashi pointed down the hallway.

"Avinashi, have you been crying?" said Ayers. "Do you want to talk?"

"No, just a little too close to the fountains," said Avinashi. "Laughed until I cried."

"Oh, fun. Wish I had been there. Guess what? We're at the head table." She grinned and gave an excited little lift to her shoulders. Avinashi thought she might squeal. "See you there." Green was right behind her.

"Good god, Avinashi," said Green. "Get a handle on that boy. Hardly the time or the place to announce our prize technology was developed with slave labor. Half a mind to send the two of you home right now. He's over at our table right now, please tell him to quiet down. I need a drink."

"Are you alright?" asked Yazdani.

"Never better," said Avinashi. She had turned her fate over to a higher power, Dame Thatcher.

The empty throne sat ominously at the end of the room on a low platform. It was spare for a royal seat, more like a large chair with a red velvet seat and arms. On either side of the chair were two crossed flags. The only one she recognized was the flag of the Russian Path party.

The tables were ten tops. The head table was at the front of the room, near the flags and in front of a small podium. Yazdani caused her usual commotion when she arrived, so Avinashi was able to quietly introduce herself to the table with little fanfare.

To her left sat Alexandrov, the head of the Arctic and Antarctic Institute, a tall, greasy man wrapped in a too-small tuxedo and with thin gray hair that looked like he combed it every other day. Next to him was Flannery, back and chatting wide-eyed with Ted, on her left. Then Shirin, and the well-lubricated Green. And then her old friend Telnov, a general called Titov, Phelps and then someone from Gazprom, a young man that had to be someone's nephew or ex-bodyguard.

After she exchanged a cursory handshake with Telnov, she grabbed Ted by the shoulder and pulled him aside. "Ted, what did you say? Everyone's upset."

"I'm sorry Avinashi," he said. "I told the truth. I promised myself I would, at the right opportunity. Kolotkov developed this in a special prison camp for scientists. In the Gulag. I owed it to him. That's why I was hiding from you. I didn't want you to talk me out of it."

She realized she would have. "Oh, Ted. What did you say exactly? Never mind, we'll talk about it later. Try to keep it safe for the rest of tonight. Please? Green is really coming down on me."

"That prick. Okay, for you."

Avinashi found her seat and sat down. The lights of the Throne Room had been turned up with the onset of the extended twilight. The chandeliers and the sconces, like the candles on the tables, were lit but threw no light to match the Arctic evening sun. A quartet in the corner played a slow, melancholy score. Smartly dressed waiters with sour faces wandered among the tables.

At the head table, the guests twittered quietly with their seatmates. The man from Gazprom was lecturing Phelps on the finer points of tactical security, so Avinashi was left with the voluble Alexandrov.

"You must come to the Institute offices," said Alexandrov. "I will show you our facilities, very extensive, fantastic facilities devoted exclusively to the study of the polar regions. Budgets are tight, yes, but we have recently purchased several new machines for studying the physics of ice. They are now state-of-the-art! The better to engineer Arctic technology. Perhaps we could work with KarLap on projects, yes?"

Avinashi could picture Alexandrov as a very effective bureaucrat, an amiable amasser of facilities and people and responsibility, gorging on new grants and concessions and budgets like the prime rib dribbling down his poorly shaved chin.

"When are you leaving Peter?" said Alexandrov. "Tomorrow night? You must visit us during the day. I am unfortunately engaged, but I will have my very senior colleague escort you. He lives at the Institute, he loves it so. Or at our old Museum, down on Marata Street, he still spends time there. Dr. Tarasov knows our research history intimately, everything we've done over the past forty years. I will make all the arrangements. Please, I insist. We will welcome you into our fraternity of polar explorers. We are first and foremost men and women of science, rather than of nations. Have you heard of our great cooperative endeavors with the Americans? I must brief you."

"That would be wonderful, Yan Timurovich," said Avinashi. "Perhaps in the morning?"

He babbled about Arctic drift stations all through the salad.

Telnov waited until the entrée was served, and until Green had tired of waiting for the sullen wait staff to return with more wine and gone off on his own to search.

"Dr. Crawford," said Telnov. Telnov paused, waiting for table's attention to settle in upon him. "So you discovered the unfortunate history of our poor Dr. Kolotkov?"

"Yes," said Ted. "Portions of it. Not a tremendous amount in the public domain on the Gulag."

"One unfortunate Russian's loss is a fortunate American's gain, it would appear."

"I don't know if I would look at it that way." Ted was going to say something, then he looked over at Avinashi. He paused. "I'm just happy someone was able to continue his work. That it wasn't lost."

"But you say you want to honor our Kolotkov, should you not acknowledge how much he has done for you personally?"

"The opportunity to develop ideas with this kind of impact is every grad student's dream."

"Oh, but it meant so much more for you, didn't it?"

"I'm not sure I know what you mean." Ted shifted in his seat. He had stopped looking at Avinashi, and was staring at Telnov. The rest of the table was staring at Ted.

"You had dropped out of school, hadn't you? You couldn't finish. At the University of California. In Santa Barbara, yes? You were doing physics. We have been studying you, Dr. Crawford. How am I doing? Am I passing?"

"I was a few credits short of graduation at the end of four years. I couldn't figure out what to do. Somewhat common in the US. Too many opportunities."

"Yes, like lying on the beach, playing in the water with the girls, and taking the drugs. Wonderful opportunities. But then too much fun and you had to go to that hospital. Where there was professional help, I assume? Did they try to help you figure it out, there, Dr. Crawford?"

"I'm not too ashamed to ask for help. And yes, I did finally figure it out."

"Oh? Perhaps we are misinformed. Our information suggests that it was figured out for you by your father's good friend, Mr. Joiner. He checked you out of the hospital and then into the care of his good friend Dr. Friedel at Stanford. Dr. Friedel put you to work as a volunteer in his lab. Washing rock specimens, I believe?"

"And I worked my way up from there. I earned my way into that program, and I think I've shown that I was worthy of the spot."

"How much does the Stanford Exploration Project receive from Texso every year, Dr. Crawford? A substantial sum, I understand. More than enough for them to take on an additional rock washer. And to incent them to drop a promising Russian technology in his lap."

Ted was staring at the table, his face flush. Telnov took a slow drink of his wine, then shifted his chair and waved one hand dramatically in the air.

"My only point, Dr. Crawford, is that those to whom everything is handed should be careful of criticizing others. Not so much just you, but everyone in the US. Blessed with favorable geography, resources, security. All of our Creator's blessings. Russia is not America."

"You're right. Russia has been unfortunate." His eyes were locked in on the chandelier. "So unfortunate as to make me wonder whether you shouldn't just cut your losses. Shut it down. Really, what's the point?"

"Outrageous!" yelled Titov. Phelps lifted his eyebrows and rolled his eyes.

"Ted, let's go find some darts," said Avinashi.

"No," said Telnov, "I would like to hear Dr. Crawford's theory. Please."

"Look, let's face it. Russia may just be a mistake," said Ted. "It's too big. It's too cold. It's not viable economically. It can't be defended. It should probably just be disbanded. In fact, it might have been better if you would have been conquered by the Poles in the Time of Troubles."

"The Poles, drobhit!" said the Gazprom man, following with a rich stream of epithets directed at his western neighbors.

"No, hear me out for a second," said Ted. "First of all, you have too much land and too few people. It's so thinly populated, you should almost have to surrender territory by forfeit. Everything is way too far apart. Outside of Moscow, there's no critical mass anywhere to the people or the supporting infrastructure. Transportation costs kill you, and make trade and transport, everything, too expensive. You have no highways between cities. Well, one two-lane between Moscow and St. Petersburg, but that's it. Your rail lines are falling apart. And there's no maritime transportation. You barely have three seaports worth mentioning, none in a great location, and rivers that only run north to the Arctic. Everything has to go by land. Expensive.

"Furthermore, the pieces you do have are all mismatched. You have your biggest cities in the north, where it's just too damn cold. Heating costs are triple what they are in the rest of Europe. Buildings have to be built much more sturdily but then they last half as long. And god knows what role winter plays in the alcoholism rate.

"And you can't grow food that far north. The growing season is 60 percent of what they have in Germany. In Eurasia, as you surely know, it doesn't get colder so much north to south as west to east, the further you get away from the warm North Atlantic currents. Not only are your cities all further north, they're an ungodly distance further east. Moscow is as far north as Helsinki, but it's a thousand miles further east and so has the climate of northern Norway. What little good farming land there is, it's in the far southern corner. Again, the cost of shipping that food to the northern cities? Astronomic.

"The rest of the country, east of the Urals, Siberia, East Siberia, the Arctic, are barely populated. 85 percent of the country with 5 percent of the population. It has a lower population density than the Amazon. And yet, you insist on trying to develop it."

"Russia flourishes in the Arctic," said Alexandrov. "You say we are not a maritime country but we have the longest coastline in the world! Thanks to the Institute, and its predecessor the Glavsermorput, we had two hundred thousand people in the Arctic at our peak. Cities, airstrips, weather stations. Over a hundred research stations on the Arctic ice. Over ninety years of intense development, you must come to our Museum, you overlook our history."

"You do build cities above the Arctic Circle," said Ted. "At huge costs. Where the Australians might develop a mine in the Outback with fifty guys they fly in and out in two-week shifts, you move ten thousand people and their families to a city you build in frozen mud around a single mine. And then you pay them three times the going rate to live a miserable existence there. You bribe people to live there. And for what? You can't get anything in or out except by air. Roads and rail are impossible to lay across the permafrost. The ports are frozen most of the year. In fact, I bet you've never turned a profit on any development in the Siberia. You could buy gold in London and ship it to Yakutsk for less money than it costs you to mine it there. But of course you would never know any of this because you've never had a functioning market with real prices.

"And before that, what did you do? When you didn't have the money to waste, you just used slave labor. Many of these cities, now gone, were built with slaves. Prisoners, sent to Siberia to work and then die. Hard to argue with free."

"Just like American," said Telnov.

"No, very different. We had outlawed slavery about fifty years earlier. In the 1930s you were just perfecting it. If there is any justice in it, at least you were enslaving your own. But then that opens up another whole set of issues. Oh, and when the Gulag was rolled back, you just started using the army. You had a lot of men at arms, but the dirty secret is that many of the conscripts were glorified slave labor for the North. Again, you had no idea how to price anything, so you went the safe route and paid nothing for your labor.

"But then, the crowning irony? This unholy mess of a country, the one you can't make any money on, where you can barely scratch out an existence, you can't even defend it. Am I right, General?"

"Russia has always appeared vulnerable to its enemies," said Titov. "History has shown this not to be true."

"Well, let's see. You have no protective oceans, no formidable mountain ranges to hide behind. Your borders are open, and the ground is flat. I've played on pool tables with a steeper grade. The Black Sea canal covers 2500 miles and only needs two locks. The enemies pour right in, on ponies from the east or panzers from West. They come for your oil down in Baku, or maybe for your farms, maybe just for that very small consumer surplus available after the average Russian downs his starvation rations. But you're right, by the time they figure out it wasn't worth it, they're getting strung out and killed on the long, potholed road to Moscow. Your terrible infrastructure really helps with that strategy, by the way. By the time they've crossed three isotherms it's too late.

"And all your experience in the Arctic? None of it has helped you defend it. You think you own it because you're up there and no one else is. The truth is, no one else wanted to waste their time or money in the Arctic.

"And now that development is becoming economical, you can't defend it, either. The US submarine fleet would need about six hours to destroy all your surface and subsurface vessels.

"Really, what you need instead of a defense department is a better marketing department. You need to broadcast the idea—don't invade, you'll be sorry. There's nothing here, it's really a crappy country. Go south instead.

"But no. Instead, in the height of insanity, what do you do? You decide that the only way you can manage and defend this country is with an iron fist. How else will you force the south to starve to feed the north. Or to conquer buffer states, to subjugate an empire with over a hundred ethnic groups. The country makes no sense. It can only make sense in the mind of a madman, some crazed poet or cleric, or on one of Peter's or Ivan's maps. And they rule it accordingly. Ivan, the father of your country, spent his idle hours devising specially made man-size frying pans for the boyars, for crying out loud. A hundred million of your own citizens killed over the last hundred years, half by other Russians. Many more imprisoned in the Gulag, like Kolotkov. Your fiance, Minister Telnov, shot for losing her maps. Yes, I have also done some research. Sixty years holding the threat of nuclear annihilation over the rest of the world. The need for control, the paranoia generated by this vulnerable country has exacted a severe costs on its own citizens, and the entire world.

"And why would you continue it? Will it ever be a viable country? Rigid police states have never been great for developing a modern, competitive society. You have no transportation infrastructure that will allow you to trade well. You have no manufactured goods that anyone wants to buy. All you have are minerals, raw materials that you can sell, if someone can figure out how to do it profitably. So you'll never be able to integrate into the modern world. It's going to be a long, slow slide.

"So, I return to my original thesis. The country should be disbanded. Perhaps the European portion remains Russian. Let the laws of market economics dismantle the rest. I think Russian Path has it exactly upside down, by the way. Russia should rent out Siberia and the Arctic to whoever thinks they can manage it profitably. Like the Australians. Or Texso. Somewhat neocolonial, I know, but it's the only way you're going to attract the necessarily capital. Again, with the right packaging, I think you could sell it."

He paused.

"Anyway, just one man's opinion. A tip from a lucky guy."

Flannery's mouth was hanging open. Shirin had pulled out a small notebook and was jotting things down, but now she gently laid it on the table. Phelps was twiddling his thumbs, trying to remain invisible. Ted took a drink.

Green returned. "Finally found the waiter. Had to use your name, Minister, but they said they would be around shortly, fill us all up. Damn, now my meat's cold, too. If I were Tsar, heads would be rolling, hah!" No one laughed.

Telnov stood up from the table and walked over to stand next to the podium. He took the microphone from the stand. A waiter appeared to fill his glass, and he made a broad gesture to fill everyone's glasses.

"I have it in my mind," said Telnov. "To offer a toast to our guests from KarLap. Then I will offer them the opportunity to offer some words in reply, if they wish." He bowed to the head table.

"First, on behalf of Minister Lazarev, I extend his apologies. As it has always been, the guardians of Russia must be ever vigilant. Never more so than now. And so he is off on urgent matters, I am sorry." An interpreter repeated his words in French, then English.

"We have had a very spirited discussion at our table, which does inspire my toast. To our guests, please understand that to Russians, to be out in the expanses, to experience God in nature, away from the corruption of the cities, from the Europeans..." He waited for the laughter to subside. "This, this is to be Russian. Not to be above all economical, to be rational. To Russians, our land is our bond with God. And only the divine is infinite. Other countries come and go. Russia endures, because of this bond. And because of this bond, Russia must endure." He raised his glass and drank with one swallow.

The room burst into applause. Telnov walked over to the table and handed the microphone to Ted. Avinashi took a breath, stood up and held out her hand. Telnov and Ted looked at her, then Telnov handed her the microphone.

This time no Maggie Thatcher, just Avinashi Sharma. In a calm, gracious voice, she began to explain to the room what a tremendous opportunity it had been for her and KarLap to work in Russia to develop this land.

So she began, but then she stopped. As Telnov walked out of the room.

In the complex, arcane canons of diplomatic protocol, walking out on a toast ranks right below recalling an ambassador as an insult. Even at this stage in her career, Flannery Ayers understood this and, on top of the definitively undiplomatic exchange at dinner, she was wondering whether she would be needing to call for a Marine evacuation of the embassy. For decades, she would dine out on her embellished recollection of these events for horrified diplomatic colleagues.

Quickly, Avinashi raised her glass and yelled at the top of her small but powerful lungs, "Na Zdrovia!" She downed her drink in one graceful swallow. But no one was watching, they were on their feet, looking out the door, wildly applauding, louder than before.

Ted was quickly at her ear. "Great toast, Avi. Spunky. And I am so, so sorry. I couldn't control myself. I won't bother you anymore, I promise." And he stole out the door.

To leave her with Green, relishing his unpleasant task. "Ms. Sharma, in light of recent events, I am afraid you leave me no choice but to terminate your position immediately. You are clearly in over your head here, and I blame myself for not seeing that earlier as much as I blame anyone else, including you. I must ask for your company phone. I will have someone be in touch with you for final processing. Please do not communicate with anyone at the company with my permission, or legal's."

She was too numb, so it must have been someone else who took her phone out of her purse and handed it to Green. She was still standing near the table when four dour men in green uniforms with red epaulets and large, peaked hats appeared before her. The leader lifted one of two large photographs he was carrying, studying the photograph and her face as if the room was filled with hundreds of small, brown women.

"Ms. Avinashi Sharma," he said.

"Yes?"

"I have an order for your arrest, on evidence of your violation of relevant laws relating to bribery of public officials. You will come with us, please. And I am instructed in this case to follow our processes strictly. And so my lieutenant will restrain your wrists. I am sorry."

The part of Flannery's story where the militia officers handcuffed and led away the poor little Texso vice president in her ruined, green formal gown always left them speechless.

CHAPTER 8

TIME OF TROUBLES

Priozersk
Friday night

Charlie followed Kirill onto the narrow bridge. The sun was dying behind the trees, surrendering the river and its banks to a quiet gloom. The northern landscape could not hold onto the day's warmth, and the air was cooling rapidly. Kirill was dressed like a common laborer, in dirty coveralls and boots. Charlie recognized him from the fishing trip but didn't say anything to Dickinson's Secret Service unit, which had already spread out across the grounds.

Dickinson was close on Charlie's heels. Nervous outside of his staff cocoon, he couldn't stop talking. "I heard he looks like a real freak. Unnatural." The footbridge was all cables and wooden slats, and bounced lightly beneath their feet. "So he thinks you're the devil? Welcome to the club. Not a week goes by I don't hear that."

Charlie had been stuck in one of the two decoy choppers. They had not taken a direct route. Three abreast in a wide formation, they first headed north across the Gulf of Finland, then east all the way to Lake Ladoga. A mere spot on the Russian map, Ladoga was a vast expanse, the second largest lake in Europe, and ringed with islands of pines. They flew north along the west shore for half an hour until they reached the Vuoksa River. Just up from the mouth of the river, on the north bank, lay Priozersk. *Lake City.* They landed on the grounds of

an old Swedish insane asylum, a three-story white stone building just a
short distance from the bridge. The bank of the river here was irregular, jogging in and out. Several islands were just offshore, the river winding around them in dark channels. According to what little Charlie
heard of the threat assessment, the whole area was locked down by two
companies of Neftepolk, including some in boats far out on the river.

The bridge led out to a tiny island nearly filled by a church. The
base of the church was in the shape of a squat rectangle. It had a tall,
round tower in the center, nearly as wide as the base, and smaller
towers on each of the corners, all topped by fat, blood-red onion
domes, themselves topped by three-barred gold crosses. The walls of
the church were wood, elaborately carved and stained a dark, natural
tone. Scaffolding climbed high up three sides of the church, reaching
just up to the base of the domes. On the side nearest them, the large
double doors of the church were thrown open, spilling warm light
down the short flight of steps and onto the grass. Kirill motioned for
them to remain while he climbed the steps and disappeared inside.

"All we need is a graveyard and the scene would be complete,"
said Dickinson.

"This is Russia," said Charlie. "Just dig, anywhere."

The instructions were to dress down. Dickinson wore a blazer over
a pale pink and yellow striped sport shirt, immaculately pressed slacks
and tasseled loafers. Charlie was wearing the field clothes that he carried everywhere. Heavy khakis with reinforced knees, a light shirt and
a pair of tramping boots worn so soft he could sleep in them.

"Well, where do you think the conference room is?" said Dickinson.
"Time to get this show on the road."

A long, thin shadow jumped across the grass. Lazarev stood at the
doorway in dark, paint-spattered coveralls, wiping his hands on a rag.

"Mr. Vice President," said Lazarev. "We thought you were lost."

Dickinson had pulled the same routine on Lazarev that he pulled
on Charlie. Peeved by the last-minute schedule change, the VP and
his staff had taken a one hour trip and stretched it into five. If he had
known, Charlie could have made the dinner and this meeting.

"Security," said Dickinson, shrugging. "Sometimes it seems my whole day is spent avoiding the latest hypothetical threat."

"No hypothetical threats here. Now come. I must show you something." Lazarev tossed the rag to the side and disappeared around the side of the church with a few long strides.

"Nice to meet you, too," said Dickinson.

The narrow strip of ground between the scaffolding and the bank was sloped and muddy. Charlie couldn't see how they could get machinery on the island, much less maneuver it. They must be building the church by hand. He waited for Dickinson, who was picking his way across the wet ground. Lazarev was already on a second bridge, at the other end of the island.

"When do we get to the part where we all start drinking and toasting?" said Dickinson.

"All business tonight," said Charlie. "C'mon."

"And that guy has an eating disorder if I've ever seen one. Reminds me of one of our neighbor girls. There are places you can send them. Fix him right up. Might improve his disposition."

"I don't think that's it."

There was another footbridge that led off the back of the island, from behind the church. Lazarev was waiting for them in the middle, and they joined him. The water ran fast and silent beneath their feet.

Charlie could see that this second bridge ended at the corner of a spit of land sticking out into the river. Protecting the area was a high stone wall, two or three times as tall as a man. Behind the wall at the corner was a round stone building, about three stories high, with a red, conical roof topped by a watchtower. Cut into the wall at the foot of the bridge was a massive brick doorway fronted with broken masonry. The two large doors, painted with black and white diagonal stripes, were swung inwards, offering passage into the tower. The stones were worn and the wall ran closer to the ground as it went left so that at the end you could have jumped over it. The whole site appeared to be settling in and on its way to becoming an archaeological dig.

"Every child needs a place of escape," said Lazarev, staring at the site from the bridge. "This was mine, this abandoned fort. I would spend days here, alone, walking the grounds. It was always my dream that it be restored. Several years ago I founded a brotherhood, the Defenders of Karela, to fund this effort. The work we do here for the Brotherhood is my greatest privilege." He took off down the bridge.

"Too much information," said Dickinson, grabbing the handrail. "I thought you said this would be all business."

Lazarev didn't enter the gate. He walked to the right along a dirt path at the foot of the wall. As he followed, Charlie looked up. The wall would have been difficult to climb, but not impossible. There was a strip of land about twenty feet wide between the wall and the river. The wall along the river was not straight, but cut in and out. A portion of the wall halfway down thrust out, almost reaching the river. At its base was a low entrance topped by an iron gate that had been pulled up.

"This was a secret passage into the fort, under the bastion," said Lazarev. "Come."

He ducked inside and they followed him through a dark passage until they were on the other side of the walls. On the inside, the ground sloped up gradually right to the top of the walls. Lazarev walked up the slope and stood at the top of the wall. Dickinson stopped at a spot just as high. Charlie stopped lower. The sun had set, but the pale quarter moon remained, and the fort and grounds appeared like an old black and white photograph in its reflected, silvery light.

Lazarev was looking over the fort, as if he were inspecting it for missing items. Apparently satisfied, he turned to Dickinson. "Charlie is not the first foreigner to extort a contract from Russia in her moment of weakness, Mr. Vice President," said Lazarev. "This fort, this ground, is soaked in Russian blood. Blood shed in defiance of another such contract, a long time ago. In the Time of Troubles. I think knowing something about this would be instructive for you."

"Please, Minister," said Dickinson. "First, I insist you call me Tom. We are all friends here. And may I call you Oleg Maksimovich?

Second, we do now–and forever after will, I swear–view the KarLap PSA as just a simple business transaction. No blood. Just oil."

"Nothing here is just business, Mr. Vice President," said Lazarev. "Perhaps I am wasting my time."

"No, please continue," said Dickinson. "I'm here first of all to listen. Mouth closed, ears open. That's what they're always telling me."

"Very well." As Lazarev looked out towards the river, Dickinson turned and rolled his eyes at Charlie.

Lazarev pointed right, up the river. "The Vuoksa runs up across the border to Finland, which for most of history was part of Sweden, its 'Eastland.' For over a thousand years, the Vuoksa carried murderous Swedes into Russia. If they even had to paddle a little bit, history might have been different, because the Swedes are very lazy. As it was, if they wanted to kill Russians, all they had to do was step into a boat and it floated right here. Only this fort, Karela, stood between the Swedes and their total control of the Karelian Isthmus, all the land between Lake Ladoga and the Gulf of Finland. Karela guarded the path to our ancient city of Novgorod, and Moscow, and later St. Petersburg."

Dickinson looked around, probably for someplace to sit down. As he did, Lazarev started out across the top of the wall, continuing his story as he walked.

"The history of this place is not widely known. But I had an uncle, a brother at the monastery out on Konevets Island. He knew the stories, and when he came to visit my father he would bring me here and tell them to me."

He reached the tower and stopped. "This tower is over six hundred years old. It is often called 'Pugachevska,' because the family of the Cossack rebel Pugachev were imprisoned here. After he had been decapitated and dismembered down in Moscow. That was the 1700s when the fort was old and no longer useful. My story takes place much earlier, when Karela was still very important." He ran his hands over the stone wall of the tower. Then he walked down and around it, back up to the wall and stopped. Dickinson had a difficult time keeping up, sliding on the damp ground in his loafers.

"For hundreds of years, the people of Karela stood against the Swedes who came down the Vuoksa to steal Russian land. Endless years of fighting. The very worst was the War of Long Hate. 1570 to 1595. Fleming, the Swedish general, was very cruel. For years, he hunted and killed Russians on the Isthmus. He spared no one. He burned every farm and building, no matter how small. And he was relentless. Near the end, all the Russians ran to this fortress for shelter. But a large group of families to the East were cut off. They fled to the islands on Lake Ladoga and hid. A young boy was asked to burn his family's extra boats but in his panic and fear he forgot. Fleming found the boats and sent his men in them out to the islands. They found the Russian families and killed them all. Even the women and the children. We know about the boy because the Swedes found out about his mistake and made him watch before they killed him. Finally, the Swedes came for Karela.

"At this time was appointed a new general for the Swedes, worse than Fleming. Not more brutal, because Fleming could not be surpassed. But this man was more cunning, and so much more dangerous. He was French and a mercenary. De la Gardie. The Danes had paid him to fight the Swedes. Then he was captured by the Swedes and they paid him to fight Russians. It was all the same to de le Gardie. You understand this, don't you Charlie? You understand de le Gardie."

"No, I wouldn't think so," said Charlie.

Lazarev laughed and kept walking down the wall. At the point at which the wall disappeared under the ground they stopped. Up ahead in the dark they could make out the trees on the mainland.

"De le Gardie, he brought technology to the fight against Karela," said Lazarev. "The latest siege machines and tactics from the European wars. All around here, on shore, he set up his instruments of death. Eventually it was fire, from incendiary shells, that forced Karela to surrender.

"We did not give up. We still fought the Swedes in the forests, a guerilla war. Rogozin. The brothers Rasanen. They terrified the Swedes. But the Swedes held Karela for fifteen years."

He walked back into the interior of the fort and stopped at a long, low building. He spat on it.

"The Swedes built this during their occupation. The brotherhood is tearing it down. The bricks will be broken down into powder and poured back into the Vuoksa."

Lazarev walked out to the center of the fort and looked around, turning a slow circle. Charlie wondered how many times Lazarev had performed this ritual.

"Finally, after fifteen years, came the armies of the Tsar. And then the Swedish King died. As a result of our success on the battlefields, Sweden was forced to return Karela to Russia. And the people prepared to return to their homes. But the suffering for Karela was just beginning."

"It gets worse?" said Dickinson. "Time for intermission. Mind if I light up?" He produced a pack of cigarettes, and extended it to Lazarev. "Minister?" Dickinson was not completely without skills. The two of them lit each other's cigarettes.

"Thank you, Tom. Russians know, it can always get worse." This time Lazarev stayed put, pulling on his cigarette, staring into the ground.

"For seven hundred years, the Riurik dynasty of Tsars had ruled Russia. The last real Riurik Tsar was Ivan Grozny, which you know as Ivan 'the Terrible,' a very poor translation. What it means is that he inspired the same fear and awe one would have of the divine, so great was his power. Shortly after the recovery of Karela, the Riurik line died out, and Russia fell into years of chaos. The Time of Troubles.

"Seeing Russia without a strong leader, of course all of its enemies pounced. The lazy Swedes finally took Novgorod. The Polish and their German mercenaries took Moscow, set it on fire and slaughtered its citizens. Tatars attacked from the south. For fifteen years, the country was complete anarchy. Armed bands and mercenaries roamed freely. Entire cities were slaughtered. There was no order at all. For fifteen years, terror reigned.

"And yet, it can always get worse. In the middle of this manmade violence, a volcano erupts. On the other side of the world, in Peru. Thirty million tons of earth explodes into the atmosphere, blocking the sun. The earth cools, and of course Russia is most vulnerable. Years ago our people fled to the forests of the north to escape the Tatars, but now we are too far north. Our short growing season disappears to nothing. Crops will not grow, and famine spreads. For two years, the people starve. A third of the country dies. Millions and millions."

Lazarev looks up at Dickinson, then Charlie. As he speaks, he punches the night air with his cigarette.

"In the middle of this horror, who now appears, ready to bargain for Russia's soul? Who would relish such suffering by Russia, and seek to profit from it? Charlie?"

"I have no idea."

"A de la Gardie, of course. Not the father, but his demon son, born out of a bastard daughter of the Swedish king. The son now commands the Swedish troops, and he forces a devil's pact on the weak Tsar Vasili. Sweden would fight for Russia against the Poles. This is possible because de la Gardie is 'flexible,' as Charlie would say. In exchange, he wants only a small trifle, almost not worth mentioning, he says. He only asks for the Isthmus, and Karela.

"The shameful Vasili agrees. And so the Swedes fight for Russia, although poorly and are in fact of no help. Russia must later rid itself of the Poles. But de la Gardie holds Vasili to his agreement and the coward yields. The Tsar sends his message to Karela. Surrender.

"The people of Karela, only just back on their land, cannot believe their ears. For them, it is their worst nightmare. Surrender to the Swedes, who slaughtered their ancestors. To the son of de la Gardie, no less. They will have none of it. They say no. They refuse even to meet with the Tsar's messenger. They are Russian, this is Russian land, it will stay Russian. How can it be otherwise? They defy the Tsar and his contract, and they prepare to hold Karela against de la Gardie. For a year there is a stalemate. Then the pathetic Vasili is deposed and dies in a Polish prison, leaving behind no Tsar, only tens of thousands of vicious Swedes still deep in Russia. Russia appears dead, finished. De le Gardie decides the time is right to claim his prize.

"In Karela, the people stand against impossible odds. There is no Russian army. There are only townspeople and peasants. The good Bishop Silvester sends word to the people in the countryside, come together and fight the Swedes. And they gather inside this fort, right here, where we are standing. There are maybe two or three thousand packed into this ground, with as much material as they can gather. Men, women, children. Maybe five hundred men fit to fight. Against tens of thousands of de le Gardie's hardened, professional soldiers. De la Gardie's troops arrive in mass by September. He expects the end to be quick. But Karela is not easily overrun. Come."

Quickly he is back on top of the wall, looking out over the river. This time Dickinson falls with a hard thump and lets loose with a string of obscenities. Charlie helps him the rest of the way up the slope.

Lazarev is at the very edge of the wall, pointing down below and to the sides with both hands. "Before the Bolshevik conspiracy tried to change the flow of the river in the 1930s, the water levels here were much higher than they are now. This land was an island. It was separated from the mainland by wide channels. The river came up and covered the base of the walls, here. The water runs so fast that it never froze, it was open all winter. The fort could be reached only by boat, and there was no way to scale the walls from the water, in a boat. Usually de la Gardie would dig under fortifications, plant a charge and blow the walls. But here the base of the walls were under water. The fort was impregnable.

"Like his father, de la Gardie tried to burn them out, but they knew his tricks. The defense of the fort was organized by Ivan Pushkin, the ancestor of our great poet. He had prepared them to fight the fires. And they had an endless supply of water. It became a siege of attrition.

"The devil de la Gardie then relied on yet another siege weapon to claim Karela—disease. It always comes in these situations. At Karela, the people started to suffer from scurvy. A terrible disease. First come painful bruises on the legs. Then you start to bleed from your gums. Your joints begin to swell, and it becomes too painful to walk or even move. Then your eyes start to cry blood, you start to go blind. Finally, your internal organs begin to bleed out, at which point you begin to scream for God to release you from this earth. Then you die."

Lazarev walked down the slope back onto the grounds of the fort and back in the direction of the tower. Charlie and Dickinson followed him in the darkness. "Be sure to take your multivitamin, Joiner," said Dickinson, chuckling.

"Of the Russians in Karela that survived the Swedish shelling," said Lazarev, "hundreds and hundreds began to die horribly from scurvy in the dark, bitterly cold winter. Here, in the winter, there is no more than five hours of daylight. The ground was too hard to bury the dead, so after the bodies froze they dragged them out into the yard. Imagine surviving that, here." He spread his arms out, palms up. "Frozen bodies everywhere. Shells falling on you. The Swedes trying to set you on fire. Imagine the suffering."

He walked slowly towards the tower. On the side of the tower facing the interior, the main door was a heavy, unfinished wooden affair, wide enough for two men abreast. "In the spring, de la Gardie still saw no end to the siege and offered terms. He tells the Russians they can leave the fort alive with the clothes on their backs." He entered the tower. Lazarev struck his lighter and held it over his head. The tower was open to the roof, high above them.

"Pushkin gathered the survivors here. He tells him of de la Gardie's offer. All we know is that they rejected this shameful offer out of hand. They still have some supplies. Sick and dying, they make a solemn vow to each other. They tell de la Gardie they will fight until the last, then blow themselves up along with the fort and everything in it and the Swedes will get nothing. They have already placed charges under all the walls. Every last one of them will die before they surrender dishonorably.

"De la Gardie has of course already promised all of the Russians' property to his mercenaries. But in the face of this Russian bravery, he sees he has no choice. He tells them they can leave with as much as they can carry out. Pushkin agrees."

Lazarev walks over and stands in the large exterior doorway, looking out over the river. "When these gates are finally opened, the Swedes are horrified. Bodies and the stench of death are everywhere. And there are less than a hundred left alive in the fort, mostly children. No more than ten men capable of lifting a weapon. Had he known, they could have taken the fort easily.

"The story of Karela inspires our country. Encouraged, the people organize themselves and rout the Poles. The Romanov dynasty assumes power. The Time of Troubles comes to a close. A hundred years later, Peter seizes Karela back from the Swedes in the Great Northern War.

"The story of Karela was the story of all Russia. Throughout our history, in every district, there has been a Karela. This time it was the Swedes. But in other times, in other places, it was the Mongols, the Poles at Smolensk, the Germans at Stalingrad, the Bolsheviks with their Gulag or the Chechens at Grozny. But the story of Karela is that as long as even one Russian survives, so we all survive."

With his hands clasped behind his back, Lazarev walks silently back along the bank and then halfway back across the bridge. He leans back on the rail and lights a cigarette from his own pack.

Dickinson stands at the gate, watching Lazarev. "Is there a point to this, Joiner?"

"He thinks there is," said Charlie. "I'm hoping there isn't."

They walked out onto the bridge.

"It is coming again," said Lazarev.

"What's coming?" said Dickinson.

"A horrible, dark time. A complete breakdown in order. A new Time of Troubles."

"I'm sorry, what are you referring to?" said Dickinson. "The Swedes again?" He looked up the river.

"You mock me," said Lazarev. "That is fine, it just shows how little you understand. Charlie knows, though. Tell him, Charlie." Lazarev took a long draw on his cigarette.

"He means the end of oil," said Charlie. "Oleg Maksimovich believes we are at the end of the oil age."

"Impossible," said Dickinson, laughing. "I won't allow it. Not until I sell my Texso stock."

Lazarev's face was barely visible in the darkness behind his light cigarette. "Ask Charlie why he is looking for oil in the Arctic."

"What?" said Dickinson. "Oh, alright. Charlie? Wait, hold on." He reached out his hand. "Say, Oleg Maksimovich, would you have another one of those?" Dickinson pulled a cigarette of the offered pack and Lazarev lit it for him with the lighter. "Okay, shoot."

"Because that's the last place left to look," said Charlie.

"I always said, when they come for our Arctic, the end is at hand," said Lazarev. "The Arctic is the final play."

"Oh, come on," said Dickinson. "I've been briefed. Now that we're fracking in the Permian, the US is drowning the world in oil. You should worry more about prices, not supply."

"The Permian is a stopgap," said Lazarev. "All the Tier 1 acreage has already been drilled. It only gets harder and harder from here, Tom. And much more expensive. The Permian will play out more quickly than you realize."

"Okay, whatever," said Dickinson. "I'm at a disadvantage with you two talking the gritty details. But, up at my level, I know that half the oil is still in the ground."

"Exactly," said Lazarev.

One hand in the pocket of his slacks, Dickinson drew on his cigarette with the other. He was squinting at Charlie, like the whole discussion was causing him pain. "Translation, Joiner?"

"Production in an oil field peaks about halfway through depletion. Our production peaked in the US in 1970," said Charlie. "Oleg Maksimovich believes the world is peaking."

"Peaked," said Lazarev. "We have already peaked. The Arabs lie about their oil. They lie about Ghawar."

"So what?" said Dickinson.

"So every year from now we will now produce less oil," said

Lazarev. "World demand continues to grow, but our supply contracts. The gap gets larger and larger. Every year there will be more pain. It is like a famine that grows worse every year, that never ends. Do you know what oil means, Tom? Oil is food, oil is medicine, oil is all modern technology. Agriculture is only a process by which oil is turned into food. Your healthcare system, your transportation system, your manufacturing, they all disappear without oil. And there are no substitutes."

"The market will adapt," said Dickinson. "You just haven't experienced a strong market economy."

"There is no time," said Lazarev. "Oil is unique. Stable, cheap and it has a high energy density, which means it is portable. It is uniquely suited for transportation applications. There are no coal-fired airplanes. Natural gas, solar or wind could perhaps be partial alternatives, but there is not the time nor money to convert any meaningful portion of your engines or other infrastructure, particularly in a depressed post-oil economy."

"So what? We have another oil shock, we've survived those," said Dickinson.

"No, this is a permanent shock, from which there is no recovery," said Lazarev. "In twenty years, you will not recognize the world. For one, there will be far fewer people. The Swede, Borlaug, won the Nobel Peace Prize for introducing modern agricultural techniques to the developing world."

"Norwegian," said Charlie. "From Minnesota."

Lazarev dismissed him with a wave. "All the same. Norwegians are Swedes. Borlaug's methods worked, too well. And the population of the world exploded with the food supply, growing from two to eight billion people in just over fifty years. His secrets were pesticides, fertilizers and mechanized cultivation. All oil-based. All will disappear. Borlaug collected the awards, but he also condemned these people to die."

"So you're saying six billion people are going to die," said Dickinson.

"Billions," said Lazarev. "It is unavoidable. An absolute certainty. There will be no way to feed them. Borlaug's methods are
unsustainable."

Dickinson was speechless. Charlie wouldn't have thought it was
possible.

"Russia is humanity's only hope for survival," said Lazarev. "Russia
must survive. It must survive for us all." He drew on his cigarette and
then blew the smoke hard up into the night air, defiantly. "That is why
we must keep our oil. What we have left."

Dickinson spun around on his heels and looked at Charlie for
help. Charlie just listened.

"Throwing in the towel kind of quickly, aren't you?" said
Dickinson. "Of course, since you're the one with the oil, you're telling us to throw in the towel."

"Would you expect America to survive? As much as Russia has
been bred to endure, America has been bred to grow. If it does not
grow, it will die. America exists for material progress. Americans live
for the bigger house, the more expensive car. Childish amusement
parks. Fantasy. This is the essence of what they live for, their very soul.
The economy and the financial system have been built around this.
High consumer spending. High levels of debt paid down with growing profits, increasing salaries–business debt, borrowing for homes.
With an overly specialized workforce that lacks basic life skills. And
the economy is so energy-intensive. Transport is based on car, truck
and air. Very little rail or mass transit. If there is no oil, Americans
literally cannot move. The US military is the single largest consumer
of oil in the world, consuming five hundred thousand barrels a day,
8 percent of all imports, just to secure the oil pipeline to the Gulf.
And finally, the society is also highly racist, and divided by class, with
the highest incarceration rate in the world. Take away the oil, it all
collapses, violently.

"Russians have never lived for material things. It has never been
as important to us. Time with friends. Our books. Learning, knowledge. Being in nature, out on our land. Most of all our faith, being

present with God. It is said that the worst Russian atheist is closer
to God than the most religious American." He shrugged. "We are a
more spiritual people, it is in our nature. All these we treasure, this is
what it is to be Russian. Our public institutions, they do not provide
us with much, and we ask for little beside a strong leader, for order.
But we have housing, which we don't own but which no one can take
from us, even if we stop paying. If they turn off the heat every other
day, we wear a sweater and bathe in cold water. Give a Russian ten
square meters, he can feed himself. If we have no gas, we can always
take the train. We are patient to a fault. We endure.

"It is not for me or you to choose Russia. We were chosen long
ago. As the monk Filofei wrote to Vasili III, 'for two Romes have
fallen, but the Third stands, and a Fourth shall not be.' This was after
the fall of Constantinople, the second Rome, to the Ottoman Empire
in 1453. After the first Rome fell, Constantinople had been declared
the new Rome in 330. For a thousand years she ruled, and protected
the faith. After she fell, Ivan the Great married the Greek princess,
Sophia, the descendent of Constantine, and Russia became the Third
Rome. The white cowl that passed from Rome to Constantinople,
passed to Moscow. Only Russia could synthesize the classical Western
civilization of the first Rome with the mysticism and spirituality of
the Eastern Rome, the better to defend both and continue the true
faith. That is why there will be no Fourth Rome, the synthesis being
complete.

"Do you think all of our suffering could be for no reason? God
would not allow such a thing. We have proven ourselves to be worthy
through our suffering. A Russian proverb says 'God endured, he orders us to endure also.' Only Russia has proven it is strong enough,
proven its ability to suffer, Christ-like. Only Russia will always endure.

"I asked you here tonight so that you might understand what I
require of you, and why. You must understand that a collapse is coming, a time of horrors you as Americans cannot even fathom. I tell you
that Russia, perhaps only Russia, will survive. And so you will not have
our oil. Right now the siloviki are exporting so much oil that we have

to set quotas for our internal use. It is being squandered in the West, being burned to support an unsustainable society. You must understand that this must be addressed. And if we take actions which you oppose, you must also understand that Russians will bear any cost to defend our land, our faith and our oil. We will fight you, and we will not be defeated. You must understand this.

"So. The KarLap PSA must be suspended. The Ministry will take actions on Monday to do so. Do not interfere. I am trying to be as absolutely clear as I can be."

A cold damp was settling in over the waters. A large dead branch floated silently under the bridge and away down the river. Dickinson still had the pinched look on his face.

"Oleg Maksimovich, I'll be honest," said Dickinson. "This is a lot for me to digest. I'm not even sure what to say. You should know, my first choice would have been to delay Firebird. Until we've had a chance to discuss this. All of this. Unfortunately, Charlie has taken away that option. Look, I know he's an insufferable prick. And for that I apologize.

"But we must focus on the immediate issue at hand. Firebird is a project of strong mutual interests between our countries. I understand that you have legitimate grievances. But unfortunately the decision is now a binary one. It either goes forward or it doesn't.

"Perhaps there is a way to work out our differences. The US believes your views on Russian territorial claims to the areas of the test being conducted in international waters have merit. If you would see your way to letting Firebird proceed, we could express our support for the appropriate process at the UN."

"So, you agree our position on the Gakkel is the correct one," said Lazarev. "Very well. This acknowledgment of our rights is a first principle. Without it, there could be no discussion."

"Wait, my intention was not simply to acknowledge your rights. I was proposing a trade, an accommodation. Win, win."

"Either you accept our rights or you do not. Shall we not decide these things as matters of principle, Tom? Or shall we haggle like two old crones over a turnip?"

Dickinson's face darkened against his light-colored shirt. It was likely getting red, but in the dim light it just looked like it was blackening.

"I didn't concede anything," said Dickinson. "You win, we win. Why can't you see that? We both want what's best for our countries, what could be simpler than that?"

"So you pretend to tell me what is good for Russia, Tom? I can see how this deal is tremendous for the United States, Mr. Vice President. For Russia, I am still searching for a reason, other than to further feather the nest of certain siloviki. You bring me nothing but your ignorance, and pretend to tell me what I should do. Why should I listen to you, the representative of this culture that wastes so wantonly? You have burned through all your own oil, now you come with your mercenaries for Russia's?"

They stood together on the bridge, between the ancient fort and the new church. Charlie said nothing.

"Life is not a just another bargain, Tom, not just another business deal," said Lazarev. "Come, you will see."

They navigated back through the mud to the front of the church. The light from inside was coming entirely from candlelight. No power yet, thought Charlie. Inside, he could see ladders, more scaffolding, drop clothes, tables and barrels overflowing with boards and other scrap. Beardless Aleksei stood inside with his spoon at the ready, watching him.

"Come inside," said Lazarev. He climbed the short flight of stairs, made a sign of the cross with two fingers, right shoulder then left and crossed the threshold. Dickinson followed suit, except his cross was the Catholic left to right. The two of them stood inside the entrance, waiting.

Charlie climbed the steps and stood just outside the entrance. He could see two men hunched over a long table, under lamps with bright flames. Other men were up on the scaffolding, painting the walls and ceiling. They all stopped their work and lifted or turned their heads, looking at him. Charlie took a deep breath and stepped across the threshold. The smell of paint and fumes was overpowering. None of the men was wearing a mask.

"Well, that settles that," said Dickinson. "Just another lapsed Catholic. Nothing worse."

"Or perhaps worse than I thought," said Lazarev. He looked up around the interior. "Have you been inside an Orthodox Church, Tom?"

"No, I have not had the privilege," said Dickinson.

"Privilege, I believe, is the right sense," said Lazarev. "We believe it is a blessing to be here with God. Western churches, with their steeples, point away from us, up to the heavens, to a God far away. Here, in the Eastern church, we come to be with God, to be received, with his permission, and with great humility, into his divine presence.

"And so the interior of the church represents the entirety of all the universe. You see above us a dome, representing the heavens. All around us will be images of Christ, his mother, the saints. Behind a screen at the front will be God's altar, where a lit candle signifies his presence, the light he brings to our lives. The faithful, living and dead, gather here in the center, in God's presence. You will have to use your imagination, Tom, we are not quite finished, as you can see. The rectangular shape of the church suggests a ship, to carry us across stormy seas. Very powerful given the island setting, don't you think?"

Lazarev seemed peaceful, almost happy. Charlie hardly recognized him. The two painters at the table were Arkady and Yakov from the boat, coloring small boards. The sweet smell of paint and thinner was making Charlie sick to his stomach. Arkady gave him a quick smile and a nod, then he went back to his work. The butt of a rifle was sticking out from under the drop cloth at his feet.

"Are you familiar with icons, Tom?"

"Only a little. The gospel in paint, I believe." Someone read his briefing book, thought Charlie.

"Yes, that is quite right. Please, come and consider this piece I am working on." He lifted a board from the table and set it up on an easel. Lazarev moved one of the large lamps over to light the small image painted on the board.

"I am copying here a very famous icon, 'Vsekh Skorbiashchikh Radost,' *The Joy of All Who Sorrow*. Tell me what you see," said Lazarev.

"Well, it's a mother, with her baby, and you have that cross in the back," said Dickinson. "Gotta be Mary and Jesus, right?"

"Yes, now see her face, filled with sorrow. The infant Jesus reaches out to her. He looks wise. Not a child. But frightened. The crucifixion, it is coming, see the cross! She suffers, from knowing her child will suffer. She looks upon him with the joy of a parent, but also with the knowledge of the sacrifice that her child will make, for mankind. Here, in this sacred place, the virtuous Christian will sit and contemplate the Virgin and her suffering, and Christ's sacrifice."

"The image," said Charlie. "When the virtuous contemplate it, whose perspective are they assuming? The child's?"

"What do you mean?" said Lazarev.

"Mothers don't typically foresee the future. Usually, they assume the worst, but they don't know what's going to happen. But a child might project this ability onto the imagined, omniscient parent. Is it asking us to assume a childish perspective?"

"His suffering was a fact."

"But not at the time of this image. And His later suffering for us was voluntary. Would a child seek to suffer to somehow please the parent, to justify her pain and suffering? Does he believe that it is almost a condition of her love that he suffer?"

"Little late for you to start getting religious, don't you think, Charlie?" said Dickinson. He laughed. "Beautiful work, just beautiful, Oleg Maksimovich. Inspirational. Can't wait to see it finished."

Charlie was about to pass out. It was now or never.

"Okay, Olezka," said Charlie. "It is late. Thanks for the walk through your tragic history. Even I get the point. By the way, you left out the part where Ivan Grozny killed his one capable son in a paranoid rage. You know, the son that wasn't an idiot, who could have maintained order? If you're wondering how your suffering could have been avoided, you might take a look at that."

"Joiner, that's enough," said Dickinson.

"I agree. And I've got real work to get back to, so can we talk business? Firebird is going forward on Tuesday, Olezka, with or without your Ministry's approval. There is some benefit to us from avoiding a confrontation at this time, so we are willing to make certain concessions. First, as Tom has already offered up, the US is willing to support your claims to the Gakkel. Separately, I can tell you that the President's office is also willing to promote your man Titov to the head of the Moscow Defense District. You should also know that we are changing the economic terms of the PSA to favor Russian interests, regardless of what you decide. But you could publicize that as a win, too. So that's it. Take it or leave it. We're leaving now. If you don't accept before we leave, we'll take that as a no. You will not have another chance to accept this offer. Frankly, I don't care which you choose. It's all the same to me."

He had barely gotten the words out when the tall white Russian and the partially painted walls and the icon and the table and the paint all began to spin. Charlie lurched to the side, put out his hands and somehow caught the table. His knees buckled, but Arkady grabbed him under the arms and dragged him into a chair.

Charlie stared dumbly at the box of paint covered rags in the box at his feet. The red and blue of the Virgin Mary's robes were mixed in with gold, and greens and purple and yellow. As Charlie stared, dizzy and numb, the colors all gave way to encroaching blacks and browns, which were devouring the rags and the box.

"Get some water, he's passing out," said Dickinson.

"No water here yet," said Lazarev. "Arkady, some vodka."

He felt it before he could see it. Charlie felt a fiery, burning sensation on his legs. Then his face was warm. Then his hands shrieked with pain.

"Fire! Olezka, fire!" yelled Arkady. He grabbed a bucket of brushes and dumped them out, scattering them across the table and onto the ground, then ran towards the door.

"No, no! Arkady, Yakov!" Lazarev was wrestling with a barrel. The others helped him dump it over and then carry it out to the river.

Charlie staggered to his feet. The flames were visible now, and exploding around the room. The surface of the tables, the icons, the supplies, were all licked with fire. Dickinson was nowhere to be seen, slipped out already by his invisible team.

When they returned carrying the dark, cold waters of the Vuoksa, it was far too late. The fire was consuming the church. With all the fresh paint and stain and exposed wood, the church lit up as quickly as a torch soaked in kerosene. Arkady grabbed Charlie by the back of his shirt and pulled him outside, down to the water's edge.

Lazarev and Dickinson gazed up at the structure, engulfed in flames. The heat forced them all across the bridge back towards the asylum.

The church was a huge torch. Bathed in the reflected light, the walls of the old fort seemed consumed again in de la Gardie's fire. Through the flames, the dark outline of the church was still visible. The onion domes danced inside the fire, flickering up towards the heavens.

"You devil, what have you done?" screamed Lazarev. He was making the sign of the cross repeatedly. "All you can do is destroy! I curse you and the whore country that bore you!"

"I want your answer now!" Charlie screamed back at him. "You tell me now, what will it be. Otherwise, I am finished with you."

Lazarev yelled at Dickinson. "Is this what you bring me? Is this jackal what you bring to deal with Russia?"

"Don't look at him, Olezka," said Charlie. "Look at me. You are dealing with me. Only I can make this deal."

Lazarev's face seethed with anger and hate in the jumping, reflected flames of his burning church. His chest heaved without stop. He screamed a long, anguished cry into the night.

"Yes, yes," said Lazarev. "The territory. Titov. And, we inspect the charges. You do not explode eight megaton charges in our Arctic without our supervision."

"No," said Charlie. "We don't have time for a goddamned inspection. That's not the deal."

"Christ, Joiner, what are you doing?" said Dickinson. "It's a fucking inspection. Do it or I'm pulling the territory off the table." Charlie stared at him.

"Okay," said Charlie. "Done." He looked over to the muddy, sweaty Dickinson. "We're finished here. Let's go."

This time Dickinson held his chopper for Charlie, and an empty seat next to him.

"What the hell happened back there, Joiner?"

"They were using enough paint thinner to float a battleship," said Charlie. "Old rags and paint thinner will spontaneously combust. Flames are nearly invisible. Very dangerous."

"So you're denying you burned his church intentionally? Didn't zap that box with your pitchfork?"

Charlie head still throbbed. He looked at Dickinson with a pained grin. "Maybe someday they'll stop whining and start taking some basic HSE precautions. Their churches wouldn't go up in flames so often."

"HSE?"

"Health, safety and environmental. They are closer to God, if only because their safety record is crap. You notice there wasn't a single fire extinguisher in the entire building? You take one step closer to the Almighty every time you walk into a Russian facility."

"I feel like I need to take a shower," said Dickinson. "Or go to confession. Stare into the abyss on all your deals, Joiner?"

"All the ones that matter."

CHAPTER 9

WHITE NIGHTS

St. Petersburg
Late Friday night

T hey handcuffed Avinashi's hands over the shower curtain rod
in a decrepit hotel room and took turns screaming at her in
Russian. The militia officers stripped down to their sweaty, stained un-
dershirts like they were going to beat her or worse. None of the questions were about KAL. They wanted to know where Ted was. How did
he get away from Peterhof? Where would he go? How could she contact him? She listened to them tell her she was a stupid girl who could
disappear as she watched herself in the mirror over the sink, hanging
by her wrists in her gown. Avinashi thought she was going to die and
was happy that she had something not to tell them. She grabbed a
glass from the sink with her toes and broke it against the wall. When
they came close enough she kicked at them with a large shard.

After a few minutes of this stalemate one of them came back holding the key in his raised hand. They unlocked her from the rod and
put her blindfolded and handcuffed again in the van. First she was
on a plain bench seat and then on the floor because the driver was
suicidal and they didn't belt her in. After a short, violent ride they
picked her up off the floor, took off her handcuffs and blindfold and
pushed her out on the street, telling her not to leave the city.

She was sitting dazed on a stoop when a young couple stopped and offered to call the militia. Avinashi asked them if they would just tell her where she was and help her find a cab. She was on Sredny Prospekt, they said, on Vasilievsky Island, and there would be cabs at a hotel just around the corner. It was an old section of town, just west across the river from the city center. The advantage of not having a purse was that she still had her cash and cards tucked inside her gown so in twenty minutes she was back at the Grand walking bloody, barefoot and defiant through the lobby. In her suite, she tried to call Ted and then Charlie but neither answered, so she left messages. She washed and bandaged her wrists. Then she showered, changed into jeans, a long-sleeved running shirt, running shoes and a gray shell and went out to find Ted.

Even if he hadn't mentioned it, the first place anyone would look for a young, single American in St. Petersburg would be the Cynic. It was about a mile from the hotel, on Antonenko, near the Blue Bridge. She ran nearly all the way, through the trash-strewn streets and along stinking canals. The Cynic was an underground dive bar popular with ex-pats and students, and nearly every one in the city was now crowded into one of the small, low-ceilinged rooms. She pushed her way through the crowds and the wide, arched doorways until she found Ted sitting at a long table in the corner of the last room drinking with some spirited Aussies and a queer-looking Brit.

"Ted, we have to go, now," she told him. "It's not safe, they're looking for you."

"Sit down, sit down." He slapped one of the Aussies on the shoulder and with a wide, obliging smile for Avinashi he slid down the table. "What are you talking about? Who's looking for me? Vadim is right over there, everything's fine." Through the crowd Avinashi could just see the professorial and very out-of-place Vadim reading a book at the bar with a cup of tea. He looked up and waved at Avinashi.

"You had a rough night, but you'll be okay," said Charlie. "C'mon, have a drink with us. You can be part of history. I took Charlie's recipe and substituted vodka for the white rum, plum brandy for the apricot. Add Cointreau, lemon juice, soda and you have a Russian dry hole. Something gets lost in the translation but it's sweet, I think you'll like it. I'll have to go get them, service is not the Cynic's strong suit. Have some fried garlic bread. And gentlemen, behave."

The largest Aussie offered a loud, rude toast to the Sheilas back home that he had to start three times because he was barely co- herent. As he finally crossed the finish line his mates shouted and downed another shot of the water of life. It was Friday night in the criminally-short St. Petersburg summer and the Cynic was in a frenzy. Bottles and glasses clinked with abandon and slapped down on tables. Desperate, giddy shouts and laughs burst through the live band's re- lentless rockabilly. Avinashi briefly allowed herself to forget she had been handcuffed in a shower, and then Ted was back at the table.

"Here you go," he said, setting in front of them two tumbler-sized glasses filled with ice and a deep purple liquid topped with a curling cone of whipped cream. He handed her a thin straw.

"Try your luck," he said.

The Australians chanted "Drill, baby, drill!" and inexplicably started imitating a short standing wave back and forth on their side of the table.

"Guys, put a cork in it," said Ted. "The patient needs rest and plenty of fluids." He turned back to Avinashi and slid her drink closer. "Sorry, some geophysicists from Chevron. Okay, try it, tell me what you think."

She held the straw and looked at Ted, soaking up his happy, ea- ger grin. "Okay," she said. The Australians cheered as she plunged her straw into the frothy whiteness and sucked up the light, sweet distil- lates. And then in an uncharacteristic, irresponsible and to her mind unexplainable act of indulgence, Avinashi drained the glass. Slowed by nothing more than that morning's single bite of a dry English muffin, the supercharged syrups flowed right into her bloodstream. A warm glow filled her insides, quieting her panic, releasing her tension, numb- ing her bruised wrists, and tried hard to banish her better judgment.

"There, how's that then?" said Ted. "Better? Hey, let me help you there." With a folded napkin he touched away some errant whip from the tip of her nose and she shocked herself by giggling. "No worries, happens to all the rooks. Hey, Avi's back! To the resurrection!" He lifted his tumbler and they clinked each other and then around the table, with more than a few misses on the Aussie side in the process.

"Avi, I am so sorry about tonight," said Ted. "I'm sorry I didn't wait, I was so embarrassed. I started to walk back when I ran into my good friends Lord and Lady Peterhof. Lord Peterhof was so drunk on my Jagermeister that he let me drive them back into town. I'm afraid this ends my dream of a diplomatic career."

"You were awful," she said. "But at least you didn't get fired."

"Not as long as I keep my phone off. That's my long-term career strategy. What about you? You plan to live north of sixty for the next fifty years? Must be running from something. That's always the way it is with people on the frontier. Crime of passion, I'll bet."

"Sort of. Annoying co-worker."

"Duly noted. So that's the grand plan? Lots of long, dark winters and sable coats in your future?"

"No, I'm a career girl. The long-term plan was Russia, London, then back to Houston. Why not me? That's what my mother kept telling me."

"Your mom's right, aim high. That's what Charlie keeps telling me, God knows why. I'm cheering for you, good for me to have friends in high places."

"You're the last person that needs that. Your dad knows where all the Texso bodies are buried. That should keep you on the payroll, somewhere."

"Like Siberia? No, thanks. Yes, dear old dad. I don't know, I think he and mum would just as soon wash their hands of me."

"Stop it. That's ridiculous. Look at you, Mr. Firebird. Saving the company, that's got to count for something."

"Telnov's right, damn lucky break is all. Or, I owe it all to Charlie for pulling me out of the gutter. When I fell off the map I think my parents appreciated the break from all our yelling. Well, you can't pick your parents, or your son. Even when you can you never know.

But I think if they could do it again, they would have picked a good Indian girl such as yourself."

"Bad Indian girl, more like it."

"Mmmm. Even better."

"Okay, really now, stop it," she said, laughing again and slapping him on the leg. Oh, my God, she thought. Did I really do that? She touched his leg again. "Seriously, Ted, we have to get out of here, now." Vadim was still reading at the bar. In minutes they could be safely away.

"Right, to hell with the policy." She was still trying to make sense of his comment when her thoughts were interrupted by the disturbing sight of Don Sanders hopping by at the head of a conga line.

"Polyarniks, the next generation!" shouted Sanders, as he jigged back and mostly forth to a rocking song about melancholy cowboys while the laughing Ekaterina latched onto his thick waist and flicked her long black hair back and forth to the music. "Ms. Sharma, now that you're out, can I impress you into my little chain gang?" He winked at her and she hoped his ridiculous, convulsive laughter would split him at the seams, but although sweaty as a pig he remained otherwise perfectly composed and attired as one could be while leading an idiotic dance.

"C'mon, who doesn't love a conga line?" yelled Ted, jumping up from the table. He grabbed Avinashi's hand and pulled her up. The dry hole got the better of her and Ted had to catch her as the room swirled.

"That's okay," he said. "Grab onto something." He made space for them behind Ekaterina and placed Avinashi's hands on her wriggling hips, and then he put his hands on her own, and they all danced off, bumping and swaying and singing, on a tour of the Cynic.

The band was in the larger room next to them, Russians in sunglasses, zoot suits and red cowboy hats. Sanders ordered another round for each table as he passed, yelling out to the waitress that followed in his wake. He was the most popular man in the place, the cool dad that let all the kids drink at his house, laws and decency be damned. Ekaterina occasionally slipped out of Avinashi's grasp and squeezed Sanders with hugs from behind, calling him Uncle Don. The last place Avinashi wanted to die was in a conga line with Uncle Don. She broke out of the line and pulled Ted along with her.

"We need to talk, Ted. Now."

She held his hand all the way back to the table. The Australians were gone, and two Russian men and a tall, pretty blond girl had taken their place. But it was the only table with empty seats, so they sat down. Vadim was gone, but his book and his tea were still at the bar. He must have gone to the restroom, she thought.

The three of them were all smoking, with a nearly full bottle of vodka in front of them, and five glasses. The Russians were young, but older than students, with long hair and beards. The blond girl's arms were draped over the older of the two, the one with light-blue, luminescent eyes. She was unmistakably American. Somehow, Ted ended up next to the girl with Avinashi across the table.

"Hello, how are you?" said the older Russian. "I like your dancing, you know how to have fun. My name is Nikolai. These are my friends, Arkady and Olivia. Have a drink with us."

"That would be much appreciated," said Ted. "Ted and Avinashi. I think we're ready to give up on the dry holes."

"Dry holes?" said Nikolai.

"Oil joke. Rum, brandy, some Cointreau, a little lemon juice."

"Ah, a woman's drink. Here, I make a toast." He filled the five glasses with one swooping pour. The barman arrived with several pans of hot garlic toast and slid them onto the table.

Nikolai held up his glass to the others, his eyes drilling into Avinashi. "Let us drink like we are going to die."

"From the day we were born," said Ted, as he threw back his drink.

Avinashi left her glass on the table. The toast brought her back nearer to reality. As soon as Vadim got back she was going to play the victim of the dry hole and get the two of them out of here.

"So you work for an oil company?" said Nikolai. "Which one?"

"Texso," said Ted. "On the KarLap project."

"Arktika! So, is that what you will find up there? Dry holes?"

"If it's there, we'll find it. If it's not there, that's God's fault, not mine."

"You know, I was also in the oil business."

"You were? With who?"

"The Russian Army. Yes, Arkady and I were in Chechnya back in 2000. Babies, we were. Fighting for the Mafia, for their oil. The most important part of the oil business, security. Like your army in the desert, no?"

"I think that was supposed to be something about Islamic terrorism."

He laughed. "You're as bad as the damn Muslims, they always think it's about them. The damn ghosts were caught in a Mafia fight, dying under our tanks and artillery, and we would laugh because they thought they were fighting for their independence. The blacks, too stupid to live. Which would be fine, except in their stupidity they killed my brothers."

"All just a big mistake, huh?" said Ted.

"You should come with us to my friend's party," said Nikolai. "We were just going to leave, they're expecting us. I will introduce you to some of my friends. Very interesting people, you would like them. Also in the oil business."

"Really? Will there be any blacks there?" said Ted. "Probably not, huh? Actually, I kind of like the vibe going right here. Let's drink awhile. Got any more good toasts?"

Time to change the subject, thought Avinashi. Where was Vadim? Much longer she would get sick anyhow.

"Where are you from, Olivia?" said Avinashi. Olivia was eating all the fried garlic bread by herself.

"Ohio," she said, chasing the bread with a healthy shot. "This is my first time in St. Petersburg, and I love it! Nikolai said I had to come and I'm so glad I did. Peter in the summer, what could be better. So much energy, it's incredible. I like your hair." She was running her fingers through Ted's hair. "I just love long hair on men."

"Why, thank you, Olivia," said Ted, smirking at Avinashi. "That's very kind of you."

"Were you in the army, Ted?" said Nikolai.

"No, I did not have that privilege."

"Of course, in the US you use mercenaries. Very professional. But no passion, so in that sense still unreliable. We saw Americans, down in Chechnya."

"You did? I wasn't aware that we were involved."

"Oh, yes. Americans and Georgians, they liked to interfere. I killed a few myself, so I know. They did not die as hard as the blacks, as I remember."

"That's great, really interesting," said Ted.

"Where did you get those crazy tattoos?" said Olivia.

"South Pacific," said Ted. "Surfing sabbatical."

"Get out of here," she said, punching him in the shoulder. "I love surfing. I hooked up with this surfer when I got thrown off a boat in Cocoa Beach. He taught me, but then he hated it when I was better than he was." She leaned in on Ted and wrapped a long arm around his shoulder as she laughed at her own story. "Where do you surf in Russia, Nikolai? Let's go, I'll teach you."

Nikolai ignored her. "So Ted," he said. "If you find oil in Arktika, am I going to have to fight the surfer for it?"

"No fighting necessary," said Ted. "We're just here to help."

"Surfers just like to chill," said Olivia. "Live and let live."

"Are you kidding?" said Ted. "You've never been from out of town and tried to catch a wave at Rincon Point. Talk about a fight over scarce resources."

"You're funny," said Olivia. "That is so cute." Avinashi tried to fight a wave of nausea as Olivia's hand disappeared into Ted's lap under the table. Nikolai seemed not to notice.

"Skinny boys in shorts," said Nikolai. "Sounds dangerous. We used to see those in the Army. We had this method for finding out which new recruits were tough enough to become paratroopers. You just beat them for six months. The ones that live are the toughest. I lived, and Arkady."

"Nikolai, stop it," said Olivia. "He's joking. Sometimes he says things just to get a rise out of people."

"Good way to select for the thickest heads, if nothing else," said Ted. "Well, sometime you're wrestling in the barracks think about how tough it would be to fight a guy when you're standing on wet boards traveling down a thirty degree liquid slope at over twenty knots, while his buddy launches a fiberglass projectile at your head."

"Ted, I'm really not feeling well," said Avinashi. "I'm going to use the restroom." She needed to find Vadim.

"Sure, sure," said Ted. He pulled out his tray of darts from his pocket and poured a tumbler half full of vodka. "Say, Nikolai. How about a friendly wager? Pick any spot on that wall. If I don't hit it within the width of your hand, I drink. If I do, you drink. How about it? Game?"

"I'll go with you, Avinashi," said Olivia.

Avinashi stopped and looked around at the bar. It was hard for her to see over the crowd. Vadim's book was still at the bar, but they had removed his tea.

"This way, I think," said Olivia.

The restrooms were crude affairs, and inside every square inch bore writing in a large, looping script. Two stalls, both with lines, and two narrow sinks. One of the sinks was empty so they shared. Avinashi took a paper towel, dampened it and wiped her face.

"Your boyfriend, he looks familiar," said Olivia, combing out her hair. "What's his last name?"

Avinashi hesitated, wondering whether she should correct her, but decided against it. "Crawford."

"Huh. Looks so familiar. You are so lucky, he's cute."

"Your boyfriend," said Avinashi. "I have to say, he seems a bit dangerous."

"I know, doesn't he?" She smiled at the thought. "He's not though. He's really very gentle."

"Do you know anything about him?"

"He's a bodyguard, sort of. But not the rough kind. He only does it because he really doesn't have any other skills. Well, that's not exactly true." She smiled again. "But you know what I mean."

"Who does he work for?"

"Some politician. This skinny guy, something to do with oil. I don't ask him about it, I know enough to stay away from politics."

Avinashi suddenly had to vomit. There was a tall trash can next to the sink and she rushed to it and heaved up a lot of nothing.

"Ohmigosh, Avinashi, are you okay?" Olivia wet another paper towel and wet her face.

"I just think I really have to go back to the hotel, right away."

"Sure, here, I'll help you."

She held onto Olivia's arm as they walked out of the restroom. Defenseless, she watched the vile Sanders come towards them down the hallway trailing his niece.

"Ms. Sharma, worse for the wear?" said Sanders. "Don't worry, you'll get used to it. I did." He came closer, still smelling of that damn Scotch.

"Say, did you hear that Brad Pitt was up at the bar?" he said to Olivia. "Scout's honor. You can get your picture taken with him." Olivia practically dropped Avinashi to the floor and ran off. Sanders caught Avinashi under her arm with one fleshy mitt, pulled her close and pressed his lips to her ears.

"The owner of this establishment happened to mention to me that your ex-colleague Vadim is out back in the alley," he said. "And I don't mean ex in the sense that you were fired this evening, but ex in the sense that his throat was cut and he's lying dead behind the dumpster. Think it has something to do with your new friends?"

Avinashi's stomach felt like it was having seizures.

"I don't want to butt into your business, but you might think about some drops of this in their drinks." He held out a small clear plastic tube with a skinny black screw top. "Three or four per glass and they won't be any trouble at all."

"You couldn't just come over there and tell them to leave us alone, could you?" said Avinashi.

"When I was younger, maybe. I was a whole lot slimmer and not quite as smart." He sighed and extended his palm. "This is about all I can offer you now. Well, almost all."

Avinashi picked up the vial like it was a dead animal. "Not going to cramp your social life if I take this, am I, Don?" said Avinashi.

"What are you suggesting? I get by on my charm, Ms. Sharma." He closed up her hand and danced lightly down the hallway and back to the party.

"Arkady, my knife is filthy, give me yours," said Nikolai in Russian. At least that's what Avinashi thought he said, but he slurred his words so much she might have imagined it.

"Key is to flick your wrist as your arm moves forward," said Ted. "Basic wave physics. Brings power without loss of control."

"Otva li," swore Nikolai.

"Okay, more of a doer than a thinker, that's cool."

"I didn't see Brad Pitt anywhere," said Olivia, back at the table. "That old guy is a whack job, who is he? Nikolai, what are you doing?" Arkady was handing Nikolai something under the table.

"A lot of drinking," said Ted, filling up Nikolai's tumbler. "Nikolai, do you mind if we call time out so I can take a sip? I'm getting thirsty."

Avinashi wasn't going to waste any time. She pinned the vial under her palm with her thumb and reached for a slice of bread, sending a few drops into the drink.

"You'll get your chance," said Nikolai. "Olivia, be a good girl and take this over there by the wall and drink it." He handed her his tumbler.

"It's not going to work, I can drink you under the table," she said. But she grabbed the glass and walked over to the wall, then turned to face them and lifted the glass.

"No, no, face the bar," shouted Nikolai. "Through the arm?" he said to Ted, then he flicked his right wrist and the knife was a blur as it flew across the room, through the circle made by her drinking arm as it lifted the glass to her lips, and hit the wall with a thud. It being the Cynic, none of this attracted any attention from the crowd.

"Hey," said Olivia. "You crazy Russian shit, you could have killed me." She pulled the knife out of the wall and walked slowly back to the table, flipping the knife in her hand.

"You want to play games?" Olivia slapped the empty glass on the table. "I'll teach you one. Give me your hand." She grabbed Nikolai's hand by the wrist and forced it onto the table, palm down. "Five-finger fillet, European style. You flinch, you lose."

Nikolai was fairly anesthetized by the vodka and didn't seem worried. "What are the stakes?" he said. She slammed the knife point down onto his hand. He jumped up in pain, leaking blood from his finger. "Cyka!"

"Gee, Nikolai, you're supposed to spread your fingers, didn't I tell you?" said Olivia. "Don't ever do that to me again, or I'll put it through the bone." She held her hand to her forehead. "Oh, I've got to sit down. That vodka really hit me."

If Olivia passed out she would lose her chance, thought Avinashi. She quietly grabbed the bottle and filled two tumblers. She rested her hand briefly on top of each and emptied the tube between the two.

"We can do that, with darts," said Avinashi. "But if he does, you both have to drink." She slid the glasses across the table to Nikolai and Arkady.

"Darts? Why not the knife?" said Nikolai.

"Because he's not a soldier," said Avinashi.

"Your boy, he is too good with the little feathered things."

"Okay, I'll throw the darts. At him."

"Yes, that I like," said Nikolai, slapping the table. "Agreed. Against the wall you human ink spill."

Ted looked at Avinashi warily. "Still upset about dinner?"

"You're not the only one with hand-eye coordination." She poured another small drink and handed it to him. "Just don't wobble."

"Already with the excuses. Not a good sign."

Ted assumed the position at the wall. "Like this?" said Ted, arcing his arm as far away from his body as he could and sipping the drink through a straw.

"No straw," yelled Nikolai. Ted spit it aside. "Ready."

She said a silent prayer and let fly. "Ouch!" The dart bounced off his arm.

"You moved," she cried. "I was right on, I told you not to move."

"No big deal, I told you I was thirsty. C'mon, bottom's up. Fair's fair."

"Here you are," said Nikolai, lifting the two drinks towards them and dropping them on the table.

"No." She picked up the knife off the table. "Second chance, with the knife."

"Yes, I love this girl, you are crazy!" said Nikolai.

"Pour me another drink first, let me see how steady your hands are," said Ted. Avinashi poured a splash of vodka in his glass. "Thanks, Mom. I won't drink it all in one place. If you stick me you have to promise to call me King Ted for a month."

"Promise." Avinashi pushed him towards the wall. "But she throws it," said Avinashi, pointing at Olivia.

"No!" said Nikolai. "Oh, okay, okay, I don't care, just somebody just throw at him."

"I'm not sure if I'm feeling up to this," said Olivia, as she struggled to her feet.

"Give it your best shot," said Avinashi. "Drink up, Ted." Olivia opened and closed her eyes slowly and took the knife.

"Cheers," said Ted. The glass hadn't even touched his lips before the knife flew through the crook of his elbow and stuck in the wall. "Whoa," said Ted, staring at the knife. "Grow up in a circus?" He pulled the knife out of the wall and slapped it on the table. "Drink up boys."

"Fucking girl has been nothing but trouble," said Nikolai, as he and Arkady tipped back their mixed drinks. Ten minutes later their animated conversation about Arabs had worn them out completely and they laid their heads down next to Olivia's on the table and went to sleep, not the first patrons to pass out in the Cynic that night.

Avinashi and Ted stopped halfway back to the hotel on a bench near the university and she hugged him in relief. Then she turned on Ted's cell phone and was finally able to reach Charlie on his mobile back at the hotel. He refused her resignation and ten minutes later they were with him in a speeding SUV on the way to the airport. The safest place for both of them was back on the *Northern Ranger*.

St. Petersburg
Saturday night

Charlie stood on the terrace of his suite holding an empty glass. Down in the darkening square, Pushkin worked the passing crowds like a carnival barker.

Charlie had dragged all the lawyers in on a Saturday and they worked through the afternoon and early evening. Essential language had been agreed upon and a process had been set in motion, so that by the end of the day on Monday a memorandum of understanding for changes to the PSA would be approved, signed and delivered by all relevant parties. Charlie would present to the Texso board on Monday in London.

Avinashi had called an hour earlier from the *Northern Ranger*. Somewhere on the flight East she had finally figured out they had only let her go to lead them to Ted and she tried to quit again. But as he had figured, this was a lot harder to do from the Kara Sea and he was able to convince her to stay the course. Just keep falling forward, he told her. Almost there.

Through the thick summer air came a distant knocking. Faster now, irritated. At him? He stepped back into the suite, set down his glass and opened his door. Shirin Yazdani stood in the hallway, her dark eyes glowing like hot, angry coals.

"You attend no events to which I am invited. You refuse to take my calls. You don't return my messages. For the final humiliation, I must come begging at your door. But now you are the one that needs me. I have something that you need to see." Charlie nodded over her shoulder to the ever-present Duman, and the large Turk returned the gesture.

"Come in and let's talk," said Charlie. Shirin sent Duman down to wait in the lobby then went in and stood defiantly in the middle of the room, her hands buried in the pockets of her pale blue trench coat. She carried a thick manila envelope under her arm.

"Can I fix you a drink?" She didn't answer so he found a small bottle of champagne in the minibar and poured two glasses. "What do I need to see?"

"No, there is a price. First, you must talk to me. I want you to explain why you have abandoned me."

He motioned her to the couch and turned on some music. She picked up her champagne and drank the entire glass, then sat back in the corner of the couch, her hands jammed back in her coat pockets.

"What did you think?" said Shirin. "We would just get married and start over? Open a shop in Umbria? This is who we are. This is what we are."

"Not me. Not for much longer."

"You cannot just quit, not now."

"I may not have a choice."

"No, Charlie, only you can decide to quit." She stared away from him, shaking her head. "And what, so you will quit and just leave me to be alone? So I will be alone over here and you will be alone over there? Charlie, why are you doing this?"

"I told you what I wanted, Shirin. But what do you want? Do I even know? I want to."

"More champagne." Charlie never received an answer to his question, but he wasn't alone. She wasn't theirs, so the siloviki assumed she was a plant for the Americans, the CIA assumed she was taking Aranaco money, and the Arabs thought she was just another

Wanda Jablonski and net-net they liked what she wrote. Lazarev likely thought she conspired with all of them to destroy Russia. Charlie thought none of the above but that wasn't much of an answer. He poured her another glass.

"After next week, I just don't know what there is for me," said Charlie. "Where ever it went, I wanted to take you with me."

In March they were both at a conference in Barcelona. Afterward they had stolen away for the weekend and he had asked her to marry him on a sunny morning in Sant Sadurni. He had not expected her to say yes, although he wasn't sure he knew all the reasons why. But nearing the end, Charlie was beginning to realize that one life can only be about so much. He couldn't go on, and there would never be another for him. So he asked her to come with him.

"Don't leave me, Charlie. I still need you." She had left the champagne untouched and she was staring into it, her eyes filling with tears. He stood up and pulled her to her feet. He undid the belt to her jacket and slid it back off her shoulders. Then he reached around the small of her back. She stiffened, but he pulled her into him. He could feel her body through her thin dress. She reached her arms up around his neck and leaned her head into his shoulder. The scent of her hair reminded him of warm Augusts, roses and sunshine.

He reached down and turned out the lights. He ran his hands over her silken shape, remembering, bringing her back to him, and he felt her shudder. He told her how much he had missed her, how he thought about her every night. How nothing seemed right to him but the thought of marrying her, even if it was an illusion. He kissed her, and touched her cheek, and thought of only her soft lips and warm, smooth skin. He lifted her dress and she pulled up his shirt. She ran her hand gently up his scarred back, as she comforted him with calm, warm whispers. And they fell softly onto the couch where they joined together again, two broken halves, for as long as they could be together.

Charlie laid in the bed next to the sleeping Shirin and remembered the first time they met. He went back to work in Colombia for two weeks before getting transferred out of the country and she had met him amidst the half-packed boxes at his office. She was a reporter in her first job doing soft stories for a now defunct glossy, the Oil & Gas Executive, published out of London. Shirin had been born in Tehran but was British to the core. Her parents had fled after the fall of the Shah and she had been raised in London, graduating from Wadham College at Oxford and even marrying a young British officer she met at an Iranian embassy party.

After her first year the magazine gave her the opportunity to write her own story idea. So the new bride asked to go to Colombia to interview the thirty-two-year old widowed geologist who had been kidnapped by FARC rebels after making his second major find in only six years. It was hard for her editor to argue that there wouldn't be a story in there somewhere and he authorized the trip.

After six months in the jungle he probably still looked like hell when she arrived, although he didn't realize it at the time because by comparison after a month he was feeling nearly human. Shirin didn't know yet what could be left unasked, and so her youthful diligence gave cover to her horror and fascination as she walked him through the past few years. And Charlie was not quite yet at the point again where he cared enough to keep certain things private. He talked about his father, the everyman Texas roughneck with the famous last name, Charlie's days in College Station at Texas A&M and about Wayne Parsons and his other mentors at Texso. They did finally talk about the discovery of the Cusiana field in Colombia, and before that the Alif in Yemen. By then it was dark and everyone else had left the office but they kept right on going to the kidnapping, and how the worst part wasn't the deprivation and the fear and the torture but how much he missed his wife and son and how he couldn't think of a reason why he shouldn't just die and join them. When they finished, he walked her back to her hotel and didn't see her again for several years. Fortunately none of the more sordid details were deemed fit for a feel-good reception-area monthly so the end product was a well-crafted but fairly standard story of stiff-upper lip perseverance. Either that or Shirin did the cutting on her own, he never knew.

Like any good professional, Shirin kept in touch with him as she jumped between a couple of other trade journals. Then her husband was killed in the first Gulf War and he had tracked her down and left a message that he might not be much help but of course he had lost his wife and if she wanted to talk he wanted to help. They did speak once by phone but he didn't hear from her again for another couple of years. Then she had decided to start something of her own, the NPR, and she was wondering if he could help her. He had just signed the Caspian deal for Texso and it was huge news. *The Contract of the Century.* They met in Baku and he gave her his first interview on the deal.

They started talking regularly again and bumped into each other at the occasional conference. Two years after Baku, and a month after they had dinner at an offshore conference in Sao Paulo, Charlie rented a house in Umbria for two weeks in August, his first vacation since Yemen, and he asked her to go with him. For two weeks they played house, away from the world. Everyone at Texso was so relieved he was finally taking a vacation that they bent over backwards not to bother him. Shirin gave Duman his first break in nearly as long and he went back to be with his family in Ceyhan. Charlie and Shirin shopped in the markets and cooked. They helped the owner try to grow roses in the dusty clay. They read, went for long walks and slept in. Afterward, he knew that it would hurt NPR for their relationship to become public but he expected something to change. He was sent down to Nigeria on a troubleshooting mission and before he knew it they had snuck away once to the Azores and then it was summer again and they were looking forward to another two weeks back in Umbria. On that trip he heard the University of Perugia had a team looking at end-Triassic mollusk fossils up near Menaggio. They took a car up to see and Charlie ended up sponsoring two graduate students at the site, so he went back each year. Eventually he funded the whole project. And so it had gone every year until this March. Next week they should have been in Umbria but he couldn't pretend anymore.

Charlie got out of bed and rang the front desk to check on Duman. He was still in the lobby and they called him to the phone. Charlie apologized for the lack of a vacation this month and told him he would have the hotel find a room where he could rest until Shirin called. Then he told the night manager to provide Duman with a room and bill it to Charlie personally.

Finally, he went back to bed. He pulled Shirin closer and went to sleep.

When he woke in the morning she was gone and the manila envelope was on her pillow. He put on a robe and made some coffee and took it over to the couch to read. It was a sheaf of technical papers, mostly from Aranaco from the looks of it, with a note from her. Ghawar was dying. It was all there in gory detail. She had received it yesterday afternoon. She was sending a note to clients with a summary this afternoon. She was told the documents would be released to the public through Wikileaks Sunday evening London time.

He scanned the papers. Then he read them again, closely. It wasn't the way he had imagined the end would come, but it would do. He quickly showered and dressed and headed for their lawyers' offices. He needed to get on the phone to London.

CHAPTER 10

SUCCESSION PLAN

London
Monday morning

"Where do we start?" said Roger Crawford.

Over Roger's shoulder, through the windows of the 48th floor of One Canada Square, Texso's London headquarters, Charlie could see a sliver of the sun rising bright and clear over the flat, broad expanse of the City. They were in before any of the staff so Charlie made coffee in the break room and they had carried it through the empty hallways to Roger's office.

It was the time of day when the world seemed most susceptible to reason. That quiet, calm, forward-looking hour when any intractable problem, even the one that kept you tossing and turning all night with its career-ending potential, could be calmly discussed, dealt with and dismissed, by men and women of goodwill, vast experience and sound judgment, up early and ahead of the curve, in crisp business, not casual, attire as they sipped warm, reassuring cups of coffee. Yet Charlie knew Roger's look, and so he could not take the usual comfort from the light of a new day. The look that said he thought Charlie himself might be the problem.

Roger studied Charlie quietly. He flipped a pen end over end in his hand, every so often poking it absentmindedly at a fresh legal pad on his desk. Roger had the trim build and careful manner of a man that might take his golf seriously, and spend far too much time over each shot, both of which Charlie knew to be the case.

The legal department didn't make allowances for those on the periphery of the empire. If anything, their decisions were viewed with greater suspicion. There was a resigned acceptance of the frontier's influence. Only the strongest could remain out there forever before they became a liability. Charlie knew the chatter. He was out in the field more than his position would require. Running solo. Too close to the undesirables. The middlemen, the mercenaries, the mafia and the tin pot despots. Inured to the endless violence and graft. And to what end? Since Azeri, it had been one dry hole after another, thought Roger. Prompting a reexamination of everything they had in the Caspian, and a humiliating restatement of the too aggressive reserve amounts he had booked. Which in turn lead to a huge haircut to the stock and a long-running shareholder lawsuit that Roger had to clean up, thank you very much. Then in all the confusion, the Brits snuck in and stole Kashagan from right under Charlie's nose. And so now you had KarLap, an expensive Hail Mary, the last gamble of a man with nothing more to lose. In retrospect, it's clear he never recovered from the loss of his family in the desert or, for God's sake, the kidnapping. What had the big guy been thinking? Charlie certainly wasn't fit for the top spot, as had been widely expected even ten years ago. He should be in counseling, not a position of responsibility. His promotion after the Baku "Contract of the Century" was impulsive and misguided, the triumph of wishful thinking and a bit of guilt over cold hard common sense. Now he was the mangy dog that someone had to put down, the last one to know he was one of the walking dead after saving the family from the rabid raccoon. Spare him now, and before you knew it he would be stashing blood money in offshore accounts and spending it on soccer teams, mountains of cocaine and women that could be his daughters, taking the company down along with him. Or so Roger thought.

"Where would you like to start?" said Charlie.

"You didn't think you needed to bring Firebird back to the board when Lazarev told you he was going to stop it?"

As general counsel for Texso, Roger Crawford was the friendly face on the inflexible law, the one who would decide in the first instance whether your occasional error in judgment constituted criminality, or recklessness, or just a bad day. There was sympathy in his eyes, and concern, almost parental. But no guilt, anywhere. No hint of any hesitation to judge. Not for staying behind to tend the home fires, for having a family. For probably already having confirmed his flight back to Houston later this week. On Thursday, just so if there was a problem with flights he could get back the next day and still not miss the weekend at home.

"Why?" said Charlie. "It was just the typical noise."

"Even though it required a change to the economic terms?"

"They're not required. I'm recommending them. If the board wants to try to stand pat that's their decision. The territorial issue is all upside for us. The concession was by the US, not Texso."

Roger grimaced, like someone in his foursome had suggested they not keep score. The pen froze, point down on the pad

"This was so clearly in our interest that it's not even close," said Charlie. "There was no time to go back to the board. It was then or never. I'll stand by the decision, and I think the board will agree. It was within my authority, in fact it was my obligation, to make that call."

Roger leaned forward and his furrows disappeared. He took a sip of his coffee, conceding the point for the moment, and shook his head.

"Well, this Ghawar fiasco will make it look like small change," said Roger. "And you're right, the result would have been the same. We can argue later about the process." Charlie had no doubt he would. "So, it finally happened. Ghawar. I read your email. Is it as bad as all that?"

"We'll find out today," said Charlie. "I can only estimate the impact on future production. The market will tell us what the loss of five million barrels a day means. I'm going to call Gavin right now to get his take."

"Well, good thing he talks fast, because you've only got about ten minutes. You still need to sit with the lawyers this morning."

"Look, is this the time for that? Reschedule it. I'll do it next week."

"I don't care if the world is ending, if you want to keep any semblance of clean hands here you will respect the process. At this point, it's not so much having an answer as having a process. It's not even my call. To remind you, these lawyers are not mine, they represent an independent committee of the board. They don't answer to me. Look, your car for the board meeting will be outside at noon, so you have a hard stop. You're getting off easy."

"I'll tell them all I know, but that's not going to get them the truth. Who else are they talking to?"

"I can't discuss that with you."

The administrative staff had started to arrive outside the office. The sun was up and promising a rare hot day in the City.

"There's no good way to ask this," said Roger. "Did you look over the package? They're going to ask me."

"I was pretty busy last week."

"Christ, Charlie. I'm sorry, it's never going to be a good time. You know, maybe with all this going on you won't mind leaving it behind."

"Is that what you think of me, Roger?"

"C'mon, Charlie. I didn't mean it like that. Anyone might feel that way. Okay, fine. You're coming back to London Wednesday, after Firebird, right? Let's get together late Wednesday. Dinner, someplace new. I'm headed back Thursday morning."

Roger squirmed awkwardly in his seat. Charlie took a sip of his coffee. It was cold.

"Thanks for helping with Ted," said Roger.

Charlie just looked out the window. Roger stood up and put his hands on his hips. "Well, you should get down there, the combined billing rate is probably ten grand an hour."

Charlie let the meter run. He went to the empty office where he was camped out, closed the door and dialed his broker. Charlie met Gavin MacKenzie when Gavin was an energy analyst covering the majors, including Texso, for a no-name firm in Edinburgh. Investors might never have learned the name of his firm, but they knew Gavin from New York to Dubai to Tokyo and his opinions moved energy stocks. If he didn't like your answers on an earnings call you would be missing ten billion in market cap by the time you got back to your office. He was a small, hard, cynical man who loved to laugh, and red-faced too young from whisky and weather. Too smart for his clients, he eventually got fed up and jumped over to the buyside where he made a pot of money and retired, sort of. Still in Edinburgh, he now ran mostly his own money, but also a little for family and friends. Charlie had money with Gavin as much for the information flow as for the returns, which had been good, if you could stomach the volatility, to which Gavin was impervious. A crushing market that had other traders lining up at the ledge would just be another source of gallows humor for Gavin. Deep down he was a rock hard cuss who relished a tough market just so he could spit in its eye. Then he would ride it back up again, still laughing, over Ardbeg and a Montecristo.

He picked up on the first ring. "McKenzie."

"It's Charlie."

"Joiner, Christ. Last guy I thought would be bawling to me this morning. You'll get your money back when I've got it. I was up all night selling in Asia and trying to lay in shorts. London opens in five minutes and I'll be hitting the exits here, too."

"I don't want my money back. I just want some color, I've got a board meeting."

"The only color I got is red, all across my fucking screen," said Gavin. "Can they handle the truth? I don't want Parsons' ticker seizing up, we're way long Texso and it's a rare bright spot for us."

"Try me."

"Okay, straight up then. Mr. Market is a bit pissed at himself for letting the Saudis fuck him over so. And at first glance, he believes they have. When we got the news last night here around ten the guys in Tokyo and Hong Kong were just getting to their desks. When the markets opened, they shot first and asked questions later. When the answers started rolling in, they shot the survivors and then the corpses again for good measure. The Hang Seng ended down 40 percent, the Nikkei was off a third. Everything got hit. Transports were obliterated. Oil ended up forty. Diversified energy was all over the board, then ended up down 10 percent just to be safe. London promises to be more of the same.

"The documents appear to be genuine, or fantastic forgeries. And the Saudis have had no comment, which basically seals it. If they were forgeries, they would be screaming bloody murder. This is information only somebody on the inside would know. And if the information isn't accurate, the only way they'll be able to disprove it is by releasing the correct information, and no one wants to see that. We all preferred to remain blissfully ignorant, thank you. So there is no upside to this situation. Our largest single source of our single most important source of energy is suspect. Hence the continued prosperity of the Western world is suspect, so forecasts and valuations are being adjusted accordingly. The only thing that would help us is a new Ghawar. It would be nice if this Firebird voodoo showed anything. Any comment on that?"

"You know I can't."

"Well, if it sells off big today I'll be backing up the lorrie and buying as much of the big T as I have cash left. Just don't screw that up, for God's sake. I do have kids, you know."

"That's a surprise."

"Oh, yeah. Mean little fuckers. Couldn't be prouder."

Charlie arrived on the 47th floor only five grand late. He knocked on the door to the main conference room and walked right in on a full legal battle group. The admiral of the fleet, a short man with a wide smile, very full head of hair and a suit, shirt and tie in an overly confident mix of colors and patterns came over to Charlie and shook his hand. "Mr. Joiner, you're a hard man to track down."

"I only have one hour, so we should probably get started."

The admiral laughed. A man who lived and breathed confrontation, he seemed to be glad Charlie would at least keep him awake. "Sorry, but we've got you for three hours, with an option on the fourth. Nice try, though." He whispered into the ear of the lawyer parked at his shoulder, and the message was then whispered thrice more down the chain until a young lawyer with an exhausted, beaten down look and a haphazardly knotted tie ran out of the room, no doubt to ensure somehow that Charlie remained sequestered.

"Well, let's go then," said the admiral. "Where's your counsel?"

"Don't have any," said Charlie. "Don't need any. You work for the company. I work for the company. I'm here to tell you everything I know. And call me Charlie."

"I'll stick to Mr. Joiner, so we don't get confused. And that's what your lawyer is for, to tell you what not to say."

"Then I don't need one. Like I said."

Charlie sat down on one side of the long conference table. The admiral and his fleet kept wholly to the other side.

"My name is Paul Corbett," said the admiral. "As you know, my firm has been hired by the Special Committee of the Board to investigate Texso's relationship with the Athra partnership."

"This all seems pretty formal," said Charlie. "Couldn't Roger just have just called me up and asked me about it?"

"Well, Mr. Joiner, perhaps it's the manner in which this came to the company's attention," said Corbett. "Boards tend to get formal when the skeleton is dragged out of the closet by a shareholder lawsuit. In this case a lawsuit about a massive restatement of the company's Caspian oil & gas reserves which you had originally signed off on."

"My point is, the Athra partnership didn't just come to the company's attention," said Charlie. "I'm still part of the company, and I've known about it all along, as well as anyone else still around from those days. It wasn't in the closet. It was just a long time ago. Forgotten, not hidden."

"You didn't forget, though, did you Mr. Joiner? In fact, last year, just as you realized there might be a lawsuit, you rushed out to meet the managing partner of Athra last year in Baku. A Mr. ... Mr. ..." He flipped conspicuously through a sheaf of papers in front of him. "A Mr. Bego."

"Araz. Dr. Araz Bego. Of course I went out to see Araz, he was the one who could help us understand where we went wrong. On the reserve estimates. When we signed the deal, he was a consultant for SOCAR, Azerbaijan's state oil company. We had used some of his data. Araz is a living legend in the Azeri petroleum industry. I needed to talk to him. And why would I assume that Athra would even come up? It has nothing to do with the restatement, they just turned it up and are now trying to create the appearance of impropriety."

"So you didn't talk about Athra?"

"No, we talked about it. But it was a secondary issue. Just a loose end."

"Oh? What did you need to tie up, exactly?"

"I wanted him to close out our connection to Athra. It was supposed to have been taken care of, but the legal guy I was working with never followed up, he left the company. I have no idea where he is, but go talk to him. Mark Nolting."

"You know, we tried, but he won't talk to us," said Corbett. "Something about self-incrimination. Grand jury subpoenas and the threat of indictments for Foreign Corrupt Practices Act violations tend to get everyone all lawyered up. Except you, Mr. Joiner."

"I told you I'll tell you everything I know, right now. I've got nothing to hide."

"We're all ears. Whenever you're ready."

Charlie pushed himself back from the table. "Mind if I grab that coffee first? How about you, can I get you some Paul? Anyone else?"

"No, but thank you, Mr. Joiner." Corbett looked sternly at the rest of the team and they toed the line. Charlie could tell the boy with the dodgy knot was biting his lip. He poured two cups and loaded them with cream and sugar. He set one in front of the boy then returned to his seat.

Charlie settled into the story. "Athra was a partnership set up by Bego to purchase an interest in the deal."

"The deal," said Corbett. "The so-called 'Contract of the Century,' right? Could you recap that for us, just so we're absolutely clear?"

"Alright, I'll try. Azerbaijan was letting a contract to develop three fields in the Caspian Sea. Azeri, Chirag and Guneshli. All multi-billion barrel plays, giants. Actually, it was one interconnected supergiant, over six billion barrels in total, all contiguous parts of the Absheron Sill. But when they discovered it, the Azeris were working under a quota from the Soviets. They needed to find three fields, so that's what they found. Anyway, in the end, they were offered as a package. Texso led the winning syndicate. There were seven other members of our group, six other oil companies and a Saudi investment partnership, Qazvin. That's Arabic for Caspian. Qazvin had 5 percent. Athra was purchasing half of Qazvin's interest."

"So what was Texso's connection to Athra?" said Corbett.

"Bego had partners, but no capital. Every syndicate member was responsible for their share of the signature bonus as well as the ongoing operating losses and capital costs. The signing bonus was three hundred million. Total development costs were projected at twenty billion."

"I hear you have a quick head for math," said Corbett. "What was Athra's share?"

"Well, you also have to factor in that SOCAR was cut in for ten percent but the rest of us had to cover its share of the bonus, losses and capital contributions. So Athra's commitment was 2.5 percent of 90 percent, not 100 percent. And the math works out to ..." Charlie squinted up at the ceiling. "For the upfront bonus, $8.3 million, and around $550 million for the capital contributions over the life of the project. For a fifteen year project, that averages out to about thirty-seven million dollars per year."

"But they had no capital," said Corbett.

"That's right," said Charlie. "So Texso loaned it to them."

"You just gave them eight million plus thirty-seven million per year for fifteen years."

"No, we loaned it to them. At market rates."

"They paid interest?"

"Yes. Every year."

"How? They had no money."

"When they bought into Qazvin, they got a dividend-paying stock. It entitled them to a current return on their investment in excess of the interest on our loan. The value of the investment, and the dividend, as well as the loan, went up every time money was invested in the project. Once the other partners recovered the dividends paid to Athra back out of profits, they split everything between them 50/50. Essentially, the other partners in Qazvin covered the interest on Athra's debt plus some extra until the profits started to flow."

"Interest plus a little extra," said Corbett. "How much extra?"

"The rate on the note was 3 percent. I'm not sure what they got from the other partners, but my recollection was something around 9 percent."

"So Athra put nothing up, but was paid five hundred thousand the first year. In fact, the more they borrowed from you, the more they made. If they had borrowed a hundred million after three years they were paid six million. Even I can do that math. And this is even before they started to share in the profits. What was their share of last year's profits?"

"Just Athra's share?" Again, Charlie looked up. "Close to two hundred million. Which is why I told Bego last year that they could afford to pay off the notes."

"They didn't have a stated maturity date?"

"They did, but it was a thirty-year bullet. At the start, we didn't know when the field would come in. But we had a gentlemen's agreement. They would pay the notes as soon as they could."

"A gentlemen's agreement?" said Corbett. "five hundred fifty-eight million dollars?"

Corbett looked down at the table, then back up at Charlie. "And why, exactly, did you think this didn't violate the Foreign Corrupt Practices Act?"

"No payment, no proscribed person, no violation. It was a loan. And Araz wasn't working for the government. He was a professor at the university, semi-retired. SARCOM consulted Bego on everything, but 'living legend' isn't an official government title. There were over two hundred other Azeri nationals listed as partners. We checked them all. No government officials. And this wasn't my opinion, that was the advice I received from legal counsel. Nolting. He conferred with outside counsel and they signed off, too."

"Which firm?"

"I don't remember. I'm not sure I ever knew. This was the 11th hour. We spent all night on it, the night before our final bid was due."

"There's nothing in the files signing off on it. No memos, opinions, letters."

"I don't know what to say. My end of it was all over the phone."

"You didn't get this signed off by anyone?"

"Didn't need to. I had very broad authority. It had to be that way, things moved very fast. The deal involved an eight billion dollar commitment for Texso. Athra was a rounding error. If they defaulted on the note we could take back their share in the deal."

"Roger was also on the legal team supporting you. Why didn't you get him involved?"

"As he can tell you, he was unavailable. On vacation with his wife and son. Sailing in the South Pacific. No sat phones in those days."

"Not very sporting of him."

"The schedule changed every day. You can't put life on hold. I told him to go."

"To get him out of the way." Would Roger have told him that?

"No, so he could have a life. His son was going through a rough time. It was good for them. And Nolting was doing fine."

"Right. Let's hope the Justice Department agrees."

Corbett turned back to his sheaf of papers.

"Texso also paid a Mr. Don Sanders ninety-five million for consulting services when the deal was signed."

"It was an advisory fee," said Charlie. "He brokered the deal. Without him, we wouldn't have had a deal."

"Yes, you might be right about that last part." He studied his papers even more carefully, circling a couple of figures on the page. "The Justice Department has advised us that immediately after Mr. Sander's fee was paid, he wired forty million dollars from a Swiss account to a Jersey Islands account controlled by President Jamilov of Azerbaijan, and five million dollars to a Swiss account controlled by someone called Gasimov."

"Well, I can tell you that Gasimov was the lead negotiator for Azerbaijan. But I know nothing about those transfers. I wasn't part of that at all."

"Well, it was your money. So you were some part of it." Charlie didn't respond so Corbett continued. "And Sanders wired fifteen million to a Caymans Island account controlled by a Mr. Paul Brown. I believe you know Mr. Brown quite well, is that correct?"

"Of course. Paul obtained my release when I was captured in Colombia."

"Mr. Brown is a mercenary?"

"Paul is a US Army veteran. Retired."

"Official record says he was a clerk, but that doesn't seem to line up with his skillset. Seems ex-Special Forces, of some sort."

"Of some sort."

"I understand he was not hired by Texso."

"Texso had good people working on it. Paul was better. A friend hired him to find me."

"Yes, a Mr. Karim al-Samaha. The man behind Qazvin."

"An old friend. Karim is the CEO of Aranaco. The Saudi national oil company."

"Yes, I'm aware of who they are. At the time Mr. Sanders wired him the money, Mr. Brown was in Azerbaijan."

"Apparently he was. At least that's what was in all the papers. I never saw him."

"Yes, he got a lot of press. It was alleged that he was connected with the resignation of President Jamilov's predecessor."

"I know nothing about it. But I did not arrange for Paul to force Humbatov out. A President heading for the hills was not that unusual. The situation in those days was chaotic, to say the least. They were cut loose from the Soviet Union after seventy years. We dealt with three different governments in three years in getting that deal signed."

Corbett got up from the table, removed his jacket and started to pace back and forth, rubbing his temples.

"Let's put on our Justice Department hat for a moment, Mr. Joiner. What do we see? It's 1994. For three years, every petroleum company on the planet has been chasing a pot of gold in the Caspian. The American companies, but primarily Texso, are going at it hammer and tongs with the rest of the world, but especially the Brits, who we all know will in good conscience bribe anyone that can remotely help them get the deal, because it's not illegal for them. In fact, it's tax-deductible. The temptation for Texso to match them must have been enormous. And then, six months before the deal is signed, the liberal "People's President" Humbatov runs for his life back to Moscow, reportedly under threat of assassination by Mr. Brown, a friend of Texso's chief negotiator, Mr. Joiner. The new President, recently of the KGB, an organization well-known to be Mr. Joiner's regular deal partner, comes to the table and does a quick deal with Texso, but only after Texso sets up a lucrative, overly complicated and secret partnership to funnel money to Jamilov's entourage and shortly after which sixty million ends up in the accounts of said ex-KGB President, his flunky Gasimov, and the mercenary Brown. What do you think of that picture, Mr. Joiner?"

"I don't know all the facts, but from what I know, I can tell you it's not how it appears."

"You should be very concerned, Mr. Joiner. Because your friends Mr. Brown and Mr. Sanders are in the clear. The statute of limitations on any part they played in this process ran a long time ago. But your visit to Bego last year potentially represents a continuing conspiracy to commit violations of the Foreign Corrupt Practices Act, very much in the statute of limitations. FCRA was an orphan in the '90s, nobody loved it. But over the last twenty years careers are being made in Justice on these violations. The backlog went from a handful cases in 2000 to hundreds today. And you will be the headliner on this religious revival, Mr. Joiner. With this story, they are going to try to crucify you." He shook his head.

"One last question for you. You told us what Qazvin meant, but not Athra. Any color you can provide for us there?"

Charlie felt old, tired and ashamed. Reduced to a sad, cautionary tale for the horrified group of youths across the table. His mind wandered back to Baku. He was with Bego in the Fire Temple, listening to him talk about his faith. Bego was not Muslim like 90 percent of Azeris, he was Zoroastrian. The old religion, from Iran. It formed the basis for all the other desert religions. Islam, Judaism, Christianity. Good thoughts, good deeds, a better world, was what Charlie remembered of it. They were the first to speak of a creator, the existence of good and evil, the need to strive for good and free will. Their rituals are based around water and fire. The Zoroastrians moved to Azerbaijan three thousand years ago, attracted by the region's eternal fires. There were so many hydrocarbons seeping out of the ground you could dig a hole, light the escaping gas and purify your soul or cook your dinner. They worshiped three eternal flames fed by natural gas seeps near the ancient Fire Temple, and Azerbaijan means 'protector of the fire.'

"Mr. Joiner?"

"Athra means eternal flame."

"Good God, Mr. Joiner."

Back in his temporary office he turned on the television to the financial news channel. The British weren't culturally predisposed towards describing a panic, but they were doing their best. The London markets had dropped fifteen percent out of the gate, then the circuit breakers kicked in and trading was halted. They were going to try to open again soon. The market was braced for another slide. He dialed up Gavin.

"First, tell me again that I don't have all your money," said McKenzie. "I think I have your sworn statement to that effect around here somewhere, but just tell me again. And I'm taping our conversation."

"You mean all I have left is the boat? Gave you everything I had, even mortgaged the flat."

"We should really do this over a drink then, Joiner. Something cheap. I gotta go. Be sure to buckle up, buddy, there's turbulence ahead. And bring us something on Firebird."

Heathrow Airport
Monday midday

He grabbed his jacket and ran down to the garage. A car was waiting for him with one of their regular drivers. "Where to, Steve? Wouldn't be Heathrow, would it?"

"All I can tell you is it's a certain large airport on the periphery of the City. That's all, sir."

Sometime in the last twenty years the center of the oil world had shifted from Houston to London. UKP and Shell were headquartered in the City. Exxon, Chevron and Texso all maintained a major presence. Texso was still headquartered in Houston of course, but the board met as often as not in London. Whenever more than half of the board attended a meeting in person, company policies required that the meeting be held at a confidential, secure location. For convenience's sake, this usually meant an airport. They met in anonymous-looking Heathrow hangars a lot. Given that airports were the biggest orgies of liquid fuel consumption on the planet, Charlie always felt that it was somehow appropriate.

As befitted one of the ten largest corporations in the world, Texso had a robust board. There were eleven members. This included Wayne, although being CEO for all practical purposes he was also more often answering to the non-executive board members than acting as board member himself.

Five of the board members provided what might best be described as helpful context. There was the member of the US national security establishment. His party currently out of office, he had time on his hands and was good for the occasional anecdote or foreign contact. He was not aboard to make waves, just to collect a check until he could go back to worrying about the Chinese in the Pentagon. There was the nationally-recognized economist, good for lots of information, analysis and insight, although near-term actionability was always a question. There was the public interest-interest oriented board member, with an eye on HSE and sustainability issues, no small challenge on the Texso board. The emeritus science professor, smarter than all of them combined but only mildly interested as she continued to wrestle with larger issues than mere business. And, most benign, the dean from the top-five business school, who was savvy enough to realize that he provided no value whatsoever except as an honest broker on succession issues.

Which left the sharp edge of the board. Five CEOs of multi-billion dollar companies from a diverse range of other sectors, women and men with huge agendas. Texso had managed to snatch one each from aerospace, packaged goods, technology, agribusiness and diversified manufacturing. Serving on the board of even a company like Texso offered no real upside for them beyond professional pride, only downside, so they were perhaps even more demanding than they were of their own companies. You had better make them look good and not suck up time they didn't have. They were insanely focused on strategic issues, quarterly performance and talent development.

Steve guided the sedan into the bowels of Heathrow. Steve's special pass and their two corporate IDs got them through three checkpoints before they pulled into a parking lot of a small, cloud-colored hangar, apparently for a personal aviation company that didn't mind vacating for the afternoon. They were ushered by Texso security through a side door into the open, well-lit hangar space. The board was at the far end, on hard chairs around a long folding table. They were sweating Ed Sweeney, Texso's head of HSE. There had been an explosion at a refinery in Louisiana last month and three people were injured. The preliminary report was in and it was time for the consequences.

A pair of still-sharp eyes spotted Charlie from the board table and a tall, genteel man with a preternaturally large head and a suit from the '50s left the group and ambled across the concrete floor to him.

"Hello, Wayne."

"C'mon, Charlie, the board's taking a little recess. Why don't you keep me company?" Wayne Parsons looked around for his assistant and she pointed to a side office. "Let's sit," he said. "Jeannie, could you track down a cup of coffee for Charlie? Thanks."

Wayne sat straight-backed in a chipped wooden chair and stared at Charlie across a messy metal desk, with the same kindly but no-nonsense look that had watched over him for the past three decades. But the eyes seemed smaller now, darker and set deeper back in watery pools.

"Well, those Arabs have really fucked us over now, haven't they?" said Wayne.

"So, you think it's true?"

"Of course it's true. The only question is why it came out like this. Absolutely nothing we can do about it now but keep our heads down and do our work. It's out of our hands."

Wayne stared at him.

"You could have called me, Charlie. On Firebird. You know that."

"You would have said go ahead and then we'd both have our necks on the line. I need you to save mine."

He was going to say something when Jeannie knocked and came in with a cup of coffee for Charlie. She also laid out two pills and a glass of water in front of Wayne then stood with her hands clasped in front of her.

"You going to embarrass me now, darlin'?"

"It's just Charlie. Now get going, I'm not leaving until you take them."

Wayne tossed back the pills with a drink of water and a wink at Charlie. Jeannie closed the door again.

He seemed to have forgotten his earlier train of thought. "So tell me about Firebird," said Wayne, turning instead to his favorite topic. The next new play. "You ready to light 'er up tomorrow? I want to pump some of that cold Arctic crude before I die."

Wayne Parsons and Texso had merged at some point decades ago, and now one was indistinguishable from the other. In 1950, back when boys seemed to be able to grow up, Wayne was a newly-minted, twenty-year old petroleum geologist with an even younger wife and a baby on the way. That was the year that Enrico Mattei, the head of Italy's state oil company, first decried the 'Seven Sisters' that controlled the world of oil. Texso was one of the Sisters, the most exploration-minded, and it was the only place Wayne wanted to work. When he graduated from Oklahoma State, Wayne had a nice offer from Esso in New Jersey, arranged through his research advisor. To his pregnant wife's dismay, he turned it down. While she stayed at her parents, he drove from Tulsa down to Houston to see about a job with Texso. A week later he came to fetch her.

When the trustbusters broke Standard Oil into thirty-four separate companies, Standard Oil of Texas was an afterthought. After running afoul of the frontier justice handed out by the Texas courts and their homegrown antitrust laws, Rockefeller had always steered clear of the state, contenting himself with the rest of the world. Standard Oil of Texas was essentially just a small slice of the massive Spindletop field near Beaumont that Rockefeller had picked up from an acquisition in Louisiana.

Three of the other Seven Sisters had ended up with most of the petroleum market and most of the headlines coming out of the Standard Oil breakup. These were Standard Oil of New Jersey, also called Esso (shorthand for 'SO') and later Exxon. Standard Oil of

New York, also called SOCONY (for its telegraph address) and later called Mobil. And Standard Oil of California, also called Socal (for obvious reasons), and then Chevron.

There were no Rockefeller men in Houston to slide into Standard Oil of Texas when it was spun out, so they had to make do with whatever busted Texas wildcatters they could round up. This resulted in a rather distinct culture for the new company. With the meager cash flow from their share of Spindletop, the new executives, if they could be called that, acquired acreage and drilled wells at a pace that shocked and then terrified the buttoned-down Rockefeller clan back East who were still running the show for each of the new companies behind the scenes. But with thirty-four new and mostly larger companies to manage, they had a few irons in the fire. So Standard Oil of Texas was left to its own devices, and it thrived. Twenty years later it was generating enough cash to buy out Texaco, one of its other, larger partners in Spindletop. In a nod to the much better-known company they had acquired, and ready to lighten up on the Rockefeller heritage, Standard Oil of Texas was renamed Texso.

This hard-charging, exploration-minded company was the one that Wayne Parsons joined as a petroleum geologist in 1950. It was a perfect marriage. In ten years Wayne was the company's chief oil finder. In another eight he was CEO, a title he had held for over fifty years. Over his tenure Texso had consistently opened up more acreage to petroleum development than the other Seven Sisters combined. Everywhere from the Gulf of Mexico to Nigeria to Yemen to the Caspian to Myanmar to Thailand to China. And now the Arctic.

There was a joke going around the company. When it showed up in Charlie's email inbox the story was it started with a wiseass Texso geologist five whiskeys into the Port Harcourt-Houston shuttle. Five oil men are on a panel taking questions from the audience. Someone asks, 'With no more major fields to discover, how are you preparing for the end of oil?' The Exxon guy goes first and talks about their biofuels pilot. The Shell guy tops that with solar. The Chevron guy hypes up marine power. And the UKP guy says they're taking a real close look at manure. When they get to the Texso guy he just pulls out a gun and shoots himself dead. Everyone is shocked, but they assume the end was just too tough for the poor guy to take. The next thing the Texso man knows he's at the gates of Hell. The devil laughs at him and says "I knew you would be here eventually, welcome to your new home." The Texso guy says, "So is this where you spend all eternity in thick tar up to your neck, sulfur burning your lungs, all amid lakes of eternal fire?" The devil says "Yes, exactly." The Texso guy says, "Good. The rest of my crew will be here shortly, we think this basin sounds damn prospective for oil."

Charlie had finished giving Wayne the update on Firebird. Wayne looked like he was going to tip over he was so excited. "Good for you, Charlie. You bring that one in, damn it, you bring that one in." Then he paused and for the first time Charlie thought the watery eyes might be something other than age.

"I wish I could save you, Charlie. I'm goddamned sorry about what we're asking you to do, goddamned sorry. You know I didn't vote for it, but with all this Baku business and then this Lazarev mess I got outvoted. They railroaded it through. I blame myself, I can tell you that.

"I gave you a real hard time after Sheila died, I know that." Sheila, his youngest child. A late, blessed surprise and the apple of his eye. "Because I was mad at myself. Being mad at you is like being mad at myself, you know that. You and I are the same, and we made the same mistake. I should have pulled you both out of Yemen, and you should have left. And then you did the same thing I would have done, burying yourself in Colombia and then that flaming cesspool in Baku. Now you're getting Monday-morning quarterbacked and kicked to the street and the company is in an awful sorry state and I'm thinking how the hell did I let this happen? I don't even recognize my own company anymore.

"They're throwing in the towel on you, Charlie. You've been selling all our best producers to buy new leases in every unexplored hellhole on earth and you ain't hardly found a thing. When you do find anything you say it's too small and you sell it to buy another lease. Well they say we're not covering our cost of capital anymore, so they want to reverse direction completely. They say we should milk the existing fields to generate cash and go searchin' for oil on Wall Street. Buy up the small fry and squeeze 'em dry. Then when we run out, just shut 'er down. But you know what really boils me? They're right. We haven't done a damn thing in ten years. All we've done is destroy value. And Firebird? They hate the Arctic, they absolutely hate it. They say it's exactly what's wrong with this company, this business. Over two billion dollars gone in the ocean, more than half of it ours. They want to pull you out yesterday. They say this is the last straw and that frankly we don't need you anymore. Which is a polite way of saying they don't need me anymore. I think they've got it ass backwards. I think we need you more than ever, Charlie, and now you're not going to be here. You were the best goddamn oil finder I had. Better than me, that's for damn sure. And I messed it up all to hell. I kept waiting and waiting for someone who could grab the wheel and finally there you were. But then Sheila died and I couldn't see straight, so I became just another stupid old fool who hung on too long. Now what's going to happen to this place? They're going to turn it over to some accountant, and the thing will cruise on autopilot until it runs out of fuel and crashes. How did I let this happen?"

Wayne was bent over and breathing hard. Charlie wondered if he should call Jeannie.

"Sorry," said Wayne. "The worst part of growing old is that you get so fucking sentimental. We can cry all we want later. You just focus on bringing in Firebird. With this goddamn business at Ghawar, everybody needs that to come in, and come in big. C'mon, we'd better get back out there."

Texso board meetings played out with all the excitement and unpredictability of a wind-up toy. Not because issues were glossed over or missed, but because everything was so exhaustively explored in advance. All the real work was done by the time they showed up. The preparation of the board materials and the detailed agenda, a pre-meeting 'social' dinner the night before, Wayne circling up with members beforehand, following his rituals with each. That one dinner, this one breakfast, this one a week before at the club. There were no surprises.

And so with the portion of the meeting dealing with Charlie Joiner and Firebird. The packaged goods CEO was the messenger, and her message was clear and direct. The board will approve the revised terms for KarLap, but he absolutely should have had further consultation with the board before laying the geophones after Lazarev made his threat. To act as he did constituted reckless behavior in the extreme. In view also of the pending investigations into the Baku contract, the board was placing him on administrative leave, effective immediately.

Charlie provided the only excitement.

"With all due respect to the board, I believe it's in the company's interest that I be in Murmansk tomorrow so as not to create the appearance of weakness, which might provide Lazarev an opportunity to back out of our arrangement.

"However, after tomorrow it is my intention to return to London on Wednesday and resign. Roger and I have arranged some time for us to get together Wednesday evening to effect that. I haven't looked at the package but I will accept whatever the board is prepared to offer. If anything."

There was a pause while the board stared at him blankly. Then Wayne struggled to his feet, suddenly every bit of his eighty plus years, and said something to the effect that if they didn't send Charlie to Murmansk he would resign and this company could go straight to hell because it damn sure wasn't the Texso he knew. Charlie didn't remember who made the motion to approve the KarLap changes and Charlie's plan for his termination. He couldn't take his eyes off of Wayne, sitting motionless and ashen-faced at the end of the long table. They approved with a voice vote and it was announced as unanimous, although Charlie never saw Wayne say anything at all.

CHAPTER 11

FIREBIRD

Laptev Sea
Tuesday morning

When Avinashi saw Nikolai climb out of the Kulneft Mi-8 onto the heli deck she took off running. Her first stop was the bridge, where she ripped the keycard off Captain Perkin's waist before he knew what was happening. Then she ran the length of the ship to the data center where Ted was up and working with his team. Inside, she told them that the Russians had arrived and that under no circumstances were they to let anyone in. She stuck her keycard and Perkin's in a desk drawer and then looked out the window. Seeing no one, she took a deep breath, opened the door and stepped out into the cold.

On Sunday, Avinashi had not been able to raise anyone at the Ministry of Natural Resources to discuss this new inspection right. In the afternoon she took a break when Ted bet her dinner that he could hit a golf ball far enough where she couldn't shoot it. She told him if he would hit a wedge he had a deal. In half an hour she had won a week's worth of meals hitting orange dots with the First Mate's .308 at just under a hundred yards. That night Charlie copied her on his Ghawar email and called to tell her that of course it was now more important than ever that they get Firebird off on Tuesday.

By Monday midday there was still no response and she was ready to fly to Moscow and start taking hostages. A half-hour later it got worse when she finally reached a mid-level functionary at the Ministry and he informed her that they would be conducting a full review and to await further instructions. As soon as she got off the phone she had received an angry call from Rupert telling her that he had just been faxed an order to suspend the project, issued jointly by both RosPrirodNadzor and RosTekhNadzor. For good measure, the order was accompanied by an injunction issued by a judge in Krasnoyarsk that was claiming jurisdiction.

Avinashi got the Ministry representative to agree to make his team available for a conference call at eleven a.m. Moscow time. For KarLap, she managed to nail down Rupert and a junior lawyer from KarLap's outside counsel in Moscow, Charlie in London on his way out the door to Heathrow, Ed Maxwell on Sredny Ostrov, their Texso Explosives Engineer in the middle of his night in Houston and on the *Northern Ranger* Captain Mike Perkins, Ted and the ship's Master and Chief Engineer. Without explanation, no one from the Ministry joined the call and after an awkward fifteen minutes during which Rupert asked why she was still working for the company she let everyone go.

For the next five hours it was as if the Ministry had dropped off the face of the earth. Then at four p.m. Moscow time a small army of bureaucrats arrived at KarLap's headquarters with absolutely no warning and announced they were ready for the presentation. Avinashi got everyone back on the phone while she had a secretary in KarLap's Moscow office pull together a set of slides that they could throw up on a screen for something to look at. The Russian team consisted of Ministry officials as well as federal inspectors from both RosPrirodNadzor and RosTekhNadzor. After a bit of a delay they had a productive session that lasted into the evening. The Russians were particularly interested in the physics of the borehole.

Offline, she managed to convince the secretary to stay late and run out and get some food and drinks. They took only an hour off for dinner and the normal amount of drinking and by ten p.m. Moscow time, two a.m. local time at the *Northern Ranger,* it appeared that all their questions had been answered and she was in the clear. Then, for the first time, they announced that their inspection teams would be onsite at Firebird at eight a.m. local time. The Ministry did not mention that in addition to the RosPrirodNadzor and RosTekhNadzor inspectors they would be sending Neftepolk but Avinashi could swear she saw at least two other men in fatigues get off the helicopter with Nikolai.

"You think you can outrun Spetsnaz?" said Nikolai. He stood at the bottom of the flight of metal stairs outside the data room door, trying not to show he was breathing hard.

Just you, she thought. "Nikolai! What are you doing here? Do you work for the Ministry? Oh, no ... you thought? No, I just remembered I left the coffee machine plugged in after I poured the last cup. Last thing we need, a fire on board. Then I'd be in trouble."

"Yes, I work closely with Minister Lazarev, and he has directed us to assist with the inspection, to make sure there is no interference. Is Ted in there? I wish to say hello." He pushed her aside. When he couldn't turn the knob he pounded on the door, but no one answered.

"Give me your key."

She patted her waist. "Must have left it somewhere."

"I have no time for this. We are evacuating your crew from the drill operations center. The inspection teams must have complete freedom to work."

"Not sure if that's safe. Let's check with the Master."

"Is this how it will be? I would not advise delaying our work. I am told it will take several hours for us to complete our inspection."

It was 4:30 a.m. in Murmansk. She thought about it once or twice first, then she called Charlie. "I am so sorry to wake you."

"That's fine." He sounded tired. "Sun's coming up. They there?"

"Yes, and with Neftepolk. Nikolai and two friends. It's more of a takeover than an inspection."

There was a pause. He was probably rubbing his face. "Well, it's a US-flagged vessel at sea. It's highly unlikely they're going to do anything like Friday, unless there is a serious provocation. Just try not to make them mad."

Murmansk
Tuesday morning

Charlie couldn't sleep after Avinashi's call so he got dressed, laced up his boots and walked from his hotel down towards the harbor in the thin morning light. Under overcast skies, he hiked past the crumbling neoclassical train station and up onto a pedestrian bridge that crossed over the wide set of tracks. The harbor stretched as far as he could see north and south. Between dark, dirty buildings that had to be vacant he could see rusting vessels tied up two and three deep at the docks, looking like floating scrap metal.

Down the other side of the bridge he passed a metal bus shelter. On the inside hung a gray radiation detector for the convenience of the passengers. If the levels were too high, just get off at the next stop. Murmansk was on the Kola peninsula, which had the highest concentration of nuclear reactors in the world. A few of them still functional. The Russian Northern Fleet was headquartered in Severomorsk, just up the Kola Bay. Hundreds of nuclear surface vessels and submarines were built and died in the rivers, bays and fjords of the Kola. When a reactor was no longer safe to operate, and couldn't be repaired with expendable prison labor, the ship was just scuttled in the bay. Sometimes in waters so shallow the vessel didn't even sink out of sight. Kola Bay was a soup of U-235.

When he reached the bay the far shores were shrouded in fog. Two Arktika-class nuclear icebreakers were tied up at the piers. All decommissioned. It appeared to be the *Sibir* and the *Lenin*. He had read that the *Lenin* was going to be turned into a museum. It was too expensive to remove the core, so they were going to just leave it in and keep an eye on it. Maybe that was part of the experience.

Walking along the water's edge, Charlie thought of the American seamen he had read about who staggered off the *Tesso Port Arthur* and into these streets after running the Luftwaffe and Kriegsmarine gauntlet on the passage from Reykjavík. They had run with the rest of Convoy PQ-17 all the way up to the icepack north of Bear Island to avoid the Junkers and Stukas the Germans flew out of Kirkenes and other fields across the border in occupied Norway. As the convoy turned south for Murmansk and Arkhangelsk the high command in London made the ill-fated decision to disperse and in the cruel twenty-four hour daylight of an Arctic July they were picked off one by one from air and sea all the way down the Barents. The *Tesso* sustained heavy damage but survived with four other ships by slapping on some white paint and hiding in the ice. They limped into Murmansk in the Black Summer of 1942. Germany was at the gates of Leningrad, Moscow and Stalingrad, and it was trying to deliver a fatal blow by driving through the Caucasus Mountains to take Baku, which was providing 80 percent of the oil the Soviet Union needed to fight.

After finally reaching Murmansk the crew of the *Tesso* began to wonder why they had risked their lives. When the commissars boarded the *Tesso* they refused to believe so many ships could be lost and accused them all of lying. They grandly announced ruble bonuses which were never paid, warned the seamen to strictly obey all rules and posted armed sentries at the end of their gangplanks. Then the Soviets quickly pumped the aviation fuel from the hold. The Russians still had oil from Baku but they lacked the ability to make sufficient high-octane fuels that could close the performance gap between Soviet and German machines. All-women gangs of stevedores unloaded the ships, and young schoolgirls were charged with laying in ballast for the return trip. A small blond girl was caught stealing a pair of boots for her brother from the cargo so she was lined up at the end of the dock and shot in front of everyone. The American wounded were brought ashore and languished or died in makeshift Soviet hospitals where the doctors refused to acknowledge any problems or deficiencies. If the arms or legs did become undeniably and inconveniently gangrenous they were sliced off with no anesthetic in a procedure they called the 'guillotine.' The merchantmen soon learned that trading cigarettes or throwing a punch would get you arrested and three years of hard labor which meant that you would disappear into the Siberian mines forever and there was nothing the US Navy could do about it. The only safe places to go were the Intourist Hotel for tea and black bread and the International Club for socializing. Safe for the Americans. The NKVD sent Russian women to the 'InterKlub' to collect what intelligence there was to be had from Texas roustabouts and Brooklyn street toughs. Corrupted by such close contact with Americans, the rumor in Arkhangelsk was that the women were lured onto an old cargo ship with the promise of being sent to their friends in America and then sunk in the White Sea. The crew of the *Tesso* hunkered down and counted the days until the winter darkness when they could make their escape. Then on the way back two days out of New York all but three went to the bottom of the North Atlantic carrying their load of Kola ore.

It could be a very dirty business working in Russia. Not everyone made it back. But you did what you had to do, if it meant stopping Fascism or keeping the lights of civilization burning. With nothing waiting for him back home but a trial, Charlie wouldn't have minded if all ended right here, if only he could get the look on Wayne's face out of his head.

Murmansk
Tuesday early afternoon

From the window of his room at the Meridian, Charlie could see hundreds of people on the steps of the S.M. Kirov Palace of Culture. Conference attendees were elbowing their way through the crowds to the doors, and others looking for tickets milling about with the few protesters. Federov's, most likely. It was undoubtedly wall-to-wall inside. The conference had sold out weeks ago. A few were regulars back for more at the annual Arctic Oil & Gas Conference. But most had come for Firebird.

The first Palace of Culture was destroyed by German planes just weeks before the *Tesso Port Arthur* arrived in Murmansk, but the American 'opportunists' would not have been allowed in anyway. Rebuilt after the war, it was the all-purpose, centrally-controlled entertainment venue for this 'advanced post of socialism in the extreme north,' offering movies, lectures, theater and music to fisherman and sailors. But then with the fall of this media monopoly with glasnost and the need to develop the bones of a business environment, the Palace had been turned into a conference center. For the last several years, it had also hosted the Arctic Oil & Gas Conference, where promoters, politicians and protesters joined with the geologists to discuss how best to tap the new riches of the north.

Progress in finding oil & gas in the offshore Arctic had been fitful. Exploration began in earnest in the late '60s. The Americans hit the jackpot right away in '68 with Prudhoe Bay, a twenty-five billion barrel supergiant. The '74 oil crisis provided additional motivation and funding, and the level of technology and expertise in working in the polar regions made huge advances. The oil finders met with less success in the Russian and Canadian sectors. The Canadians really took a step back when oil prices crashed in the mid '80s. And the American sector also had its disappointments, with the Mukluk well offshore from Prudhoe Bay becoming the biggest dry hole in history in 1981. A perfect prospect, but in the final analysis they had arrived only thirty million years too late, the caps on the traps having lost their seals over the millenniums, and the oil seeped out into the sea.

In the early '80s, things were looking grim in the Russian zones as well. After fifteen years of exploration the Russians and Norwegians figured out that the West Barents was nearly barren. When the North Atlantic opened up fifty million years ago with the breakup of the supercontinent Pangea the West Barents region was lifted up exposing it to erosion. Two hundred million years of oil-bearing sediment was exposed to erosion and washed away.

But in the '80s they finally learned where to look for the pockets of gas that were still there. In 1984 the Norwegians hit a nice-sized field, Snohvit, 150 kilometers off their northern shores and then in 1988 the Russians hit a supergiant gas field, Shtokman, in the East Barents five hundred miles northeast of Murmansk, just off Novaya Zemlya. But the gas was effectively stranded because the technology did not exist to transport it from such remote locations. By 2000, liquefied natural gas technology had developed to the point where the fields could be developed. Snohvit shipped its first gas in 2008. Shtokman was slated for 2010, then postponed three years, then postponed again. Too much gas in Texas. But with Firebird the buzz around the Arctic had returned.

To open up a remote region like the Arctic, you needed more than a large gas field. You needed an oil supergiant that on its own could justify the initial build-out of infrastructure. The pipelines, the processing facilities, tanker ships, drillships. In the Barents it had taken over twenty years to find just Shtokman. Firebird could conceivably give birth to multiple supergiants in the North Kara and Laptev Seas between 2:00 and 2:15 this afternoon, right in the Spirinov Room of the S.M. Kirov Palace of Culture. And you could watch it happen live if you were lucky enough to have been one of the forty people invited. Or if you had an internet connection.

People were fairly excited about it.

At 1:15 Avinashi finally called with the news that the inspection teams had finished their work and were leaving the ships, apparently with no further comment.

Ready to go. Just in time.

Back in suit and tie, feeling like he was dressed for his own funeral, Charlie walked together with a member of his local protection team from the Meridian Hotel across the leafy square towards the S.M. Kirov Palace of Culture.

"Let's head around the corner, Charlie," said Stepan. "There's a better way in."

Regardless of the present situation, the Firebird results, once public, would have a direct and immediate impact on world oil prices. Fortunes would be made and lost. The partners in KarLap were all demanding immediate access, and as a practical matter keeping the results secret until they could be broadly disseminated was an impossibility. The pressure from commodity speculators was intense, and the temptation for those with access to the information would be overwhelming. This included twenty to thirty individuals at each of the KarLap partners, the FSB who would undoubtedly wire the Kirov or any other venue they could have chosen, all the way down to anyone on the kitchen staff with a cell phone. The information was certain to leak. So the KarLap board, or really Charlie, had decided that it would be prudent to let everyone in on the secret. All at once. The results would be available in real-time online, and they were making passwords available to all plausibly credible parties.

But only the forty attendees would be able to get the full 3-D view. The partners. Some press. Telnov. Not Lazarev. But Charlie was dead certain he would be watching, somewhere.

Charlie and Stepan ducked through a side entrance. Down the hall Shirin was with Andrew Bell from UKP. Bell was sharing a joke and providing his own laugh track. Shirin had been in and out of Charlie's room last night like a dream. They had an unspoken agreement to make no big decisions until after 2:15.

Bell spotted Charlie. Gathering himself for his most productive moment of the day, he homed in on Charlie like a mindless torpedo.

"Say, Joiner, my end is a bit cheesed off at this cutback. You didn't see fit to communicate and confer with your partners on this?"

"Did you remind your end about the part where you and your checkbook agreed to come along for the ride? See you downstairs, Andrew."

Bell grabbed Charlie's arm. "Did you catch Lazarev's news conference this morning? I thought you had him taken care of. So why is he on television saying he forced necessary changes in the PSA but remains opposed, terrible idea, fails to meet minimum standards of safety, blah, blah, blah?"

"Covering his ass. I'm sure you're familiar with the strategy. But did he announce any action that would stop us?"

"No."

"Well then. Excuse me, I'm working."

He hurried down the stairwell with Stepan close behind. When Charlie had checked in when he arrived close to midnight they were still unpacking crates. There was now some semblance of order established in the Spirinov room. Long tables had been set up in a U-shaped pattern around a large screen. At each of forty seats was a pair of thick goggles attached to cable.

The Texso technician from London walked up to him with another pair of goggles. "Alright, here we are then. Care to have a go?"

"No going back now."

He put on the goggles and was instantly transported to a point high above Severnaya Zemlya, looking east across the Kara Sea, to Novaya Zemlya and just beyond into the Barents.

The overwhelming abundance of digital information available from 3-D seismic and other surveys of fields had compelled engineers to develop advanced methods for displaying the information. With special goggles, or on the walls of special rooms, users could now view three-dimensional images of the field. Engineers and users could walk through and around oil fields, discuss layers and strata, traps and caps and run an endless host of analyses, all in a colorful, collaborative environment. When you were trying to sell someone on a play, it was indispensable.

He pulled the goggles off and looked to make sure the path ahead of him was clear.

"Is it okay if I walk around?" said Charlie.

"Only for you. During the actual test we're going to make them sit, and I'll drive. Can't have them all bumping around now, could we? Over here, start in the middle."

He hung his jacket over a chair and moved out into some open space. Then he pulled his goggles back on and jumped back into the Arctic. The skies were black and the seas were blue. The Russian

Spreading pools of bright red and green appeared here and there in the ocean's crust. Immediately, a large show appeared about a hundred kilometers northeast of Schmidt Island. Another in the shallow waters of the southern Laptev. Then everywhere, it was Christmas.

"We can discriminate between gas and oil shows. Not methane hydrates yet, but we're working on it. Oil red, gas green. As soon as we have enough data for a field size estimate, it will appear on the screen, in BOE." Barrels of oil equivalent. "We'll put a number on any concentrated show that pencils out to over a hundred million BOE. Other shows will just look faint red or green. Smears, really."

"Ok, got it."

Size estimates started to appear next to the fields. One hundred and thirty million barrels here. Four hundred and fifty million barrels there. He walked over to the largest show to read the number. Twenty-five billion barrels.

"Is that a running sum in the corner?"

"Spot on."

Two hundred and fifty billion barrels. Ten Prudhoe Bays.

"What case is this?"

"Overall totals are based on the USGS estimates. Good as any. They had estimates down to assessment units. We used that as a starting point and further randomized it."

"Well, I guess we'll find out how good they are. Should have made them come and watch."

"So we good to go, sir?"

Charlie would take it. "Yeah, nice job. Say, would you mind turning the sim off for a second?"

The red and green disappeared, leaving just sea and earth. Charlie walked east to the Lomonosov Ridge, then up to the North Pole, around to the Pole of Inaccessibility, all the out to Wrangel Island, back through the East Siberian Sea, past Delong Island, until he was back in the Laptev, looking across Severnaya Zemlya and the Kara.

Could you know too much? Was is it better not to know?

Laptev Sea
Tuesday afternoon

It was only minutes to detonation and Avinashi was sweating in the data center with Ted and his team. The power from the server farm had the room over eighty degrees she was sure, so she reluctantly shed her parka. The explosives team was in the drilling operations center, and the crew in the data center listened to them count down over the radio.

"D minus sixty," the radio sparked. Thirty seconds later another radio crackled with a similar message. "D minus thirty."

Ted was glued to a screen and hadn't spoken to her in over an hour. She found it hard to believe, but he seemed a bit sour about losing to her in the golf and shooting game on Sunday. She was mad at herself for being so upset about it. She even tried to lose to him at darts on Sunday night. Then on Monday, all any of them could think about was the test, and then from lunch on the rest of the day was a blur.

"D minus ten." Pause. "D minus nine."

The inspection teams had finished their work and then couldn't get out of there fast enough, but for one of Nikolai's goons that apparently drew the short straw. Arkady, Nikolai had called him. If the charges weren't 1500 meters underground she would have been concerned. It should be a law that the last one that touches the charge has to stick around for the detonation. But this was Russia. No one trusted their work.

"D minus five." Pause. "D minus...oh my God." Their entire world moved as the room shot up into the air, and then down.

Avinashi flew to one side and tried to brace herself before hitting the wall. Ted instinctively reached out and grabbed the nearest piece of equipment.

"What was that, what was that?" said Ted, angry, clutching a server.

Just one shock, apparently, and it was over.

"ABCD's, somebody talk to me. I still have functional systems here, I think. Avi, what's going on out there?"

She ran over to the window and looked outside. Something had blown up right through the Derrick, splitting it in two, with the sides rolled back like a banana peel. Water was rushing off the decks and streaming back into the moon pool. Emergency lights were flashing. Other than that she couldn't see anything.

The radio crackled to life. "Bridge, we have had a catastrophic malfunction of the explosive device. We have major structural damage in drill operations and what appears to be a compromise of the port sponson."

Ted wasn't listening at all. "That's it, that's our first response. We got one, we got one."

The room started to list to port.

"Thirty seconds in we have a 98 percent open water response rate, 94 percent response from geophones detonating their charge. And we are processing."

The radio burst in. "We are taking on water in the port sponson. We also appear to have a hull breach on the port side of the moon pool."

With no external point of reference, it was hard to be sure, but the room had to be listing at least thirty degrees to port.

Ted grabbed the radio. "We have got to stabilize the ship," yelled Ted. "The results are coming in, and everything is working great. We are getting tremendous resolution, even from the fringes. The detonation is measuring out at a 5.5. What the hell happened down there? What kind of rock did we detonate in?"

Or what did we detonate, thought Avinashi. She ran over to the window and looked out. They felt like they were moving. The whole platform was moving, being dragged out to sea.

"We're moving," she yelled.

"What?"

"The whole ship, it's starting to move to port."

"Shut that door!"

The ship claxons began an assault on their ears. "This is the bridge, abandon ship, abandon ship. Captain's orders, assemble at the starboard lifeboat immediately. Repeat, Captain's orders, abandon ship."

"Everybody out," yelled Avinashi. She ran over and physically started hauling the ABCDs to the door.

"Go, everyone," said Ted. "I can handle this."

"Ted, you're coming, too," she said.

"I can't. I didn't have time to fully automate everything. I know, I know, would have been nice, but frankly I didn't expect the ship to sink, ok? I can't leave it now. We might lose the data. I've got to stay here and burst it to Houston and Murmansk. Go, I got this."

She ran back to the window. The Captain was standing by the starboard lifeboat as everyone onboard filed in. Two were being carried. There was a steep list in the deck to port. They couldn't use the port lifeboat, the ship looked like it was ready to fall over and smash it on the ice. And the boat was being dragged out through the ice, to the north.

"Ted, there must have been a landslide. The detonation was too large, it's loosened the bottom and now it's going over into the abyss and will drag us over with it, if we don't sink first. We need to get out."

"Get in the lifeboat. I'll be right there. The results are coming in, I only need thirty more seconds."

She ran out to the door. Captain Mike was standing next to the open hatch of the lifeboat, waving at her. The ship had stopped moving in the water. The anchors seemed to have been torn free of the bottom. And there was still another boat. Avinashi waved him off. Arkady pushed Captain Mike into the lifeboat and pulled the hatch shut after them. The boat started to lower into the sea.

"First oil, we've got first oil," yelled Ted. "We've got the first hundred million barrels, out in the Kara. Now we've got two hundred million. Oh, no. 80 percent processed. We're only at eight hundred million barrels. 90 percent processed, 1.5 billion barrels. Something's wrong. Nothing's wrong. But we're only at two billion barrels. That's it. 100 percent processed. 2.4 billion barrels. What happened? What happened?"

Suddenly the whole room rolled sharply to starboard and in seconds they were sliding with all the equipment against the starboard wall. Ted ignored it all, staring quizzically at the screen, as he tipped over, nearly ready to collapse onto the monitor.

"Okay, time to go," said Ted. He grabbed her and they started climbing back up the door. The peered out onto the decks. Now the starboard side of the ship was submerged. Near the stern, they could see the lifeboat pinned under the icy water by the davits.

"C'mon," said Avinashi, They climbed into the port lifeboat, lowered it around the bottom of the boat to the ice and cut themselves loose. Twenty minutes later the *Northern Ranger* slipped to its grave at the bottom of the Kara, taking the other lifeboat with it.

Murmansk
Tuesday afternoon

Charlie pushed away the unseen table and walked out across the Laptev. If you stared closely, you could see that the sea was flecked with specks of green. No red. He would have thought that the sounding had malfunctioned if not for the trillion cubic feet of gas stranded in the far northeast corner of the Laptev, where it was likely to remain forever. The last hydrocarbons would never be extracted. Either they wouldn't need them or they couldn't afford to. Now it appeared it would be the latter. Standing over the stranded gas, he gazed back across the Laptev and the Kara. Mukluk was one, very expensive, dry hole at a billion dollars. Firebird cost twice that, but revealed fifteen distinct petroleum basins spread across the Russian Arctic to be just as devoid of hydrocarbons. The tally in the corner of his view totaled 2.5 billion barrels of oil equivalent, scattered across 1.2 million square kilometers in pockets so small none of it was likely ever to be recovered. Charlie had drilled, quite efficiently, the largest dry hole in the long history of global oil exploration. Decades worth of dry holes in one afternoon.

His goggles sagged, sliding on sweat. He wanted to take them off, but he was having difficulty raising his arms. After he pushed them

off, he still could not see. And the room was off-kilter, and out of
focus.

In Charlie's life and given his chosen profession, the manufacture
of hope was always a long and gradual process. Its loss, however, was
like a long fall off a precipice. Not quite instantaneous, but the end
came quickly enough, interrupted only by a few last stubborn questions, protests and denials, jarring but passed inevitably by like the
pins in a pachinko machine, only briefly delaying the inevitable gut-
wrenching and fairly rapid descent to the bottom.

Charlie was falling.

By the time they had learned to listen for oil there was none left.
Only silence. He hated himself. He was the worst man in the world.

Along the way, he managed to lift a sleeve to wipe his face. The
others were all looking at him. He yanked and pulled at his tie,
which was suffocating him. The professionals were ashen-faced. They
looked to him for some reason to believe he hadn't just sealed all
their fates. The journalists just looked confused for the most part,
pencils poised. Except for Shirin, whose eyes glistened.

Telnov was on his phone. The doors were opened by several militia members. Telnov closed up his phone and beckoned to them as
he approached Charlie.

"Mr. Joiner," said Telnov. "I have been informed by Ros Prirod Nadzor
that the explosive devices utilized at Firebird exceeded agreed-upon
parameters. Additionally, traces of radioactivity were detected at the
site, raising other concerns. They have recommended that the officers of KarLap be detained immediately so that inquiries can be
made. I ask you to please go with these officers."

Telnov appeared as in a dream, and Charlie watched and listened
to him impassively. A bad dream, he decided, as the officers spun him
around and wrenched his arms into handcuffs.

CHAPTER 12

WE'RE YOUR FUTURE

Murmansk
Tuesday early evening

His cracked, gray cell stunk of sour stomachs and bowels. They had taken all his personal effects, his belt, his shoes. Charlie stood for as long as he could, then he sat on the cold floor and stared through the bars. The stone at the base of the iron posts had been worked by generations of wretched occupants. Charlie wanted out, too. But only like an animal that sensed it was time to go off to the woods and die, quietly and alone.

A fleshy guard with bloodshot eyes unlocked his cell and yanked the door open, making it groan and wail. A pimply young soldier with a baton stood nervously behind the guard, ready to beat Charlie senseless.

They dragged him to a small, low room where the young embassy woman who was at the demonstration sat under fluorescent tubes. Her arms and knees were drawn in tight, and her hands clasped atop the cheap leather case on her lap. The pimply one stayed in the room.

"Mr. Joiner, we didn't have a chance to meet. I'm Flannery Ayers, the ranking embassy member on site. I insisted on being able to see you." She looked pleased with herself.

"Thank you," he said. "What do know about my status?"

"You're welcome. Well, you're under arrest in connection with a

RosPrirodNadzor investigation. You know, into the explosions, and what may have happened at the *Northern Ranger*."

"Did something happen?"

"They didn't tell you?" Flannery leaned forward and made her most earnest eye contact. "They've lost contact with the ship. Nothing. It's been hours. It's awful. You know, I was just out there last week. I had become very close with one of the women on the ship. I am worried sick about her. But look at me. You probably knew people on board as well."

He could die later. "Ms. Ayers, I need you to get me released as soon as possible."

"I knew you would ask me that, so I consulted on that very issue with the Deputy Chief of Mission. You know, very nearly the top." She waited for a compliment on her initiative. None forthcoming, she proceeded. "His assessment was that there's really nothing we can do except let it . . ." She emphasized the next words, as if they carried special meaning, if you listened closely enough. ". . . play out." She leaned back, wisdom having been imparted. "There's really no precedent for this sort of infraction, as you can imagine. You know, given the suggestion of a nuclear device. Or haven't they told you?"

"They mentioned something about detecting radioactivity at the test site. About which I know nothing. This is the Russian Arctic. There's radioactivity everywhere."

"Excellent point, duly noted. In any event, at this point our recommendation is just to stand pat. The embassy is sending one of our senior staff members up from Moscow tomorrow. We'll work all available channels, but I'm afraid we may just have to let the wheels of Russian justice turn."

Charlie tried hard to digest all the implications of that statement.

"Ms. Ayers, I appreciate your assistance. If I could trouble you just a bit more. Would you please contact Wayne Parsons, our CEO, and Jacob Stoyan, at the National Security Council, and give them the details of our meeting? Just let them know that you saw me, where I was, what we talked about. Please let them know I have no idea what happened. Would you tell them that?"

"Of course. Anyone else? Family?"

"No. I'm afraid not."

"I just wish there was something more I could do."

Flannery was relieved she managed to get out of the room without touching anything.

In Charlie's experience, once you had run afoul of local authorities there was a narrow window of time during which alternatives remained available. Once closed, days easily stretched to weeks, then weeks to months. Unlike in the developed world, the longer you were held out on the frontier, the less pressure anyone felt to hurry. Once you had been locked up for several months, what was one more, or another? Charlie called the guard, and in his best phrasebook Russian, asked for the *Polkovnik*. The Colonel.

Ten minutes later he was shown back to the same room. In another ten minutes, the door was opened for a militia officer entered the cell. His uniform was worn, but everywhere properly fastened and straightened. His hair was neatly oiled and combed back away from his face.

"You are comfortable, Mr. Joiner?"

"I can help you," said Charlie. "And you need help." The officer watched him steadily, his eyes betraying nothing.

"My project is sponsored by Viktor Ilyich Chernov. The project, as you know, has suffered a setback. I need to be released at once to contain the damage to Mr. Chernov. Your ill-advised and unauthorized detention of me puts him at risk. I will certainly tell him that when I am eventually released. This puts you in a very dangerous position. I would highly recommend that you either release me or silence me. Immediately." The colonel continued to stare at him.

"Who asked you to pick me up?" said Charlie. "I think I know. And why did they ask you? I am a foreigner, this should be an FSB matter. Because Chernov is the FSB? There is no benefit for you in all of this. You have much to lose."

Another cell door groaned open down the hallway.

"I am very close to Chernov. I know his wife, Ninochka. I know his daughter. I held his grandchild in my arms just last week."

Down the hall, the pimply-faced one was swinging his baton.

"I have four private numbers for Chernov on my cell phone. Call the first one. Tell them you are me, and see if they put you through. Let me go now and I will make sure he does not ruin your life. You picked me up as instructed, asked me questions, released me. You determined there was no real authorization to hold me. The promised paperwork did not arrive. Maybe it got lost. Where was I going to go? It is an FSB matter."

Without another word, he got up from the table and left. In ten minutes, the sour guard returned with Charlie's shoes and jacket but none of the other personal effects. He led him down the hallway and through a pool of blood to a door and opened it onto the street.

Charlie took a roundabout way to the hotel and entered through a side door. At the front desk he explained that he lost his wallet and needed another key to his room. They could check him against his passport which was in the hotel safe which, by the way, he would also need. They pulled the passport and gave it to him with a key. He always kept cash tucked in his passport and he gave some to the clerk and the manager. If he got any calls, he wasn't there.

He ran all the way up the stairwell to his room. He pulled a nylon duffel bag out of his suitcase and packed it with some essentials, then he left the room and everything else behind. He went back down the stairwell and out into the alley. He needed someplace where he could wait. Someplace he would not stand out, and not where they would look for him. He retraced his route past the train station and over the pedestrian bridge. But then he cut right, to the marine passenger terminal. Inside the sparsely occupied waiting area, he sat down on a bench. From his bag, he pulled out one of his backup cell phones. He put in the battery and called Vicki.

She picked up on the first ring.

"We've been worried about you." She was doing her best to sound calm.

"I'm fine. Any word on the *Ranger?*"

"I don't think they have been able to find out anything. They've got Ed Maxwell working on it."

"Everything's going to be fine, okay?"

"Alright."

"I'm still in Murmansk. I just need to come back so I can straighten everything out. I'll need a car and driver for a longer trip. I'll call you back in thirty minutes to tell them where to meet me. Everything's going to be fine. I'll talk to you soon."

He dialed Maxwell. "What's being done? What's the status of the rescue team?"

"Absolutely nothing," said Maxwell. "I got two choppers of Neftepolk about half an hour ago and they've shut everything down. They're saying it's not safe to go out to the *Ranger*, they need to bring in a special nuclear remediation team, won't be here until tomorrow. Won't let the *Papanin* or the *Hnoss* in, either. Seized them. So nothing is happening. Oh, shit, I have company. Gotta go."

The line went dead. He dialed another number at Sredny. For Roy Cook, a pilot he had met back in Baku.

"Hey Roy, it's me."

"Hey, Chief. This your one phone call?"

"Released pending execution. What's your status?"

"Well, they put a big chain around my skid. But I did get clearance for a flight at five a.m. local time to rendezvous with Wayne's jet arriving seven a.m. in Khatanga."

"Wayne's coming?"

"No, but that's the best I could think of. Shortly after takeoff I expect to receive news of his flight being canceled and then not being of entirely sound mind I will on my own initiative divert for search-and-rescue at Firebird. Sorry, Chief, that's the soonest I can get up there."

"That's all I can ask. Thanks, Roy."

Charlie removed the battery and put the phone in his pocket. He walked to a seat by the side entrance where he could watch the main door, then pulled a journal out of his bag and pretended to read.

"It's me," said Charlie.

"I found a driver," said Vicki. "I called the Hotel Arktika and told them we had a package that had to be driven to Kandalaska. Tonight. It's about 150 kilometers. The found a driver, they say he's reliable. He would do it for ten thousand rubles. Half in advance."

"Good. Tell them to pick up the package at 7:30 on the street behind the hotel. Northwest corner. Wait for a Schmidt."

"Okay. Are you going to be alright? What else can I do?"

"That's it for now. I'll call you when I'm headed out of town. 7:45 my time. That's 4:45 your time, right?"

He reached into his duffel bag and found the stack of rubles he had pulled from the lining of his briefcase. He counted out five thousand and thirty thousand rubles, folded them into two separate bundles and put them in his pocket. Then he walked back over the pedestrian bridge towards the hotel. He detoured around the sports stadium and timed his arrival so that he could arrive near the hotel ten minutes early. Inside a dismal bar from which he could watch the hotel from across the street he ordered vodka.

A dirty white Lada sedan pulled up ten minutes late. The driver stepped out of the car, a short, heavy man with a mustache. He made a quick call on a mobile phone then lit a cigarette and leaned against the back of the car, enjoying the summer evening.

Charlie watched the street for another five minutes. Seeing nothing obvious, he walked over to the car.

When the driver turned, Charlie said "I'm Schmidt" and climbed in the back. The driver started to protest but Charlie already had the door closed, so he got behind the wheel.

"Just drive," said Charlie, handing him five thousand rubles.

Reluctantly, the driver took the money and started the car. They had driven a few blocks when the man pulled out his cell phone.

"No phone," said Charlie. "No phone." The driver put the phone slowly back into the pocket of his jacket.

The driver wound his way west, through the ghetto of Communist-era apartment buildings on that side of town, out to the main road heading south down the peninsula, and upon which, after a couple of days of hard driving, you could reach St. Petersburg.

They were outside and just a ways south of Murmansk proper when Charlie leaned over the seat, holding out the stack of thirty thousand rubles.

"Nikel," said Charlie. Somewhere off to the right was the bridge across Kola Bay, and the road that led into mining country, and Nikel.

The driver looked at him, then the money. He turned back to watch the road and think. Then he reached up and grabbed the stack. But Charlie did not let go.

"Then Kirkenes," said Charlie. He held on to the stack as the Russian tugged at it, to make his point. Then he let him yank it out of this hand.

"That's all I have. Same again for you when we arrive, safely."

Kirkenes. Norway.

As they were pulling out onto the bridge over the Kola Bay, Charlie called Vicki.

"Find our man in Kirkenes and tell him to be at the border crossing in two hours. I should be there within an hour after that. Tell him to bring thirty thousand rubles. Got it? Thirty thousand rubles."

"I assume you're not serious about that last part?"

"Yes, that's right. Thirty thousand. I'll also need a charter from Kirkenes to London. I want to be wheels up by midnight. Why don't you see what you can do."

"I'll start making calls."

"Good. I'll call you back when I can get a signal. Might be awhile. Sound good? Thanks." Then he pulled the battery.

Two hundred kilometers to the border crossing at Kirkenes. He would be there within three hours, or never. On the other side of the bridge Charlie pointed at the road sign which indicated the fork to Kirkenes and repeated the name a few times. The driver nodded animatedly but pointed to his fuel gauge. To fill up he apparently needed to make a call, because he was wiggling his phone. Charlie nodded and the driver made his call to whichever uncle's neighbor's friend sold fuel on this side of the city.

The road to Kirkenes cut back north up along the river. After five minutes they pulled over in front of a set of low, forlorn buildings still wearing their first and only coat of paint. The only maintenance they had received were the crude attempts to prop them up with scraps of wood. A poorly dressed but intelligent-looking man with smudged glasses emerged from one of the listing structures and unlocked a rusted fuel tank. The driver seemed too happy as he grinned and nodded his head at Charlie while he topped off his tank. Money changed hands and then the driver indicated in graphic terms that he needed to relieve himself.

"Phone," said Charlie, handing out his hand. The driver gave it to him but took way too long behind the building. Then they were back on the road.

They cut away from the river and climbed up into the dark boreal forests. The sun was beginning to lower ahead of them, throwing shadows in front of the dark pines. In the harsh climate, the trees struggled to grow. He knew a modest-sized larch here could be over five hundred years old. Born in the last Time of Troubles. There were a few spots early on where the forests had been cleared for poor farms to feed Murmansk. Whatever could not be grown here in the two-month growing season had to come by rail from the south.

The pitiful Lada ground through its gears up and down the rolling hills. Charlie insisted they drive fast, or relatively so for a Lada, so the driver had to react quickly to avoid the axle-breaking holes that jumped out at them. Soon they had established an intense, irregular rhythm and they were making acceptable time.

The road made huge, sweeping turns through the forests and climbed long rises offering broad vistas at its crests. To the west he could see a line of low fells, barren hills that even at their modest heights rose above the tree line here in the far north. They grunted and groaned their way by still lakes, their empty surfaces like dark glass. They crossed over a crumbling dam, still holding back water but its forgotten towers stripped of conducting cables. Dirt roads lead regularly north or south, to played-out mines and abandoned military installations, but there was never any traffic.

Trapped in his bucket of rust as it labored towards the border, Charlie struggled to hold back the feelings of hopelessness that sought to overwhelm him. His calling was to bring energy, order and hope, yet undeniably, despite his talents and dedication, he had managed only failure and despair. It was as if mankind had come up short, in him. Thousands of years of hope and struggle ended with his foolishness at the ends of the earth, where man had long pushed to find his limits, and Charlie had found them. He looked out over the mean, darkening landscape, and he began to see the future he had wrought.

The sun was low but still up as they limped into the town of Sputnik. This particular Sputnik was a Soviet military town, from the looks of it, long forgotten and impotent. A man was walking towards them on the other side of the road, the first person they had seen in miles. As they got close, he picked up a large rock and threw it at the car. Drunk, he yelled and cursed at the Lada as the driver swerved to avoid man and stone.

Stan and Lucy Joiner had welcomed their fifth son Charles Ernest into the world on October 3, 1957, in the middle of a bright and pleasantly cool fall afternoon in Beaumont, Texas. As everyone learned in the next day's papers, Charlie Joiner was born just hours after the Soviets launched Sputnik and the Space Race from remote rocket bases in Kazakhstan shortly after their midnight on October 4. For weeks afterward, Charlie's proud father marched proudly around

Beaumont on his prosthetic leg, bragging that he and Lucy had launched their own little answer to Sputnik, and their Chucknik was going to be a world-beater, for sure. Throughout all of those happy days in Beaumont, his proud, smiling parents were a constant fixture, cheering him on the ball fields, singing next to him in church, walking him to school. His mother had passed away, but Stan was still able to wheel himself down to the park to watch ball games when it wasn't too hot. Tomorrow's papers would not be kind to Stan, and Charlie knew that he would be relieved that Lucy was in a better place and didn't have to read the news anymore. Stan, he had gotten through tough times before.

From Sputnik the road continued west but mostly north until it turned sharply south just short of Pechenga. The site of the northernmost monastery in the world, an experiment by Russian monks to see if they could convert the local Laplanders to Christianity, abruptly ended when the Swedes massacred them all during the War of Long Hate, which Charlie had briefly researched after meeting Lazarev at Karela, until it became just too depressing. The town also gave its name to the Pechenga Belt, the massive strip of volcanosedimentary rock which extended from here to the border, famous worldwide among geologists for its large nickel-sulfide deposits.

The sun lingered as the road curved back north again, then south. At the top of a rise Charlie looked out the left-hand window and strained to see if he could spot a tower in the fading light. In their game of strategic one-upmanship, the Soviets had decided in the early '60s to race the United States down as well as up, and they announced the Kola Superdeep Borehole. Communist man would drill down to the Mohorovii discontinuity, or the Mojo, where the earth's crust floats on the mantle. For fifteen years they drilled, down about 8 miles, still the deepest hole ever drilled. Finnish news outlets, perhaps still stewing about the Winter War, or the Continuation War, or the indignity of being made the namesake of Finlandization, reported that at the bottom the Soviets had hit a pocket of air heated to over two thousand degrees. As the story went, the Russians lowered a special heat-resistant microphone, of all things, and recorded human screams. The shrieking of the damned. It played well with US tabloids. Work on the borehole was abandoned, short of its goal. The official story was that subterranean earth was much hotter than they expected. Charlie thought he saw the two hundred-foot tower in the distance, a cold war ghost rising over the barren land. Whatever happened out there, the Soviets had truly opened a gateway to hell on the Kola.

All around the trees were weak and dying. Then they entered the kill zone, and there were no trees at all. Only poles and power lines remained standing along the road on the rocky, lunar landscape. Ahead Charlie saw three towering stacks, tips lit red by the setting sun. The Nikel-Norilsk plant, where the death cloud was spawned. Here, in its large smelters, nickel-sulfide ore was fired in massive buckets to release the precious nickel. Hundreds of thousands of tons of sulfur and heavy metals poured into the sky every year from the gigantic stacks, mixing with the clouds to make acid rain so strong it melted umbrellas. The smelters were only a local menace until the Soviets starting shipping even more sulfurous nickel ore from the mines in deep Siberia, at Norilsk. Sulfur dioxide emissions quadrupled, and now the plant threatened the entire region, becoming a strategic flashpoint for relations with Norway and Finland. The Russians were happy to install any improvements the Scandinavians were willing to pay for, otherwise, quit meddling. Nikel was the most godforsaken town in a world that was too full of them.

Like all Russian industrial developments, the plant was fully and efficiently integrated into the town. No buffer zone, no boundaries. The damned of Nikel lived and died right in the thick of it. The happy and prosperous Finns and Norwegians summering across the border at their northern lake homes likely had little appreciation for the depths to which mankind could descend in the modern age, much less only a stone's throw across the border. As the driver slowed to pick his way through the broken streets, dirty, barefoot children ran out of the weeds and broken buildings beside the road, beating on the windows and offering to sell them tiny toxic berries out of old tin cans. Adults to whom this was an everyday sight hurried to nowhere over the black ground.

Up ahead three men stood beside a truck blocking the road, all roughly dressed but none of whom looked he drove trucks for a living. A thug and an unemployed teacher and engineer with no hope of resuming their professions, if Charlie had to guess. His driver ran right up to the truck and stopped his engine. He did his best to feign surprise and frustration, gesturing and yelling loudly out the window. Until the thug pulled out a pistol and stuck it in his face.

The teacher also pulled a vintage pistol and slid in beside Charlie in the back, snapping at him in Russian, while the engineer jumped into the passenger seat. The thug motioned for Charlie's driver to follow his truck and that was the last thing Charlie saw because they shoved his head in a bag.

They drove a short way on horrible roads that almost snapped his neck and then stopped on smooth concrete. The teacher untied his blindfold and Charlie was in a dark warehouse. The thug snapped on a dingy light. A supply shed of some sort, but with a table and three chairs. They stuck Charlie and the driver on chairs at the table, then talked among themselves.

The plan was quickly confirmed. Charlie's driver helped with the interpretation. He now apparently spoke quite passable English.

"They need five hundred thousand dollars. Or they will kill us both."

Charlie doubted that both of them were at risk. He pulled out his cell phone and checked the reception. They must have intentionally driven near a cell tower. He held up his phone, indicating he would like to make a call and they nodded.

"Vicki, it's Charlie. Yep, we're getting close. Nikel, I think. Okay, that sounds good. Listen, I'm going to need one more thing. I need him to bring real cash this time, as much as he can get his hands on. Dollars, rubles, kroners, anything. I know it's late, just check and see what he has on hand. Also, find out what kind of car he's driving. No, everything's fine. Promise. Just trying to swing a deal. Picking you up some sable. Call me back. Thanks."

Charlie hung up the phone and turned to the driver. "Five hundred thousand is impossible. Impossible." He let his words hang in the air. There was apparently no need to translate.

His phone rang. "Yep. Okay, thanks Vicki. Nope, all set for now. Can you hang around a bit? Thanks."

He turned to his new business partners. "Okay. Twelve thousand dollars and a Land Rover. And I have three thousand dollars and one hundred sixty-five thousand rubles in my bag. But you will need to use some of that to get me across the border to get the rest. That's everything I have. It's a good deal, right? Take it and let's all be friends, okay?"

Charlie retrieved his bag from the car and dumped the contents on the table. Clothes, boots, books, phones and an envelope of cash. He slid the envelope across the table. While they were busy opening the envelope, he repacked his clothes and the phones. Then he stacked the books, pocket Bible on top, and left them on the table.

They were an inexperienced team, and kidnapping was a complicated business. He listened to them talk in Russian as they discussed in all likelihood the value of the Land Rover, the likely price of guards at the border, the probability of the contact bringing twelve thousand dollars. If they shot him now for the bird in hand would someone come looking for him? How effective was the driver as a cutout? If they let him go, did Charlie seem like the vengeful type, were they getting too much money, an amount that he would bother coming back for? They asked him what year the Land Rover was. Charlie said he didn't know but that he was sure it was bought new in the past year or so. Only driven in Norway. Corporate car.

Understanding not a word, but watching them closely, Charlie gathered that the thug was trying to educate the teacher and the engineer on the harsh, practical realities of the business. Charlie's Bible seemed to figure in their conversation, as he had hoped. Like all good deals, the discussion ended with neither side happy. But they accepted Charlie's offer, and soon he was back in a convoy headed for the border in the dark, the Lada leading the way.

They swung south around the lake just east of Nikel and then north under a bright moon for Kirkenes. The border was only ten miles away. The terrain was more rugged than earlier and thick with sparkling lakes. Out of nowhere an Orthodox church appeared on the side of the road, painted a simple white and blue, but cared for. Then it was gone, a brief beacon.

Near the border the thug stopped his truck at the side of the road. He climbed out of the cab and marched towards the Lada with clenched fists, apparently having had a change of heart, if it could be called that. He prevailed in a short roadside argument with his colleagues, and then they asked him to step out of the car.

Charlie pulled out his bible and held it up, then he pointed back to the church. He wanted to make his peace with God first. The engineer barked at the thug for his lack of decency and pushed Charlie back in the car. He would not have this on his conscience. There were limits.

They pulled around and drove back to the church. Charlie grabbed his bag with the Bible and they let him go inside to say his peace while they waited outside with their guns.

Charlie walked to the middle of the sanctuary and dropped to his knees. And in some fashion he did pray.

Then he unzipped his bag and pulled out his field clothes and boots. He took off his funeral suit and tossed it aside. Then he dressed again and stood in the presence of God and all the heavenly hosts. As a geologist. Taming the world with a pickaxe and boot leather. In the field, Charlie could log fifty miles in a day, with five thousand feet of vertical and fifty pounds of rock samples thrown in for good measure. Making his way east across the border to the abandoned iron mine at Bjornevatn, then north along the mining road to Kirkenes, around five miles, with a full moon, would be just a quiet, reflective walk.

He left the Bible on top of his bag and slipped out the back door into the dark woods.

CHAPTER 13

THIN ICE

Laptev Sea
Tuesday night

Avinashi was watching when the lifeboat somehow bobbed back up to the surface under the midnight sun. It appeared more submarine than boat, with only its conning tower and top reappearing above the water. Avinashi was cold, even inside the mammoth immersion suit. Ted must have been frigid. She climbed with great difficulty down out of the narrow tower, which had the only windows on the lifeboat, to check on him.

"I'm okay, really," he said, sitting on the bench in his shorts and t-shirt and with only a life vest for warmth. "I have a fast motor, high natural body temp. They'll be here soon. Just glad I'm not out there. Although you would think they would put some damn winter clothing on an Arctic lifeboat. Where's the customer feedback form? Gotta talk to someone about that."

After their heart rates returned to normal, they had conducted a quick inventory. They had ropes, buckets, first aid kits, flashlights and whistles. Even a seasickness bag and a can opener, although no cans, and inexplicably a small box of white knit hats with Texso logos. But no other clothing, no blankets.

"Not dressed entirely right for this outing, in hindsight," he said, rocking back and forth.

"Ted, you're nearly blue. Take a turn in the suit. Please." She started to unzip the suit.

"Stop right there," he said, zipping her suit back up. "Before we do something we both regret. And not what you're thinking. You know how long you would last in the cold. You get frostbite shopping in the freezer aisle."

She looked at her watch. "At the top of the hour, we start taking turns. That's five minutes. Then ten minutes for you, twenty minutes for me."

"Five and twenty-five. Don't want to overheat."

"Ten and twenty. If you get the vapors, Scarlett, we can revisit the issue."

A loud thump sounded on the side of the lifeboat. Avinashi waddled up into the tower in her moon suit to check it out.

"You know, there wasn't really much to go on," said Ted. "Only a hint of a hint of an idea. It's not like he wrote it all out like some recipe."

"Ted, what are you talking about?"

"Kolotkov. I really made it work, Avi, I did."

"Oh, I know you did, Ted."

"Okay, I appreciate that, but let me just say it sounded a tad patronizing. No, I mean I really figured it out. It was a highly complex problem, I'm not kidding you. I worked on it for months and got nowhere. One day I just flat out gave up. There was monster surf at Mavericks so I headed out to Half Moon Bay to do some serious damage to myself. And I did. Because I couldn't stop thinking about the damn math and being distracted is not something you should let happen when you're on a fifty-foot wave. I ended upside down underwater getting my head pounded on the bottom. Nearly died. It was peaceful in a way, just rolling and rolling along with the waves, back and forth in the coda of the wave, nearly still but still rocking, rocking. And that's when it happened. I had all the pieces in my head, but it was like someone reached in and rearranged them all. Put them in order. Threw a few out. And then, all sweetness and light. And yes, better than any drug, I have to admit, and I know of what I speak. Anyway, next thing I remember I'm floating face up in the surf with some rugrat telling me to get off his wave. I drove back to Palo Alto and finished it up in a week. I played a part. I did."

She crawled down and put her arm around his shoulders. "I know you did, Ted. Thanks for telling me." She sighed. "Pack ice moving in. It's closing up the lead. Do you think we'll be safe here?"

Avi thought about Mike waiting for them outside the lifeboat and letting them go. If they had made it they would be dead.

"Ted, I can see the other lifeboat. The hull must have been compromised, but it's floating. Do you think there could be survivors?"

"They were under for several hours. And with the hull breached? Even if they had air they would have died from exposure, even with suits." But he still considered the issue. "If no one comes, we can go check it out if the lead freezes up.

"Well, at least we know where the oil isn't," said Ted. "That's what Charlie's thinking, I'm sure. We certainly did a lot of work for someone else. Now they can just focus on Chuchki or West Greenland, maybe the Antarctic. They'll be getting all the glory, but no thanks for us, I'm sure." He rubbed his hands together. "But that's enough for me anyway, I've had it. Petroleum industry leaves something to be desired, in my opinion, and I'm sure the feeling is mutual. Time for a fresh start, don't you think? Maybe life sciences. I hear that's computationally intensive."

"Hold that thought. Time to switch." Avinashi zipped off the suit. Ted slipped his frozen limbs inside the neoprene while she took a turn on the bench. She still had her white silks under her jeans and fleece shirt, so she wasn't too cold, yet.

"Ah, toasty," said Ted. "You do throw off a little body heat."

Thumps sounded from above, on the deck. Heavy, muffled steps.

"Okay, here's our rescue," said Ted. "Didn't even hear the chopper. Ice must have been too thin to land nearby. Great, they're going to think I wore this the whole time. Quick, let's switch back."

"Let me check first," said Avinashi. She was rapidly cooling, and she needed to keep moving anyway.

She climbed back up in the tower and looked around. She saw no one walking on the boat, or anywhere. The pack ice had closed around the boat, bottom and top. How much pressure was there? Hopefully if it got too much, they would pop up out of the ice like the *Fram*.

"I don't see them anywhere," she said. "That's odd."

Glass shattered into her ear, and despite herself, she screamed. Ted was already at the bottom of the steps when she dropped into his lap.

"What's wrong?" he yelled. But they looked up, and the white, long-clawed paw exploring the dome made that clear.

"Are you alright?" he said, dragging them both away from the tower. "He must have come in with the pack ice. That's okay, we're good. They'll just have one more thing on their list once they get here. And stop encouraging him, will you? You look like a seal. Skinny harp seal. C'mon. Your turn in the sweatbox."

She was worried about how cold she had gotten so quickly. The suit helped a little. But they couldn't last all night out here.

"Now the heat's going to escape through the broken window," she said.

"Good point. I'll fix it." Proceeding carefully to make sure that the bear wasn't lurking outside the tower like a seal breathing hole, Ted stuck an extra life preserver in the broken window. "Well, it's a partial fix."

He sat back on the bench.

"What time is it? One a.m. Ain't that something? Where are these guys? Did they forget we're out here?"

"Let's not talk about that," said Avinashi. "They'll get here when they get here. I'm sure your Dad's raising holy hell right now."

"I don't know. Might be. Truth is, I was born under a bad sign and he might think he's well rid of me."

"Ted, stop it."

"No, can I be honest with you and indulge in a moment of complete and utter self-pity? Nothing ever goes quite right for me. It's true. And not just for me, but for my family, everyone around me. You're going to say that's ridiculous, but let me remind you that you are sitting out over a dry hole in the Arctic in a lifeboat with an idiot cripple in shorts surrounded by a sunken ship, dead people and a killer bear. So who's making things up? Connect the dots.

"I'm not bringing this up to complain, too. I just wonder, why is this so? I have no idea. Take a shot, you're pretty perceptive. Is it a character flaw? Do you see anything? Minor, major, anything? Does everyone get it but me? If so, please clue me in, I'm just missing it. There doesn't seem to be a huge correlation between my many flaws and my many failures, I can't find the pattern. You're Hindu, is it just karma? Enlighten me if you can."

"Okay, stop it. Time's up, let's switch. I don't even have to check my watch. I can tell your body temperature by what comes out of your mouth."

This was truer than what she let on, and she was concerned he was becoming hypothermic. His voice had a distant, plaintive quality. He was talking very fast, but she thought she heard his teeth chattering. And his exposed skin was very pale, almost bluish. The problem was, she was feeling all these things herself. Without the suit on she felt sleepy, and sick, at the same time.

"Avinashi, please," he said, looking sweetly ridiculous in the immersion suit. A large, red sad man. "You're the only one that I can talk to about this. I feel like a pro ballplayer that had that career-ending injury before I ever got to take a swing. The doted-on son that his parents secretly don't care for. A mathematician whose modest gifts only allow him to wreak greater havoc. How do I break the cycle?"

She wrapped her arms tightly around her and with deeply furrowed brows rocked hard back and forth as if her effort would heat them both. "There is no cycle, Ted. Not if you keep trying. As long as you don't give up. My family was not particularly devout, but all my life my father taught me that goodness begets goodness, evil begets evil.

"My mother had to give up her career in the foreign service when she married my father. She chose Ajay and me, instead. My father moved us to Houston when he had the chance, so we could grow up in the US. He was laid off in the mid-'80s, when I was three, and oil prices collapsed. The only work he could find was in West Siberia and he took us along. My mom died there and he brought us back to the US and he worked as a hotel night clerk, and that became his life. But it allowed me to get here. And I am not going to let him down. He's had his setbacks, but I've never seen him do anything but good his entire life. There is no way to comprehend our accumulated karma, over many lifetimes, but from wherever we are we must work to improve ourselves."

Her temperature was dropping further. She got up to walk back and forth in the cabin, but she almost fell over so she sat back down.

"I see the same things in you, too, Ted. You may get lost from time to time, but you're always trying to find your way. This is not all your fault. But if you do want to jumpstart things, we do believe you can get a quick karma shot with Yoga. Or pilgrimages. I'll send you some links."

"Yoga? You've got to be kidding. I'd rather go back to being a cricket."

Without thinking, Avinashi lay down and curled up in a ball on the bench. Ted pulled an arm out of his sleeve and laid the back of his hand on her cheek.

"I'm chattering away about my feelings and here you're early onset hypothermia," said Ted. "Okay, no more games or false modesty. Strip down and get inside the suit with me. We can both fit. Sometimes I think I could carry you in my pocket. We need to keep each other warm or we're going to die waiting for that chopper."

Ted laid out several life vests along the middle of the floor. He took off the immersion suit and undressed to his boxers, then stepped back in. Avinashi could not stand by herself, so he lifted her upright.

She wriggled out of her jeans and he pulled off her fleece, then he stripped off her silks and added them to the pile. Then he helped her step in the feet of the suit, facing him.

"Sorry, this is no joke," he said. "Skin on skin." He lifted her tank over her head, wrapped her arms back around his chest and zipped up the suit, then wrapped his arms around her.

For a minute, they just stood together, as she absorbed his warmth. Unselfconsciously, she tried to wiggle her frozen feet up onto his. He squeezed her lightly and lifted her up the rest of the way.

"Let's lay down," he said. He shuffled to the end of the cabin, then she shrieked as he rolled backward onto the foam vests, with Avinashi landing on top of him, laughing.

"Making you laugh again," he said. "Order has been restored."

"I don't remember this being part of the old order," she said.

"That's right," he said. "I keep forgetting those were just dreams. So vivid."

She laid her cheek on his chest and tucked her head under his chin, where it seemed to fit quite well.

"How could your parents not absolutely love you?" she said. "My father, on the other hand, would be terrified of you. But just at first."

"Buyer's remorse, I would say."

"What are you talking about?" she laughed.

"I first remember noticing the 'look' the summer after we moved to Sugarland. I was seven. Two years later we had the 'talk.' I was a blind adoption. Absent Sherlock Holmes or random DNA sampling I'll never know my real parents. That's the way they wanted it, apparently."

She lifted her head and looked into his eyes. "I'm sorry, Ted."

"It's okay. At least it explained the 'look.' It was creepy, I'll tell you. Started checking my scalp for tattoos."

She laid her cheek back down on his chest. He felt each of her hands, then her feet between his.

"You're warming up," he said. "A little."

He slid his hands up and down her cold arms. Then he ran them along her back and her sides. Then down along the outside of her thighs, and up her back again. She still had her head tucked under his chin, but her lips were on his neck. He kissed her cheek, then pulled her up to his lips, and he kissed her deeply. She wrapped herself around him in their very small cocoon as it grew warmer and warmer until she was sweating and panting and the cold air burned her lungs. They rocked together for a long time, a small, warm bundle in an ocean of ice, until she shook again and again, screaming with her face in his neck, her arms around his warm, hard sides. Whereupon she fell into a dream without first falling asleep.

"Avi," said Ted gently. "We may have an ice management issue." They were trying to study in the engineering library at Stanford but he was making her laugh, and now he was talking to her about ice. He was strange sometimes, but very sweet, she thought.

"Avi, are you awake? I don't want to ruin our moment here, but I should go out and check the ice. It seems like the hull is under a bit of pressure."

Then she was leaving the library, off on a long journey. And Ted was with her. Where were they going? They were traveling together, close and wet. Very close. Zipped together, naked, in a Texso survival suit. Oh. My. God.

A savage, ripping sound like a tree being torn in half whipped her eyes open, as the interior of the lifeboat snapped upwards and downwards at the same time. Water trickled from a crack running the length of the hull. In seconds, it was a torrent.

She pounded his sides. "C'mon! Unzip us, unzip us!" She pounded harder. "Go, go!"

He tore down the zipper and the cold, damp air reached in and groped her like a giant, perverted hand. Standing in ankle-deep water, she pulled on her silks as water rushed into the cabin, then she skipped across the benches and the steps and poked her head up in the dome.

They were caught between the business end of two multi-year floes. The other lifeboat was up against the far edge of a newly-frozen lead, about a hundred yards away. In the cabin, they already had six inches of water and more every second. The sides caved in again to the sound of crushing fiberglass, and the width of the boat was diminished by half.

Ted stood in the immersion suit, unzipped to his waist. "All in favor of abandoning ship?"

Just one problem, she thought. "Do you think the bear is still out there?"

"Are you kidding me? Those bastards will sit and stare at a seal hole for three days straight if they have to."

"Ricky was carrying his gun, right?"

"Ricky always carries his gun. Just for such occasions. And I ripped him for it constantly. But it's a bit waterlogged now I would think."

"What are the odds you ever empty your pockets?"

"Very approximately zero."

"You were carrying shells on Sunday. You put them in your pocket." She grabbed his shorts and shook them, and they clinked. She dug into the noisy pocket and pulled out a handful of .308 shells. Dry shells. "Five."

"You don't have a very high opinion of me, do you?" said Ted. "I suppose now you want me to run over there and borrow his rifle."

"No. I'm going to get it."

"With your invisibility cloak? I'll go, you distract. I'll be like a ghost. Arctic ninja."

The ice squeezed the boat again, making it scream. The water was up to the bottom of the seats. In a few minutes they might not be able to get out the hatch.

"You'll never make it," she said. "Give me your shoes and start getting your plan together."

"You're going to outrun a bear? Cheetahs of the north. No way."

She grabbed his waffle trainers and two Texso hats.

"You've never seen me run," she said.

Faster than the ice bear can grab a harp seal, she had her feet inside the hats and laced up in the trainers and was up at the hatch. He grabbed her arm.

"You'll have to work your way around the lead," he said. "That ice is only hours old, it won't hold you. If they spot you, I'll bang all hell on the boat. That's your starting gun."

"Good plan," she said.

He tucked her hair up under her hat. "I do believe in you," he said. "If anyone can outrun my bad luck, it's you." She leaned over and kissed him.

All the windows but the forward one were obstructed by ice. But there were no bears that she could see, so she popped the hatch. No teeth or claws. She popped her head out and back in.

"Nothing," she said. "The boat is caught inside a good-sized pressure ridge. But I can get out. Here I go."

She climbed out onto the jagged, jumble of ice around the top of the lifeboat. The strong early morning light hurt her eyes, and she couldn't see well. The light, wet wind was enough to remind her how cold she was. Just below freezing. She could tell now. Her muscles started to tighten.

She made her way carefully down onto the floe in front of the lifeboat. The newly-frozen lead lay between her and the other lifeboat. It was farther than it had looked, and wider. At least a hundred meters straight across, and probably twice as much around. She scanned the horizon. With the *Ranger* gone, there was only ice now, out to the edge of the world.

She walked down to the lead. The ice was dark and clear and covered by the barest dusting of blown snow. She slid out her toe and pressed down gingerly. It deformed under her touch, plastic, bending rather than cracking.

She looked back. Ted was standing in the tower in his t-shirt and shorts, holding a wrench. He gave her a quiet and grimly serious thumbs up.

The pressure ridge blocked the shorter path around the left. She went right, up onto a raised flat section of the floe. A quick look around.

They were already running at her.

Two white, graceful forms, running like a dream, with long, rolling strides. Ted was beating, beating on the boat.

Avinashi walked towards the bears.

"Avi what are you doing!" screamed Ted. "Hey, you big pieces of white trash, get over here, time to get your furry asses kicked. Yeahhhh!" Avinashi heard him fall out onto the ice.

She was a few meters back from the lead now. She stopped and waited.

Until their beautiful, streamlined heads were just a few strides away.

Now. Avinashi turned and ran hard straight towards the lead.

She pumped her arms and drove her legs against the rough surface of the floe. With her short, quick strides, she hit the lead already at full speed. Then she lightened her step, and danced over the ice with long, easy strides. She was running over a snowy field, she told herself, disturbing not a single flake. She was a light, flat stone, skipping, skipping, skipping endlessly on a still pond. She was lighter, her pads were bigger, she was faster. She could fly, she could fly, she could fly.

She heard grunts as the bears pulled up just before they hit the lead, then crashing through the thin ice and into the sea. She ran faster, trying not to get sucked back into the soup of ice and claws and teeth.

She hit the lip of the floe at the other side of the lead very fast and with the tip of her toe so she did take flight, for a moment. Then crashed hard on the floe. The bears were still splashing across the lead. Coming.

She leaped from the floe onto the lifeboat and threw open the hatch, to see them trapped in cold water, sealed under a thin layer of ice. But Ricky loved his rifle. And kept it safe and dry and strapped down in the overhead rack. In its case. Just for such occasions.

The gun was heavier than she remembered. She was so cold. Her fingers hardly worked. The shells were like chunks of ice. She was going to drop them. No, they were going in. She was with her father.

At the ranch. It was sunny and warm. Almost too hot. She loved it. She was going to shoot with her father. Only five. Not enough. Five is plenty. Two is plenty. Done.

She dropped the forestock hard on the edge of the tower, chambered the first round and without hesitation shot the closer bear square in the chest. She hit the second bear from the side near the spine. Now the first bear is down, and she hits it again just behind the shoulder. The second bear is coming again. She hits it in the chest. It is still coming. She hits it again in the throat. She drops inside the lifeboat, and falls through the ice, into the water.

When she climbed out there was a helicopter overhead but it was Russian. She ducked behind the lifeboat and she could see Ted doing the same across the lead. Maggie is insistent. Avi knows what she must do. How can you save him if they take you? Avi stands on the ice to the side of the lifeboat and waves at the helicopter. She can see Nikolai at the cargo door. Avi points over to the other lifeboat. Then she holds up the gun so Nikolai can see. Their sniper lowers his rifle on her, but Nikolai waves him off. He laughs. They take Ted. Nikolai is still laughing as they fly off.

The expanses are endless. It's as if she is on the moon alone, cast free in space. Her mother is crying. But Maggie won't let her quit. She is screaming at her. Find a knife! Don't you dare quit. You know what to do.

CHAPTER 14

WELL ABLE

Bjørnevatn
Wednesday early morning

His mobile picked up a signal as he was walking out of the mine in the dark.

"Roy, it's Charlie."

"Hey, Chief. What's with the huffing and puffing? Early for a run."

"Clearing my head. What can you tell me?"

"No joy. Still locked down. And no sign of any SAR or Hazmat teams."

"Any workaround?"

"Well, we left out a case of vodka for them to steal and they threw themselves one hell of a party, but they still managed to post a guard on my bird. Keep hoping he'll freeze to death but I think he drank too much antifreeze. We're a little undermanned and under-gunned to launch a frontal assault. Just me and Lee and a couple of bolt actions."

"Don't even think about it. I got us some leverage. Sit tight."

Lazarev's staff was still monitoring the phones in the middle of the night in Moscow. By the time Charlie was able to find his way through the darkened buildings and out to the entrance road, he had a call back.

"You are in Norway," said Lazarev.

"Yeah. Needed to get back to the office."

"You have much to answer for in Russia, Charlie. You should not have left."

"Plenty of time for that. My immediate concern is the welfare of my people on the *Ranger*. Why is nothing being done?"

"Special precautions are being taken. This requires time. Thankfully we had the proper equipment in place to detect the radiation."

"Somehow we didn't think that would be necessary."

"If you are so concerned about your people, why are you not in Sredny?"

"If I knew I could go to Sredny and not Lubyanka, I would."

"That could wait."

"Okay," he said. "I'll need you to clear my flight from Kirkenes to Khatanga. And I want you to unlock my helo so it can meet me there. And no Neftepolk. Like I said, I want to go to Sredny, not Moscow."

Lazarev hesitated, but he did want Charlie very badly. "Of course."

Charlie had reached the front gate. The Land Rover was parked just outside.

"I just want my people taken care of, Oleg Maksimovich. I don't care about the rest. It's over. I know that."

"It's not over, Charlie. It's just beginning for you." The line went dead. Russians never say goodbye.

Inside the Land Rover the driver poured hot coffee for Charlie from a thermos as morning dawned.

Kirkenes
Wednesday morning

At twice the usual rate Vicki had been able to charter a long-range Hawker that was waiting on a shipping exec in Kirkenes. Charlie sat in the plane on the tarmac at the airport, waiting.

Finally Ed Maxwell called and patched him through to Roy.

"Your check must have cleared because we are now airborne and outbound for Khatanga. Once we're over the horizon we'll circle back."

"Can they track you?"

"They never used to spot us back in the day, not if we stay low and fast. I doubt they've been upgrading."

"Roy, they can't go back to Sredny. You understand that."

"Roger that. We have an alternate exfil route. But I'd rather not discuss that over the radio."

Ten minutes later Charlie was wheels up in the Hawker, heading east. As they banked right, for London, he could see the small town of Kirkenes below, on an elbow of land jutting out into a branch of the immense Varanger Fjord. Neat rows of houses in bright Nordic reds, yellows and blues huddled together on deep green lawns. Fishing boats, large and small, filled the harbor. Russian vessels were frequent visitors to Kirkenes, for refits and repairs unavailable at home. But the small port, on Norway's far northern shoreline, was being remade in anticipation of Firebird. The Norwegians were building massive additions to the harbor, to better serve as a reloading point for oil coming out of the Russian Arctic.

The accompanying influx of new wealth likely also accounted for the egregiously large sportfisher at anchor in the harbor, its graceful white hull and lofty flying bridge out of place among the sturdy working vessels. Another guy that got lucky and now fancied himself the ultimate big game hunter, thought Charlie. He was embarrassed for the man, for the foolish spectacle of this huge warm water boat tied up in a fjord that led into the Arctic Ocean, to be a sheet of ice in two months time.

London
Wednesday midday

When he arrived in London the markets were open. He called Gavin from his taxi on the way into the City.

"Well, the infamous man of the hour, the decade, the century. Spectacular failure, first rate! You do nothing in a small way, my friend. What a spectacular short this would have been, but then you know, not sure what there would be to spend it on at the end. Just when you think you've seen it all, Charlie, you learn something new. The latest game is to look at long-term rates of decline and their impact on discounted cash flow models. Do you know how wicked it is to discount even a mid-single digit declining earnings stream. The market is down 20 percent before it got stopped out by the circuit breakers and it's still a massive short. Everyone's dusting off their Malthus and we don't like what we see. I have children Charlie, so I can only joke so much. Couldn't you have found just a little bit of oil up there? Or at least have kept this bit of bad news to yourself? Ignorance is sometimes bliss, my friend. Did you catch your buddy Lazarev this morning? Funny how massive failure puts a flush on that man's cheeks. New Energy Policy for Russia! Nationalism on steroids. With a double bagger on oil prices today and still climbing, you think he'd be wanting to sell as much as he could but they're stopping exports. Fuck contracts, he's keeping it all! Excuse me, Charlie, but your little adventure makes me want to go cry now."

He called Sanders.

"Charlie! Didn't expect those Russian cops to hold you! Although you're lucky it wasn't the FSB, you'd be on your way to Chernov's torture chamber right now. You're bringing their whole house of cards down, Charlie. Lazarev's got their balls in a vice and he is turning the handle as hard and fast as he can. The military is moving to his side. They are not where they wanted to be, but they can tell a new wind is blowing. This New Energy Policy isn't the end. This is just the tip of the iceberg. What happened yesterday? Maybe we go too greedy, Charlie. Is that possible? Christ, Charlie, maybe this time we've really gone too far."

It was a glorious, not-too-hot August day in the City, the kind that was ordinarily impervious to gloom. He intended to head for the office, but the thought made him sick and he decided to stop at his flat to shower and gather his strength. He knew he had no food, so he had the taxi drop him at the market around the corner. He had not eaten since breakfast yesterday.

As Charlie walked in to the sound of bells, Father McGlynn from Holy Redeemer arose from his deliberations over the small produce cooler in the corner. He was a small, friendly man that practically begged to be underestimated. Holding a tomato, he walked right over to Charlie and pulled him close, looking up with clear blue eyes.

"Charlie, how are you? Good to see you, it's been too long. Have you stopped in to see the progress on the choral room? It's going to be gorgeous, thank you again. They'll be making beautiful music there for generations, long after you and I have moved on. Come on by this afternoon, I'll give you the tour and we can talk. I'm not going to accept a no. That's straight from the top."

"I would like that, Father. Let me try. If I can make it I'll call."

"You do that, Charlie. By the way, I am informed there were two gentlemen in the neighborhood this morning asking for you. Two Arab fellows. Know what that's about?"

He had no idea. "Just some friends from the oil patch," said Charlie. "Wondering when they would show up. Must have gotten lost, thanks."

Father McGlynn grabbed Charlie's elbow. "Jesus called strong men to do his work. Fisherman. Men who would go out on the angry sea. He loves you, Charlie."

"That's someone."

"Liang loves you, too, Charlie. But he's stuck on one of those rocks. He won't sleep, he won't go to class. He got all the others. Can you call it off? He's eleven. It's not healthy."

The meteorite, thought Charlie. "I need to know if he can figure it out. He needs to know."

Charlie's cell phone rang. "Sorry, Father, I have to take this. If I can, I'll stop by."

It was Roy. He stepped outside. "Not good news. *Ranger* was a total loss. Both lifeboats launched. One failed, two survivors in the other. Crawford and Sharma. I got Sharma. But the Russians were there first and they got Crawford. So I got the one. Looks like she might lose some toes but otherwise okay. Sorry, that's it."

Charlie paused. "Thanks, Roy. Thank you for going."

He decided not to go to his flat right away, after all. He took his bag of scones and coffee down to the Thames and sat on a bench, facing south and the sun. A young mother slowly pushed a pram, followed somewhat by another child, a small boy distracted by each and every treasure to be discovered along a city walk. It was a day the memories of which were needed to sustain you through a long, dark winter.

He called his flat.

"Hello?" The voice was English, not Arab.

"Is Charlie there?" asked Charlie.

"No, can I take a message?"

"Who am I speaking with?"

"Maintenance. There was a water problem. Lots of damage, unfortunately. Do you know how we can find him? It's urgent, you see. Can't track him down."

"No, sorry. Good luck."

He called Roger in Houston.

"Charlie, where are you?"

"I'm in London."

"What's going on? The embassy told us you'd been arrested, then you disappeared. The Russians are going ballistic. We need to get out to the *Ranger,* and you're not helping at all. Ted is on that ship, God damn it."

"Ted's okay. The Russians picked him up. He was one of only two survivors. We got the other one. Sharma."

"Oh, thank God. Wait, we each got one? What the hell happened out there, Charlie? The Russians are saying they detected radiation. They're implying we detonated some sort of nuclear device."

"I have no idea how that could have happened, Roger. You have to believe me."

"We are well past that now, Charlie. We are talking about a nuclear detonation on Russian soil. Do you have any idea what that means? The FBI is camped out in one of our conference rooms here. Special

Branch has taken over our London office. You need to get over there immediately, Charlie. They're accusing us of hiding you." That explained who was at the flat.

"I'm not sure what I can tell them. I told you, I don't know what is going on."

"It's not for you to figure out, Charlie. Get yourself to the office. Now. That's an order."

"I want to talk to Wayne first."

The line was silent, except for a soft background hiss. "Charlie," said Roger. "I wanted to tell you in person. Wayne is gone. Lydia said he was upset and went down early. She went to check on him and he had passed. I'm sorry. Don't blame yourself, Charlie. He hadn't been well, it was just his time. Lydia is still informing family. We're making an announcement tonight after the market close."

Charlie closed up the phone. He walked to the water's edge and dropped it in the river. As he watched the water flow by, he felt that his time had also passed. Too early, but that is what happened sometimes.

He heard two sets of footsteps approaching. They stopped right behind him, but he didn't turn around. Too tired, he just waited for the touch of cold steel on his neck, or blackness.

"Mr. Joiner?" An Arab voice.

"Yes."

He still didn't turn around. A well-dressed Arab gentleman walked around into his field of vision and handed him a cell phone.

"Hello?"

"Charlie, it's Karim. I am so pleased we have found you."

In his most desperate hours, there was always Karim. "What have I done, Karim? What have I done?" He raised his hand to his eyes. "I have brought us to the end."

"Charlie. It is not for us to despair. Well able is Allah to save. Well able." Words from long ago.

"Come to me, Charlie. There are things you need to hear, and I have waited too long. My cousin has a plane at Biggin Hill. Hassan will take you. Go, now. We may not have much time."

CHAPTER 15

POISON WIND

Eastern Province, Saudi Arabia
Wednesday night

The SUV jumped off the highway at full throttle and bounded across the open desert. The driver must have been steering from memory, or have been a man of great faith, because he went so fast the headlights were useless. And then he turned them off, and also his dashboard lights, and piloted by the moonlight and perhaps his GPS, or his compass. Out the window the moon made a flickering, silver path on the passing sand, and the desert appeared to Charlie as a calm, black sea.

He had slept on the flight and was still not quite awake when he had stepped out into the wet, suffocating heat of coastal Dharan and wordlessly fled the airport with his reticent driver and two bodyguards. As he sat quietly in the back of the car, his mind was cut loose of time and drifted recklessly through his memories. And so now this bone dry sea became instead sands soaked in oil, like the makeshift golf courses where Karim had invited him to play years ago at Udhailiyah, and then the dark earth of the sabkha into which he had dug deep to find crystalline sand roses for Sheila, and then inevitably the blood-soaked sands of the Empty Quarter in Yemen, where she lay forever dying, crying and pleading with him to save their son. Where he stayed with her until lights appeared far ahead, over some secular temple built over the god of modern civilization and commerce. Ghawar.

They were weaving now, still at high speed. Charlie thought he could make out wellheads, and pipelines heading out over the horizon to distant gas-oil separation plants. The driver spoke low, sharp words into his radio as they coasted into a large desert tent camp fully illuminated with brilliant floodlights. At the edge of this oasis of light stood a drilling rig, its derrick rising high into the night sky. Modern trailers off all sizes ringed the site out in the shadows. The sides of the tents were rolled up, and everywhere men scurried back and forth or huddled together in small groups. Some were dressed in traditional flowing white thawbs. Others, like the large, grim Saudi coming towards Charlie as he stepped out of the car, wore rough khaki field clothes.

The Saudi grabbed Charlie's right hand with his and clamped his other hand on Charlie's shoulder before giving him a kiss on both cheeks. "As-Salaam `Alaykum, Charlie."

"Wa `Alaykum As-Salaam, Abdul."

This imposing man with small, quick eyes was Charlie's counterpart at Aranaco, its Senior Vice President for Exploration and Producing. Abdul al-Rahman was also the close protégé of Aranaco's Chairman, the Saudi Minister of Petroleum and Mineral Resources Karim al-Samaha, also a geologist by training. Because of this relationship Abdul was also rumored to be the likely successor to the current CEO of Saudi Aranaco, but these outside observers did not appreciate the situation at all and it would have taken the King himself to force Abdul to give up his current position.

"You put your feet up on the desk to think, Charlie. He drags us from our air-conditioned offices out into the desert."

"That bad?"

"The situation has indeed become desperate. And now we have no more time."

"Where are we exactly, Abdul?"

"Where it began." He pointed back to the last wellhead Charlie had passed on the way into camp. "'Ain-Dar No. 1."

Many years ago the French had studied the distribution and discovery of oil fields in basins around the world. They observed regular patterns and expressed them in simple, yet aristocratic, terms. In any basin there usually proved to be a single King, one field that was much larger than any other. In the same basin, there would also be found two or three Queens, each two to five times smaller than the King. Then there would be three to five times as many Lords, each again significantly smaller than the Queens. And finally, scattered about everywhere in great numbers, but often of inconsequential size, were the poor peasants.

After a few years of hard work in a new basin a Queen would be discovered. Only years later, the King would be revealed. Finally, after many years, all the Lords would be pinpointed. Along the way, at any point, you would have to force your way through all the peasants.

The Arabian Basin was no exception to these rules. The first Lord, possessed of seventeen billion barrels, was discovered up in Iraq at Kirkuk in 1927. Eight years later the first Queen appeared in Kuwait at Burgan, holding fifty billion easily recoverable barrels. During the war, in 1941, Saudi Arabia finally got on the board with its first Lord of the Eastern Provinces, the 'father of the sand flies,' Abqaiq, home to thirteen billion barrels under the sands just west of Dharan.

After the war, when exploration began again in earnest, the American geologists Ernie Berg and Max Steineke identified a low anticline structure deep in the desert at Haradh. The layers of sediment here were very nearly flat, but the slightest wrinkle had formed as the Arabian plate had pushed up against the Eurasian. An anticline, a perfect oil trap. This wrinkle appeared to run north and slightly east for well over a hundred miles, to a point up near Abqaiq. For convenience's sake, they drilled the first well at the northern end closer to the infrastructure available at Abqaiq. There, in 1948 at Ain Dar No. 1, they struck oil on their first attempt and lifted the first crude from the mighty King of the Arabian Basin, Ghawar. Original estimates of the ultimately recoverable oil from Ghawar were over eighty billion barrels. Now, with fifty-five billion barrels produced to date, and still flowing over two million barrels per day, many analysts had lifted their estimates for Ghawar to over a hundred billion barrels.

The Arabian Basin would yield twelve supergiants, each with over ten billion barrels of oil, and prove to be the greatest petroleum province in the world. And Ghawar was first among them. The King of Kings.

"Flowing steady for over seventy years, still from the original casing," said Abdul. "One hundred forty million barrels from one well. It has been no secret that the water cut has been up and down over the years. Now what everyone knows is that in March it jumped to over 70 percent. It is the same at wells all over Ain-Dar."

Ghawar was believed to be one continuous field stretching 175 miles long and thirty miles wide, just larger than Delaware. But the field varied greatly across its vast extent, and so was broken into six distinct regions. Two small areas in the north proved to be the most productive. Shedgrum and the first, Ain-Dar.

Abdul turned back to Charlie. "But what no one knows, Charlie, is that we have no idea why. And the water cut is still increasing. Ghawar is dying and we have not been able to stop it. Come, and see."

Charlie followed Abdul under the pyramid-shaped dome of a red and pale blue striped desert tent as large as an infield. The sides of the tent were rolled up in the hot summer night, but the interior space was divided in the usual fashion by walls of additional woven cloth. They entered a spacious room where a group of younger Saudi men wearing stereoscopic goggles and long white tunics sat on deep red pillows and thick, gold carpets in front of a massive rear projection screen which filled the entire back wall. The screen was displaying two nearly identical images that looked like long, high, rounded-off ridges, built up from of a rainbow of layers, blue on the bottom, then aquas, greens, yellows, reds and pinks. The men had a keyboard and controller, and they were spinning the images in tandem, and zooming in and out, and then layering in and out lines and dots and purple plumes that Charlie guessed were rock layers and faults and long, spidery horizontal wells and injected water or gas, all the while engaged in a very tense, animated discussion in Arabic.

"These solutions are two of the best fits, but neither has a very high confidence level. The only thing that we know for certain is that neither of them is right. After two months of working with our simulator we had no high-confidence solutions and nothing that we could clearly test to get there. So in desperation we brought rigs back out in May to take new core samples," said Abdul, pointing to a smooth, fence-post-sized cylinder of rock laid out next to the men on a pillow. "Whole cores, so we can measure directional permeability, and add that to our data set."

Saudi Aranaco had custom-built a reservoir simulation program for Ghawar. Few fields could justify the huge investment the Saudis made in the program, but Ghawar certainly did. The simulator had a trillion cells and ran on a massively parallel processing system running back at EXPEC, Aranaco's Exploration and Petroleum Engineering Center, in Dharan.

Rather than forcing Aranaco scientists to divine the one deterministic model that could fit all of its fifty-years of observed data for Ghawar, and then test it for accuracy, the simulator could sift through thousands and thousands of possible fits, or solutions, created by random variations of variables, and select the two or three most likely. These type of analyses are referred to as stochastic, from the Greek word for 'guess.'

After reviewing the best several models and their differences, Saudi Aranaco scientists could acquire and input additional data, like directional permeability data from new core samples, that they thought could best further narrow the choice. In this iterative fashion, the most likely model, and explanation, of the observed oil flows and water cuts could be pinpointed. This model would tell them how best to reach the oil, and where to pump and not pump the water.

"And we still aren't getting answers. We're missing something, and we don't know what it is. Two weeks ago Karim moved everyone out here, and we have been breathing, eating and sleeping this problem. We have been working all night every night and rest only a little during the day."

Charlie knelt beside the core and ran his hand along the smooth surface. "Arab D?"

"That's right," said Abdul. "Zone 2-B."

For all of its vast hydrocarbon wealth, over 80 percent of Saudi Arabia's oil production had come from a single two hundred-foot layer of carbonate reservoir rock buried over six thousand feet below the shifting sands, the Arab D formation. Arab D was divided into six additional zones, and of these Zone 2-B was by far the most prolific.

The oil from the original wells in Ghawar flowed so abundantly that Aranaco geologists naturally assumed that the Zone 2-B was homogenous across the length and breadth of the field. Only such a vast area could support such a strong, continuous flow.

The first collision with reality occurred in the late-'80s as the fairly simple simulation models became worthless, completely divorced from the reality of the observed jump in water cut. What followed was a painful education in the real-world complexities of Ghawar. They discovered the Super K, or 'thief' zones, which were the highly permeable layers of rock, 'K' being the geologists' symbol for permeability, through which the water that was supposed to sweep oil to producing wells instead swept around it through the Super K zones, leaving the oil trapped behind. They discovered the mysterious tilt of Ghawar's oil-water contact surface, not perfectly flat but instead varying over 800 feet between its highest and lowest points. Far from being homogenous, Aranaco scientists discovered that Ghawar was a wondrously complicated structure rife with horizontal and vertical fractures, tar caps that prevented oil flow, with rock of widely varying permeability and porosity, and oil of greatly varying weights. Complex, as life itself. All of which made the task of predicting and responding to the water flows in the field an exceptionally challenging endeavor.

"He comes here and touches it, just like you," said Abdul. "Looking for answers, which will come in time as before, Inshallah. I just hope that we are given the time."

"Why would you not?"

Abdul pulled Charlie back out under the stars and spoke very quietly. "I am a scientist, Charlie, not a politician, you know this. But even I can tell you things are very, very bad right now. If we cannot solve this problem, we may have to adjust our reserves, massively. It is not just Ain-Dar, Charlie. Shedgum is also starting to exhibit the same problems. And Haradh has not been going well for some time. Husam al Dim al-Kassab is using all of this against Karim, claiming mismanagement, and even against the King. It is the same story. He says that the King has lied about how much oil is left, so he can give it away cheaply to buy American protection. But now, al-Kassab has most of the ulema, the scholars, with him."

Al-Kassab. A minor and by all accounts dim-witted prince who had only enough sense to realize his best play for power was to ally himself with recalcitrant members of the clergy. There had been no small amount of dissatisfaction with the King's attempts to introduce some minor attempts at modernization. He was seizing the opportunity.

"Me, I think that is part of the reason we are not in Dharan," said Abdul. "Karim, he does not want to get trapped in the city. He has been told he must stay mobile. So we are here, ready to fly away on a moment's notice."

There were no other sounds, just a voice in their ears, so by all rights it should only have come from someone that was standing with them all along. "No one ever likes off sites, do they? Personally, I kind of like it out here."

Charlie turned to his direct left and spied a familiar face with calm, watchful blue eyes. The man was a youthful-looking forty, if Charlie remembered correctly. He sported his usual very short hair and was dressed in a pale, light dress shirt, loose jeans and light boots. Mr. Brown.

"Paul," said Charlie. "How are you?"

"Same old. More importantly, how are you?" said Paul. "I was going to come up and see you, but then you went all walkabout on us."

"Well, they'll just let anyone in then, won't they?" said Charlie.

"With my special green visa, yes. You should try it next time. Save you a walk in the dark. Could have twisted your ankle."

"Yeah, well, see I lost my wallet."

"Abdul, do you mind if I steal Charlie from you? Karim would like to have a chat."

"As long as you bring him back," said Abdul. "Maybe he can figure this out."

"Straight away," said Paul. He looked at Charlie. "Ready to go for a drive?"

Several more SUVs were parked at the northern edge of the camp. Paul climbed in one and pulled down the keys from the over the visor and started it. He pulled some sort of device out of his pocket and set it on top of the dashboard. Then he pulled away out into the desert.

"So what happened, Paul?" said Charlie, as they drove slowly out into the darkness. Paul also drove without headlights, navigating by the full moon.

"Come again?"

"How did it get out? Who leaked it? Was it al-Kassab? And why?"

"Oh, is that all? I thought you were going to ask me about the Kennedy assassination again." He drove on in silence, calmly checking the device on the dash.

"Okay. I'll ask Karim."

"Let's not do that, Charlie. Let's not." Paul shifted in his seat. "I'll tell you the how, then you can ask him the why and tell me. The how is that one of the twenty-eight men who had access to that information was incented to release it to a third party, unknown even to him. This was determined by us after twenty-eight separate conversations, several of which were unfortunately very stressful for all parties."

"Incented? For money? That's insane."

"That would be. Coerce might be a better word than incent. Five years ago, on a business trip to Geneva, our man managed to find time to father a child by an Italian woman. This man tried to keep the whole matter secret, from us, from everyone. But someone found out, because the boy went missing in December. In January, our man started receiving pieces of the boy in the mail. They told him they were keeping the boy alive, and would cut pieces off one by one unless he gave them what they wanted. You know how this went. After the first package, he hired someone. The illusion of action. After another package, he offered money. And so on. After they sent him an arm he sent them what they wanted."

Charlie just stared out the window, watching the desert roll past. Finally, he asked. "The boy?"

Paul shook his head. "I had someone look at the packages, all of which he still had. The boy had been dead the whole time. They killed him, cut him up, and put the pieces in a freezer. Then they just mailed them one by one until they got what they wanted."

Paul slowed the SUV as they came up the slope of a very low rise. At the crest, facing away, stood a small, solitary figure. Even in the heat, he wore a heavy, dark cloak, or mishlah, over his white thawb and a white headdress, the ghutra. About him darted graceful figures, ghostly in the moonlight. Paul stopped the car halfway up the rise. Under the horizon, thought Charlie, hidden. Paul stopped the car but didn't get out.

"Don't ask him about this," said Paul. "The boy was born of Zina, outside of marriage, and so under Islamic law he is not considered part of the family. But the boy was still his grandson. By blood at least."

"Oh, no. Khaleel?" Karim's son.

Paul nodded again. "Go on, I'll wait here. He wants to talk to you alone."

Charlie sat still in the car for a moment. "Thanks, Paul." Then he stepped out onto the sand.

Charlie walked up the rise toward the diminutive, robed figure. The cloud and sand-colored shapes were salukis, the elegant desert hounds. At least half a dozen. They raced back and forth across the deserts tracing streaks of moonlight, chasing after rabbits visible only to their keen eyes.

"As-Salaam `Alaykum, Karim," said Charlie. The man turned and raised his arms high and wide until they almost seemed to encompass the starry heavens. His coarsely-bearded face was dark and fractured with deep, crisscrossed furrows, the consequence of a life spent out in the oil fields of the Arabian Basin.

"Wa `Alaykum As-Salaam, my son." He came to Charlie and kissed him on both cheeks, slowly, and with emphasis. "You are back, safe. Again. All praise belongs to Allah, Most Merciful."

"It does indeed." Charlie thought back, for an instant, to a church in Karelia. "It's good to see you again, Karim. I wish the circumstances were happier."

Karim's smile remained but lost its joy, as his eyes broke away from Charlie and drifted back to his dogs. A slender, silken creature carried a live hare back to them and offered it to Karim. He grabbed the animal and quickly twisted its neck, then slipped it in a pouch at his feet. The saluki bounded off after more prey. Karim looked on with his hands clasped behind his back.

"They are beautiful, are they not, Charlie? Their form, their intelligence, all focused to one end. Only the hunt for them, nothing else. I envy their singleness of purpose, the freedom, the joy of this." Another hunter returned with his prey, of which Karim again made short work.

"I enjoy some of the old ways, Charlie. But I have no illusions, unlike some others. Any nobility we Bedouins possessed came with a heavy price. We feared not war because we had nothing to lose but what we could carry. We feared not death because it was our constant companion. We buried more children than we raised. There would be nothing good in returning to that. Nothing at all. This Lazarev, he is mad. Come, let us walk."

Karim blew on a high-pitched whistle and the dogs circled up and followed him as the two of them walked across the sands. A large, buff-colored dog kept particularly close, glancing back at Karim with dark, intelligent eyes. Karim stopped and gathered the dog up, lifting it up on its hind legs, and ruffling its feathery chest.

"This is Harim, we have hunted together for many years. See this white mark, on his chest? The Kiss of Allah, it is called. He made these dogs special, like no other." He released the dog, and it drifted off into the dark. "Although the true Kiss of Allah lays a mile below our feet. So I believe."

They walked out onto the flat void. Charlie had a hard time keeping pace with Karim, who seemed to glide over the desert with long, invisible strides.

"Charlie, did they take care of you on the flight? Have you eaten? We cannot talk if we are not refreshed."

When Charlie wasn't sleeping on the plane they were plying him with food and drink, in the Arab fashion. "Thank you, Karim, your cousin was very hospitable, my thanks to the both of you."

"Paul was ready to go in after you," said Karim. "Of course, we were following the situation very closely. When we heard you were arrested we considered our options very closely."

"Hopefully, Paul has had to rescue me for the last time. Fortunately, I was able to work something out on my own."

The dogs circled them silently in the dark like sharks beneath the water.

"A bit of a disappointment for us up there," said Charlie.

Karim shrugged. "Still, a very efficient means of exploration. Very cost-effective. So you look somewhere else now. Saves everybody time."

"The market isn't quite looking at it that way."

"No. The market has too much information to process right now. So it panics. The market was never rational, contrary to common wisdom, and know you and I have pushed it to the brink of insanity. We have not always been as transparent as they would like, but transparency is a fantasy. We are the most valuable business in the world. We could never release enough information to satisfy them. In any event, is not the best evidence of a man's ability what he has actually done? We have never failed to deliver the oil we promised. If we have enough time, Charlie, we will solve this problem. We always have. The market is too short-term, it panics. The number one concern of the Kingdom has never been supply, it has always been demand. Why should we feed the rumors to speculators, who can profit for doing nothing, while we destroy, uneconomically, the demand for this bounty of Allah? Demand destruction, that was our greatest fear." Was, thought Charlie.

"We have been good stewards of this resource, Charlie, and a good partner to the US. We managed the transition to national ownership reasonably. We have invested in our infrastructure, including the maintenance of very expensive spare capacity to soothe the market and ensure against disruptions. The price shock in '74 was an unfortunate, but probably unavoidable, part of the nationalization process. Prices were artificially low. And when it came to it, we proved our commitment to our common path with the West. You were there, Charlie. You were part of it, in '85, although I do not believe you quite fully understood your role, or the play, at the time. But you of course remember our audience with the King at Khobar?"

Charlie remembered Khobar. It was July 1985 and he was still in Yemen. Texso was a year into the production process at Alif. Sheila was tiring of raising a two-year old in the Empty Quarter and the politics were spiraling out of control, but Charlie was dead set on getting it started off right and refused to leave. There had been noises about another assignment, and he was worried he was going to get pulled off. West Africa. Peru. Maybe Colombia. He was in a production meeting when a call came in from his CEO, Wayne Parsons. Wayne happened to be his wife's father, too, though that didn't count for much as Wayne ran more of a meritocracy. And daughter-stealing baseball players started out in the penalty box. Wayne had backed him on the Alif play and they had begun to develop a relationship, although they still spoke only infrequently. This had to be it, the next assignment. But no. Wayne wanted him to help someone out. I want you to meet a man from the government. He needs an expert he can lean on. Someone that knows oil, knows deals, knows the Soviets, has credibility with the Saudis. Guess who I thought of? Give him a hand. See what you can do. He'll be at the strip in Marib this afternoon.

Charlie was still waiting at the airstrip at ten that night when a huge, black Starlifter cargo jet with no markings finally roared in, nearly invisible, out of the night sky. Ten minutes later he was seated at a table in the vast hold, which seemed to be outfitted in equal parts with living accommodations and exotic communications gear. There were no windows, but the muffled engine noise and the way he was thrown around at the table made it clear that they were soon back in the air, to Charlie's surprise. Across the table from him was a much older man, at least in his '70s. He had very little chin, a steeply receding forehead and only faint, white wisps of hair behind his ears. Soft, fleshy skin sagged on his features. As the man peered at him through large glasses with thin wire rims, Charlie had the impression of watching a wise, old fish in a bowl, with the fish watching him back.

"Sorry about keeping you in the dark, but I don't entirely trust your man Hashidi." The President of Charlie's host government, the Arab Republic of Yemen, and the leader of the ruling pro-Nasser Arab nationalists. "I know you weren't planning on it, but I hope you don't mind taking a short trip with me."

"Not at all, Director Casey. Wayne asked me to help you in whatever way I can."

"You know who I am? No moss grows on you."

Of course he did. Bill Casey, Reagan's Director of the Central Intelligence Agency. First wielder of the oil weapon, against the Germans in WWII. First at the Bureau of Economic Warfare, later at the OSS, the WWII predecessor to the CIA. Charlie knew immediately the sword was coming back out of the scabbard.

"You're even younger than I expected," said Casey. Charlie probably looked his twenty-seven years. "That's okay. I was thirty-two when I ran Europe for Donovan." Wild Bill Donovan, founder of the OSS. "I've got a meeting coming up with the Saudis," he said. "King Fahd, actually. We've got a proposition for him, but we need to run it by someone that knows what he's doing. I've got lots of oil experts, but no oil men, if you know what I mean. I need someone that can get into the weeds a bit, think through some of the details. Then help us pitch it. Give us some credibility. Wayne says you're my man. Are you?"

"What's the proposition?"

"Alright, that's fair. Wayne said I could trust you. First, let me ask you, what's your experience with the Soviets?"

"Very limited. They've been prospecting across the border in the PDRY since before I arrived." The People's Democratic Republic of Yemen, the Marxist half of the divided country. "I reached out to their head guy, tried to explore a joint development arrangement. Could have saved us some time, they've collected a lot of data. He wasn't very interested. Although he said they would consider it if we gave them all our seismic first as a good will gesture."

Casey shuffled around in a stack of papers on the table. "This man of goodwill. Who is that?"

"His name is Lazarev. He's a key operator in their fields in West Siberia, around Samotlor. They brought him down to jumpstart their exploration in the PDRY, which has been flailing. He's considered their best new guy."

"And then you beat him to the punch, back there, at Alif?"

"By a bit. I think they're going to hit around Shabwah soon. That would be my guess."

"After you showed him the way? It's on the same trend, just across the border?" The ends of Casey's mouth lifted like folds of drapery being raised, as if he were smiling.

"You could say that," said Charlie. "Anyway, that's the sum of my experience with the Soviets."

"Well, that's not entirely true, is it?" said Casey.

"I'm not sure what you mean."

"What about your dad? Did he ever talk about his little sojourn? I'm told he spent some downtime in the Soviet Union. Summer of '42. He was what, seventeen? Sailed into Murmansk on the *Tesso Port*

Arthur. Jerries shot most of his leg off, Russians got rid of the rest. That couldn't have been pretty. On the way back he ended up in the North Atlantic. With two arms and one leg he dragged two other men onto a piece of wreckage and somehow kept them together and alive for twenty-four hours until they got picked up. Tough son of a bitch."

"That's right. Particularly the last part. And he did talk about it, a little."

"And? What did he think about Russia?"

"He thought it was hell on earth."

"That's to the point. And what's your take?"

Charlie shrugged. "Sounds like every other oil region around the world."

Casey was slumped back in his chair, and his limbs stuck out at all odd angles. Still, he gave the impression of being awkwardly effective, like a human utility knife.

"You seem like a kid that can get his mind around a big idea. So try this on. We're going to finish the Soviets off. No one thinks we can do it, but we can. We've been playing defense so long, we forgot how to play offense. The Soviet Union is nearly bankrupt, and the whole insane system is collapsing. The signs are all there. They've been selling their gold at fire-sale prices and it's almost gone. Then the only thing that will be propping them up will be oil exports. Without that, they'll starve to death. You mentioned Samotlor. Well, it's on the decline, and they're going to need technology they don't have to keep production rates up. Same for the whole basin. We've taken the fight out of the Red Army in Afghanistan. We've cracked the myth of the Steel Curtain in Poland. Now we just need to kick out the oil stool and let them hang. We need to collapse oil prices. And for that we need the Saudis."

"When you say collapse, what does that mean?" asked Charlie. "You planning on taking Texso down, too? The whole sector? Just asking."

Casey leaned forward, coming right up against the side of the bowl. He unfolded an arm and swung it around, jabbing two thin fingers at Charlie.

"You get this straight. You could find a hundred billion barrels of high octane under the streets of Manhattan tomorrow and it means goddamn shit if we can't defend it. Nothing is more important than national security, nothing. Agents younger than you disappeared into Himmler's *Nacht und Nebel* or took their seven grams in the Lubyanka just so you could still have a Texso. And it can all be gone tomorrow if we forget that, if young people like you don't understand that. And you're out here, for Christ's sake. If you don't get it, who will? Wayne gets it. And next time you're home in Beaumont you ask your dad what he thinks. But I think you already know."

The plane had leveled off, cruising somewhere high over the desert, invisible in the night.

"There's no time to think about it," said Casey. "Yes or no. I gotta figure out some way to get the Saudis on board. If we can figure out some way to keep Big Oil from going belly up, of course we need that, too."

Charlie looked straight back into the big glasses. "I don't need any time to think about it," he said. "Show me what you've got."

Casey took an hour and ran him through their proposals, all of which Charlie thought were unworkable. He asked Casey if there a place he could put his feet up for a minute and think. Casey had someone show him to Casey's private office. After a short spell, Charlie came back and told Casey they should suggest an arrangement he had heard of called a netback. The oil majors would get paid by Saudi Aranaco based on their costs plus a guaranteed profit, rather than just paying for the oil and having to resell it in a falling market. This gave the majors a slim but guaranteed profit, enough to keep them going, and it ensured they would commit to keep selling Saudi oil, rather than someone else's. It also incented them to sell more oil, regardless of price, driving it down, and ensuring Casey's goal. He sketched out how it would work. Casey, the former lawyer, loved it.

They went first to Saudi Aranaco headquarters in Dharan where Charlie helped Casey sell it to the Saudi oil minister Yamani, and his chief deputy, Karim al-Samaha. They all in turn pitched it to King Fahd who happened to be nearby in Khobar, at one of his minor palaces, a three hundred million dollar beachfront affair on the Gulf. Charlie was not too focused on it at the time given the intervening events, but four months later, in October, Yamani announced the Saudis were abandoning OPEC quotas to massively increase their oil production. Too many OPEC members were cheating on quotas, Yamani said, and they would no longer be the only country to abide by them. Then entered into netback arrangements with their major foreign distributors, including Texso. Oil prices collapsed from thirty-one dollars a barrel to ten. The global oil industry entered a ten-year deep sleep. Hundreds of thousands of jobs were lost. Casey died two years later. Three years after that, the Soviet Union formally dissolved.

"What don't I know about Khobar?" asked Charlie. He and Karim were far out on the empty sands, alone. The dogs had vanished, off hunting distant prey. The bright, colorless moonlight turned the landscape into an antique black and white photo.

"That the next day the Russians were there, too. Led by Shevardnadze, the Soviet Foreign Minister, also the head of the Geology Ministry. What you never knew is that we had been in discussions with them for months, and we were close to announcing a new Saudi-Soviet OPEC. Charlie, Lazarev was the architect of the whole thing, he made all the presentations. He was Deputy Minister at MinGeo, and they were trying to do an end-run around the Oil Ministry with Shevardnadze and Gorbachev. Only Allah knows why, but I am sure it served some bureaucratic purpose of theirs. This new OPEC would be led by the Soviet Union and the Kingdom, although I think the Russians assumed, as they always do, that they would be in charge. So we had to choose a path. As hard as it might be to believe now, there were good arguments on either side. But we chose to continue our partnership with the US, the West, who were the best and highest value consumers of the oil. It was the right choice. I'd like to tell you it was all about supporting our brothers in Afghanistan, but that only helped us sell it to the ulema.

"So Fahd told the Russians that we needed more time, that we were now considering leaving OPEC altogether. The Russians exploded. Such rude people. I thought Lazarev was going to throttle Fahd right in the throne room. They argued with us, told us why it wouldn't work. Yamani looked to me, and I tried to argue back, I talked about our ideas. Your ideas. I mentioned you by name, Charlie. To Lazarev. I told Lazarev you had thought it all up, that Texso was behind it. I was much younger, oh, even less wise than today."

It didn't seem that important. "That's fine," said Charlie. "He already didn't like me. He hated me for the fact that they had been skunked in Yemen for nine years and we hit Alif after one."

"No, Charlie. It is much worse than that. The day of the accident. When your car was bombed. That was not the only attack that day."

"I never heard about any others."

"We kept them quiet. But there were four others. One of the King's decoy cars was destroyed in Riyadh. Minutes later someone fired an RPG into Yamani's house in Jeddah but, Praise be to Allah, he had just left. A package was sent to me at my office, but it detonated in the mailroom. Then, that night, a Russian surface-to-air missile was launched against Casey's black plane, but it too failed, defeated by countermeasures. We have always believed that all these attacks, and yours, were connected. We believe it was the Russians. Charlie, we believe the Russians killed Sheila, and your son. Lazarev killed them."

"No, that doesn't make sense," said Charlie. "It was just part of the civil war, our project was going to fund the government, the South was trying to slow it down. We knew it could happen. It happened. It's over." The same words he had been telling himself for over twenty years.

"No, Charlie," said Karim. "Listen to my words, think on them. The Russians were sending us a warning. They were right to be terrified, this meant the end of their empire. We could not tell you or Casey, because we could not disclose the Russian option. And you know what they are capable of. It was this Lazarev, then and now. You know what they did to that boy. Who does these things so easily? This is exactly what they did in Beirut. Everyone knows that."

In 1985, when it seemed every foreigner in Beirut was being held hostage, the Islamists had kidnapped four Soviet 'diplomats.' The Russians sent a team to Beirut which promptly grabbed twenty terrorists in return. Their negotiations consisted of sending them back, one by one, in pieces. The Russians got three of theirs back, and no Russians were ever kidnapped again. The Islamists kept to kidnapping the more civilized Italians, Germans and Brits. Russia's reputation for brutality in the Mideast lingered.

"And the timing of this leak, right before Firebird," said Karim. "He was counting on you to fail. Then his quick announcement of their new energy policy. He is striking back at the US and the West. And you, again."

They had been walking thoughtlessly, aimlessly, and now Karim stopped. For the first time, he seemed out of breath and old.

"It is all my fault, Charlie," said Karim. "That is why I extended you my protection, my dakheel. I convinced Wayne you needed time away, that the Marxist rebels were still a threat. I did not mention Lazarev. I did not know he would send you to Colombia. Then, when you were kidnapped there, I spared no expense, looked for the very best, and found Paul to bring you back. I have tried to atone for my error, Charlie."

Charlie looked up into Karim's ancient face and eyes. "Karim, I volunteered to go to Colombia. And you are not responsible for my wife's death."

"Thank you, my friend, but Allah shall be my judge, all Praise and Honor to him."

A hot, dusty wind kicked up, blowing traces of sand across the flat earth.

"As Allah would have it now, Charlie, it falls to you to stop this Lazarev. I will do whatever I can, but only you have been in Russia, know his enemies, his weaknesses, where he might be vulnerable. Use your government. The King will make whatever calls you desire. But only you can do this."

"I was only ever good at one thing, Karim. And I don't even do that very well anymore."

"You need to find a way, Charlie. The world needs time. Not this. The situation has become critical, even in the Kingdom. Al-Kassab has begun moving against the Royal Family. This morning his forces slaughtered the entire village of Dhurma in the Nejd, a city with many connections to the House of Saud. Thousands were killed in an artillery attack. I came here with Abdul in a last attempt to revive Ghawar, but it is dying and we cannot stop it without more time that we do not have. I must tell you I have considered staying and dying here with it. Then I suspect we would see those four US divisions in Dharan after all." The last resort considered by the US in '74. Outright seizure of the Eastern Province.

Charlie wanted to walk into the desert, find his family and leave this all behind. He stared up at the impersonal heavens, and they mocked him with their memories of his wife and child. Sheila screaming, crying at him. Save our son. Save him.

"Charlie, you must try. You must think of something."

"I will try Karim." He knew the threads to pull. Bego. Ivanov.

Impossibly, his cell phone began to ring. He pulled it out of his pocket.

"A cell tower at the camp," said Karim. "It carries in the desert."

Charlie answered it. Avinashi. Roy had gone east, hitting backup fuel depots all the way along Novaya Zemlya. She was calling from Varandey, a small port on the Arctic coast, in the Pechora Sea.

"Avinashi, I need you to go to Nizhnevartovsk." The home of Samotlor, the now-dying King of the West Siberian Basin. "See a man called Ivanov. Sanders can connect you. Ivanov may be able to help us with Lazarev. To get Ted back. I need you to see what you can figure out. I need to go see a man in Baku."

She said she could get there by tomorrow afternoon. Charlie ended the call. Karim was scenting the air, like one of the salukis, who had returned and were now howling.

"Charlie, we must hurry. Back to the car. We must not get caught out in the open." He blew the kennel signal into his whistle. The dogs raced away for home, leaving them behind. "Do you smell it, Charlie? The sulfur? Simoom." The Poison Wind. Small, local cyclones of extremely hot air and sand. They appear without warning and disappear in a flash. The fast, hot winds strip a body of its moisture and bring on heatstroke in minutes, killing from the inside, like a poison.

"Simoom? At night?" said Charlie.

Karim pulled Charlie by the elbow and they started running across the sand. "You are a bad Catholic, Charlie, not reading your Bible. Go see what happened to the Assyrians. Yes, they can come at night."

Karim must have signaled Paul because Charlie could see a plume of dust rising from the sand ahead of them, silver in the moonlight.

Karim faltered, and bent over, clutching his knees. "Go, leave me," he said. Charlie looked back. A wall of dust hundreds of feet high had leapt out of nowhere to obscure the northern horizon. "No," said Charlie. "We're almost there."

He pulled him toward the racing SUV. He was sure Paul had the accelerator floored, but the simoom was closer. Sand nipped at his face, and visibility was plummeting. Then it was gone to zero. He closed his useless eyes as the sand whipped at his face. He fell to the ground and pulled Karim down.

Charlie was insanely hot and choking on the sand. He felt it in his stomach and his lungs. He tried to cover his mouth with his shirt but there was no air, only thick dust, everywhere. In his ear, he heard a yell, a call to action, to right old wrongs. Karim yanked his mishlah over Charlie, against the wind. He pushed his hand back through and clamped a small respirator over Charlie's mouth and nose. Charlie tried to push it off, but Karim pushed back harder, and gripped also with the other hand, until Charlie was bound as if with iron bands. True to his bond, Karim then lay upon Charlie, protecting him against the Poison Wind.

CHAPTER 16

BLACK GARDEN

Baku, Azerbaijan
Thursday early morning

Charlie stared at the tarnished copper samovar sitting sphinx-like on the high cupboard, trying to decipher the proper way to fire it up. "I've gotten pretty good at those," said Paul. "Let me give it a try." He found a battered can of oil and some matches and set to work.

Charlie wanted to set a particular mood. Hot tea would be part of it, Paul's presence another. They were in the forlorn teacher's lounge of the State Oil Academy of Azerbaijan, amidst the furniture too broken and soiled to be worth taking for an office, posters for old geology conferences, extra copies of books and bound copies of forgotten theses. The school was housed in a faceless, Stalin-era edifice that squatted on a whole city block in the center of Baku, close to the old, baroque rail station and two blocks and a world away from the modern, golden glass tower of the central bank. Founded during the first oil boom in the 1880s, the school was home to Azerbaijan's top technical talent, including one Dr. Araz Bego, emeritus professor of geology and author of the definitive six-volume treatise, *Petroleum Geology of the Kura and South Caspian Basins.*

During his years in Baku, Charlie would often meet Bego here at his office as the sun was coming up over the Caspian. By natural

inclination and deliberate strategy, Texso was reaching out to the
Azeri academics, the thought leaders in the geological community,
and Bego was the dean. The two men would take their tea and walk
down to the harbor, discussing lens sediments and lithofacies, production costs and royalty rates. Thirty years older now, it was unlikely
that Bego was sleeping any later. Paul opened up Bego's locked office
across the hall so Charlie could peek inside. Towering stacks of books
covered the floor and the desk like stalagmites. Drafts of technical papers in handwritten Cyrillic and English scrawls were scattered across
his desk. A laptop locked to the desk. Thick woolen slippers behind
the door. He would come. They just had to wait.

Academics rarely became rich as Saudi sheiks, but Bego was an
exception. When Russians had nightmares about being cheated by
clever, dark men from the Caucasus, they were thinking of Bego.
Stalin had sent Bego's father to the Gulag and the rest of the family to Kazakhstan, and when he returned Bego's only passion other
than geology was stealing oil from the Commissars. Still, from what
Charlie could see, all his wealth had paid for was the restoration of
a pre-Soviet oil baron's mansion in the city and a security detail of
nephews and distant cousins. Most of the new money had moved up
in the hills or down the coast, to escape the noxious fumes of the
world's most polluted city. Even now inside the school it smelled
like someone was burning tires in the basement. But Araz liked to
stay below the radar and besides, Bego had lived with the poisons
so long that any withdrawal would probably kill him. Charlie and
Paul had discussed tactics briefly, and Paul had immediately focused on this location for the meet. A soft target easily breached,
where they could wait for Bego to come to them. Somewhere he
felt safe, where his men might wait outside or even leave him for
the day.

Charlie pulled a one-armed green wooden chair over to the window, where someone was trying to grow a pepper plant on the sill. He
peered out the dirty windows into the plaza in front of the train station, where a handful of people were starting their day under night

skies just turning pink. He had to sit. His airways felt like they were
coated with fine grit, and he was still having trouble catching his
breath. In the shadows outside the window he could see Karim lying
in the desert, an old Bedouin at last, coated with dust and dirt and
sand and united with the constant companion, death.

Karim's dakheel survived his passing. Paul was instructed to assist
Charlie, and after he dug Charlie out of the sand he cleaned him up
and bundled him into the jump seat of a cargo plane that somehow
was permitted to traverse Iranian airspace on a direct flight to Baku.
To the military airport no less, where travel documents were not required. An old, cadaverous Azeri missing an ear greeted Paul with a
kiss on both cheeks and drove them into town in the dark in a boxy
Zil delivery truck, three across in the grimy front seat.

In 1990, when Charlie arrived in Baku with his guide Don Sanders
for the first oil show, ethnic Armenians had just finished fleeing the
city after the Azeris started throwing them out of high rises and
running them down in the streets. Old hatreds between Christian
Armenians and Muslim Azeris had blossomed anew two years prior,
when an Armenian-dominated enclave of Azerbaijan voted to secede.
The region had a prototypically-Caucasus name, *Nagorno-Karabakh.*
Mountainous Black Garden. The use of weapons abandoned or sold
by the disintegrating Red Army punctuated the discussions. The
Soviet Army moved back in to stop the pogroms and restore order, or
perhaps just to secure said weapons caches, or rather, some said, to
send a message to other vassals in the near abroad looking to stretch
their wings. It is not clear which. Fact and truth were in short supply,
agent provocateurs abundant. Here at the intersection of NATO's
Turkey, Islamist Iran and the fatally-wounded Soviets, where loose
nukes, abandoned Cold War weapons and untapped pools of oil lay
everywhere underfoot, intentions were complex, ever-changing, and
often indeterminate. Whatever the reason, the intervening Soviets
mowed down demonstrating Azeris in an attempt to cool their pas-
sions. Black January, 1990.

By the time he got to the oil show that October, both Charlie and the Azeris were playing catch up. When the Soviet order collapsed, the Azeris started with more weapons and more men under arms. But the Russians had never trusted them, and Azeri men in the Red Army were not allowed into actual combat positions. However, the Armenians knew exactly what they were doing and, moreover, were fighting on their own Mountainous Black Garden turf. They seized the upper hand and key territory early on and never let go. Azeris were dying in the Black Garden, including hundreds of Azeri civilians massacred while trying to evacuate Khojaly. Azeri families in Baku were demoralized and wailing in the streets of Baku. The violence also crept down from the mountains into the city, and dead bodies would sprout in the filthy streets overnight.

Jamilov, a wily ex-communist in semi-retirement, saw that Azerbaijan still held the high card. Oil. Suddenly, the weak, populist Humbatov had run at news of a rumored coup, and the survivor Jamilov was seizing the reigns and cutting deals. With the oil, or promise thereof, he could buy protection. For himself, for Azerbaijan, both arms and high-level, strategic sponsorship. Soon the Azeris were flush with Russian, British and American weapons, mercenaries from southern US states and mujahedin from Afghanistan.

While Charlie was discovering Cusiana in Colombia, the British were getting shut out by Chevron across the Caspian at Tengiz in Kazakhstan. As consolation, Gorbachev told UKP to go pick something out in Baku. By the time of the oil show, they were close to a deal. But the game was changing, and UKP's upper lip went wobbly when the quasi-independent Azeris announced at the conference that the key offshore fields were being opened to competitive bid. Charlie and Don went to work, kicking off a three-year battle with UKP, Pennzoil, Unocal and a host of others for the remains of the Baku fields.

The Azeris were delighted to entertain Western offers for developing the fields. The Soviets gave them nothing but what they could steal while the supermajors were only asking for a third of what they could find. Not that the Azeris still didn't try to get more. And it wasn't as if the stealing wasn't quite lucrative. They were all doing it, the Soviets even from themselves. In fact, they budgeted for it. One expert reviewed the Soviet allowances for 'spillage' from operations and noted that if in fact these amounts were lost in operations the pools should be so large as to be visible from space. But after a hundred years of exploitation and eighty years of Soviet mismanagement, the onshore fields were dying. And offshore development required money, which the Soviets certainly didn't have. So a deal would get done.

In the end, Charlie and Sanders had dispatched all comers, including the Brits. In October 1994, Texso and its junior partners signed the 'Contract of the Century' for the development of the Azeri, Chirag and Guneshli fields. Six billion barrels. Twenty years later, the Texso consortium had invested twenty billion dollars in Azerbaijan. Given the assumed multiple of three, that was sixty billion dollars of economic activity pumped into the state. The Azeri economy had gone from flat on its back after the breakup of the Soviet Union to coming around and nursing a killer hangover. The conflict with Armenia had been reduced to a simmer. After a last-ditch coup effort, Russia had retreated from Azerbaijan to Chechnya.

And, not insignificantly, a million barrels of oil a day were pumped into the global economy.

The Caspian was not the next Kuwait, as it had been promoted by the Clinton administration, to better drive US investment and make sure the breakaway republics stayed broken. There were no 200 billion barrels of oil, no Burgan. Unless Kashagan really came in better than expected. Not likely, as its new nickname, 'Cash-All-Gone', would suggest. After the Azeri-Chirag-Guneshli field, the majors were drilling dry hole after dry hole in the Southern Caspian.

On the drive into the city they passed the same forests of abandoned oil derricks, leaking pipelines and infant-killing processing plants that Charlie remembered from before. And also new construction to service the rich, including designer shops, car dealerships, and hastily-built apartment towers suitable only for laundering drug and dirty oil money and killing their occupants in the first earthquake.

It was progress on a geologic time scale.

Thirty years later his schedule was exactly the same. Just after six-thirty they heard muffled conversation and two pairs of footsteps coming down the hallway. The door across the hallway opened and more books thumped down on the desk, as one of the pairs of footsteps walked away. Then the other pair, attracted by the aroma of hot tea and the unusual and welcome prospect of a little early morning conversation, walked to the door of the teacher's lounge and opened it.

Dr. Araz Bego was small, trim and handsome, like a three-quarters scale model of a Hollywood leading man. Well past his prime now, though, and with his sad, dark eyes and the hint of droop to his thick mustache, he projected the endearing vulnerability of a figurine that might be collected by sentimental old women. He was dressed in the universal academic uniform, an assemblage of shirt, tie, cardigan, coat, pants and shoes that was simultaneously casual, dressed-up and hopelessly mismatched.

"What, are you here about Athra again?" asked Bego. "I would think you have more important matters to deal with than ancient debts."

"I do, Araz. That's why we need to talk."

"So why is he here?" Bego was looking at Paul. "Have you decided now it is time for Jamilov to go? You will find that he is not so quick to run as Humbatov."

"Which is why the Brits picked him," said Paul. "Don't look at me, Araz, all I did was ferry in some fellow travelers. Friends of the King."

"Your Arab mujahedin," said Bego. "Some help. All they did was kill every blue-eyed Russian Azeri they came across." Azeris were Muslim, but not fundamentalists.

"Paul is here to do whatever I ask him," said Charlie. He poured a cup of tea for Bego and handed it to him.

"Perhaps to take me back to the United States?" said Bego, looking at his tea suspiciously. "To save you from going to jail? Are you try-ing to save yourself, Charlie? Things are not going well for you, so perhaps you forget old friendships. I have seen what terrible times can do to friends, to families. The Bakhar restatement, Athra, now Firebird."

"This is not about me, Araz," said Charlie. "It's about everything. Everything's gone wrong, and I need to fix it. I haven't come to take you with me. I need your help, right now, right here."

"If that is true, then you can only be here to ask me about Lazarev," said Bego. "But then you are too late. You should have come to me before." He set his cup on the counter and pulled several white cubes from a pocket and dropped them into his tea and swirled the cup. He took a sip, peering over his cup at the pepper plant. "Ach, my pepper, it does not look well." He gently picked up the plant and moved it to the next window. "They tease me, you know. No one else will eat food grown in the city. Believe me, I have eaten much worse." He rotated it carefully on the sill. "You know, the American government has been very interested in talking to me. About you. There is so much you did not tell me on your last visit."

"I couldn't tell you much, it wasn't public yet. You should talk to them. Tell them whatever you can."

Bego turned around portentously, his eyes squeezed down to a sliver. "Perhaps I should. And remind them why we chose the com-pany from America, the superpower. Let me ask you, Mr. Brown." He turned to face Paul, but then turned his head to Charlie. "If Lazarev comes back to reclaim our fields, how many divisions would your US Army send to protect a million barrels of oil a day? Particularly now that the Saudis are shipping only four, not eight?"

"We just built that pipeline to Turkey, it would be a shame to lose it," said Paul. "But I'm retired now, so I wouldn't know. Why don't I leave you two alone." He slipped out a second door at the end of the room.

"You can mention it," said Charlie. "But I don't think that's what they want to talk about."

"But they should. Because that's what Athra was all about. That's what it took. To squeeze out the Russians."

"Out of what?"

"Jamilov was nervous, he wanted to bring the Russians in. Lazarev's company, Kulneft, for 20 percent! After they sat on our fields like vultures, picking at them, shitting on them, for eighty years." His voice trailed off, and he seemed to be traveling the decades again in his mind. He snapped his fingers. "So I bought him a spine. I put together a list, everyone he knew, everyone he talked to. His mother, every cousin I could find, his imam, his grocer, all his whoring buddies, everyone that his son owes money. I told them all that either they would get rich, or the Russians. Only one. That they should tell Jamilov what to do. Go with the Americans, not the impotent Brits. That night I knocked on your door at the Old Intourist. This was the list I brought to you for Athra."

UKP was Charlie's most serious competition. United Kingdom Petroleum Company plc had been put back into private hands, but as the name suggested it was still a national institution and for all practical purposes an instrument of state policy. Or, rather, state policy was an instrument of UKP. It was thick with retired British officers and the revolving door between MI-6 and UKP never stopped spinning. The Brits were still bare-knuckled, even dirty, competitors abroad, true to their colonial legacy. In fact, just before UKP almost stole off with the first offshore Baku field they had to hastily rename it 'Azeri,' from the original '26 Baku Kommissars,' which commemorated some Azeris the Brits may have massacred, although no one could remember for sure. Of course, they were not constrained by such idealistic notions as anti-bribery laws. Very little was illegal for them, even less was off-limits. Free shopping trips to Harrods, cocaine and hookers in Dubai, crates of RPGs and mines that happened to fall off the back of lorries, UKP could expense it all, just be sure to get a receipt! And of course you weren't really using all resources at your disposal unless you had the fellows at the security service pitch in with some electronic eavesdropping, a little blackmail and perhaps a coup or two.

A week before Bego showed up at Charlie's door at the Intourist, the Azeris lead negotiator, an ex-KGB tough named Gasimov, had demanded an outright bribe from Texso of twenty-five million dollars, threatened the lives of Charlie's entire team, then promptly flown off to Thailand for a week in the sex trade with his buddies from UKP. *I know the way you drive to work, I know where you eat, I know where you drink, I know where you fuck.* The next rounds of bids were due when he returned, but Charlie sent all of his staff to the relative safety of Istanbul. He was with them on the phone in the Intourist finalizing their bid for the next day, talking in code because all the rooms were bugged, typing it all up himself, when Araz knocked on his door.

In the end, his rough proposal, whiteout and all, won the day. The Brits could throw a party, but they weren't at the time projecting power around the world. Not like the old days.

"Araz," said Charlie. "We could have put Lazarev in the deal. For something."

"And you would have, which is why I didn't tell you what I was doing. You don't know, you have no idea what is right. You think this is just about me, my own family, but it is not."

A set of his multi-volume treatise was in a bookcase in the lounge. He pulled down the last volume and cracked it open along the spine, holding the pages open to the last section, up close to Charlie. The acknowledgements section. A list of names that filled two pages and continued on. *Dedicated to our dear colleagues, victims of the Repression.*

"It is about a whole generation, many from right here in this building. 'Bourgeois specialists' who were pulled from these offices or their homes in the night and tortured by the NKVD at the prison down by the waterfront. Out in Black City they had prisons for the wives, and special prisons just for children."

Black City was the industrial zone outside Baku.

"Where you and I used to walk," said Bego, "I can see the spot where my mother held me when she waved the last time to my father, on his way in 1937 to Magadan and Kolyma in the Gulag. They made him look for diamonds and gold in the snow with no shoes, eating only bark off the trees, over an area six times the size of France. That year Moscow hosted the International Geological Congress. All the prestigious names were in the Gulag. Vydrin, Kozlov, Popov, many others. They had to bring them back to fill out the Congress. They delivered their papers and were sent back to die."

He put the volume back up on the shelf.

"This is why you didn't put Lazarev in the deal. For anything. In fact, Russia should be giving fields to Azerbaijan. The Volga perhaps, West Siberia. They killed all our best people and then they took our ideas, our land, our oil. Then they took our technology to develop their own fields. The Soviets couldn't build quality drilling pipe to save their lives. Anything quality, anything difficult, we built it right here. Drilling pipe, drill bits, seismic equipment, right here."

"Araz," said Charlie. "Sanders made payments to Jamilov and Gasimov. Big amounts."

Bego's brow furrowed, he held still, and seemed to shrink even further. "How do you know about this?"

"Talk to the US Justice Department and they'll tell you."

He darkened, a tiny storm cloud. "Jamilov and Gasimov, they still wouldn't do it. They wanted additional 'insurance.' I could pull together only so much of the money myself. I convinced Sanders to front me the forty million. He would lose his fee if you didn't get the deal. But he still made me pay him back double. I am having to steal much oil. A little bit from you, now, too. But that seems appropriate."

"I will get it back from Sanders if I have to."

"That may also be appropriate. There is something else. You asked me to consider where we could have gone wrong on Bakhar. What I found is that Lazarev was not leaving as much on the table as he claimed. He had fake data produced for Shafranik, to convince him that they were giving up more than they were. When he lost, he gave this data to your team."

The door at the end of the room swung open. A thick Azeri in tight slacks and a leather jacket burst into the room. He had a gag in his mouth and his hands were bound behind his back. Paul was pushing him along by the back of his neck.

"Worthless," said Bego, shaking his head.

"At least he was watching for your pepper signal, give him that," said Paul. He marched the man across the room to the other door. "He's going to wait for you in your office."

Charlie refilled Bego's cup. "Araz, how did you know I wanted to talk about Lazarev?" asked Charlie. "You said I should have come sooner to talk to you about Lazarev."

"This is all about Lazarev," said Bego. "Well, you and Lazarev."

"I keep hearing that."

"Tell me, were you surprised by the radioactivity that I hear about?"

"Of course I was surprised. Why wouldn't I be?"

"You might not be. If this Firebird was a continuation of Program 7."

"I have no idea what you are talking about."

"Ah." He settled back into his chair, smiling.

The door opened and another old man, a professor as well from the looks of him, walked in and then quickly out again.

"Out with it, Araz, we don't have much time. What is Program 7?"

Bego ignored Charlie's pleas and settled into his story.

"A monument to the noblest intentions of man, and its basest," said Bego. "You Americans started it. 'Atoms for Peace' Eisenhower called it. 'Peaceful' nuclear explosions. Dig canals and harbors. Blast underground storage spaces for oil, water. Eisenhower was locked in a nuclear arms race and he had to sell the American people on a massive spending program on atomic weapons and labs and underground tests. So the US created 'Operation Plowshare.' They conducted a couple of dozen explosions in the desert, mostly small, a couple of kilotons. They realized the applications weren't practical, they weren't stupid. Mostly, there was this little problem of radioactive fallout. But they collected valuable weapons data, and it put a better face on the nuclear age.

"But for the Soviets, well, the idea was a perfect fit. They constantly needed new, exciting stories that could show they were keeping up with the Americans. In fact, they were far behind on every meaningful measure. But easy, simple things done in an enormous way would do just fine. Something that would impress the man on the street, something about the Motherland to console him as he drank himself to sleep at night. Big metro stations, tractors, mines, bombs, countries. 'Gigantism,' they called it. Palchinsky, from a geological perspective, called it the 'gusher' mentality. The Motherland moving a mountain? How soon can we get started? Radiation? Not a problem! The first explosion was a hundred kiloton device they used to make a lake near the nuclear testing grounds in Kazakhstan. Instantly, they had a lake four hundred meters across and a hundred deep. The explosion was so shallow, the fallout was detected in Japan. But they just cut a channel through the lip of the crater to the Chagan River and filled it up. The chief scientist, he was the first to take a swim. Or so he said. They watered their cows at it!"

Charlie wondered where Paul was. Full daylight reigned outside the window. There were more footsteps out in the hallway, but no one came in. Undoubtedly word had traveled that Bego had a guest. Charlie might even have been recognized.

"Araz, we don't have much time," said Charlie. "What does this have to do with Firebird? What is the point?"

"The point is, they exploded over 120 nuclear devices. And mostly for what? For the mineral industries. Oil & gas, mining, geology. Over a hundred. Mining excavation, breaking up ore, oil & gas stimulation, blowing out well fires, underground storage. But the biggest single program? Over thirty-nine devices? The Geology Ministry. And for what?"

"For seismic."

Bego smiled at his quick pupil. "For deep seismic sounding. They had a huge frontier, with vast mineral resources, and they had huge programs underway to catalog it. They needed to catch up! They were behind, think big! There were thirty thousand geologists crawling over the vast Eastern spaces, taking samples. They drilled over five hundred thousand cores! And they wanted, they needed, huge seismic sounding lines. To cover thousands of kilometers of territory. They wanted to discover everything, right now, overnight!

"The nuclear devices were perfect seismic sources for this purpose. They could generate magnitude five seismic events which you could measure over three thousand kilometers away, and which allowed for long listening times, over ten minutes. They placed seismometers along endless seismic lines, stretching five, six thousand kilometers. Hundreds of devices, laying them with helicopters every twenty kilometers. They could cover the whole line with two or three nuclear devices. And, more importantly, the nuclear devices could probe all the way through the crust and down into the upper mantle, four to eight hundred kilometers down.

"Russian scientists always had to go deeper, farther than the rest. And you know that the whole Mendeleev school still had this idea that oil was created in the mantle, and leaked up into the crust. Never mind the fact that all the theories about how this wasn't true seemed to neatly predict exactly where oil was actually found. They wanted seismic that would penetrate down to the mantle.

"For ten years this was going on, starting in '65. We were building some of the seismometers. Not all of them, but they needed many, so we got involved along with others. It was good work, lots of opportunities to skim." He rubbed his fingers together.

"Then, MinGeo sends this new man, Lazarev, down to see me. It was the first time I meet him. Mid '70s. We had built four special marine seismometers a couple of years before. Now he wants us to build two hundred. But it's all very secret. This is a special group at MinGeo, no one else at MinGeo or certainly anywhere else, like the Ministry of Oil, is supposed to know anything about it. Only talk to he and Telnov. We know they come to us because it is easier to keep it secret. We do many special projects.

"And, most telling, what do Telnov and Lazarev want to focus on? They are interested only in the coda. They want long recordings, the whole thing. And only a few channels of data, just four! We knew that nuclear explosions had exceptionally robust codas, from the continuing build-up of all the late-arriving waves that were scattered in the crust. That's what they were studying, that's the part they were measuring!"

"Firebird," said Charlie.

"Yes, of course! And so we built them. In all, we built over five hundred. Remember, these weren't fancy ones like your Golden Feathers, these were big boxy things with a loop on top. You had to lower them on a cable from a boat. How you managed to use over five hundred of those things I can't imagine. What, five hundred ships at once? But they tried, apparently. It went on for years. They must have had trouble funding it because they screamed at me about costs, all the time. Our credits just wouldn't show up. So I just started shipping them seismometers that were missing parts. Ninety percent of them wouldn't even work. They never checked. Then in '83, it stopped. Nothing. They told us to destroy all our equipment. Our labs, our lines. Whatever I couldn't sell we loaded on a boat and dumped in the sea."

He walked over to the samovar and filled his cup.

"So, Charlie," said Bego. "What does this sound like to you?"

"It sounds like they were looking for something. And they never found it."

"So," said Bego. "Do you think they concluded it was not there?"

"No. Because the radiation at Firebird means he wanted me to look for him. Again."

"Yes. That is what I thought. But you also found nothing."

Someone on the staff had not gotten the word because the door opened and two youthful academics wearing atypically fashionable clothing walked into the room. Charlie was again wondering where Paul was and where and how he should move Bego when one of the young professors oddly backed up against the door while the other pulled a pistol out of his waistband. And then they were not academics but Kirill and Bearded Aleksei from the boat, which dawned on him just as red gashes opened up on their foreheads and they knelt on their knees and then rolled over to sleep on the floor. Paul Brown walked over from the other door and shot them again, twice each in the chest, his pistol making muffled bleats each time.

Paul grabbed Charlie and Bego and dragged them out the side door to the stairwell and down to the street and into the back of the delivery truck. The sat on a carpet in the back and rolled around with the cabbages until they stopped in a warehouse somewhere in Black City.

"He blamed you for the Caspian deal," said Bego. "Of course he considered the fields theirs, Russian. Then you came in, Charlie, and you took his children from him. So he thought. He never traced it back to me. He made me report to him every time you and I met. Every time you stopped for fucking tea I had to sit with one of his drunken bobos for a two-hour rectal exam. All these years I kept it secret. Now he is after me, too. So, Charlie, what do you do now?"

"I do what I can," said Charlie.

CHAPTER 17

FIRST CIRCLE

Nizhnevartovsk, West Siberia Basin
Thursday afternoon

Avinashi limped across the tarmac. The air was cool. Gray clouds hung low and full. The toes on her left foot hurt like someone was pinching them and would not let go. She found the cargo company offices in a low, concrete building separate from the passenger terminal. She looked inside for the sort Sanders might know and immediately settled on the swarthy man leaning over one of the desks up front. His gray suit was complemented by a purple shirt and gold tie, and he was talking on a cell phone while at the same time trying to sell a riot baton to the woman at the desk. Absolutely necessary for a beautiful woman such as herself, he was telling her, as he flicked a switch and it expanded to full length with a snap. That's her man.

"Yusup Sangov?"

The man turned towards Avinashi with the phone still at his ear and holding the baton as if he were in the middle of ordering more to meet the exceptional demand. He muffled the phone up against his chest and looked her up and down. He spoke to her in English.

"Miss Amy of Texso? Yes, of course it is you. I have worked for all the major oil companies. UKP? You are familiar? Now also I work for Texso. Mr. Don Sanders has assured us of your generosity and insisted we spare no expense for your trip. Miss Vicki has confirmed the same. I have arranged everything first-class. Our cars are outside. Come." He collapsed the baton, threw it in his briefcase and snapped it shut, clicking the latches, then swung it off the desk and charged the door like he was headed for the sales call of his life. Avinashi hobbled after him.

Three grimy vehicles were lined up at the curb. One of the ubiquitous Ladas, what appeared to be a four-wheel-drive van and, at the front, a white Volga sedan.

"You choose, Miss Amy. Any of the three, you choose. All are included."

The drivers currently rousing themselves to attention all looked vaguely Persian, like Yusup. Probably Tajik. What purpose three cars served she had no idea, other than he was doing his best to provide full employment for the clan. Avinashi chose the Volga, and she climbed in the back. The teenaged girl driver got behind the wheel, and Yusup sat beside her. They pulled out of the airport at a purposeful speed and motored into the city, a collection of generic apartment and office buildings, many new. On the boulevards, thin birches and alders hurried to grow before summer's end. Avi remembered her mother had tried to grow roses in Nizh like she had back in Houston but the land was cruel and unforgiving and they all died. Then six months later she was dead as well and her father raced with her and baby Ajay back to Houston, defeated but not broken.

Still on the phone, Yusup threw his free arm over the back of the seat and yelled to her from three feet away. "I have made all the arrangements for your visit to Nizh. This afternoon we show you everything. There is the Palace of Art now. Right there, quick!" He jabbed his arm left, through the driver's field of vision, at a glass-and-stone pyramid, then settled back in his seat. "Then you will eat. My brother has the finest restaurant in the city. Later this evening the puppet theater. Asal knew you would enjoy this." He nodded at their young driver, who indeed smiled knowingly. "Tomorrow, meetings with very important figures in the local oil associations. But this is still in the process of arranging. We did not know you were coming until this morning."

Avinashi addressed him in her most presumptuous, matter-of-fact Russian. "My plans have changed. I'll be having just one meeting. Tonight. With Boris Ivanov. Let me know when you have set it up. Now just take me to the hotel."

"Ivanov? No, impossible! Miss Amy, do you know who Ivanov is? All this, all this is Ivanov's." He swept his hand in front of the windshield. "Nizh is Nizneft, Nizneft is Ivanov. No one would be here if not for Nizneft. There is no other reason to be here. Back there is Nizneft headquarters, you just missed it. My cousin gives tours, we can add that to your schedule. Just a little extra. But no Ivanov. Now, you must also go shopping. Perhaps in the morning."

Dame Thatcher had absolutely no patience for this. She was taking her carrier group south to get her island back and those Argentineans had better start swimming.

"I need you to find someone in Ivanov's office right now," said Avinashi. "Tell them that Charlie Joiner asks that Ivanov meet with me tonight. Tonight. Not tomorrow, or the day after that. Do not take no for an answer. Mr. Joiner is a very senior executive at Texso, a personal friend of Ivanov. Firebird? You've heard of it? That Charlie Joiner. If you can't do it I can have Sanders call, it's just that he told me you were connected around here."

"Okay, okay," said Yusup. "I do know someone who works in the Nizneft head office." He barked at Asal and then into the phone line that he kept permanently open. Then he finally hung up. A minute later he had a call back and he began an animated discussion in what she assumed was Tajiki.

She had cut open the bear, gutted it and wriggled inside. The chopper had arrived an hour or so later and she crawled out, a bloody mess. Roy didn't land but lowered Lee on a harness. He rolled her into the basket and they hauled them both up. Lee produced some dry clothes, wrapped her in blankets and gave her hot water to drink. Tom tucked chemical heating packs into a pair of boots and slipped her feet inside. He said he couldn't promise anything about her toes, but she should make sure they didn't freeze again soon.

First they headed north. Roy topped off the tanks at an emergency fuel bladder KarLap had prepositioned on Ushakov Island and by late afternoon they had made Rogachevo on Novaya Zemlya. The airfield had been used to supply Shtokman but was down to a skeleton crew. The men gave the lost bird from Sredny a quick once over, shaking their heads and laughing. They scratched their heads at the bloody brown girl but scrounged up a shower and some too big clothes. Before anyone had a chance to ask too many questions she had talked her way on to a cargo flight headed back to Tyumen. No warm blankets or hot tea, just three and a half hours in a cold cargo hold with her hands over her ears, wondering if she would ever see Ted again. She indulged herself only once to cry. She had decided on ten minutes but then it stretched to twenty before she could stop. Then she put her emotions in a box and tied it up tight. She spent the night in Tyumen on a couch in the KarLap offices near the airport and in the morning she caught the first flight to Nizhnevartovsk. Tyumen was the original center of the West Siberian oil industry. Nizhnevartovsk was in the middle of the best fields, five hundred miles further east.

"He will see you," said Yusup, leaning away from the phone just for a moment. He stopped her with a finger in the air as he listened for details. "Yes, at the hotel tonight. In lobby. They will send a car. Yes, this is confirmed." He was nodding into the phone, then ended the call and turned around. "You are fortunate I was able to make these plans for you. No one else could have done this. Perhaps this is worth a bonus? Yes, I think so."

They stopped at the Samotlor Hotel with a jerk.

"Very well," said Yusup. "We will come in and wait with you in your room. But then you must go alone. Those are the instructions. I have a bag for you, some things that Miss Vicki asked we obtain for you, spare no expense. Asal will carry it up."

Avinashi told them she would manage. But there was one thing he could do for her.

Vicki must have thought it would be hard for them to go wrong with black. Tight black wool slacks, black cotton tee, light black jacket, black slip-ons. Give her a headset and she would be ready to work the door at a Moscow club.

The Samotlor Hotel was not fashionable. It was a no-frills business class hotel that would have blended right in outside Bush Intercontinental. Only the liberal use of blond wood paneling suggested the taiga. The lobby was filled with geeky purveyors of foreign expertise and technologies. Security tags dangled from their necks on lanyards, spelling out the names of international oil services companies. At intervals they were collected at rally points and marched off to hired shuttles.

She was unable to get a firm time from Yusup. When he said eight she could tell he was making it up. She picked at some vegetarian kebabs in the restaurant and was in the lobby by seven.

Avinashi was alarmed to find that a man in one of the red leather chairs looked familiar. She did not look away quickly enough, and now he was staring back at her. Oh god, she thought, now what does he think? He was late-middle-aged, with unkempt, thinning hair and smart eyeglasses. With his wrinkled suit and tie pulled down, he looked like a banker from the City that had gotten horribly lost on the wrong end of town looking for action. Between his knees he was protecting a thick, expandable briefcase. He had an ID around his neck but there was no way she was going to try to get a look at that. She sat in one of the red chairs and pretended to read the copy of *Russia Oil & Gas* she found on the table next to her.

By nine traffic had thinned in the lobby but he was still there, stealing obvious glances at her. Worse, he seemed to be getting feverish. He was sweating horribly and kept pulling at the neck of his open shirt. She wished Vicki had asked them to pack pepper spray.

Three hard-faced men entered the lobby. They spread out and scanned the room. One gave a sour nod to Avinashi and jerked his head towards the door. Whatever awaited her, she thought, at least she was leaving her lurker behind.

But no, here he was, following her outside! Now Avinashi started to sweat. She tried to escape into the back of their black Land Rover, but he just climbed right in after her. And the other men followed, two sitting upfront and the other in the third seat behind them. Did they think he was with her? They tore away from the curb like they were late.

No choice now but to go on the offensive, she thought. "I'm sorry, but you look so familiar," said Avinashi.

"Oh, I'm sorry, hullo," he said, acting as if he just noticed her. "Why, now that you mention it, you do a bit as well." He pinched his chin between thumb and forefinger. "Ever been to the Cynic? In Peter? Is that it?"

Of course, the odd Brit with the Aussies. She had not recognized him without his vodka.

"Oh, yes," she said.

"We were never properly introduced," he said. "Owen Crouch. Upstream production. UKP. And you are?"

"Amy Baker," she said. There was no way she was going to mention Texso, that might set off alarm bells all the way back to St. James Square. She couldn't pull off an oil services cover. Only one other option. "National Petroleum Weekly."

His face flushed and he reflexively licked his lips. Of course.

"Oh, yes, isn't that Shirin Yazdani's paper?" He went on and on about seeing her speak in Geneva. Tremendous insights, greatest respect for her work, reads it every week. And so on.

"Well, we're both off to see Generalissimo Ivanov then, is that it?" he said.

"I hope so," said Avinashi. "Any idea where we're headed?"

He peered out the window warily. They were speeding through town, headed north and east. In the distance, plumes of smoke rose thick and dark all the way to the low cloud cover. Somewhere, the sun was sinking below the horizon. It would be a dark night.

"Not a clue, I'm afraid. Usually we meet at his office. But an awful lot of cloak and dagger tonight, guess he's gone to ground already, with this Lazarev business. So much so our security just washed their hands of me. Taking no responsibility whatsoever, they said. Wankers only provide security when you don't need it." He shook his head.

Then, as if a thought had just occurred, he looked at her askance. "What, doing a story on the death of NN-UKP already? That was quick. Well, I think you're underestimating Ivanov. I hope you are." He gazed out the window, conspicuously balancing and rebalancing the multitude of factors at play, only observable to old hands like himself. "These oil generals, they're tough old birds, and they've got more money than the Army or the KGB combined. Add their dash of mafia connections, and they're not so easy to mess with. Even for someone like Lazarev. You don't get to the top out here by being a pushover. No, I wouldn't count him out yet."

"We are doing a piece on the work you're doing at Samotlor," said Avinashi. "But no preconceived notions, we'll just follow the story where it takes us."

No time for half-measures. Pull on the string, Charlie said. Pull, pull.

"Lazarev's new policy would seem to be the end of UKP at Samotlor though," said Avinashi. "No exports, no money for UKP. Other than rubles. You're not worried, Owen? May I call you Owen?"

"Oh, yes, please," he said. He pushed his glasses up the bridge of his sweaty nose and laughed nervously. "But I'm afraid that's all you'll get out of me. They wouldn't like my two cents showing up in the NPR, you can be dead certain of that. Some of those secret service boys would come talk to me. Not a pleasant conversation, I expect."

Okay, she thought, no other choice.

"Oh, of course," said Avinashi. "We never want that. But if you know anyone we should talk to, give me a nudge, will you? We never get anywhere without good-hearted people willing to point us in the right direction. Shirin spends all her time at that, frankly. All these meetings at dark, out-of-the-way restaurants. Super-confidential, you know. Not my sort of thing. Luckily she handles it all herself. Of course, to justify her personal attention, it has to be someone really in the know."

Immediately his brows unfurrowed and his head tilted to the side at a wistful angle, and she knew he was already picturing he and Shirin in a dark bistro in Chiswick.

"Yes, I will give that some thought," he said. "Avinashi, you say? Avinashi, now you describe it that way, it puts an entirely different perspective on the matter. Good-hearted person in the know, yes." He laughed. "Some would say that describes me, in fact. To a tee."

"Oh, really? In the know? But what is your role, Owen? What brings you out here, among the cloaks and daggers? Oh, sorry, I shouldn't be prying. Listen to me, hard to turn it off."

"No, no, that's quite alright, perhaps I am being too guarded. You look like the sort I can trust to use her discretion." He snuck a glance at their escorts in his obvious fashion, but if they even noticed the two of them it was not apparent. "Fact is, I have to know everything. See, UKP puts up all the money for NN-UKP, but we don't make a move at Samotlor without Nizneft's say so. Ivanov's say so. Otherwise there's always a confiscatory tax or lowball buyout offer Chernov or his other friends at the Kremlin can hit us with. Anyway, it's my job to get it. I update him on our plans every week. Keep him happy, they tell me. Like it was that easy. The man's a hoover for detail. Every new pump, every single wrench, every bloody barrel of oil, he wants to know about it. And he never forgets a word, and he'll hold you to it. Raging paranoid. Kind of fellow thinks his mother had him for ulterior motives, yet to be revealed. Every Thursday night, here I go. Not that I'm missing much action out in ol' Nizh. And besides, it had to be a senior guy, and I'm sixth man at NN-UKP overall, well, fifth now that Thompson's leaving."

The driver had his window open halfway, and the cool, damp evening air was blasting in, flipping Crouch's tie back and forth. They turned left off the pavement and headed north and west on a raised, gravel road.

"Oh bloody hell, we're going to the fields," said Crouch. "A rat hiding in the sewers. That's what we've got." His mood seemed to sink again.

The road carried them over low, open wetlands dotted with pools of water. Here and there, stranded on scattered islands of dry land rising mere feet above the water table, were stands of birch, larch and spruce. Avinashi picked up the scent of sweet, low-sulfur West Siberian crude. The driver rolled up his window and turned on the air conditioning.

"You be sure to tell Ms. Yazdani that Crouch swore this was the absolute worst place in the world to produce oil. The worst. Arctic conditions half the year, rest of the year it's like working on a goddamned sponge. Too wet to drive, too dry to float. Just water, bog and mud. See this road? Sand and silt dredged out of the floodplains. Two billion cubic meters to make all these roads and drilling pads. Do you know how expensive that is? And after all that, it still sinks. But without 'em you're not getting anywhere. Unless it's all frozen. But when it gets to fifty below, you have other problems. Some areas up north you have to heat the oil just to make it flow. But then, it sinks again, into the permafrost."

"The amount of water is shocking," said Avinashi. "There were dikes around the runway."

"This whole area is drained by the Ob," said Crouch. "But if you ask me, it does a piss poor job. Flows north to the Arctic, like all their big rivers out here. But in the spring, the river stays frozen up north and so of course the water backs up and floods the whole basin, which by the way is as flat as a billiard table. And the bog will grab that water and hold it for dear life. If you stopped all the rain and snow tomorrow, it would take you two years of normal flow to drain the basin. Sixth largest river in the world, two years! That's how much water there is here. Freezing, flooding, sinking. Lovely."

The skies were getting dark, and the black pools of water looked foul and forbidding. The road was getting worse, now single track and pockmarked. The driver slowed, but they still pitched back and forth inside the car. Fighting a losing battle to stay upright, Crouch banged his head against the window as he jammed his heel down on Avinashi's left foot.

"Ouch! Bloody hell! Oh, sorry, was that your foot?" said Crouch. "Rotten roads."

Avinashi bit her lip and gripped the door handle so hard she thought it would break.

She let out her breath slowly. "No worries," said Avinashi. "So, what miracles is UKP working out here, then? Something amazing, I'm sure."

"Miracles is right," said Crouch, rubbing his shiny head. "But we're ending up no better than the last fellow known for that particular specialty. Since we bought into Nizneft, Ivanov has stripped out the best new fields and handed them to cronies. We suckers at NN-UKP are left to care for the dead and dying, like the spinster changing dear old dad's diapers while the other kids are off spending the inheritance."

"So unfair," said Avinashi. Crouch was generating discussion now between the two men in front, something about whether to tell Ivanov something. But Crouch was oblivious and not to be stopped.

"Well, I don't care so much about how tough the job is," he said. "No, you tell Shirin, do you think she would mind if I called her that, when we meet? I expect not, she doesn't seem the sort. You tell Shirin, that for Crouch, the hardest part is seeing what we've been left to work with here. The conditions may be hellish, but this is the greatest oil basin in the world, next to the Arabian. And they've nearly ruined it with haste and half measures. It's a petroleum tragedy.

"Of course, being Russian it's the biggest oil basin, if not the absolute best. Thirteen times the size of England, thirteen times! A gargantuan, shallow bowl with deep, deep sediments. Perfect. You would have to be the unluckiest man in the world to drill out here and not hit hydrocarbons. Someone like that Joiner fellow from Texso, you would have to be that miserable." He laughed uproariously. "Tell that to Shirin."

"Absolutely," said Avinashi. A stand of trees ran right up beside the road. The Land Rover slowed to walking speed. A spotlight flashed on them from the trees. When it turned off Avinashi could just see the outlines of half a dozen men carrying automatic rifles and long tubes. One of the men approached the car and talked in low tones to the driver. The smell of oil was more pervasive, and no longer so sweet. She heard the men mention UKP and Texso, Crouch and Baker, but Crouch wasn't listening. He talked all the way through the checkpoint. The men argued about the headlights, and then the driver shut them off. He was handed a pair of night-vision goggles by the sentry but he tossed them on the seat. They pulled back on to the road, carefully.

"They discovered it by accident, you know," said Crouch. "Oh, Gubkin always told them there would be oil here, but they laughed at him. Besides, it was east of east, on the edge of the world, it was too far to care. Then in '53 there was a drilling team floating down the Ob, and they stop for lunch. They still had a quota of feet to drill they hadn't met. So, being good Sovs, they thought, hey, this place is as good as any other, feet is feet. Before anything could break, they hit gas, the Berezovskoye field. By '65 they had found their King, Samotlor. Ultimately, Samotlor will be twenty-five billion barrels, we hope and pray, with six billion yet to find. But again, this basin is typically Russian. Very egalitarian. There are half a dozen fields around five billion barrels, plus or minus, then loads and loads of peasants and minor lords, small giants, if you will. In the '60s, you couldn't turn around without bumping into a billion barrel giant."

"What a gift," said Avinashi. More trees, another checkpoint, complete with flashlight and weapons.

"God's blessing on the Russians, it seems there's oil everywhere. Brezhnev, noted petroleum geologist, says it might never run out. So they attack it in typically Russian fashion, on a massive scale and subtlety be damned. Of course, everything was controlled from

Moscow. And, in their infinite wisdom, the planners just laid out the drill sites in a square grid. No accounting for local geology, nothing. They called it the Siberian box. Just put wells everywhere, every four to five hundred meters. They drilled tens of thousands of wells. And water flooding, right from the get-go. Hard to blame them, the wells here have always been slow flowing. But then in the late '70s the easy growth in production is gone, things start to get a little tougher. But the Sovs need hard currency to prop up the likes of Cuba and Angola, buy grain and to keep the Red Army in rockets. And that only comes from oil exports. To complicate matters, the Soviet Union's own industry was using up oil like it was free, no thought for conservation or efficiency, because of course for all they knew it was free, no one ever knew the true cost of anything. But don't think Moscow is cutting the Plan. You'll make it and, by the way, did we tell you you'll have to do it with no money. No new technology, no new equipment. Well, the guys in the field, they just do what they can—drill more wells and pump more water. After the next round of drilling, the new wells are so close together you could piss on the fellow at the one over. It was like sticking a hundred straws in a milkshake. Then of course they pumped water into the fields like Hercules sending the river through the stables. The water swept past the oil, leaving millions if not billions of barrels trapped behind."

"Oh my," said Avinashi.

"Not only that, but a lot of the oil that wasn't left behind was spilled on top. Every one of those wellheads needed to be attached to the pipeline. Can you imagine how much pipe that is? Remember what I said about no money? Remember how everything freezes or sinks? The pipelines were crap and they had an impossible operating environment to begin with, so of course they broke and leaked all the time. It was like a big drip irrigation system spread out over the whole basin, except with oil. They tried to fix them, they didn't want to lose the crude. They had more people in repair than production. But they could only do so much. Oh, and if it did leak, they never cleaned up the spill. Not really their style. Moscow certainly didn't care. The

workers didn't care, they were all hoping to be back in Moscow themselves in two years. The old-timers convinced themselves it would all
just wash out to the Arctic in a few decades or so. Anyway, Russians
are very keen on the idea of acceptable losses. You may have picked
up a little of that from their history. We keep telling them that we
can't budget deaths in our plans, but still a bit of a cultural discon-
nect there."

"Hence the smell," said Avinashi.

"That back there?" said Crouch. "Just wait. Fact is, oil has con-
taminated all the water around here, on the surface and in the near
subsurface. And it's not all just going to wash out. It's stuck there,
in their drinking water, the water they use to clean, the water the
plants and animals drink. All fine as long as you don't mind a little
naphthalene or cresol in your tea or your shower. I wouldn't be out
here, frankly, if I was your age. You had children yet? Sorry, is that too
personal? Well, I can tell you, not too healthy for the kids or women
of childbearing age. I'm surprised to see single gals like yourself running around these parts, doesn't seem prudent. Rough lot out in the
fields, people tend to fall off the map. Shirin comes out here I should
show her around. She's got that big Turkish fellow, I hear, but muscle
isn't going to get you in and out. You need your wits." He tapped his
head.

"I'll be sure to mention that," said Avinashi.

"Anyway, with this sort of history, you might expect there's something left to find out here, and we hope that's six billion barrels in
Samotlor. Not the easy stuff, though, the hard stuff. We're doing full
3-D seismic, going back and rechecking for any left behind accumula-
tions, subtle, overlooked traps. We'll find it, but what a bloody mess.
And don't forget, the weather hasn't improved any. And we have to
deal with Nizneft ripping us off at every opportunity. Like having the
mafia for your business partner. They don't see it that way, of course.
For them everything is a zero-sum game, and that they should end up
ahead at the end is only right and good. Anytime we try to do something that makes business sense for us, or helps our return, of course

they feel it's coming out of their pocket. No win-win. Win-lose, or lose-win. Only options. And they lie all the time. Just habit for them, keeping things from their superiors, outsiders. We can't even get real maps, everything has to be encoded and decoded by specialists, so it can be protected from James Bond or CIA spies, but not any kid with Google Earth. Ah, here we are, the King's Lair."

The road cut out onto an embankment running out into a large lake, a few miles across. The expanse was crisscrossed by roads connecting all the drilling pads.

"Ground zero. Lake Samotlor. Know what that means? It's Khanty for 'Black Lake.' Appropriate, wouldn't you say?" Low, inky waves swept across the surface. Out in the middle, a towering flame was visible.

"Flaring gas from the gas-oil separation plant," said Crouch. "How easy do you think that was to build out here? At least they're using one. Sometimes they just skipped that stage, shipped water, oil, condensate all out in the pipeline. Hate to see what sort of twisted uneconomic logic suggested that."

"So, Owen, what is your update for this week?" said Avinashi. "Shirin would be very keen on knowing, I'm sure. Not for attribution, of course, just deep background."

"Alright, well you tell Shirin that Crouch is on a bit of a suicide mission, you could say," said Crouch, puffing his chest. "He drew the short straw, gets to float the post-Lazarev trial balloon. 'Tell him it's only prudent to slow investment down, now that Lazarev's laid down the gauntlet on exports,' they say. 'Just until it sorts itself out.' I don't need to float that one to know how he'll react, he's going to bloody explode. He knows what the real message is, we can't put another pound into this until Lazarev is put in a cage. And who's going to do that? You can see how confident Ivanov is, holed up out here. This whole Lazarev thing has gotten him a bit unhinged. Sworn enemies, those two are, goes way back, apparently. Not good for Ivanov to see Lazarev's star rising, not at all. If he does hole up, not surprised to see him holed up out here, though. Home turf. Toxic maze, this is."

Have to work out here to know your way around. And maps are not readily available, as I said. You'd need an air force and a couple of amphibious divisions to take it, which I don't believe the Neftepolk have. Not yet."

They had crossed the lake and entered another marsh with dozens of black pools and more checkpoints. Soon they were back out on another lake, smaller, with several drilling pads scattered about the surface. They pulled onto a road that dead-ended at one of the pads. Like all the others, it had a 'nodding donkey' pump, a Christmas tree wellhead and a pipeline. This pad also had a drilling rig and four crew trailers. The trailers were arranged in two pairs, the two members of each pair joined up, side-to-side. A handful of workers were onsite, working mostly over at the drilling rig. Russians and some Khanty, she thought.

"Believe me, I'll try to keep this short, then he's all yours," said Crouch. "Sorry I can't wait, but maybe I'll see you back in town." He opened his door and got out.

Avinashi climbed out the other side and stepped onto the hard gravel. Her toe was still throbbing, but then she forgot all about it because the thick, heady smell of oil hit her like someone had forced her nose into the neck of a gas can. If someone lit a match, it felt like the air would ignite.

"Oh, bollocks, this is bad," said Crouch, covering his mouth and nose with a handkerchief. "They must have had a pipe burst on the lake."

The noise of the pumping unit was oppressive, grinding and whining with every lift and dip of the horse head. Two men in fatigues, both smoking and carrying shouldered rifles, approached the car. They spoke briefly with the men from the Land Rover, who then retired to the near set of trailers.

The taller of the two men in fatigues, a balding man, seemed to be in charge. "Owen Crouch, you will brief me first. You, Sharma, go with him."

"Hullo, what's this? Sharma? Look Sergei, Ivanov can wait on his puff piece, I've got to get back. I demand to see him immediately.

Where is he?" The bald man hit Crouch in the face with the heel of his hand, dropping him to the ground.

"That's not necessary, not at all," yelled Avinashi, in Russian.

"This is none of your affair," said Sergei, kicking Crouch with his boot again for good measure. Crouch was curled up in the sand and retching. She kneeled down beside him and felt for his glasses on the ground. Until the second soldier grabbed her by the arm and dragged her over to the far set of trailers, practically lifting her off the ground.

Inside, the two connected trailers had been opened up to each other, to make one space. The interior had clearly been furnished by and for men. A cheap bookcase jammed with bottles stood against the far wall. Two men sat on a couch watching a pornographic movie on a big screen TV. They looked at her indolently then returned to watching the film. She could still hear the pump through the thin walls, a continuous cycle of moaning and straining that when mixed with the noises from the TV made it sound like huge machines were outside having laborious sex with the earth. Other male detritus littered the room. Parts of machinery degreasing in buckets of solvent. A bloody t-shirt thrown over the back of a chair. Cardboard boxes filled with DVDs. Pornographic pictures hung on the walls, together with seismic traces and maps with hand-drawn boxes and arrows. There were bags of trash in the small kitchen, but no dirty dishes. The other trailers must have the mess hall. There was only one interior room, a bedroom, where she could see a young woman in her panties and bra lying on the large bed watching *When Harry Met Sally* dubbed in Russian. Avinashi wanted to retch.

At the far side of the room a bear of a man sat at a metal desk yelling into a cell phone. An old bear with gray hair growing thick and straight up in wavy, silver flames from the top of his square, statuesque head. He wore an expensive pale blue dress shirt matted with sweat, with half the buttons undone to reveal thick masses of salt and pepper chest hair. Inside dark rings, his eyes were volcanic. He continuously doused them with drops as if to keep them cool and operational.

When he finally saw her his eyes bulged and flashed at her minder. He barked a final threat into the phone and slammed it down on the desk. In the other hand he held a radio handset, connected to a large radio with a coiled cord. Radio traffic sounded over the speaker in sharp bursts of voices and static.

He yelled at the minder in Russian. "Fucking Joiner can't do anything right. He destroys everything, and then this is what he sends me?"

The harder they press on me, thought Avinashi, the harder I shall become. Like steel.

"I apologize for wasting your time," said Avinashi, in Russian. "I can see that you don't need Texso's help. You will be happy and content to hide in the swamp until the end of your days."

He stopped and looked at her again, more closely, trying to see who would talk to him this way.

"You wanted to help me, you should have found some oil," said Ivanov. He picked up a dirty towel and wiped the sweat off his face. "I always thought Joiner was smarter than Lazarev. That's the only reason I helped him. But now he has failed and put me in a very dangerous situation."

"We haven't failed. Just taken a detour. We need to adapt. Quickly."

"Hah! You do work for Joiner. Same shit he would be telling me right now." Inexplicably he undid his belt and dropped his pants, kicking them aside. "Do you mind? I feel constrained. Or is it just you, Miss Sharma? I have always had affection for the black ones, My only weakness, I believe."

"That's too bad, if only I had affection for the fat ones, we would be a perfect match."

He yelled at the two men watching TV. They shut it off and went outside, leaving them with only the sounds and smells of copulating metal. He squirted into his open eyes again. He never seemed to blink.

"Okay, all business," said Ivanov. "The situation. Perhaps you have better sources in Moscow than what I buy with all my money. Mine, they say the Army is moving behind Russian Path. The whole world is going to be a shithole, but ours will once again be the biggest, most glorious shithole of all. Same old joke. 'Commissar, my neighbor has a cow, I don't. So you want a cow? No, I want you to shoot his!' Lazarev is shooting your cow right now. Shooting it and leaving it to rot. And so I also will have no cow. No new pumps, no money for 3-D seismic, no reservoir management, no new pipelines. Those siloviki good-for-nothing fucks are losing control of the situation. What else are they good for, and now they can't even do that? They got soft, too much time fucking Romanian gymnasts and getting fitted for English suits. And now he will try to shoot me also, right after your cow."

"No he won't," said Avinashi. "He still needs you to produce oil for Russia."

"Did Joiner tell you anything?" said Ivanov. Actually, no, thought Avinashi. "Or could he only get someone completely ignorant to come here? Someone who has no idea how fucking dangerous it is to be here right now?"

"I've been in worse spots," said Avinashi. Multiple times, but only in the last week, she thought. "And right now I don't really care how dangerous it is."

"Icy, she is. Like the Snow Maiden, maybe. Okay, how am I supposed to help you help me?"

"Why don't we start with you rescuing me from my ignorance, and tell me just what it is I seem to be missing. Unless you are too busy."

He smiled, but more as if he had finally figured her out than that she was amusing. "What you are missing? As many years as in a man's grown life, I am afraid. That is how long I have been tangled with Olezka."

Ivanov poured himself a glass from the bottle on the table and slammed it back. He filled it up again, and also another dirty glass on the desk, which he pushed over to her. She hesitated. There was an explosions of voices on the radio, excited. She picked up the glass. It now seemed like such a small thing.

"Na Zdrovia," she said, and swallowed it all. Ivanov reciprocated.

"My men, they say it is because all I can think about is oil. I am obsessed by blackness. I find it exciting. Does this flatter you? To be the object of so much desire?"

"Let me think. No, not at all. Get to it, you're wasting our time."

A few more drops in his eyes and he settled into his story.

"My entire life, Olezka has been nothing but a curse to me, from the very first time my crew arrived to take over one of his drilling operations. November '73, it was up near Pokachi. It's forty below, and this MinGeo guy who came from Tyumen all of six months ago is walking me all over his rig, telling me how to do this, how to do that, like I hadn't been doing this for two years already. Well, we beat him right there and then. Pretty bad. Maybe not the wisest thing to do, but you had to know him. He was this tall thing, and I guess he had trouble finding boots big enough for his feet, which were like boats if you must know, because he had this funny, annoying walk. And of course, the worst, he knew more than everyone, as he would tell you. Not only that, but he thought petroleum was a dirty business, and though he could do it better than all of us he would rather be back in Moscow, studying mathematics. Well, he was practically begging us to beat him. And yes, truth be told, it was not the last time we beat him. It may have happened a few times after that. It was long ago.

"You have to understand, I was with MinNeft, the Ministry of Oil, Lazarev was with MinGeo. We had to work together, but we were always fighting. We were not then organized like the Western integrated oil companies, not like Nizneft today. Every function was in a different Ministry. Imagine that your Ford built only engines, and General Motors built only the rest of the car. Now, work together! Compete, cooperate! It was chaos. Finger-pointing, scapegoats, secret battles. And so it was nearly my obligation on behalf of MinNeft to beat him for being so insolent. And, of course, he was not singled out for this treatment, we beat many of them. It was so easy. They could do math, but they were not so good at swinging chains and hammers.

"Besides, MinGeo had the easy work, why is he making mine so much more difficult? Exploration in the Siberian basin, it was child's play. Find an anticline, drill a shallow hole down to the Upper Cretaceous. That's it! Oil, gas, it's right there! And it was all within a stone's throw of the Ob. It's easy, it's cheap. Then, of course, MinGeo they drill some delineation wells, make a wild guess at the recoverable hydrocarbons, multiply it by two, maybe three, give that to the Ministry of Oil to produce, copy to Gosplan. If MinNeft can't find it, well, then they are slackers and wreckers.

"And there we are, with the impossible task of pumping oil out of a frozen swamp with worthless equipment designed twenty years ago. The ministry finding the oil always got more money that the ministry pumping the oil out of the ground, is that not always the way? It's the finding that makes money, right? Not the pumping. That is the stupidity of Moscow. This is what happens to the brains in the cities. MinNeft suppliers were always the lowest priority of the Central Committee, and so we had nothing, but were expected to do everything. So we had to build everything ourselves. MinNeft had to build its own factories to do what the Ministry for Oil & Gas Machinery would have done, if it had received sufficient funds.

"And then MinGeo tries to take our responsibilities. Well, they say, in virgin territories it is only natural that the explorers should have greater responsibilities. So they start drilling and producing oil out of all the best fields and then they bill us for the service! And what they charge! And they leave us with the rest, the hardest. Tell me, who does this?"

Avinashi had an answer but kept it to herself. He poured them both another drink, and this time he made the toast and they drank. The radio had gone silent, but the pumping continued.

"What you must understand also is that we were all a bit crazy out here back then. Living was very difficult. There was nothing. It was cold, it was dark, it was dirty, there was no civilization for a thousand miles. Americans can live without culture, without feeding the mind, it doesn't bother them. You could give that box of shitty DVDs to an American and he would be happy and mentally challenged for the rest of his life. Russians, we need great books, we need great music. Not just pop, but great works of Art! Important films, concerts, profound books and lectures. We had none of that. Not like today. Today, in Nizh, thanks to Nizneft, thanks to me, yes, we have the Art Institute, a ballet, an orchestra, a world-class library. I can be fair as well, because I will say that I think Lazarev in particular, he suffered out here more than any of us, back in those days. He was always a clever one, I can say that, even though I beat him for it. There is nothing inconsistent in that.

"He went to the Arctic to get away from us, I think. Of course, he got lost. He should have died up there, would have served him right and saved us all a lot of trouble. Particularly me. But that's how he is. He refuses to die, he is like a cockroach. Can't be killed, and a constant irritation. He was going to a drift station, to be a great MinGeo polyarnik, he tells us. He thought he would become like Papanin, a true superman, a hero, and leave us all behind. Instead he was the same little shit. He drove everyone crazy up there just like he did here and they all killed themselves. He survives, but a little of him dies as well and he did come back different. You have seen the movie, so you know the story. But there is some truth to the myth. He was more focused, more ruthless. Not so easy to beat, maybe.

"In the years when he got back, the late '70s, it was very difficult for all of us. For MinGeo, the rate of growth in discoveries begins to decline. MinNeft, our production also starts to level off. The Plan, however, stays the same. Production targets do not yield so easily to reality.

"We complained about the Plan and the planners, but for those of us who grew up in those days, there was something mystical about it, about the whole exercise. We planned every activity down to the hour of labor, down to each individual nut to be used, each milliliter of lubricant. It was a complete cataloging of our entire world, known and unknown, a guide for one's life and presented by unseen distant forces. For me, myself, it was the closest I will ever come to being religious. Of course, the Plan bore none but a distant relation to reality. One engineering plan suitable for every well? Laughable. But can you not say the same thing about Lazarev's feverish icon worship, that it too was divorced from reality? We lost something when the Plan was put aside. Lost our vision of life. That is my opinion.

"MinNeft, we were struggling with the Plan in those days. There is much finger-pointing. But Lazarev, he fulfills the Plan. He comes back from the Arctic and then boom, boom, boom, three supergiant discoveries, twelve billion barrels by himself! I told you he came back different. Now he is New Soviet Man, superman. He goes to Moscow, top job in MinGeo, where he can scheme with his fellow egghead geologists against MinNeft, against everyone. He had this crazy idea to create another cartel, just like OPEC. It will save the Soviet Union from going bankrupt. A MinNeft friend in Moscow tells me this. But then, it all falls apart, oil prices crash. Then he gives the Caspian away! Lets Joiner and the blackarse Azeris outsmart him. Russian fields, gone, now to Texso. So he is out, out of MinGeo, back in Siberia, holed up in Kogalym, working in some despicable MinGeo exploration office, doing nothing from what I can see.

"Then, of course, in '91 we had the chaos. It was unimaginable, the great unwinding of everything, of the Empire. Lazarev, to his credit, sees the opportunities. As do I. We have talked about this in calmer moments. The benefits to an oil company of cooperation and integrated control of all key elements. Each of us wants to finally build an integrated oil company, like Texso, a Russian Texso. We end up competing for all the best assets in the Siberian basin, one by one. Loans-for-shares, auctions, outright sales, we do it every which way. And yes, there is also blackmail, kidnappings and bloodshed, you may have heard. But not as bad maybe as that, and more by Lazarev than me. Fundamentally, I am a civil person. Lazarev, he started in Kogalym, and the Povkhovskoye Field, which he had discovered. Then he added more fields, pipelines, refineries,

distribution. Very good assets, always cheap. There was so much to
be had, we both did well, to tell the truth. His became Kulneft, mine
became Nizneft.

"Kogalym, it became practically a closed city again. Everyone
worked for Kulneft, the city was Kulneft. He never left the city. Even
inside the city, he was nearly invisible. They revered him there like a
god, and he was about as mysterious. Stalin was never worshiped like
Lazarev is. And he made them go to church! Three, four hours! If
that does not show Russians are the most spiritual of all I don't know
what does. He limited their drinking, closed all the casinos, no fun
at all in Kogalym, they say. His company runs like a fine watch. The
church they protected him, too. He also started working on the Army.
He donated to the Church, built his brotherhood, stocked it with military. Money and religion, pride. Powerful combination. Remember,
this is the late '90s, the country was falling apart, the KGB was weak,
they were in retreat."

The door to the trailer opens without a knock and Sergei enters
the room. He whispers in Ivanov's ear, then waits for him to consider.
Not long, as he quickly whispers back in Sergei's ear.

"After ten years of this, he was so big the siloviki, by the time they
get into power, it is too late. They cannot touch him. They send six
of their hard men out to see him in 2002, to tell him how it will be,
their plans for re-nationalization of key strategic industries, and they
were never heard from again. Balls! Even I cheered for him a little
bit. We found them the next year in the spring, south of Langepas.
They were hanging from an abandoned wellhead and they had no
skin. They probably remembered things they had forgotten when
they were two!" He laughed loudly.

"Those fucking siloviki. Lazarev made them afraid of all of us.
They tried to station a brigade of KGB in Surgut. Their aircraft
started exploding every time they tried to fly back to Moscow, their
cars exploded on the street. He was worse than the mujahedin in
Afghanistan. He killed judges, federal inspectors. He kidnapped the
mother of the head of the FSB, for crying out loud. I think the siloviki

they would have nuked the entire town of Kogalym but the oil was too valuable, they couldn't risk the fallout.

"You know the rest. He created Russian Path, bought a TV station, started talking about all this Third Rome shit to his Brotherhood, all that Old Believer crap. Is any of this helping? I can't imagine what good this could be to anyone now."

The vodka and the smell of the oil were making Avinashi sick. She wanted to find an armored room somewhere and lie down.

"We are told he was using nuclear weapons to look for oil," she said. "What do you know about that?"

First, he said nothing. He rolled his glass back and forth on the desk.

"There were rumors that MinGeo was using nuclear. I don't know about Lazarev. MinGeo was conducting nuclear tests, to see if they can fracture structures to free up the oil formations. Big disaster, all they managed to do was irradiate about a dozen major fields. I put my worst teams on production for those fields and we sold the oil to the Albanians, who sold it to the Italian mafia. God knows what they did with it."

Just ask it, she thought. We won't be passing by this way again.

"Charlie thinks Lazarev found something in the Arctic," said Avinashi. "When he was up north. Don't ask us why. Just a hunch."

"Why, why do you ask me? Where else have you stopped? Who else have you been talking to?"

"What do you know? You do know something." She sat forward in her chair. "You have to decide, Boris Romanovich. Are you going to be able to hide forever, or are you going to fight him? If you are going to fight him, we can help you. But you need to tell me what you know."

"Who? Who are you? How can you help me, why should I even try?"

"Lazarev, he probably is coming for you. You think you can hide out here? His Neftepolk will find you. They'll fly out and drop down on you from helicopters. They'll buy the local army commander off. He'll think you're on the way out. Particularly if you keep hiding like this. Your only chance is to fight back. With everything at your disposal. That includes us."

The bald Sergei returns. He has blood on his sleeve. He whispers in Ivanov.

"Suka!" He turns to Avinashi. "Lazarev has paid off the British. They are cutting their funding in concert with Lazarev's policy announcement. They are all in league against Russia!"

Avinashi could try to press Crouch's case, to clarify. Would it change his mind? It certainly would not help her find what she needed. And what did she know about UKP's true intentions? She hated herself. So this is how you die, a little bit at a time.

"Yes, your circle is getting smaller, Boris Romanovich."

"Okay, fine. I will tell you this, but no one else is to know, except Joiner.

He sends Sergei back out the door.

"I told you in the late '70s MinGeo, for the most part, was struggling to find oil. Of course, this was natural, but Moscow was not so understanding and they were screaming mad. We could hear them yelling all the way out here.

"No one could find oil except for Lazarev, that is. He had discovered Sutorminskoye in '75, right after he got back from the Arctic. That is when he first started to become a big shot. 2.5 billion barrels. Then, the dry period began. But then, in '81, Lazarev again. He drills Verkhne-Kolikyeganskoye, 5 billion barrels! Then the next year, Priobskoye, over 4 billion barrels! No one is discovering anything but Lazarev. He starts to get anything he wants out of MinGeo, and Moscow. He meets with Brezhnev himself.

"Well, I was most curious. I know him. Clearly, this was not all Lazarev. He had some trick, something extra, that he was keeping from us. We made it known that we would pay to discover what it is. Eventually we were approached by an ex-KGB officer from Novosibirsk. He tells us a story, about a scientist. A scientist that he sold to MinGeo back in the early '70s. This KGB was running a *sharashka* in Novosibirsk. Do you know what this is, a sharashka? Do you read, Miss Baker? Have you read Solzhenitsyn, Dante? I expect not. Solzhenitsyn wrote a book, the *First Circle*, about a sharashka. These were the Gulags for scientists, where they could be repressed, but still work for the State and not starve to death. They were too valuable. Solzhenitsyn called them the First Circle, after Dante's First Circle of Hell. A favorable spot only in comparison to the rest of hell.

"Anyway, this officer, he recalls selling this scientist to MinGeo back in the early '60s, before they were all disbanded. He knows that this man is now working for Lazarev. Up in Kogalym. If we want to know what is going on, he said, we needed to find this scientist. So we paid him. You know this officer. Yes, your Chernov." He clapped his hands and laughed. "You are surprised, I can see this.

"So we find this person up in Kogalym. The first team I send up never comes back and they move the scientist. But money talks, even in Kogalym, and our second team grabs him. We beat him a little, he tells us everything. The scientist, Kolotkov, he has developed this technology that Lazarev is using to find oil. Some witchcraft, that he and two other scientists dreamed up. Kolotkov himself is a musician, really, but he studies music more like a mathematician. The other two, they are a geophysicist, naturally, but then a fucking botanist! A botanist! What? Crazy! But together, these fucking prisoners figure out a way to listen for oil. God only knows how this happened.

"But he was afraid of Lazarev, and just a little reluctant to talk to us. And perhaps we hit him just a little too hard. Who is to know? First he started telling us everything, then he started making things up, then he goes and dies on us before we figure out which is which. I keep telling them, interrogate for truth, torture to verify, but they never listen. No discipline. But, he dies. Too bad, we think. But then, no more Lazarev supergiants. All is very quiet up in Kogalym. Lazarev suspects this is me, but he never knows for sure."

"What, what was Kolotkov making up? What did he tell you?"

"He tries to tell us that the biggest find ever, the highest reading they ever had, the biggest sound, if you will, bigger than all the rest, was from this box Lazarev carried back from the Arctic. The one he carried out on his back, or his sled, or whatever."

The door flew open and one of Ivanov's men came into the room with electronic goggles pushed up on his head and an exotic rifle. Boris Romanovich, men on the lakeshore, he said. Come, see.

"I am almost finished," said Ivanov. "But not just yet." He got up from behind the desk and started advancing on Avinashi.

"You may have noticed that I cannot stop staring at you, Avinashi. You are attractive, yes, and so pleasingly black, but the truth is that I stare at you because I indeed have no eyelids. Yes, none! How does this happen? Well, it is because a black devil in the office pool pounces on me and seduces me, bewitches me. I am driven completely insane and of course I chase her, and I start fucking her, I make her mine. I fuck that deep, dark blackness. She is not so happy with this, and she fucking rips my eyelids off."

He is backing her into the bedroom. The Russian woman runs out.

"After she ripped my eyelids off I never stared so hard at anyone as I did when I fucked her. And when I was done I had her sunk deep in the black lake. Where I would have put her husband and children if he hadn't run so fast. The whole experience left me so...unsatisfied. But you look very, very much like her, so..." He continues toward her and gives her a hard shove back on the bed, yanks his shorts off and falls down on top of her.

Avinashi pulled the riot baton out of her waistband and flicked it open. Then it is a blur as she whips it back and forth against that stone block of a lidless head, again and again and again. He howls in pain. She swings as hard and as fast as she can. For her mother, for her self. Like her mother before her, she strips the flesh from his head as he screams.

The right wall of the trailer disappears in blistering fireball. They are thrown together against the opposite wall. She is dazed, but struggles to stand. The trailer is on fire. She staggers towards the door, with Ivanov close behind her.

She still couldn't hear, but it was cool outside, even cold, and dark as a cave. No stars, no moon. A soldier handed the goggles to a bloody Ivanov, who pulled them over his eyes, cursed, and handed them back to the soldier.

"See how I pay out vengeance to my enemies, Miss Sharma, so you know what awaits you." He rips a rifle from a soldier, rests it on the hood of one of the SUVs and starts firing, in methodical, regular shots. They rang out over the lake, disappearing. He checked his handiwork with the night-vision goggles. Gone, he said. Then he ripped them off, yelling in surprise.

"A fire, on the far shore," he said, wailing. "Where are my fucking drops!"

Avinashi could see them now, unaided. Small circles of light, strung out along the far shore. Far apart and irregular, like a string of cheap Christmas lights. Now they were growing.

"Gavno!" said Ivanov. "They're trying to light the lake. Now we know why the pipes all sprung leaks at once."

One of the SUVs exploded. Avinashi could feel her face burn, a small piece of metal caught her in the neck. She dove for the ground as the other vehicles started to light up, one by one. Then the trailer. And the other trailer. The platform was an inferno of burning metal. The nodding donkey groaned and pumped through it all.

Ivanov was crouched with two of his men behind the diesel generator for the pump. She crawled over to him. Her best chance of survival was to stay close to him. If anyone was getting out, it was Ivanov.

"They want to flush us out along the road," yelled Sergei. "Surely an ambush. Our helicopter is five minutes away. We will wait for evacuation by air. We will have to be quick. The men will lay suppressing fire."

The lake was a ring of fire, and it was closing. Avinashi stared into the flames and black smoke, a vision of hell. The smell of burnt oil and char was overwhelming. The only straw to cling to was the thumping of the helicopter approaching, lights out, through the blackness. She couldn't see it, but it was close. Now, the thumping completely drowned out the sound of the pumps.

The helicopter appeared, finally, but as another ball of fire exploding over them. The burning hulk of metal fell into the flaming lake, throwing hot oil and water up on the pad, all around them.

"You, you have done this," yelled Ivanov, at Avinashi. "You have brought this upon us. There is no way out for us now. I can only buy my way out. You will be part of my offer. And if I had Joiner here, I would gut him and sell his head on a stake. But you'll do. Take her."

Sergei grabbed her and pinned her head against the ground. She could see Ivanov getting up from their hiding place and yelling and cursing at unseen ears out in the lake. There was no way anyone was going to hear that, she thought. They had not come to listen.

Ivanov ran into the water with a rifle and started shooting at the opposite shore, more defiantly than effectively. Neftepolk tracer rounds raked the lake and Ivanov, setting both aflame. Oil and water from the black lake turned Ivanov into a fiery onion dome, bright and brilliant.

Sergei took a wrench to the head and went down in a heap. A strong hand grabbed Avinashi's arm so firmly she yelped in pain. One of the Khanty workers pulled her along so hard and so fast she thought he was going to dislocate her shoulder. At a run, he pulled her all the way across the pad and around the other side of the derrick. There was a small boat pulled up, in a section of the lake that was not burning so much. He threw her in the bottom, covered her with a damp tarp and pushed the boat out into the lake.

Avinahsi's mother kept her daughter warm while she burned Ivanov and his men. Burned them all as they screamed and turned them into dark billowing clouds that disappeared into the black skies.

CHAPTER 18

POLYARNIKS

St. Petersburg
Friday late afternoon

C harlie pounded the door so hard it danced on its hinges. Avinashi could see others inside through the dark, arched windows, but the door was locked. If anyone was moved to look outside, she doubted they would be further inclined to open up. With his haggard face and bloodshot eyes and his banging, Charlie did not look like he was interested in a casual stroll through polar history.

Avinashi still felt cold and damp from the shower. After the Khanty smuggled her out of Nizh, she had made her way back to Pete and met Charlie at a gaudy, pink palace where Sanders had secured a couple of quick, anonymous rooms. With the worn-out women and tasteless décor, Avinashi could only assume it was a bordello. She was disappointed when a blonde woman with a bandaged face hugged Charlie and overall seemed entirely too friendly with him, and Avinashi wondered how well she really knew him. But they made her a quick lunch of pickled vegetables and cheese and bread and there was a place to clean up and close her eyes for an hour while someone washed her clothes. When she awoke she was tired and sore but alert.

Sanders had met them downstairs in the empty bar. It was mid-afternoon but he was already drunk from his bottomless glass of scotch. Lazarev had made his move overnight, he told them, and the tanks had rolled into Moscow. The Black Purge was underway and the President was dead.

"Story is Lazarev shot Putin himself. Stuck the pistol in his mouth and splattered his brains all over a Nevsky portrait. I don't get it. Gotta hate somebody to do it up close like that. Something personal."

"You're probably right," said Charlie.

Sanders said he was getting out. A mafia plane, leaving from a private airstrip and then onto Sweden. They could come if they wanted. This was it, the last helicopter out of Saigon. Charlie and Avinashi had looked at each other, but only briefly. They were too close. Paul seemed completely unperturbed. If it wasn't dangerous, what good was he?

Avinashi had called the concierge at the Europa and was told the Arctic and Antarctic Museum was open until six o'clock. Shortly after five they were in one of the bordello's black SUVs heading back towards the city center. After they passed the Moscow Rail Terminal they turned left off Nevsky Prospekt and drove a few blocks down Marata. The driver dropped the three of them across the street from a dingy yellow building with white columns and a green, copper dome. It stood apart from its surroundings, rising just above the neighboring five-story buildings and sitting at an angle to them, facing the corner of the block. Above the columns, in large gold, Cyrillic letters, were the words 'Arctic Museum.'

Charlie kept pounding, and Avinashi was worried that someone would stop them. She was turning to look at Paul who was watching the street when the latch threw open with a shot, and the door pulled open just a few inches. A tiny woman with short gray hair and a broad, flat Slavic face stepped halfway through the crack and stared at them with small black eyes the size of peas. She was dressed in thick, dull clothes, and a pair of black-framed glasses hung around her neck on a steel chain.

"Did it not occur to you that perhaps we are closed?" she said. Apparently they were that obvious, thought Avinashi, because she was addressing them in English. "Come back tomorrow. It will be my day off." The woman stared at them, calm, blameless and triumphant.

Charlie looked to Avinashi. "I'm sorry, we thought you were open until six," she said. "There do appear to be others inside."

"That is correct," said the woman. "But tickets are sold until five. So, there you are. Good evening." With a nod, she backed in behind the door.

Avinashi put her foot in the door. Her left, unfortunately. "Director Alexandrov insisted we stop in to see the Museum," she said. "He said that Dr. Tarasov would be delighted to show us around."

"Very doubtful," yelled the woman from behind the door, now banging it on Avinashi's sore foot with surprising strength.

"Perhaps I should call the Director," said Charlie. "And with whom shall I say we spoke?" The woman stopped banging on Avinashi's foot and pulled it open.

"He would know, instantly," said the woman, putting on her glasses to get a better look at them. "You may call me Tatiana, as everyone does. I am the curator. Come in, if you must." She turned and limped away into the dark foyer.

But it was not a foyer, Avinashi thought, as she followed Tatiana through the darkness and into the bright whites and blues of the open center. That is why the building was at an angle to the street. It was aligned latitudinally, and they were entering from the darkness of the West into the truth of the East. Except that up in the dome, at the top of the tan and yellow marble columns, instead of Christ looking down from heaven, there was a mosaic of Antarctica, adorned with the Russian words for 'Continent of Peace and Friendship.' A slogan that perhaps said more about the other continents than the one with no people.

Directly beneath the high dome, on the ground in front of them, sat another. The top portion of a globe, several feet across, lay on a low stone table. It displayed a relief map of the Arctic, showing the five nations facing each other across the abyss. More so than the other oceans, it was dominated by its large, continental shelves, covering half of its total area. The Siberian shelf was the largest on earth. But in the center, the big basins—the Nansen, Amundsen, Makarov and Canada—reached depths of over four thousand meters. You could sink the State of California in the Amundsen, bury it in ice and never see it again. Splitting the basins were the big ridges, the spreading Gakkel Ridge between the Amundsen and the Nansen, and the Lomonosov Ridge, reaching up and across the Pole, splitting the Amundsen from the Makarov. Further towards the Pacific end, also the Mendeleev and the Alpha.

A handful of tourists were spread out around the nave exploring other icons of the polar world. Dioramas of reindeer and penguins, models of ships and tents in glass cases, gigantic landscapes of men struggling with ships and sleds and ice, and everywhere photographs of serious men in beards wearing leather trimmed with sheepskin. Paul was inspecting a stuffed polar bear lunging off a white stand. Tatiana waited on them next to the low Arctic map, hands behind her back, seemingly eager to see her inconveniently important guests in and out.

"A church," said Avinashi.

"Yes, that is correct," said Tatiana, humming her approval. "Although not so long ago the proper term was 'architectural monument.' Early nineteenth century."

At the head of the space, in the sanctuary, was a tent. It was rectangular, and low with a slight peak, not much taller than Avinashi. 'CCCP' was stitched on the side, in large letters.

"Oh my," said Avinashi, rushing as best she could around the low dome towards the tent, doing her best to appear properly excited. Charlie and Tatiana followed. "Which station would this tent be from? It looks old, it wouldn't be SP-1, would it?"

"You are not a novice in these matters," said Tatiana, somewhat warily. "Yes, this is a tent used by the great Papanin in 1937 to reach the Pole. The structure is not large, as you can see. But then he was a small man, not much taller than yourself. Small, but quite capable. A vigorous man."

Tatiana appeared to flush and Avinashi started to do some quick math before she stopped herself, it being none of her business. The articles of daily life on the ice were displayed around the tent. Log books and a sextant. A slim pickax and a spade with a canvas cover. An insulated bottle and a small, oil-burning stove. Wooden radios and a phonograph. An ammunition belt that must have held two dozen shells. And thin wool and cotton clothing that made Avinashi shiver just to look at it. Not much between man and Arctic.

"Your English," said Avinashi. "You must have spent time abroad."

"Yes, at Cambridge. Three years in the early '90s. But I returned."

"Of course," said Avinashi, pausing for a moment to appropriately acknowledge Tatiana's loyalties. "We are quite interested in the drift stations," she continued. "Director Alexandrov's stories made the whole topic seem very compelling. That's why we wanted to see Dr. Tarasov. The director said that he was directly involved in their operation."

"Tarasov was involved, but not directly" said Tatiana. "He was never on the ice. No, he organized all logistics from right here, in Leningrad. This was until the stations were suspended in 1987, before the unpleasantness. Now he plays full time with his toys in my basement, from which it is my deepest desire that he be removed, which you may feel free to tell the Director."

"Logistics," said Avinashi, eyeing Charlie. "He sounds like just the person we should talk to."

"Trust me, you do not. I can help you. You see, I was on the ice, with SP-21. You are surprised, I know, I appear too young. But yes, I had just graduated from the Shirsov Institute, in Oceanology. I was selected personally by Director Papanin."

Of course, thought Avinashi. Vigorous indeed. She tried to imagine young Tatiana, a cute, quick little pixie.

"Fascinating," said Avinashi. "Could that perhaps be why you limp ever so slightly."

A hint of a smile appeared on Tatiana's face, like the restrained pride of a teacher not wishing to spoil her prize pupil. "Yes, correct again. And from your similar walk, shall I assume you have spent time on the ice as well? Perhaps quite recently?"

"Yes," said Avinashi. "A very short time, nothing like yourself. But we are fascinated, we must hear all about it. We are also most interested in SP-19. Director Alexandrov was telling us some of this tragic story, we simply had to hear the rest. And of course, with Minister Lazarev's involvement, it's just so timely, you must agree."

Tatiana crumpled her nose. "SP-19, the whole affair was disgraceful. Much like Lazarev himself, I am not afraid to say. And likewise, as you may know, Minister Lazarev is no friend of the Institute. Yes, you would have to speak to Tarasov regarding this. I was on the ice with SP-21 during the whole incident. But I must be frank with you, Tarasov speaks with no one. He is a very odd man. Why would the Director suggest this, I wonder?"

"Because the director thinks that I will buy him new toys," said Charlie.

"And why would you do this?" said Tatiana.

"Because we are working to develop petroleum production in the Russian Arctic," said Charlie. "I am the Chairman of KarLap, and Avinashi works with me."

"Yes, of course," said Tatiana, eyeing Charlie. "I know you. Although not this little polyarnik, or your dangerous friend over there. Well, your task has become impossible now, has it not? What with this Lazarev foolishness? Another fit of Russian madness, when will they end? Only when we destroy the entire world, I am afraid."

"Well, see, that's what we're afraid of, too," said Charlie. "That's why you must get Tarasov to tell us about SP-19."

"I see." She fixed Avinashi with a hard stare. "Director Papanin survived the Great Purge, as you know, when Schmidt did not. He always told me, 'Let them underestimate you, then do what you can.' Please stay while I close up."

Ignoring their protests, she shoved the remaining visitors out onto the street thirty minutes early and locked the doors.

In the narthex, behind a curtain, were stairs that led to the basement. There were several flights down and it was dark, but on the first landing there was a switch. Tatiana flipped it and a weak light showed the rest of the way down.

"He's down here," said Tatiana. "He never leaves. I'm not sure where else he lives."

At the bottom was a battered and rusted steel door. Charlie helped Tatiana pull it open, scraping the bottom across the concrete floor. She stepped inside a dark room, and flipped on another light. A large, windowless room, painted gray. The ceiling was double-height, and large metal shelving reached all the way up. Boxes and cabinets packed the shelves to overflowing, with rolling ladders providing access.

"All our old Institute records, if you can believe that," said Tatiana. "The paper copies, at least. No money to store them properly, as you can imagine."

Across the room was another steel door.

"He doesn't use this door, there's another straight out the back, to the alley," said Tatiana.

Charlie pulled the door out, and it swung a bit easier this time. This room was even larger. It was only just adequately lit by three high floodlights, from which she could see that it had been painted very badly, in white. Lab tables with lamps and high stools filled the center of the room. On the right, a stairway led up to a catwalk that ran in front of a series of doors on the level above. On the far wall, there were what looked like four large glass-fronted coolers, their interiors lit with stark white fluorescent lights. And against the left wall were three gleaming machines.

"Dmitri Stepanovich," said Tatiana. "Come, you have visitors. Dmitri Stepanovich!"

A small head, white and plaintive, peered from around the edge of the door on the far side of the room.

"Come, come," said Tatiana. "These good people have come to buy you things if you could bother yourself to answer a few idle questions. Are you hiding something back there, Dmitri Stepanovich?"

"Of course not," said the man, stepping quickly inside and shutting the door. "But I have no time for visitors, I am very busy."

"Yes, yes," said Tatiana. "Friday night lab time, when else could you possibly squeeze it in? Come, sit, meet your guests. Yan Timurovich wished that you should see them. I will make tea."

Tatiana introduced them then sat them at a table while she boiled the water. Tarasov wiped his hand on his slacks, but it was still sticky when Avinashi shook it. He was an older man, but short and thin like he had gone directly from adolescence to old age. Like his hands, his clothes were no longer being washed. Uncombed tufts of white hair grew forgotten behind his ears, and his thin beard also seemed an unconscious decision. His skin was almost translucent and underneath she could clearly see the thin, fragile blood vessels. Behind large aviator style frames, his eyes had a fearful, sad expression like he had just been hit.

"I am sure I could not help you," said Tarasov.

"Perhaps we can help you," said Charlie. "This looks like expensive equipment you have here." He peered at the machines against the wall, focusing in particular on a stainless steel box the size of a sauna, with a large metal door and a window about four or five feet square. "What is this?"

"The world's fastest ice maker," said Tatiana. "Very useful at the anniversary party."

"That is a blast chiller," said Tarasov. "German, for quick freezing food. I use it to make ice." He folded his arms and looked nervously around the room.

"And other items, I suspect," said Tatiana, setting tea before him with obvious disapproval.

"You could always use another one of those, right?" said Charlie. "And I think I've seen one of these before." He tapped the tall machine on the right. About ten feet in the air a plunger was suspended from a thick steel beam hung between two vertical steel rods, presumably meant to be forced down with some extreme mechanical pressure on a second plunger below. "It's a testing machine, isn't it? Applies compression and torsion forces. Very expensive."

"Yes, it is American, so of course," said Tarasov. He wrapped his palms around the hot tea but did not drink. "And the other is a simple cold room. My field of study is ice physics and mechanics. Deformation under pressure, compressive failure of ice surfaces, ice friction, these sorts of things. Why would any of this interest you? This must be a mistake. Please, you must leave. I have much to do."

"These people are from KarLap," said Tatiana. "They might be interested in funding your research."

"Funding it?" said Tarasov. His head shrunk into his shoulders and he looked away, seething with impotent rage. "KarLap has ended it. That's what you have done. You have done enough."

"Why have we ended it?" said Charlie. "Why would anything change, all the way down here?"

"Please," said Tarasov, looking up at Charlie with disgust. "Lazarev hates the Institute. Everyone knows this. They left him on the ice. So we will all suffer now. What would you expect?"

Charlie looked quickly at Avinashi, like she should know something, then back at Tarasov. "Well, not quite 'they'," said Charlie. "You didn't always crush ice, did you Dmitri Stepanovich? You were in charge of logistics for the drift stations back then."

"Anyone not on the ice was involved in logistics," said Tarasov. "The entire Institute was involved. I had no special role."

"But Tatiana said that you were in charge," said Charlie. Tarasov glared furtively at Tatiana, but he offered no other protest. "So Dmitri Stepanovich left him on the ice. You left him out there. Will he be coming for you now?"

"Why, why me?" said Tarasov, spitting his protest. "That would be unfair. If I did, I would only have been following orders."

Charlie dragged his stool right next to Tarasov, who shriveled further down onto his seat. "We can stop him," said Charlie, calmly. "But we need your help. We need you to tell us about SP-19."

"No one can stop him," said Tarasov. "There is nothing to be done. He is coming, after all this time. Why should I make things worse?"

"Either you make them worse, or I shall," said Charlie. "Should I call him, Dmitri Stepanovich?" Charlie's expression did not change, nor his voice, noted Avinashi. "He has so much to do. But perhaps I can get him to decide more quickly on your fate. Make it a priority. Before things get any worse for you."

"You wouldn't do that," said Tarasov.

"Yes I would," said Charlie. "I might even tell him how helpful you were regardless. Do you think I might do that, Avinashi? Tell him."

She hoped not. But she wasn't sure. "Yes, I think he would," she said.

"It was the others, all of them," said Tarasov, becoming a small, sputtering spasm of fear and panic. "Alexandrov, the others, it came from the highest levels. Why should I have to suffer for this? I was only following orders."

"There is no reason you should have to suffer," said Charlie. "We can protect you. All we need to know is the last location of SP-19, before it was destroyed. That's all. No one needs to know you told us anything. Then we'll go."

"The location, that's all?" Tarasov laughed with small, dry shakes, which seemed for him a momentary relief, yet still anguished and painful. "But that was the great secret, don't you understand?"

"Understand what?" said Charlie. "No, I don't understand at all, Dmitry Stepanovich. Tell me, why was that a secret?"

"Because we had to protect the drift stations, that's why," said Tarasov. "They were the Institute's sole reason for being. They had to be protected at all costs."

"What, you were trying to protect them from the Americans, from NATO?" said Charlie.

Tarasov laughed, shaking again. "No, no, don't you understand anything? Not from the Americans. From the other Ministries, of course. They all wanted to be on the ice, but we had the sole exclusive right to them, as long as we protected it. They were always trying to encroach on our territory."

"But how would keeping the location secret keep the other Ministries out?" said Charlie. "I don't get it."

"Because you do not understand the rules we played by," said Tarasov. "So let me explain. Shorty after we launched SP-19, back in 1968, the Ministry of Defense wanted to launch its own drift station, to spy on the Americans in the Beaufort. But why should they be able to do this, Alexandrov and the others argued, when we already had a drift station in the Beaufort, SP-19! Why not just make use of this station, already fully operational under the capable leadership of the experienced Dr. Pleskov?

"Again in '74, when MinGeo sought authority to establish a station in the Laptev Sea, for God knows what purpose. Why, we argued, should they be permitted to do such a thing when SP-19 was already there? Right there! We could easily accommodate a single researcher plus equipment from MinGeo. We would even make our personnel available to assist him in the conduct of his experiments!"

"So the location was not secret?" said Avinashi.

"No, it was," said Charlie. "Because SP-19 was not in the Laptev. And I expect it wasn't in the Beaufort, either."

"Of course not!" said Tarasov, shrieking, and swinging his tiny, clenched his fists up and down in the air. "It was all a lie, a great deception, to protect the Institute. SP-19 had been a failure from the beginning. It was launched in the Chuchki Sea, like many others, where the currents carry up over the pole. But you cannot predict where they will drift, and sometimes they veer south, and east, sometimes they pace back and forth before heading out. The motion of the ice is like God, divine, it defies understanding! Not all are like SP-22, which traveled thousands of kilometers over eight years. SP-26 wandered for three years and moved only five hundred kilometers. SP-15 went south and was broke up in ice hitting up against the New Siberia Islands.

"SP-19, right away it became trapped in an gyre. For three years, it didn't move out of a three hundred kilometer box in the East Siberia Sea, it just went around and around, around and around. Completely possible, but against all probabilities. It was cursed, cursed, that's all I can say. We did not publicize it at all, it would have been a huge embarrassment. We were instructed not to talk about it, not until we had something good to say.

"So, when we heard of Defense Ministry plans, someone surely thought, why not finally put SP-19 to some use? It could be in the Beaufort. You have to understand, we lied to each other all the time. Lies were not bad, there were just good and bad lies, effective and ineffective. You understand, I am sure. SP-19 in the Beaufort? A very good lie.

"The lie was easy. We just flew the MinDef personnel around and around in circles and dropped them in the East Siberia Sea. Looks exactly like the Beaufort. Then we 'fixed' their radios so they wouldn't work. By the time they got back with no data due to their own incompetence, interest in whatever project which was so important had waned and we never heard from them again. For all we knew, they started their own ice stations, secretly. But you see, that was alright. We didn't mind if they had any, we just didn't want them to be officially permitted to have any.

"We expected a similar experience with MinGeo in '75. Lipatov was under strict orders to 'interrupt' Lazarev's project, whatever it was. In fact, shortly before we dropped Lazarev on the ice in May, SP-19 had finally broken out of its spell and was headed East. Certainly he was much closer to the Laptev than MinDef was to the Beaufort! But beyond that, I have no idea where he was. All location data was kept compartmentalized and distributed only when you had an absolute need to know. The last time I needed to know the location was May 4, when I dropped Lazarev at the station. After that, I have no knowledge."

"There must be records somewhere," said Charlie.

"No, almost certainly not," said Tarasov. "Soviet institutions were well-practiced at burying secrets. The records are surely destroyed, by Alexandrov and the others, particularly with Lazarev rising.

"You see, the whole affair was most embarrassing. They had tried to get rid of Lazarev over the summer, as before, disrupt his work.

But Lipatov was distracted, some internal, petty squabble out on the ice, we never knew exactly what. And then there was a catastrophic ice emergency. At certain levels this was viewed as providence, given the circumstances. A decision was made to let the situation 'play out,' as you would say. I had the last communication with the camp, then we just listened. They called for two days, then all radio calls stopped. Two weeks later, we flew out to the last known location, a very small group. I tried to avoid it, but they made me go. To keep the circle small, to keep it secret."

"You see," said Tatiana. "Dmitri Stepanovich hates the ice and the cold. He actually fears it, I believe, which I have always found very amusing. Not a good Russian, not at all. But it explains his morbid habits, perhaps."

Tarasov appeared not to hear her. He stared at the wall as he continued his story. "We found them, or what remained," he said. "I am not quite sure how, or even where we were. I didn't want to know. The scene was horrifying. Many of the bodies had been butchered and were still bloody and frozen. It didn't appear to be bears, but it was impossible to believe that polyarniks would do that to each other. We found Lipatov cut in half, next to a bloody shovel. Others were found naked and frozen on the ice. You know one will do that, in extreme hypothermia. At the end your skin feels like it is burning, and you tear off all your clothes. I will never forget it. You must understand, I knew these people. They were friends, colleagues. What could have happened to them? We cut a hole in the ice and pushed them all into the sea, sending everything to the bottom. The official story was that we never found the camp. We thought that was the end of it. And it was, until Lazarev appeared, weeks later. If only he had perished. That scene was horrific, nothing should have been allowed to escape that day. Nothing good could have come out of it, only evil.

"But he didn't. Not only that, but he managed to bring his cursed tapes back with him, so now they were screaming to get the position data. It was Telnov, and he kept calling, demanding the data, threatening. Lazarev, too, he called. He called everyone at the Institute, hundreds! Just one conversation with each. I never took his calls, he was looking for me, my voice, I know it. I had my assistant tell him I was elderly and often home sick. We told them we didn't know exactly where the station was destroyed. Alexandrov didn't want to get pinned down. So we gave them position data that faked the route all the way until two weeks prior. We told them everything else was lost with the station. I saw it before it was delivered, but I understood it to be completely fabricated. It didn't even include the last location I knew of, in May. But it showed them south and east of the end of the Gakkel Ridge, and just east of the shelf off Severnaya Zemlya. We knew they would assume the station was near the Gakkel, because of the volcanic activity. And this did seem to satisfy them, because Telnov stopped calling."

Charlie got up from his stool, walked back around the table and sat on another. His head dropped down to the table, and he extended his arms and clasped his hands, like he was praying.

"Why is this so important," said Tatiana. "Why do you need to know now? How will this help?" Charlie remained silent, his head bowed.

"Lazarev found a petroleum field," said Avinashi. "The morning the station was destroyed. At that location, wherever it was."

"What, with his little seismometers?" said Tarasov. "Ridiculous."

"We believe he did," said Avinashi, looking to Tatiana. "With the same technology that we used at KarLap. And we believe the field was quite large. Very large. We need to find it."

"There is no oil in the Arctic," said Tarasov. "If there was oil, it would be where you have already established it is not. On the shelf. Elsewhere, the geology is not favorable. No, this is impossible. He did not find anything. You have made a mistake."

"But what if it were true?" said Charlie, raising his head. "If we find it, we can use it to stop Lazarev. Don't you see? He's used Firebird and Ghawar to create a panic. If we can find this field, we can turn the situation around." Charlie looked at each of them in turn, but he found no encouragement.

"Let's imagine for a minute it were true," he said. "That Lazarev found a massive field. How could this be possible? And let's face it, only a massive field helps any of us right now. So forget about anything small. Tell me, how could Lazarev have found a massive supergiant?"

"He didn't," said Tarasov. "To say otherwise is madness."

Charlie ignored him. "Do you have a good chart?" he said. "Something large?"

"I will see what we have." Tatiana hopped off her stool and disappeared into the storeroom.

"Avinashi," said Charlie. "What do we need?"

"Proliferous source rock," said Avinashi. "Buried to the oil kitchen, with a path to good reservoir rock, sealed by a cap that hasn't ruptured or been eroded away."

"Where's our proliferous source rock?" said Charlie.

"We could assume the Azolla source rock isn't a penny-stock fantasy," said Avinashi.

Tatiana returned carrying a long paper tube. "Oh, they aren't fantasy," she said. "Every one of the few cores in the basin picked it up."

She snapped a large, rolled-up map out on the table, revealing the Kara and East Siberian Seas, all the way from Severnaya Zemlya in the West to Wrangel Island in the East, and from the coast of Siberia to the Pole.

"Your problem is going to be finding enough sedimentation to bury and cook the source rock," said Tatiana.

"Right, that's a challenge," said Charlie. "But then it could in fact help us. Constrain the search. Remember, we're assuming it's there. Anything I could draw with?" With Tatiana's prodding, Tarasov turned up a chewed felt-tip pen.

"Okay," said Charlie. "Here we go. Dmitry Stepanovich, where was SP-19 on May 4?"

"Seventy-five degrees North, 164 degrees and 30 seconds East. I have tried to forget, but I cannot."

"Lucky for us," said Charlie. He made a mark midway between the New Siberian Islands and Wrangel, and as far north as the former. "Okay, how fast could they have been going?"

"It is impossible to know," said Tarasov. "It was completely variable."

"I only need a top-end estimate," said Charlie. "What is the fastest the drift stations moved?"

"Director Papanin told me he once traveled thirty-five kilometers per day," said Tatiana, flushing again.

"The average was more like five kilometers," said Tarasov.

"May 4 to July 18, that's what Avinashi?" She started doing the math in her head. "Seventy-five days," he said. "Is that right? So just over 2600 kilometers?" He was right, of course. "But they never traveled in a straight line. Should we just say 80 percent of that?"

"Even 50 percent puts them up over the Pole," said Tarasov, shrugging.

"You're right," said Charlie. "And Lazarev is only human, let's assume. So he isn't walking back from there. Let's start with that, instead. How far could he travel? He left on July 18, hits land on September 4. Forty-eight days. How far could he have gone in that time? Assume the currents are transpolar, trending north, max of thirty-five kilometers per day, that's about 1.5 kilometers per hour. Let's call it one to be conservative and make the math easy. Tatiana, how fast can he move across the ice?"

"Sometimes fast, sometimes slow," she said. "On average, average. He was likely pulling heavy gear. Say a very slow walk. Two or three kilometers per hour."

"Let's assume three," said Charlie.

"Near shore there is no ice," said Tarasov. "He paddled. And near the shore, currents run south, not up to the Pole."

"Okay, let's ballpark this. Say he paddles 3 kilometers per hour, plus a current, call it four. Before that he walks at three kilometers per hour, less a current, call it two. Assume the trip was two thirds ice, one third water. Travel ten good hours a day, the rest of the day hunting, sleeping, getting lost and praying. What's the solution?"

Avinashi was determined to beat him this time. "Total time walking plus paddling equals 480 hours," she said. "If you walk twice the distance you paddle, at half the speed, then your time spent walking is four times that spent paddling. Average speed is four plus four times two divided by eight, which is three. So you walk for four-fifths of 480 at two, paddle for one-fifth of 480 at four." She thought for a moment. "Just over 1150 kilometers."

"Straight edge?" said Charlie. Tarasov fetched a long ruler. "His landfall was here, near corner of the Taymyr Peninsula. Let's draw an arc with a radius of 1200 kilometers." Charlie checked the scale and set the ruler on the map. He anchored one end on the Taymyr, and traced an arc across the map with the pen held fast most of the way up the other end. Inside the arc was all of the Laptev and western East Siberian Sea, and major portions of the Gakkel Ridge, the Amundsen Basin, the Lomonosov Ridge and the Makarov Basin. It reached up the Lomonosov Ridge all the way to the 88th parallel.

"Lots of territory," said Charlie. "But thanks to KarLap, we can cross off where we know the oil isn't." Starting at a point north of Severnaya Zemlya at about the 85th parallel, he drew a line east through the Gakkel Ridge, then down through the Amundsen Basin as far as the coastal shelf, and all the way along the shelf east to 160 degrees east, just west of the last known position of SP-19. Below the line, he drew diagonal lines.

"Expensive lines," he said, grimacing. "Each about twenty-five million dollars, I'd say. And what's left?"

"The eastern half of the Amundsen," said Avinashi. "The Lomonosov Ridge, and the Western half of the Makarov Basin." She paused. "But not the Gakkel Ridge," she added. We ruled out any areas near the Gakkel with Firebird."

"Right," said Charlie. "They kept looking near the Gakkel, using the geophones Araz made for them. All the shelf areas near the Gakkel, where they simply had to be. It made sense, and that's what the Institute was telling them. When Firebird came along, Lazarev was worried we would succeed where he had failed. And if it was near the Gakkel, it would have been in international waters. Unless the US agreed to support their claims to the Gakkel, Russia could have lost rights to the field. That's why he tried to stop Firebird, and then when he couldn't stop it he demanded we agreed to support their claims before the test went forward."

"But it wasn't there," said Avinashi.

"No," said Charlie. "It never did make sense that it was near the Gakkel. The crust is too new, too thin. It would have been very improbable. So where else could we find a hotspot and sufficient sedimentation?"

"The Lomonosov," said Tatiana. "There has been volcanic activity on the ridge, over on the Canadian side. And there areas of sedimentation that come close to what is necessary."

"How much information can you get me on the Ridge?" said Charlie, looking at the two Russians. "What's available?"

"What, you are going to find it, right here, right now?" said Tarasov, looking to Tatiana and Avinashi for support. "You think Lazarev is mad, well. Even if it exists, to think you might find it from a few scattered clues over hundreds of thousands of kilometers of ocean bottom is the definition of insanity."

"Still worth a try, don't you think?" said Charlie. "Remember, I'm not looking for a small field. That wouldn't help even if we found it. We need to plan for success. This may be a needle in a haystack, but my haystack is six hundred by four hundred kilometers and I only care about needles that are at least fifty kilometers long."

"And the areas with sufficient sedimentation are even smaller," said Tatiana. "If in fact, there are any."

"There is at least one," said Charlie.

"But how will you be sure?" said Tarasov. "You could not possibly ever be sure."

"Of course not," said Charlie. "We won't be until we drill. We just need to be able to believe enough to try." He looked at all of them, but there were no further protests.

"We are quite fortunate, in fact," said Tatiana. "We have a complete copy of our latest draft of our revised UN application that supports our claim that the Lomonosov Ridge is part of Russia's continental shelf. It has an index of all the available data. But I am not sure that it will help you. There is both too much and too little information, I am afraid."

"I want to see everything," said Charlie. "And let's make some more tea. You wouldn't have any coffee, would you?"

Tatiana pulled the index of data on the ridge from the soon-to-be amended Russian UN application for its ownership. She spread all the pages of the index on a table, of which there were at least two or three dozen, and they gathered around it to assess the hand they had been dealt.

"There may not be everything you would want," said Tatiana. "But what has been collected has been government-funded and is in the public domain. The only proprietary data will be what we collect on the *Sevmorput*."

"Seismic will the most critical," said Charlie. "But I want to see everything. Gravity, magnetic, bathymetric. What is there in the way of coring?"

"We have thousands of core samples," said Tatiana. "But few that are deep. All the drift stations, Soviet, American, Canadian took cores, but most were less than five meters. Anything beyond that, the core and the equipment are too heavy for the ice. You need a ship to drill deep cores, and the only drillship that has gone out is the *Vidar Viking* in 2004, for the international ocean drilling program. They took cores down to four hundred meters, and there were only four. That's all there is."

"I want everything you can get on those four cores," said Charlie. "Let's hold off on any others until we start to zero in on an area."

Tatiana and Avinashi exchanged a quick glance. Charlie was actually assuming they were going to find something.

"And what do we have for seismic?" said Charlie.

"All together for the Arctic ice pack there are about twenty thousand kilometers of seismic," said Tatiana.

"After all those decades?" said Charlie. "I could collect that in three months in the open water."

"The ice is more complicated," said Tatiana. "For the ridge, there were five lines taken by crossing drift stations, and ten lines taken by icebreakers. One of those lines is deep seismic refraction data."

"That's it?" said Charlie. His eyes widened, and he looked down, into the mid-distance, at no one. "No, okay, that's fine. We'll start there. I want all that seismic in hard copy. Also, in addition to this bathy chart I want the USGS geological map, also in large format. Do you have that on hand? Also, there must be something that shows sediment thicknesses. And good gravity and magnetic maps. Also large format. Let's start with those, and then Avinashi, if you could just download everything else from the list that you can find I'll let you know if I want hard copies. Okay, what am I missing?"

Tatiana quickly collected large copies of the gravity, magnetic and geological maps from her office and laid them out on the other tables. Charlie immediately descended on them and became lost in thought. Tatiana dragged Tarasov with her into the storeroom to pull hard copies of seismic traces and Avinashi went to work pulling electronic copies of the other items on the index.

For a last, gallant but likely empty gesture, thought Avinashi, there was an enormous amount of data to digest. Mountains of bathymetric data collected by NATO subs with time to kill under the ice during the long Cold War. Endless aeromagnetic data collected separately by the American and Soviet militaries, then co-mingled during the anything-goes '90s. And loads of gravity data collected first from the ice, then later from the air, and finally from under the ice by high-speed subs. And of course the seismic. Tatiana and Tarasov came out of the storeroom again and again with their arms full of red bound volumes.

"We have paper copies of nearly every shot," said Tatiana. "Reflection seismic, both the high-frequency, high-resolution but shallow variety as well as the low-frequency, lower-resolution, deep penetrating sort. Also the very deep sounding refraction seismic, although less of that. There was no 3-D seismic, of course, because you cannot tow wide arrays of hydrophones through the ice. Only a simple 2-D array towed straight back, close to the boat. And there were limitations even with regards to the 2-D, what with the higher ambient noise at the collection point due to the ice and the proximity to the towing vessel. If you tow it deep under the ice, you get a surface reflection from the top, but if you tow it shallow. Well, they call that 'suicide' mode. The refraction seismic data was collected off of ships but by ocean-bottom seismometers and explosives delivered by helicopters. The charges used were modest, usually no more than twenty-five kilograms of explosives."

Charlie nodded his head politely but remained deep in thought over the bathymetric and geologic maps.

"On second thought," said Charlie. "Let me see the long core data first. Is there some sort of summary?"

Avinashi pulled the raw core data and the few published papers she could find and printed them out. Then she went to work on filling in the rest of the holes. Tatiana brought her laptop from her office and put Tarasov to work pulling and printing the gravity data. Then she went back to the storeroom to see what else she could turn up.

They buried Charlie under layers and layers of data. He didn't say much, except to ask for this or that, for help finding these or those, or to ask Avinashi to translate the Russian documents. Mostly, he seemed lost in his own world.

Several hours later everyone except Charlie had hit a wall. Tarasov had pulled a cot out and gone to sleep in the corner. Avinashi had finished working her way through the index. She got up to stretch her legs and limped back and forth across the lab. Her foot had swollen up again and was very painful.

"Come, let me see your foot," said Tatiana. "We must make certain the tissue is not becoming gangrenous."

Avinashi was going to protest when she heard a bark. Tarasov awoke with a start. Tatiana jumped off her stool and scurried over to the back door. She ducked outside and returned carrying a small black and white dog.

"You disgusting man," said Tatiana to Tarasov, making him flush. "This one will come with us. And where is your medical kit?"

"In my office," said Tarasov, looking ashamed. "In one of the cabinets. Somewhere."

"There should be one out in the lab," said Tatiana. "Come, Avinashi."

She led Avinashi up the iron stairs, carrying the small dog.

Tarasov's office was a converted storage room, with no windows or electrical. He had run a cord in through the door to power the desk lamp and computer. Tatiana found the medical kit in a box and retrieved a bowl of water and a towel from downstairs.

"Come," said Tatiana. "Up on the desk, off with your shoe."

Avinashi sat up on the desk while Tatiana pulled up a chair. Avinashi slipped off her shoe and pulled off her sock. The foot was red, and her second and third toes were twice normal size and filled with fluid. Tatiana leaned over to inspect something on Avinashi's heel. The older woman wet a cloth in the bowl and wiped away a dark smudge. She held the cloth up to the light, then sniffed it. "What have we here? Not the blood of a young woman." She lifted her eyebrows. "Well, even though she can defeat the Great Bear the formidable Miss Sharma must attend to her toes."

There was a scalpel of sorts in the kit. Tatiana washed it in the bowl and rinsed it with iodine. She lanced Avinashi's toes, and the fluid ran out, mostly clear but mixed with a bit of blood. She cleaned them in the water, then wrapped them with bandages and taped them.

"There," she said. "You are fortunate, they should be fine. But watch them closely." Avinashi was not so sure. Tatiana closed the door and pulled up a chair to sit in front of Avinashi. Unfazed by the lack of ventilation, she lit a cigarette.

"How long were you out?" said Tatiana.

"Overnight. I'm not well suited to the cold, I'm afraid."

She lifted her eyebrows. "None of us are. Some take longer to figure this out. But Tarasov, he is acutely aware. It drives him mad. Perhaps that is why he conducts his 'research,' freezing innocents like this one in his chiller."

"You're joking," said Avinashi, looking at the small dog asleep on an old lab coat in the corner.

"I am sorry that I am not," said Tatiana. "We find them in the trash."

She gazed at Avinashi through the thin cloud of her tobacco.

"Your friend," said Tatiana. "If he does not realize by the morning that this exercise is hopeless, then you may consider him to be mad."

Avinashi hopped down onto her good foot, then sat down in one of the other chairs.

"He doesn't know what else to do," said Avinashi. "He feels responsible, and there's nothing else he knows how to do."

"So you, why are you with him?" said Tatiana. "Why are you running around Russia, with this crazy man? He is not still the man that was your boss."

"Someone was taken from me," said Avinashi. "Charlie told me we could get him back."

"He is one man," said Tatiana. "Looking in his mind for something which does not exist. I don't see how this can help you get your man back. Yes, I know it is a man. I, too, once looked like you. Go back to America. Perhaps your government can help you. But not this man." She dropped her cigarette on the floor and ground it out with her foot. "I must go home now. There is nothing else for me to do here. You wish to come with me?"

Avinashi shook her head.

"Very well. It is my day off tomorrow, but I may come in. Later in the morning. For now, goodnight. Think about what I have said."

She kissed Avinashi on both cheeks.

Downstairs, Charlie was flipping feverishly through pages of seismic traces. He had half a dozen volumes open in front of him on the table, the rest were stacked all around him on the table, the stools and the floor.

"Avinashi, look at this," said Charlie. He jabbed at a squiggle on the page and started lecturing her on the lost art of interpreting 2-D seismic. She looked at the graphs and saw next to nothing. How he hoped to interpret this without any visualization or integration tools was beyond her.

She finally noticed how old he was. He was getting that insistent, oblivious attitude of the odd, old man in the office, the one always trying to show everyone the proper way to do things, the way they had always been done. Way past a respectable retirement age, dressed in clothes that should be in a museum, unable to see or understand the way the world had changed around him. To be humored and avoided. But Avinashi was always the nice girl. The one who would talk to the old man.

"Avinashi," he said. "We need to work out how we're going to drill this. That's something you could help with, you could work on finding us a rig. Something that could drill out on the Ridge."

He really had gone mad.

"Charlie," said Avinashi softly. "Can we talk for a minute? What if it's not there? Have you thought about that? What if Lazarev just made a mistake? Bad data. Machine malfunction, maybe. A false positive."

He stared at her. "Why would you assume that?" He blinked several times in succession, his head bouncing just barely each time. "That doesn't help. That won't help stop all this. That doesn't bring Ted back."

What is he talking about, thought Avinashi? Help? If it wasn't there, this was all a waste of time. "But Charlie," she said. "Shouldn't we reassess what the likely reality is here? Doesn't that give us our best chance?"

"No, no," said Charlie. "No, that's not right." He looked at her quietly, and she felt like he was finally becoming aware of her presence.

"How are you doing?" he said. "Everything you've been through, how you are still going is beyond me. How is your foot?"

"Oh, it feels okay. So far, so good."

"Sit down, sit down. We've got a little bit of coffee left, let me get you some." He pulled up a stool for her and she climbed wearily on top. He found her cup on the table and filled it halfway from the pot. He set it on the table next to her, and sat down.

"Hey, I bought you something," he said, smiling. "It's back at the hotel, I had them put it in your room. It was Ted's idea. Your own survival suit. He seemed pretty sure about the size, hope it fits. Deluxe model, with three satellite beacons, your own heat source, the works. Even stuck a Texso patch on it. Hope you like it."

She flushed. "Thanks, Charlie, that's very generous."

"Avinashi," said Charlie. "I can't tell you that I know what is going to happen. But I can tell you one thing. The only reality we will ever know is the one we make for ourselves, right now." That was it, she thought. The clinical definition of insanity.

"This other likely reality that might be out there," he said. "The one that in some absolute way limits what you can accomplish, that might conceivably keep Avinashi Sharma in a box. You will never, ever be constrained by that reality. Because that reality is too big, it's beyond your imagination. You will never touch the sides of that box, it's not our place. The only reality you will ever know is the one that you make inside of that for yourself. When you start believing that there are no fields left to find, then that's the day you'll stop finding any, I guarantee you that. Don't think like that. Not you. There are plenty enough who can do the doubting. Not too long ago an expert, being realistic, said he would eat all the oil anyone found west of the Mississippi. That's not our job, to be realistic. Not you. Your job, your purpose, is to imagine, and to believe. And then drill. Can you do that?"

"I want to, Charlie," she said. "I really do. I just don't know how. I don't think I know how."

"Go outside, get some air," he said. "And while you're out there, you go look up at those stars. You ponder all that space and time for a few minutes, and then you come back in and see if you can tell me that you're ready to decide that you know what our reality is. How enormous this world is. What is possible, and impossible."

She went up to Tarasov's office and peeked in on the dog. He was awake and quivering in excitement at seeing her. She picked it up and walked out down the hallway and outside into the fresh night air. The skies were clear and even through the lights and smog of St. Petersburg she could see the stars.

She looked up, at light that was billions of years old, seeing across time, across limitless space. What was possibly out there now, after billions of years? What could be, would be, billions of years into the future? There could be no end to questions, to life, she realized. It was beyond her imagination, and so anything she could imagine, could be. Why could there not be a world where she found the oil? Where she rescued Ted? Where she made her mother proud? A world of her making.

Avinashi went back inside to figure out how they could possibly drill this hole.

Charlie was still flipping through seismic. She went up to Tarasov's office to settle the dog. She turned off the light, then laid him down on the coat and petted him to calm him.

She heard voices, from downstairs. Angry voices, loud. She kept petting the dog, hoping he wouldn't bark. It seemed quiet enough, so she inched up to the door and opened it a crack, peering down.

There were two strange men in the lab, men with long hair and beards and guns. The men were doing most of the yelling, at Tarasov, demanding to know who he was. Charlie was trying to intervene, but they kept pushing him away with the muzzles of their gun. One of the men was talking on a radio.

And then, there they were, her unholy troika. Nikolai, in fatigues and with a large sidearm strapped to his hip, with another four of his men. Telnov walking slowly. And finally Lazarev, tall and white, gliding like a ghost. One of Nikolai's men was leading Paul Brown by a rope tied around his neck. His hands were bound behind him, and there were two dark holes where his eyes should have been.

Tarasov flung himself on the floor, wailing. Lazarev spoke to him in low tones, nothing that she could make out. He directed Nikolai to hand Tarasov a piece of paper and told him to read it. Tarasov protested and Nikolai hit him. In quavering Russian, Tarasov read the paper. Something about evacuation and waiting until October. A confession? Tarasov couldn't finish reading before he broke down again, begging and pleading.

Lazarev, cold and still like death, looked down at Tarasov. Then away, around the room. His eyes fixed on one of the machines. He whispered to Nikolai, who in turn barked other orders. One of the other men picked Tarasov up, while the other opened the door to the blast chiller. Telnov protested, something about this not being what they had discussed. But the men threw Tarasov and Brown inside and slammed the door shut, sealing in Tarasov's screams. Brown couldn't see enough to scream. They stuck a knife through the latch, locking the door.

Lazarev leaned down and peered in through the window. Tarasov pressed his palms and his face up against the glass. Lazarev found the switch for the interior light and turned it on. Avinashi could see Tarasov's face clearly, and his lips moving frantically, but no sound reached her. Then Lazarev turned the machine on and spun one of the dials. Charlie yelled at Lazarev, trying to get him to stop. Telnov stood off to one side

The machine began making a loud hum. Tarasov was frantic. He pounded on the door. He grabbed wire baskets and trays off the racks inside and smashed them against the window. Then he was still, up against the upper, back corner of the unit. Doing something, probably trying to disable the unit, his arm stuck up through the vent. Then he stopped and shook his arm out, and he looked wildly around. She could see him wrap his arms around himself, and hunch his head down on his shoulders. Then he huddled down into one of the corners, trying to hide from the air blasts.

Lazarev was leaning against the windows with his hands up and spread wide. Avinashi couldn't see his face, but now he was yelling, too. About how Tarasov had left him to die, about how Lazarev had suffered, how Tarasov was only feeling what he, Lazarev, had felt for weeks on end, never knowing if he would live or die. So now he, Lazarev, would leave Tarasov here, in the cold, to die. Perhaps he would come back in October and see how Tarasov had fared.

For long, horrid minutes Lazarev stared through the glass. Tarasov began shivering uncontrollably, his exposed skin turned pink and white. Then, inexplicably, he started tearing off all his clothing. Then he fell on the floor, unconscious. Lazarev spit on the glass, then turned away and left. Nikolai followed, and the other men, dragging Charlie with them.

Telnov remained, slumped down on a chair, a look of disgust on his face. He got up and walked over to the chiller and turned it off. He pulled out the knife and opened the door, standing back quickly as the cold hit him. Telnov pulled out a gun and stepped inside the chiller.

How much longer before they came back for her, thought Avinashi. She needed to get out. Now. She crept down the stairs, still holding the dog. She walked slowly up to the machine, shielded from Telnov's sight by the open door.

She heard a gunshot from inside. Avinashi ran up and slammed the door shut. She grabbed the knife and rammed it into the latch.

Telnov appeared at the window like a figure out of a nightmare. He saw her, and his eyes bulged open wide. He stepped back and raised his gun, pointing it at her. She lifted her hand and put it over the on switch. He looked down at her hand. He lowered the gun to his side. Her hand hovered over the switch.

Then she turned and ran with the dog toward the door to the alleyway. As she ran, she could hear gunshots sounding behind her.

Avinashi left the dog in the alley behind the Museum and skipped along on her sore foot for three or four blocks, then ducked down some stairs and huddled at the bottom, breathing hard. She pulled her sweater up over her head and became an invisible inky bundle. Men ran past on the street, but they didn't see her. Underneath, she pulled out her phone and punched in the number for the US Embassy in Moscow. But though she lay her thumb on the talk button, she could not press it. After she caught her breath, she got up again and walked.

Past the train station, then down Nevsky. The slow, steady succession of footfalls reminded her of her early days as a runner, padding up and down the quiet, cool, pre-dawn streets of Clear Lake City, Texas. Eight years old, preternaturally determined and, admittedly, somewhat grim. You might not have known it to look at her, but running made her happy. Her father knew, which was he got up with her before dawn and followed in the car. They both knew Avinashi was in a hurry to get somewhere, although neither could know where at that young age. But to Avinashi, running felt like progress. Fast or slow, each step was a step forward. Years later, she had found everything she wanted and now it was all taken away. Only the blessed momentum of all those steps was still carrying her forward. Once again, she did not know where she was going, but she found she could not stop. She would not stop.

She walked all the way down Nevsky until she reached the cemetery by the Alexander Nevsky Lavra. It was the darkest hour of the night, and she was dead tired and cold. Under the circumstances, she decided she could forgive herself for calling Sanders. She dialed all his numbers but he did not answer any.

She stared into the cemetery. Darker was probably safer for her right now. Avinashi passed through the gatehouse and walked on the quiet paths. Tikhvin Cemetery was Russia's most prestigious final resting place, and so the headstones were grand and packed nearly one on top of the other. Dostoevsky, Tchaikovsky, Stravinsky, Lomonosov. And there, in a dark, hard spot next to Russia's giant, she retreated into her inky bundle, said a prayer and closed her eyes.

CHAPTER 19

MINDS OF MEN

St. Petersburg Harbor
Saturday early morning

From somewhere up in the darkness, the devil's excrement dripped onto Charlie's broken body. Drop after drop, in an accidental and redundant act of torture.

Nikolai and Leonid beat him for most of the ride in the van so when they arrived they had to drag him inside. In a dark, hollow space they stripped off his clothes and tied his outstretched arms to a long pipe. Each grabbing an end, they hoisted him off the ground and hung him on a rack, where his own weight was tearing him apart. The thick industrial odor of machines and fuel and foul water crowded out the air so he could hardly breathe. He was numb from the cold, and his mouth was parched and swollen. A fresh stench made him think he had lost control of his bowels. His was not the only account being settled that night. From behind him, in another room, he heard shouting. Two familiar voices. Then a man's scream, followed by a woman's, hers long and anguished. Then nothing. As the unbearable minutes stretched into hours, he began to sob uncontrollably. In the pit of his despair, he pleaded for forgiveness. From Sheila. From his son and his father. From Wayne and God.

A door opened behind him. A shaft of light entered the room. Two sets of footsteps followed, and the faint smell of the sea. A familiar face was illuminated for an instant in the beam, a monster revealed by a flash of lightning. The monster walked up to him until they were almost touching, chest to chest, and put his lips to Charlie's ear.

"Is anything good left inside? Or only lust? For more and more and more. Do you not see it now, for what it was? Your Godless life?"

Charlie struggled to block the pain, to think, to move his tongue. "Olezka."

"It is not too late, Charlie, to renounce this life. God may hear you. He may have mercy."

"It isn't too late," said Charlie, in a whisper. "Olezka."

Lazarev put his ear up to Charlie's lips, playing the confessor. "Yes, Charlie?"

"It's not too late to stop, Olezka. Don't do this."

"You are an abomination," said Lazarev, turning away. "A hideous, evil thing. Turn on the lights, Nikolai. I want to see it."

A switch snapped and light filled the room, pure white and devoid of warmth. Charlie squinted into the large, decrepit space. Tables and boxes were strewn about haphazardly, and tools and machines that were barely recognizable under layers of dirt and grease. There were skinny tanks of gas on wheels for welding, and fat plastic tanks on wheels for washing out the holds of tankers. Coils of hoses for the cleaning machines, dripping with crude, were stacked on the ground and, he surmised, hung above him on the rack.

Over on the floor he spied something wrapped in a woolen blanket, a fine one in a light brown shade, wholly out of place. Now he could see it was a jacket, and that the flashes of clean white poking out of its sleeves were cuffs. But the something wrapped inside seemed too small to be a man, until he saw shoes on the other half of the body up on the table. The jacket opened toward him, but Sanders' head had been wrenched all the way around the other way until all Charlie could see was the back of it, and the still-perfect hair. Charlie had not lost control of his bowels, but Sanders had, before the end.

"Sorry you have to share a room," said Nikolai. "We are all full tonight. At least he finally shut up."

"Yes, your acolyte," said Lazarev. "What a fitting companion for you. A fornicator, a drunk, a schemer. And you made him what he was. Well, now I have caught you both. And here you are at last, Charlie, hung in my hall of devils. Charlie Joiner, the great American oil finder."

Lazarev walked around behind him. Charlie knew he was staring at the purple lines of scar tissue on his back. Dozens of short scars, together making a crude and vicious circle around the whole of it. Inside this, two long scars. A thick purple bar crossing inside the circle across the top. And dropping from the middle of this, a long, cruel line down one side of his spine, all the way to the bottom of the circle. A familiar symbol, except to those who could not accept finding it carved on a back, rather than atop a filling station, or in the pages of a glossy magazine. But here it was, FARC's symbol of repression and exploitation, cut into Charlie's back with the jagged edge of a can and left to mend itself in the muck of the jungle.

"Does it not bother you, Charlie?" said Lazarev. Charlie felt a finger tracing the scar along his spine. "That people despise you so? Think about the hate that is required to do this to a man. Does it not give you pause?" The finger lifted, and Lazarev came up close behind him, again putting lips to ear. "Only when you are like this, I expect. And then I expect it bothers you very much." Lazarev laughed. "Don't worry, Charlie, we are almost finished. All I need to know is whether you found the field. Tarasov knew nothing, of course. But you were there all night, reviewing his data. And you met with Bego, and Ivanov. You were on the right track, you must have found something. Where is it, Charlie? What did you find? You don't want it to die with you, do you? You are too vain for that."

To his shame, Charlie could not stop the sobs. The pain was too great, the despair too complete. The convulsions made him pull harder on his arms, and his shoulders felt like they were going to break.

"Nothing," said Charlie, mouthing the words more than speaking them. "I tried. I couldn't find it."

"Well, I have too much respect for your abilities, whatever their origin or the use to which they have been put," said Lazarev. "So Nikolai will make sure. But I will return, before the end."

Lazarev handed something to Nikolai and whispered in his ear, then walked out the door.

Nikolai stood in front of Charlie holding a knife and a sheet of paper. There was bandage around his right hand, the one holding the knife. It was soaked in blood. Nikolai stared at the paper with a confused look.

"Joiner, you are a fucking pain in my ass," said Nikolai. "You thought you would come here, steal our oil, and not end up like this? Idiot. Now I have to cut this on your chest. I don't even know what the fuck this is. A mountain? Why a mountain? Some fucking joke between you and him? And that line? That's going to hurt."

He put the paper in his mouth and with his free hand dragged a table closer to Charlie. Nikolai set the paper on the table where he could see it, an artist with his model. Charlie could see it now, too. Not a mountain, he thought. A logistics curve. And a line, from the bottom all the way straight up through the peak of the curve.

"Stop me any time and tell me where our oil is," said Nikolai. "Otherwise I will be forced to complete this fucking masterpiece."

Panic and fear loosened his lips. "Nikolai, I don't know where it is," said Charlie.

He grabbed Charlie's chin and lifted his head, so he could look him in the eyes. "You know, I think I believe you," said Nikolai, before dropping his head again. "But you are not the only one who is thorough. It is not that complicated, as you like to say. If you know, you will tell me. So let us get this over with."

Nikolai glanced once more at the diagram on the paper, then started with the curve.

The Spetsnaz slumped back into a chair, exhausted. Finally, it was quiet. The knife and the sheet of paper were on the table next to him, covered in blood. Charlie was heaped in a pile against the wall. Nikolai threw the knife aside and stood up.

"So after all that you know nothing," he said. "Less good to me than a fucking ghost. Well, I will go find Oleg Maksimovich. He wants to do you himself. You wait here, okay?"

He laughed and snapped off the lights on his way out the door.

But Charlie was already gone. Fleeing from the waves of pain, his mind had stolen away along a familiar, well-worn path, leaving behind the bloody chest with its carefully traced cuts and the bones bruised on concrete. As was their habit from long practice, his thoughts ran back and forth across time, real and imagined. But this time they were beyond his control, his mind a powerful racehorse that had thrown his rider but still charges around the track, dragging him by the stirrup, full speed right through the finish line, just going around and around and around.

He was tied up in the jungle aching for his dead wife, then he was seeing her smile for the first time as she collected his overdue fines at the library. He was playing wiffle ball with his brothers under the streetlights, then he was pitching the Texso board on a play in the Russian Arctic. He was rubbing the first oil show from Alif between his fingers, then he was driving from LAX to Santa Barbara to get Ted out of rehab. Then in full stride he ran hard into the memory of standing alone in the center of the Kirov Cultural Center, and the shock cast him free of his brief, precious life, from its discoveries and dry holes, its simple happiness and sorrows.

Charlie found himself a step closer to God, outside of time. Still as eternity, he watched the planet cool, and crusts form and break over convection currents of liquid rock. Over long millenia he watched continents rift and spread, oceans form, mountains rise. Eons of rain washed rock, grain by grain, into the seas. Covering and smothering the detritus of early life, under the inconceivably slow and gradual accumulation of mass and pressure and heat. Black hydrocarbons cooked, and seeped, were trapped, and slumbered.

The geological history of the Arctic ran forward and backward in an endless loop. The Amerasian Basin opened and closed in the East like a Japanese fan. A spreading submarine ridge encroached from the West, slicing a length of the continental shelf away from Northern Europe and pushing it all the way to the Pole, before retreating again. The great rivers of Russia and Canada filled the new basins with fresh water and silt, and the northern ocean bloomed under the warm, endless sunlight until it was covered with a vast, thick green mat, before freezing again.

And then, inexplicably, he was back in Texas with his father. Running to keep up with his long, half-man, half-plastic strides as they crossed a green field. They were on the way to pick up his brother at college in Kilgore when his dad pulled off onto a side road. When they reached the town of Joinerville a few minutes later he thought his dad was just being funny. But the other side of town they pulled over and Stan got out and took off over the field.

And then, as before, his father was standing in the tall grass next to an abandoned derrick. Think about it, Charlie, he said. That broken-down old man out here in the middle of the night, with that old driller Laster and a bunch of farm kids. Tearing up bits of tire and throwing them into a boiler he got out of a sawmill. Turning drill pipe so broken and rusty they were selling it for scrap. Remember, Charlie, this was the Great Depression. People were scared, real scared. But there's Pa Joiner, seventy years old, half-bent over from the pain and he's still out here sweet-talking widows into cheap leases and stake money. Turning it all into a show, hawking hamburgers, moonshine and crop-duster rides to pay for supplies. They told him there was no oil in East Texas, and he might even have half-believed that himself, though I don't know. Gotta be easier ways to cheat people. Or maybe he conned himself first. Anyway, that night he found it. Right here. Daisy Bradford No. 3. Thirty-five hundred feet down in the Woodbine sandstone, where it ran up against the Austin Chalk. That's what they call an angular unconformity trap, Charlie, where way down deep your reservoir rock layer runs up at an angle against your cap rock laying flat over the top of the whole thing. Can't see nothing from up top. No anticline on the surface, nothing. Just flat. But somehow he found it. The East Texas Oil Field. Six billion barrels, biggest damn field in the lower forty-eight. Runs north for near a hundred miles. Won WWII for us, you know. Hauled some of it over myself. Biggest field in the whole country until Prudhoe. Which was another angular unconformity, for your information. Well, God bless Pa Joiner, I say, Charlie. And God bless old widow Bradford and her foolish, girlish heart.

Indeed, thought Charlie, feeling his dad tousle his hair again as he sat at the table in the basement of the museum, flipping quickly again through the dusty red volumes, retracing his steps, poring back over the same pictures of reflected sound.

Looking. Looking. Feeling his heart start again, now pounding hard.

There.

Giant, meet stone.

When they came for him, Charlie tried to talk. But he could not move his lips, or his hands, or his head. And that was the saddest part of all. It would die with him. Again, the same stab of light entered the door, and two sets of footsteps. But different this time. Softer.

Duman moved with surprising quickness across the room, considering the darkness and the sunglasses. He dropped to a knee beside Charlie. His large hands checked for a pulse and then gently pulled back a lid to check his pupil. Duman must have determined there was something still worth saving, because he gathered Charlie up in his arms. And then in the midst of all the horror was the scent of roses and the sound of quiet cries. "Oh, Charlie, oh, Charlie. How can it be? How, how? I did not ever want to see you like this. Never again. I am so sorry, Charlie, I am so sorry. What have I done? What have I done?" Shirin's hands danced frantically over his body, wanting to touch him, but afraid.

Then they were out the door and in a hallway with high windows along one side. Outside, it was already another bright August

morning, oblivious to the nightmares still playing out in the darkened rooms.

"So this is where you wandered off to, you fat blackarse. Were you
listening to us?" Nikolai's voice. "Well you just put him right back
down. Leonid, put Joiner back in his room while I find another one
for these two." Nestled in the giant's arms, Charlie felt tension building across Duman's huge, muscled frame, like the coiling of a great
spring. He set Charlie down carefully on the floor.

"God damn spook," said Nikolai. "Too stupid to live. Now get over
here."

Duman moved so quickly Charlie felt the breeze on his face.
A brief fight ensued. It finished with a sound like the wheeze of a
large animal, and a long crackling, twisting of bone, and a heavy
thud.

And then Charlie was picked up again, gently. "No," he said to
Duman, forcing the words to come. "A girl." He flicked his eyes at the
battered green door to the room beside his.

"Charlie," said Shirin. "We must go. Others will come. We have a
car outside."

"No."

Duman set Charlie up against the wall again and disappeared behind the green door. He reappeared quickly with a tall blonde girl,
holding one arm across her body with the other, her face bruised and
swollen and almost unrecognizable. Hurt badly, but not defeated.
But perhaps ready to go home.

She was coming, thought Charlie. He had promised her father.

Duman lost them among the other dark-windowed German sedans of
greater St. Petersburg while Shirin worked her contacts for an exit.
Olivia sat in the front passenger seat with her head resting against
the window, staring out at nothing. Duman had wrapped Charlie in
an extra set of his tent-sized clothing. The shirt was already soaked
with blood and stuck against his chest. Unable to sit, his head was in
Shirin's lap. She caressed his cheek and fingered his short strands of

hair like worry beads as she pleaded and argued in Farsi. It was clear her calls were not met with enthusiasm, and she looked thin and gray.

"That wasn't my father, you know." Olivia was still staring out the window, but now speaking to him. "The man you talked to."

"You don't have a father?" asked Charlie.

She turned back and looked at him. "Yeah. In Virginia."

"Okay then."

Finally, after an extended exchange of sharp words, a call ended in bitter agreement and Shirin murmured a location to Duman.

"One more stop," said Charlie. Polina.

An hour or so later they were all outside of the city, pulling up to a gate where two soldiers peered down at Charlie through the lowered windows. Shirin spoke briefly with them in Russian. They pointed off to something in the distance.

Duman drove on, and then right into a building where he shut off the engine. He looked briefly at Shirin, then he pulled a pack of cigarettes from his pocket and raised them to Olivia and Polina. Olivia nodded and the three of them climbed out. The car sunk on its suspension as Duman sat on the hood next to Olivia while they shared a quiet smoke.

"We must wait now," said Shirin, pressing her lips to his forehead. "Only a little while. There is a doctor in London waiting to see you tonight. A friend."

Charlie tried to talk, to ask why she looked as if she should be the one to see the doctor, but she put a finger against his lips.

"Because I am my family, Charlie," she said. "And we have been chased from our country, a country we built over hundreds of years. What should we do, but try to go back? Lazarev was offering us that chance. So yes, we were talking to him. Working with him." Shirin bent over him, caressing his face, nearby but back in the shadows, her hair shrouding her face, her eyes two deep, dark, liquid pools of sorrow.

"I have done terrible things to you, Charlie. My family, they asked these things of me, and I did them. I gave Lazarev information about you. About KarLap. Information I collected from others. And from you. I was to meet with Lazarev this morning, at Kulneft's facilities, down at the harbor. Duman heard one of the men talking about you, and we went to look for you. What have I done? I want to die, Charlie. How can you look at me?"

He managed to raise his arm and wrap it around the back of her neck and pull her toward him. As she wept, he kissed her on the cheek.

"Dial for me," he said. Taken aback, she wiped her tears on the back of her hand and looked at him curiously. He whispered some numbers to her. Charlie spoke briefly with Avinashi while Shirin held the phone to his ear.

They waited until evening when another soldier came and told them the plane was ready. Duman drove the car right out to the plane and carried Charlie on board. The skeleton army presence at the airstrip seemed to be doing a brisk business in expatriations. The medium-sized business jet was also to carry two other Russian couples, one with a small boy and a girl. The boy stared wide-eyed at Charlie, and he tried to smile back so as not to frighten him. Shirin gave Charlie two pills and that was the last thing he remembered.

St. Petersburg
Saturday morning

She made it safely through the night, but that morning a ghost did appear to Avinashi. But not Lomonosov's.

"Charlie?" said Avinashi. "Charlie, is that you? I can hardly hear you." She poked her head out her sweater and stood up, trying for better reception. She was sore all over.

"Charlie, what happened? Are you alright? You don't sound fine, Charlie. Where are you?" He spoke slowly, and she could hear the pain in his voice. "You know where it is? Oh my God, that's great, Charlie. I don't know what to say. I knew you would. Uh-huh. I see. Yes, I guess I could find Tatiana. No, I can remember. Go ahead."

She listened carefully. He told her where to look. How to verify the position.

Avinashi was about to ask him if he was sure. Why he was sure. But she didn't. Because she believed in him. She believed in him enough, anyway. Now it was time to drill.

"I'm on it, Charlie."

"What terrible times," said Tatiana, looking at Tarasov's body inside the chiller. "Come, we must hurry." Avinashi had waited across the street from the Museum until she saw the old polyarnik coming to work on her day off. The plan was to sneak Avinashi in and out of the basement before Tatiana had to sound the alarm about finding the body.

The red volumes that Charlie had been reviewing were still laid out on the table. In minutes, Avinashi had the information she needed. Find a particular set of seismic traces. Look for these particular patterns, described very particularly. Record sets of coordinates. Lay them out on the geological map. Draw a set of lines, record the intersection. That was it. Oh my God, she thought. That's really, really far north.

In an internet café back over on Nevsky, Avinashi took one last sip of her hot tea then set to work. She pulled up a commercial web site that listed all offshore drilling rigs available worldwide. There were only about 350 total, and just a couple of dozen capable of working in the ice, so their options were likely to be pretty limited. She screened for ice-class rigs currently within striking distance of the Arctic. Drilling season was in high gear, and there was a fair amount of activity in the Barents, the Chuchki and the Beaufort. But all the rigs were listed as being under active contract. None that she could see that had been pulled off or had their contracts canceled. Of course, the *Northern Ranger* was still listed as active, drilling in the Laptev. Were the other listings up to date? Maybe someone would part with a rig for a premium. A long shot, but she would have to start making calls. How was she going to get Texso to sign off on this? Hey, Vicki, can you pull together the paperwork for a rig?

What about other types of rigs, she wondered. The only drilling that far north had been scientific, part of the deep ocean drilling program. Taking cores, not oil. She did some broad internet searches, but couldn't see any active IODP ship in the Arctic.

What about as part of the UN process? All the Arctic countries were in the process of either submitting or amending their applications for extended continental shelf boundaries. There was lots of high-frequency, bathymetric type data being collected, she expected. Any coring? She checked the Danes. They might be pliable. Nothing. Likewise the Canadians, the Norwegians. She even checked the Americans. Nada. The Russians were even less likely to help, but she checked them anyway.

Well, there we go. Of course. The ship Tatiana mentioned. The *Sevmorput*, or *Northern Passage*, the world's only ice-class cargo ship had completed its retrofit into the world's first nuclear-powered drillship. It was presently engaged in collecting cores from the Gakkel Ridge, to better support the Russian Federation's God-given territorial rights to same. The responsible ministry? Ah yes, the Natural Resources Ministry. Well, isn't that something. Now, if she could only figure out how to get the Russians to drill it for her, she'd be set. Hah, that's a challenge that Charlie would like. What he'd probably do is . . .

Avinashi dialed a number from memory. The line clicked and then rang through, clear.

"Yes." A man's voice, old. Telnov.

"Yuri Markovich. It's Avinashi Sharma."

"Miss Sharma. You ran off last night. Where did you go?"

"Charlie found it. He knows where it is."

"Good. Then we will go ask him again."

"You will find him missing."

A sigh. "Of course."

"I have a proposal for you, Yuri Markovich. Not for Lazarev, for you. For Russia."

She paused. A stone-faced young woman walked a young boy and a girl down the street outside the window. "Are you listening?"

"Yes."

"The oil is on the Lomonosov Ridge. Quite far north, actually. If I were to tell the Americans, Yuri Markovich, do you think you would be able to keep the oil? Or the Ridge?"

She took a sip of her tea. Chew on that, she thought.

"Russia has no ability to control the Arctic," she continued. "The few planes you could put in the air would be shot down like target drones. Whatever submarines you could launch would never be seen again. Would you choose to use nuclear weapons to defend the high seas, which you could never hope to control? The Arctic may be Russian, but only in the realm of ideas, of history. If it comes to practical military considerations, the Arctic will be American. With some Chinese and Euros for political cover."

The woman was still waiting for the bus with her children. Her face was brave beneath a mask of pain and anguish, just waiting for a bus that wouldn't come.

"But there is a way for Russia to keep the Lomonosov, Yuri Markovich. To keep the ridge, and the Arctic, and the oil."

The bus finally pulled up, but it was full. The woman tried to push her way on.

"All you have to do, Yuri Markovich, is drill it. Just go out and drill it. We need to drill it now, the world can't wait. We don't have months, we don't have weeks. We have days. We need to drill it now. And, as fortune would have it, you have a ship. And we don't. So that means you get to keep the oil. We have told no one where the oil is. Not the Americans. Not the British. And as long as you are making progress to drill the oil, we won't. In the meantime, we will secure a deal for you, and for Texso, with the Americans, for the oil. Russia to obtain all rights to the oil and to the Ridge. The US will support all necessary actions at the UN. They'll undertake to get the Danes and the Canadians in line, not that we need them. Chernov will be asked to have the PSA extended on the same terms to cover this field. That is the deal. You are being offered this one time only. If you don't say yes right now, we are going to the Americans."

"Chernov."

"Yes. Two paths, Yuri Markovich. You must choose. They will come for the oil. Do you think now that Oleg Maksimovich will be able to stop them? To defend Russia's oil? Who will better defend Russia? Chernov or Lazarev?"

She could hear him breathing. The bus came and went. The mother couldn't get on, so she sent her children on without her. She would have cried if she had any more tears.

"What is your answer, Yuri Markovich?"

"What ship?"

"The *Sevmorput*."

"It is not possible. They are on a scientific mission. They are not equipped for this."

"Well, I expect we can make it work. But if that's the way you feel, then perhaps I should just hang up. Shall I hang up?"

"No, no." She heard him take a sharp, resigned breath before exhaling his answer. "I agree. I agree to this. For Russia."

"For Russia. Yes."

"I will need to go to the ship, myself," said Telnov. "It is the only way."

"Well, I look forward to seeing you there. As Texso's representative, to make sure appropriate progress is made, per our arrangement."

"Very well."

"Please keep this line available, Yuri Markovich. I will be in touch."

The mother was walking back down the street, slowly.

CHAPTER 20

Dr. Drill

Arctic Ocean, 82 degrees North
Monday night

The captain of the *Sevmorput* sat at the long metal table in the mess with his senior officers on either side. He had come straight in off the deck and wore a long, thick, hooded parka like a royal robe. He was the indisputable master of the boat, an immense ice-class drill-ship the length of three football fields with a nuclear-powered heart that burned as hot as the sun. He had the ship tucked up behind the nuclear icebreaker *Sovetskiy Soyuz*, which was shredding a path through the first year ice as they made their way at over ten knots towards the Pole. The captain fixed his fierce gaze on the diminutive Telnov and growled like Neptune himself.

"You ask the impossible," said the captain. "This is not a serious request."

Avinashi sat on Telnov's side of the table down on the end, where she had been pushed by the two heavily-armed Neftepolk flanking Telnov. She stared at the captain's hands, two giant fists balled up on the table. They had deep gouges, where strips of flesh had been torn out and the wounds left to scar, but the captain seemed the sort not to have noticed at the time. The tiny geologist by comparison looked old and forgotten, like something from the dead letter office.

"Oh no, more serious than you can imagine," said Telnov. "And not even a request, but an order. And your failure to carry out this order will result in the direst consequences for you and your officers. Do I need to be more specific?"

The captain laughed, low and deep. "What, are we back in 1937? Then you might as well shoot us now and save us the trouble of failing."

Whereupon Maksim pulled out a pistol and shot the captain square in the forehead, exploding the back of his head across the photos on the bulkhead, scattering blood and bone and brains all over the assembled crews of the *Sevmorput.*

The blast propelled Avinashi up out of her seat. In shock, she stumbled back against the wall, her eyes fixed on the captain. His head tipped forward like he had fallen asleep. Then his entire body slumped against the table, rolled over sideways and hit the deck.

"Which of you is next in line?" said Telnov, with the room still ringing from the discharge. My God, for what thought Avinashi? Maksim and Yakov held their weapons on the officers. After some hesitation, one of the officers spoke up.

"I am Chief Mate Bukin," said the unremarkable man across from her. The oldest, she thought, even older than the captain. A lifetime number two.

"Captain Bukin, I will leave you now to prepare your plan," said Telnov. "Please call us when you are prepared to brief. No more than thirty minutes. I trust you will look more favorably on this opportunity than your predecessor." Telnov and the Neftepolk filed out of the officer's mess. After a moment's hesitation of her own, Avinashi ran after them.

Staring at Telnov's back as he walked away down the passageway, Avinashi balled her own fists, afraid and angry but also deeply ashamed. "I will not be a party to this, Yuri Markovich," she said, yelling at him. "Our deal is off." Maksim raised his rifle to strike her, but Telnov stopped him with a sharp word. Telnov made his way with some difficulty around the Neftepolk and back down the narrow walkway, walking right up to her until their noses were nearly touching. He breathed very slowly and quietly, like he was barely alive.

"But this is your doing, Avinashi," said Telnov. "You knew I would do anything to keep our land. So you threatened to take it from us unless I drilled your well. Now, after I have made the sacrifices you demanded, you want to go back on our arrangement? No, you will see this through. There is no going back, for any of us."

Avinashi went back into the officers' mess, where the tang of burnt powder mixed with its inevitable other half, the sweet, appalling smell of blood. The Chief Mate stood over his captain, dumbfounded. The short, pudgy Second Mate made an awkward sign of the cross over the body and barked out orders to grab bedding in which to wrap it, and not say a word to anyone while they were about it. The others he set to wiping down the wall with table linens. In minutes he had the captain locked in a storage closet, the worst of the mess cleaned up and everyone back at the table.

All eyes upon him, Chief Mate Bukin sat down at the table and stared at his hands with a vacant expression. Avinashi had not heard him utter a word since he had identified himself to Telnov. The Second Mate again stepped in to fill the void.

"Drilling department, what is your plan?" asked the Second Mate. "The Chief is waiting."

The dark eyes of a neatly-dressed fat man bugged wide open. This would be the toolpusher then, thought Avinashi, the head of drilling operations. "But you heard the captain," he said. "It's impossible! This is all her fault." He pointed at Avinashi, and they all turned and stared at her. "She will be the death of us all."

Well-practiced in this sort of thing, Telnov had made Avinashi deliver the bad news. She had just finished briefing them on their objectives before the captain delivered his fatal answer. They were to make their way, she had told them, at all possible speed to a position over the Eastern shoulder of the Lomonosov Ridge. A position at eighty-five degrees north, about 250 kilometers from the North Pole. There, in water depths of over 1500 meters, they were to drill to a total depth of 2800 meters below the seafloor. They would have only the *Sovetskiy Soyuz* for ice management, and they could coordinate with her only by signal lights because they had to maintain complete radio silence. This was because others might become curious as to their whereabouts and come hunting for them. Which is why they could not expect to have more than two days to complete their mission.

"I am sorry to lay this at your feet," said Avinashi. "I have no other choice. The stakes are very high."

"Yes, we see that," said the toolpusher, pacing back and forth, shaking his head. "More so for us than for you, apparently. But why, that is the question? Suddenly there is an overwhelming scientific desire to drill a deep core on the Lomonosov?"

"Not scientific," said Avinashi. "Economic. And not cores. We're drilling for oil."

The toolpusher nearly jumped across the table. "What? There is no oil on the ridge," he said, spitting and shaking his fists up at the unseen, cruel god that tested him so. "On my mother's grave, I swear I'll eat any oil north of eighty degrees."

"Enough," said the Second Mate. "That is not your worry, Rostov. Tell us, exactly what are your concerns with the mission?"

"Gladly," said the toolpusher Rostov. "First, no one has drilled this deep from the solid pack ice. The Americans drilled to four hundred meters on the ridge, but it took them weeks to get it right and they had two icebreakers. Oh, and yes they were allowed to use radios, and helicopters and an army of meteorologists. Even then they nearly broke their arms patting themselves on the back. And the Americans, they had multiple sites identified, so they could choose the one that was the most ice-free. Yes, once they were able to maintain position for just over a week. But there is no way to stay on station long enough to drill to 2800 meters. We would have to withstand the ice for nearly a month."

"But they were taking cores. And that's with rotary," said Second Mate Rubin. "What could Masha do, just going straight in?"

"No, no, rotary is the safe choice," said the toolpusher. "Most definitely. No one could ever fault you for going with rotary."

Chief Mate Bukin snapped out of his panic attack. "We will be on station in eight hours," he said. "When we arrive, we will commence normal drilling operations, just as if we expect to be successful. If we are fortunate at all, and in all likelihood this will be the case, ice conditions will force an unavoidable suspension of drilling, and it will be clear that we could not be held responsible. We must find a way to confirm this with the *Sovetskiy Soyuz*. I believe they could be helpful in this regard."

"Hey, wait just a minute," said Avinashi. "That's not a plan."

"It's the best plan," said the Chief Mate, looking at her for the first time. "Given the circumstances."

"Second Mate Rubin," she said. "A word outside, please?"

"What is this?" said Avinashi, out in the passageway with Rubin, after she had shut the door. "You're not even trying."

"Yes, we are trying to avoid being shot," said Rubin. "A worthy objective."

"Well, it's not going to work," she said, thinking of her conversation with Telnov. "There is no going back for him, and that means for us, unless we succeed."

"We are experienced in dealing with these situations," said Rubin. "We can manage the Deputy Minister."

"No, there must be another option," she said. "You said you wanted to use someone called Masha. Can she help us? Where is she? Let's talk to her."

Rubin stared back at her silently. She felt Ted and the field drifting away from her, like they were drowning, just out of her grasp. If there was any way to get this done, it would only get done with Rubin. He was the key to anything that happened on the *Sevmorput*, she could tell already.

"Maybe there is something worth taking a risk for," said Avinashi. "Something that you want. Something I could get for you. If you help me. Is there? What is it? Tell me."

"Not to be shot?"

"More than that. Something worth living for."

"Nothing you could get for me," said Rubin. "Now we must get back, the Chief will need me to brief Telnov."

"Ah, but then there is something you want," she said. "Are you married? Yes. Children? Of course. Something for your children, then. That's it, isn't it? Tell me, what is it you want?"

There was something. A dream of a father, a northern mariner.

"If you help me drill this well," said Avinashi. "I can and I will make this happen. You have my word. Now take me to Masha."

The *Sevmorput* was mammoth, a thousand-foot cargo ship, the only one in the world designed to crush Arctic ice. She had been refitted as a drillship and now a fifty-meter drilling derrick rose from her vast, flat middle, just over a moonpool cut into her bottom. Rubin led Avinashi across the long decks to the drilling platform as the sound of breaking ice sounded all about them in the gray, dim light of the cloudy northern night, to a cold storage berth just off the floor of the drilling platform.

They stood there with the head driller, Zubov, a balding giant whose muscles were apparent even under his cold-weather gear. One of his roustabouts ripped the nailed top off a wooden box with his bare hands. Inside, nestled in gray foam, lay a long, shiny metal cylinder with three wheels at one end, each edged with jagged metal teeth that shimmered like they had been dipped in diamonds.

"My Masha," said Zubov, picking up the massive hunk of metal with one hand and kissing it the business end with his filthy lips. "Isn't she beautiful?"

Avinashi could not hide her disappointment. "Masha is a drill bit," she said.

"Yes," said Rubin. "The Kogminsk L-59. But we call her Masha. The captain named it after his wife."

"His wife?" said Avinashi. "Is that traditional?"

"Oh no," said Rubin. "The captain is the only one to do this, as far as I know. He was uniquely inspired, I believe." He leaned over and lowered his voice. "The captain's wife was very formidable. A hard woman. The captain, he was always content to be at sea." He raised his eyebrows. "Theoretically, Masha could reach 2800 meters in less than twenty-four hours."

"She, I mean it, has that rate of penetration?" asked Avinashi. "That would be over a hundred meters per hour. How is that possible?"

"Masha is a turbodrill," said Rubin. "KulNeft's latest, and very finest. And in fact she can make over 250 meters per hour, this has been proven. Once, for over twenty-five minutes continuously."

"That's it? But it could have kept going?"

"Well, no. It broke. But this model has many further improvements."

Avinashi was quite familiar with turbodrills. They were the quintessential Russian technology. Born of trying circumstances, tremendously clever, insanely complicated and wholly impractical. The rotary rigs used historically throughout the West worked by sticking a fixed drill bit on the end of the pipe and turning the whole drill stem by means of a rotary table up at the drilling platform. Not surprisingly, this puts tremendous torsional stress on the drill stem and requires that the pipe be made of high-quality steel. In the Soviet Union, high-quality steel went to the military, not to Siberia to be stuck in the ground.

With turbodrills, only the bit turned, not the drill stem. This was accomplished by utilizing the hydraulic force of the drilling mud. The mud was forced down the drilling pipe and through a series of layered rotors just above the bit that turned the bit very fast. Often too fast, such that the teeth wore down or broke too quickly, or that the rotors, or the bearings, or the gearing used to reduce the rotations to a manageable rate, all failed. But when they worked, turbodrills could be faster than rotary drilling. Much faster. Out of necessity, the Russians had perfected, if the term could be used, this black art more so than anyone else.

"But I don't see that we have any other choice," said Avinashi. "It's Masha or nothing."

"Oh no, she is too unreliable," said Rubin. "You heard them. It would be too easy to criticize the decision to use her. Better to use rotary."

"Just answer me this," said Avinashi. "Unless the Lomonosov Ridge just happens to be underlain with butter, is Masha our only chance of drilling this hole in the next forty-eight hours?"

"If you insist on looking at it that way," said Rubin. "The answer is yes."

The futility of it all danced gaily across her mind's eye, laughing at her attempts to ignore it. She closed her eyes and tried, with all her strength, to think only of the possibilities.

"Okay," she said. "What have you got to put it on the bottom and make hole? Show me."

He led her out of the storage berth onto the open deck around the drilling platform. A towering derrick rose above her, the top seeming to scrape the bottom of the thick gray clouds above. Behind a railing, under the drilling platform set underneath the derrick, was the moonpool, closed now while they were underway.

"Yes," said Rubin. "Well, this obviously is the drilling platform."

She looked around. It looked like she was in a museum. Oil field equipment of the '60s. No high-tech drilling operations center like the *Northern Ranger*, no automatic pipe handling equipment to quickly rack pipe and make connections. No bothersome fire extinguishers.

"The basics," she said. "Good enough. Tried and true, nothing wrong with that. Do you have everything you need?"

"No," said Rubin. "But somehow we always make do. There were funding issues in outfitting the ship. The captain had to be somewhat creative. We collected this equipment from various sources. Some from Uralmash, other foreign equipment from sources in Shanghai, and Africa. Almost nothing new, obviously, but yes, all in working order, with the proper attention."

They did have a derrick, clearly, with fingerboards high up for holding the upright ends of stacked pipe. Suspended from the top was a hook with blocks and drawworks for lifting and lowering stands of new pipe and the drill string. Fastened to the side of the derrick was a standpipe and hose for running the drilling mud into the drill string. If there was a serviceable engine and a mud pump around somewhere, they could drill. Rubin was looking at her ominously.

"Now, Avinashi," he said. "May I show you something in confidence? With your assurance that it will not affect our arrangement?"

The only thing she would not stomach at this point was more violence. With Rubin, she felt this was not a concern. "Okay. What?"

Rubin led her around the moonpool and through a door that opened onto a flight of metal stairs leading down into a large open berth. In the middle of the room, connected to various hoses, sat a gleaming blue machine, as big as a large van. Bright yellow letters on the side spelled out KarLap.

"My mud pump," said Avinashi. "Of course."

"I am sorry," said Rubin. "But now I am sure you agree it was necessary. For Masha, a high-quality mud pump is most essential. This was the only one available."

She looked at him askance and let it go. "How are you set for pipe? Casing? Risers?" said Avinashi. "Enough for the job?"

"The *Sevmorput* is a large ship," said Rubin. "And fuel is not an issue. Our practice is to load everything aboard which we can find and ever possibly need, there is always room. We are carrying enough pipe and casing for two years of drilling. Not all of the best quality, but it will be sufficient. Risers, too, I believe."

"The drilling crews. They are up to this?"

"Rostov, our toolpusher as you would say, has only two crews, run in twelve-hour shifts. But Zubov's can do the work of two, if necessary. And they are all extremely capable. Selected by Telnov himself from KulNeft's best. Artists with the bit."

She turned and walked back outside, Rubin close on her heels. Damp, cold air washed in from the bow. Getting colder by the hour.

"We need to get back," said Rubin. "I need to conduct the briefing."

"No, I will conduct the briefing," said Avinashi. She fixed him with a hard stare. "Go make sure everyone is assembled. Every available man, anyone that doesn't have his hand on a lever or a wheel. And I want the drilling crews there, too, both shifts. I don't care if they all have to sit on the floor or in each other's laps. And I want you to get something else, too."

"Men of the *Sevmorput,*" said Avinashi. She was back in the mess standing in front of the wall of photos. Nearly a hundred men were crowded around her, leaving not an empty spot on the floor. Telnov stood back against the wall, barely visible over other broad shoulders, with Maksim and Yakov beside him.

"Once again, outside forces descend on Russian lands. And the very fate of the world, of civilization itself, will be decided by her response." She spoke clearly and softly, drawing them in. Demanding their attention, their absolute stillness.

"Ahead of us, under the ice, beneath the cold sea, sleeps a giant," she said. "A giant discovered by a Russian. A man called Lazarev, who dragged its secret out of the cold, step by painful step. It lays buried under a submarine ridge named for another Russian, a giant himself called Lomonosov, nearly within sight of Russia's white façade, the Arctic coast." The only sound in the room was the low, distant rumbling of crashing ice.

"The age of easy oil is over," she said. "And now the world is coming for the Arctic, and her hydrocarbons. For this giant, this Russian giant. The destiny of Russia, of the world, will be determined by whether they are successful. There is only one way that Russia can stop them." She nodded at Rubin. "Second Mate, if you will."

Rubin ordered glasses passed around the room, and bottles from the captain's private store were opened. She waited until the last glass was filled, and then a little bit more. Then she continued.

"To stop them, the men of the *Sevmorput* must get there first." She accepted a glass offered to her by Rubin. "And they do not have weeks, or days. They have hours. So I wish to make a toast. A toast to the brave men of the *Sevmorput,* who are called upon by Russia, at this fateful hour." She raised her glass, and finally raised her voice to the rafters. "To you, *Sevmorput!*" Whereupon the confines of the mess were rocked by the cheers of the men, yelling out *Sevmorput* at the top of their lungs, hugging and embracing, ready to walk across the Arctic end-to-end, barefoot if necessary.

Avinashi slipped out into the passageway, where she was greeted by Telnov, Yakov and a smirking Maksim.

"Perhaps the captain was right," said Telnov, right behind her. "It does seem to be 1937. The same semblance of truth. But I toast Avinashi Sharma all the same, and her efforts, on behalf of Russia."

Arctic Ocean, 88 degrees North
Tuesday late night

The ice was at least 9/10, and heavy, much worse than she expected. Avinashi hung on the port rail looking over the side as crumpled planes of ice the size of tennis courts passed by, each as thick as she was tall. It was colder, much colder than Severnaya Zemlya, and must have been at least ten degrees below zero. It was damp, and the skies were still filled with heavy clouds. Safer from prying eyes, she thought.

The *Sovetskiy Soyuz* was doing a yeoman's job up current from the *Sevmorput.* The captain and crew were pirouetting the forty-thousand ton vessel back and forth like an angry dog, crushing the multiyear floes down into treacherous pieces just not quite large enough to knock the *Sevmorput* off station. In the heavy ice, her dynamic positioning drive, consisting of six omni-directional propulsion units that could be extended from the hull, was nearly useless. All the crew could do was try to keep the ship pointed in the direction of the ice and currents and try to stay on station with the main engine and propeller, leaving it to the heavy steel curtain extending down from the moonpool to keep ice off the drill string.

As well as they were doing, she could see that they desperately needed another icebreaker. They had been on station for twenty-four long hours already. In order to stay on for days, you needed at least one more icebreaker to catch the ones that would inevitably fall through. They could rely on luck and superior skill only for so long. Telnov and Yakov had gone aloft in the *Sevmorput*'s helo to assist in scouting ice conditions, but she had not seen them for over half an hour.

Everywhere on deck able seamen and roustabouts swung heavy hammers to break and clear the ice. The rungs of the derrick were all frozen over all the way up to the derrickman, Volvsky, who stood sixty meters in the air on the monkeyboard, pulling stands of pipe out of the rack with the elevator when it was time to join them to the drill string. In between connections, Volvsky would dance back and forth on the monkey board, holding on with one hand as he waved at her with the other while the derrick swung back and forth as the ship was knocked by the ice. Of course he was not wearing his safety belt. Zubov's crew had insisted on working two full twelve-hour shifts to start, the second of which was nearly ended. However, they appeared ready to do the entire hole themselves. Perhaps she had motivated them a bit too well.

Zubov stood concentrating, one massive hand on the brake, controlling the height of the drill string, and thus the weight of the bit, and Masha's penetration rate, as if he were making tender, terrible love to the earth. Zubov had cleared the deck, allowing only his crew, and Avinashi, to watch him in this most private act. No sophisticated drilling software to analyze and adapt to streams of data flowing back from below, just a pair of electric Russian eyes on a dirty Chinese gauge and his iron fist on the brake.

In drawing up the well plan, Rostov and his team had opted for quick and dirty over a by-the-books approach. Once on station, they had quickly tripped pipe to the bottom. With conventional riser-less rotary set-up, they drilled a hundred meter long, eighty-centimeter diameter hole and laid in structural casing and a Norwegian blow-out preventer of questionable heritage. Then they tripped the pipe out and re-deployed the riser and drill stem, this time with Masha. She was indeed a hard woman, and they were making fast hole. Zubov was already at five hundred meters. Only 2300 meters to go.

So as not to break the drill string, they needed to keep the angle of deviation from the line determined by the hole within certain limits, generally just a few degrees off normal. It was better then that they were working at such depths, because a fixed angle translated into a bigger absolute offset distance at the surface. In their case, at these depths, they had about 150 meters to wander before they snapped the pipe or the risers. If they were getting close to this angle, they had two choices. Take a chance and ride it out, or trip the drill string out of the hole. A normal deepwater operation would have a device on the bottom hole assembly that could sever the drill stem and seal in the hole in seconds if an emergency arose. That was not an option for them, because that meant losing Masha. They would have to pull the string.

A loud, distant horn started. Again, and again. The *Sovetskiy Soyuz*. From high above, Volvsky the derrickman was pointing towards the bow and yelling. Avinashi couldn't hear a word he said. She took off running for the bow, still with a slight hitch in her stride.

She ran down the decks, careful not to slip on the ice that was everywhere, then up the stairs, around the side of the forecastle, passing under the lifeboats suspended above, then out to the open foredeck, and looked over the forward edge.

The *Sovetskiy Soyuz* was still about a kilometer away but pointed in the wrong direction. Towards them. And in between them was the reason why.

Pack ice is sea ice, formed from freezing open seas. Of varying thickness, depending on age, but invariably flat to the sea, unless thrust up in pressure ridges. But when most people think of polar ice, they are most often thinking of glaciers and icebergs, ice that forms on land, not sea. In the high Arctic true icebergs are rare. The icebergs famous for sending unsinkable ocean liners to their grave are calved off the coast of West Greenland and sent down along the coasts of Newfoundland and Labrador through 'Iceberg Alley' to menace North Atlantic shipping. But occasionally, very rarely, the glaciers of the far northern Canadian and Russian islands will calve immense flat sheets of ice. Tabular icebergs. Ice islands. Huge masses of ice rising above the surrounding pack ice.

But very rare. Quite bad luck to run into one. One like that off the bow of the *Sevmorput*. An ice island. A small one. Only the size of a city block. But headed directly for them. Still breathing hard, she ran off for the drilling platform.

The driller Zubov was not yelling at the derrickman Volvsky, he was positively screaming at him.

"We have been given the order to pull the drillstring," said Zubov, seeing her. "The imbecile, he refuses. He will lose Masha for us. We must get Masha out, they are going to hold off as long as they can."

At which point ice island kissed the bow of the *Sevmorput*, shaking the entire thousand foot length of double-hulled steel like a toy, and flinging the tall stands of drill pipe across the derrick. Volvsky screamed again, this time in pain. When she looked up, Volvsky was on the back of the monkey board jammed up against the derrick, hugging a pipe. He was not moving much, just screaming.

"Get me up there," said Avinashi. She saw a safety harness and started buckling it on.

"Two lunatics in my derrick I do not need," yelled Zubov.

"I can throw pipe," she said. "Get me up there."

"Baby Masha!" he yelled, laughing. "Yes, hard woman, you go give him hell, and get me my bit back." He hit the brake and the crown block and massive hook came plummeting out of the derrick. Where was the airtugger, she thought, thinking of the small winch that usually hauled up the derrickman? Of course, she thought, up in the derrick. She held her ground, and he stopped the massive hook a foot from her head. He threw a chain around the hook and around the smaller hook on the waist of her belt, then stepped back.

"Don't touch anything," he yelled, leaning hard against the brake, sending Avinashi flying up into the cold air. Immediately she started swinging back and forth inside the derrick, the swaying of the tower being amplified as she went further up. Not touch anything? She would when she got smashed against the side, she thought. She came up hard and fast close against a side crossbeam. Instinctively, she put out her arm to protect herself. She clipped the beam hard with her forearm, protecting her head, but of course the pull on her waist did not stop. So as her arm slowed her upper body, her midsection kept traveling skyward, flipping her upside down. She closed her eyes, grabbed her harness and hung on for dear life. Seconds later she stopped abruptly, almost getting thrown off the hook, she was sure, and upside down at the top of the tower.

"Kick the hook." It was the derrickman Volvsky. "Kick it, hard now. Then grab the chain." She put her sore toes up against the hook. And pushed, and flailed wildly for the chain, just catching the icy steel in her left. "On the monkeyboard now, hurry."

She hung ten stories over the drilling platform, suspended from the hook, looking over at the monkeyboard. It was half covered in ice.

"Step carefully," he said. He was pinned up against the derrick at the back of the monkey board. A stand of pipe was jammed against his leg. At the top the stand was wedged under a beam, so frozen. His face was twisted by pain.

"Coming," she said. "Hang on." She swung back and forth a bit, wondering how she was going to get off, when she came crashing down on the monkeyboard, where Zubov, watching from below, just dropped her. "That lunatic, he's going to kill me," she said, grabbing the slippery edges of the monkeyboard. Her heart pounding, she unhooked her safety belt from the chain, and instantly the hook plummeted back to the platform below.

She looked around for an attachment point for her belt. "Where can I hook up?"

"Tie yourself to this wreck?" said Volvsky. He shook his head. "Too dangerous."

"Right," she said. "Let's get you out of here." She stood up and grabbed the railing, then stepped carefully across the slick monkey board. She reached the pipe, grabbed it and tugged. It was stuck fast.

"Not coming out," he said. "They may have to cut me out. I won't be in your way. You just start racking pipe as it comes. I'll talk you through it."

She looked forward. The *Sevmorput* was struggling against the ice island and it looked like they were being pushed back. The *Sovetskiy Soyuz* was making an arc, swooping around their starboard side. She assumed they were planning to try to slide up alongside the *Sevmorput* to face the ice island side-by-side. That maneuver would take time in the thick ice. Then she heard the crown block whirring towards her fast from the deck.

She had not actually 'worked' the tower, but she had been in one once, in West Texas, with a Texso management training group. And they had not handled pipe, of course. Just went up with the airtugger, stood on the monkeyboard with the derrickman, watched him do his thing. Just to say you did it, and also probably to scare the hell out of you, so you would learn to take HSE seriously without getting yourself killed. Now, what was she supposed to do?

"Grab that length of rope," said Volvsky. "When the stand of pipe comes up, swing the rope around it. After they have the bottom end set in the mousehole, they'll release the elevators." The elevators were the two pieces of a metal collar that wrapped around the pipe just below the joint to haul it out of the ground. "You pull your end of the pipe into the fingerboard over here. Then you do it again. And again. Simple job. And you can enjoy the view."

The massive crown block flew by her head, then stopped. The pipe hung a few feet away from her. "Now," he said. She swung the rope around the pipe but missed the end. "Get closer," he yelled. Zubov was already yelling at her. She leaned against the icy rail and whipped the rope around, grabbing the other end cleanly. The elevators released and plummeted out of sight. "Pull!" She put her boot up against the rail and put her back into it. The pipe flew over to the fingerboards, and she swung it back into the last slot just before it jammed against Volvsky. Out of the corner of her eye she saw the Sovetskiy Soyuz fly by the side of the Sevmorput, just two or three meters apart.

"Again," he said. "Here it comes."

How Zubov's crew managed to break down the connections so fast she did not know. But the ends of the pipe stands came flying out. Triples, three sections of ten meter pipe each. Eighteen stands they had to pull to get Masha out of the hole. Two minutes per. Over half an hour. They would never make it. They were still being pushed back. They had to be at five degrees now. Any minute the stem or the casing would snap and Masha would be lost.

Three. She almost slipped and fell. The pipes were flexible, particularly in triples, and this stand almost whipped her over the side when for some unexplainable reason it started to wobble. Four. It was getting harder and harder to pull the stand across. Her legs and her back and arms burned. They were still being pushed back, barely. Five. She was so tired she couldn't stop the stand and it swung all the way down and smashed against Volvsky. He screamed bloody murder before she could get it off of him and in the fingerboards. "Again," he cried. "Again." She couldn't handle them anymore, she couldn't. The next stand came flying up.

Another orange hull charged across her field of view. An icebreaker on the port side, Russian, with a shark's open jaws painted on the bow, devouring the ice, again nearly brushing their port rail. With the *Sevmorput's* helo on deck. The *Yamal*, thought Avinashi. Telnov had found the *Yamal* on its way to the Pole and commandeered it with the able assistance of the Neftepolk.

She wrapped up the stand, and somehow managed to throw it into place and not crush Volvsky.

"Hey, it's her. Up there." Someone was yelling. Down on the deck of the *Yamal*, two or three dozen people, in bright outdoor gear. Some were pointing up at the derrick. At her, the dark skinned girl in her distinctive blue and green KarLap parka and pants.

"She's drilling for oil!" Good god, she thought. The polar-trekkers. They started chanting. "No ice for oil, no ice for oil!"

Another stand came flying up. She wrapped it up and threw it into place. She was using the sway of the derrick, taking the pressure off her back.

The stand of pipes clanged loudly. More of a snap, really. She wondered if she had broken something. She looked down at the platform, then over at the *Yamal*, making its way. One of the eco-tourists was pointing a bear rifle at her. She dove behind the stands of pipe as another shot clanged off the derrick.

There was the sound of an explosion as the bow of the *Yamal* hit the ice island. Three nuclear reactors with a combined eight hundred thousand horsepower of thrust leaned into the ice, and pushed back.

The drawworks had stopped. The pipe stands had stopped coming. Avinashi peered over the monkey board down onto the platform. The driller Zubov was coming up on a harness. She peered around the stands. No sign of anyone with a rifle. She imagined Maksim and Yakov had put a quick end to that. She could see the *Yamal* and the *Sovetskiy Soyuz* were pushing off the ice island.

"We had to stop pulling the string," said Zubov. "I felt a resistance. I think the bit is stuck. No coming out. Only down now." He reached over and ripped the pipe off Volvsky with one hand. His leg was broken. They lowered him down with the airtugger.

Volvsky safe on the deck, she leaned against the rail of the monkey board and looked out at the two icebreakers as they reassumed their positions. And beyond them, to another object in the distance. Something white, and very large. Not really an object. It looked more like the coast of Greenland.

Without waiting for the airtugger, she hooked herself with the chain back onto the crown block hook and swung off the monkeyboard, yelling at them to bring her down. She had to get to the bridge, she thought. Then she dropped.

"What is that?" she asked, breathing hard. Her lungs felt like they had freezer burn.

Rubin and Chief Mate Bukin were both on the bridge. Rubin was looking out the windows through the biggest pair of binoculars she had ever seen.

"Another ice island," he said. "The section we just hit must have calved from this beast. It is directly up current from our present position."

"Can the icebreakers handle it?" she asked.

"Ten could not," said Bukin. "Millions of tons of ice. High, catching the winds, which are increasing. No chance. Tell Zubov to pull the string."

"He can't," said Avinashi. "Not without losing Masha."

She grabbed the binoculars from Rubin and almost dropped them on the floor. She had to squeeze her elbows together and prop them on her chest to hold up the heavy glasses. She propped the other ends against the windows and looked through.

The island lorded over the surrounding pack ice, its leading edge rising several meters up out of the sea. It had to be at least three kilometers across, and it was going to sweep right across their position. Years and years of ice, laid down layer by layer, then spawned on some unholy island and sent around and around the Arctic until turned up here. Now. Fate was not to be denied, it seemed.

"You would need Moses himself to part that devil," said Rubin.

Cold tears dripped uncontrollably from under the rubber shields on the binoculars. No, please, she pleaded. There has to be a way. See it, see it.

And then there it was. Just possibly.

"Get the helo over here," she said. "I need to go out to the island. Quickly."

She heaved the glasses at Rubin and ran off to her room to grab her survival suit.

Avinashi looked straight down at the ice island from the side window of the banking helicopter. Not flat like the surrounding pack ice, the island's sprawling surface rose and fell like a rolling, frozen prairie. The low peaks were deep blue, hard ice polished smooth by relentless winds, the shallow valleys filled with dim, dirty snow. She tried to pick out the right line across the island, taking mental pictures, memorizing subtle landmarks.

The first ice island was only discovered in the 1940s by the Americans. Or perhaps first by the Soviets, as they later claimed. In any event, it was dubbed T-X by the Yanks, for Target X. A secret designation. T-X was so large it showed up on the radar of a patrolling B-28. It generated considerable excitement, offering many more logistical possibilities than the fragile pack ice. It could host a large, permanent airfield. A military base, or a weather station. Much better than the primitive, dangerous Soviet drift stations. But then, after considerable excitement, it promptly disappeared. A vast island of ice, just vanished. Then it was found again, weeks later. Then promptly disappeared. Easy to hide in the Arctic if you're the right color. Eventually another was sighted, and thus T-X became T-1 and the new island T-2. Then finally there was T-3, which went on to host an American drift station for fifteen years before it broke up against the shores of northern Greenland. Other lucky countries found their own ice islands. The Canadians, the Swedes. They were all as precious and dear to their owners as prime Manhattan real estate.

The pilot pulled up and scouted for a place to land. She had asked him to target the center, close to the front. It was a short flight. The island was now less than a kilometer from the Sevmorput. In less than an hour, it would rip the ship right off the drill string.

They closest flat spot they could find was about four hundred meters off the line she had picked out. The helicopter set down, and Avinashi climbed out as the rotors kept turning. Yakov followed her. Telnov was not about to send her out unsupervised. Her companion was dressed for the ice, like herself, and carried a large rifle, although he did not make her feel safer.

She was cold to her bones, and the blast from the rotors did not help, sending icy air straight down her back. She trudged across the snow to get clear. This way, she yelled at Yakov, and they made their way across the island.

Her adrenaline having run dry, she was hit by a wave of exhaustion. She struggled to put one foot in front of the other. The island was a world of whites and grays and blues. She kept her eyes focused on the ground in front of her and counted out the steps. Four hundred should do it.

She lost her count twice, but seemed to have gone about the right distance when she spotted the deep notch in the edge that she had spied from above. Good enough. She turned to the 'inland' direction and started to count steps again. One hundred. Then another two hundred.

At the first stop, she found a spot that still had a little snow cover and formed a shallow depression with her glove. Then she pulled out one of her satellite beacons, turned it on and put down in the snow.

"We need to hurry," she said to Yakov. "One more." She started to count out steps. Until a distinct flicker ahead caught her eye. Blue, yes. Also gold, again not unusual. What was different was the way it moved. It flapped. She got up on her toes and looked again.

Prior to laying claim to their ice island the Swedes had conducted precious little Arctic research, not having an Arctic coastline, thanks to Norway hogging it all and somewhat contrary to popular misconception. But somehow a Canadian named Hobson with a knack for finding ice islands had talked the Swedes into funding his pet polar research. From among his finds he selected a beauty, subsequently dubbed 'Hobson's Choice', which gyrated around the Arctic for fifteen years until the Swedes felt they had learned enough about the Arctic and pulled Dr. Hobson's funding. He packed up his equipment and said farewell to the island, which was promptly lost again. Although he did leave one thing behind, reportedly.

A Swedish flag.

The distinctive crack of a .308 sounded from behind her, and a scarlet spray burst onto the snow and ice to her left. Yakov fell to his knees and threw his arms out across the pattern traced in front of him.

She spun around and crouched down low. A sole figure kneeled on the ice about twenty-five yards back, pointing a rifle.

The figure stood and started walking toward her, still holding the weapon on her. A man, dressed in bright red, modern polar gear. The latest technology. A young, tall man, covering the ground quickly in long strides.

Marcus, the happy-go-lucky intern from Terra Mater.

He pulled up about ten yards away. There was nowhere to run. She pulled out the second beacon from her pocket and held it high.

"Marcus, stop," she said. "Or I'll set it off."

"Set off what, Avinashi, your satellite beacon?" said Marcus. He held her other beacon up, having plucked it from its nest. "Avinashi, when will the insanity stop?" He planted the butt of the rifle hard on the ice and kneeled beside it, gasping for air. "And you make us party to this atrocity, sending your Russian goons to kidnap us and bring us here, to help you destroy the planet. Do you believe in destiny, Avinashi? Well, starting today, I do. I believe I was brought here to stop you." He started to shake violently.

"My god, Marcus, you're wet," she said. His parka and pants were soaking wet. "You're going to freeze to death."

"Finn lowered me to the ice and I came out across the pack, after you," he said, very slowly. "I slipped. I fell in the sea. But I got out. I had to. I'm sorry Avinashi. You leave me no choice. Against the fate of the world, the life of one person doesn't matter at all. My life." He tried to raise the rifle. "Your life." She looked around. She would never make it over the hill.

"Please, Marcus," she said. "Don't. You don't know what you're doing. What about billions, does that make any difference?"

He had the barrel pointed straight at her. Then she heard the hammer slam the pin home with a little click that carried over the ice. But no explosion.

Wet shells.

She turned and ran across the ice, as best she could. Two hundred steps. She turned on the second beacon and planted it in the ice. Then she ran north, to the side of the island with the helicopter. She lost count of the number of steps when the first blast wave knocked her off her feet, sending her flying out across the ice.

CHAPTER 21

MOSCOW CALLING

London
Wednesday morning

W hen Charlie awoke, the nurse called in the doctor. He appeared to be Iranian. He checked Charlie's dressings then handed him a letter and told him to stay in bed. It was a handwritten note from Shirin. A phone number in case he wanted to call her. Look for new clothes in the closet. I hope they fit.

Charlie called the Texso car service. They likely thought it odd he didn't know where he was. An address in Finchley, he told them, after a brief investigation. Was Steve available?

"You alright then, Mr. Joiner?" asked Steve, eyeing him in the rear-view mirror.

"Little tired, that's all," said Charlie. "Probably could use some time off."

Steve nodded. "I'm sure it would be well-deserved, sir."

Charlie's chest throbbed under the pain medication. Even his slow, careful movements getting dressed and out to the car had ripped the sutures, and he could feel blood soaking the bandages. He looked at his shirt, but it still appeared all white and business as usual.

The air held perfectly still as the sun burned away the morning haze. The traffic seemed unusually light, but that could have been the power of suggestion. Up ahead, he could see One Canada Tower still standing tall, a pyramid before the fall. They pulled into the underground parking garage, and Charlie tried to get out with a minimum of tearing.

His key card belonged to someone in a past life, but he was able to talk his way into the elevator, through security, past the receptionist, all the way to his office, where he sat and waited for them to arrive.

Roger was first to appear at his office door. "Charlie, what in God's name happened to you?" Charlie looked down. There were traces of red on the front of his shirt. "And where is Ted? Please tell me you know where he is."

"I can make this right, Roger."

"Charlie. We are well past that now."

"No, we're not. This is the last thing I'm ever going to ask you, Roger. But I'm asking. Help me."

Roger said nothing. He appeared truly lost.

"Alright, Charlie. But not for you. Only because no one else seems to know what to do."

Charlie's phone rang. The receptionist. "Mr. Stoyan in the lobby for you."

"Could you please show him to the conference room?" said Charlie.

Jacob Stoyan was seated at the long conference room table when they entered.

"Jacob," said Charlie. "This is Roger Crawford." They shook hands.

"My god," said Stoyan. "What did he do to you, Charlie?"

"Enough," said Charlie. He dialed the receptionist from the table phone. "Abigail, could you please find some coffee for Mr. Stoyan? Thanks."

Charlie sat down carefully in a chair. "We can turn this situation around," he said. "We can get the oil flowing again."

"The situation is beyond critical," said Stoyan. "This morning NATO forces moved into Baku from Georgia. But Russian partisans blew the fields. The facilities are useless. It will take years to get them back on line. It moved us backward. That was the last option."

"No," said Charlie. "Our last option is Chernov."

"Chernov? He's here in London, on the run. He has nothing."

"I doubt that. I think Chernov is close. It just got away from him a bit. We can tip it back."

"How?"

"We need to give Chernov the Lomonosov."

"How will that help?"

"Who can we get to run this up the flagpole?" said Charlie. "Quickly."

"Well, any idea from you would probably have to run through Phelps. The Vice President's office has been running point given his relationship with Lazarev."

"Can you get Phelps on the phone? Now?"

Stoyan dialed in from the conference room speakerphone. The White House operator tracked him down after a few clicks.

"Phelps."

"Brad, this is Jacob Stoyan. I'm calling from London, and I'm sitting here with Charlie Joiner."

"Christ, Joiner. Nothing personal, but by all rights you should be dead or in someone's fucking cell by now."

"Not yet. Maybe soon."

"Maybe sooner than you think. Your girl called me and ratted you out, Joiner. You and your deal with Lazarev. Behind our back, you go off to drill some fucking wildcat at the top of the world. You are one piece of work, Joiner. Civilization is spiraling the drain and you're blithely doing deals with the devil. Fucking amazing. Well, in case you haven't heard, we sent a little Valentine to the two of you. We had a B-2 parked over the Pole ready to send a JDAM down Lazarev's chimney should that opportunity present itself, which it had not because for some reason our prime asset went dark. In the meantime, we were looking for a way to get our point across, so we were only too happy to dump a rack of them down on his drillship. That's right, Joiner, game over. And your girl called it in for us. Unfortunately, the one honest person in your outfit had to be a casualty of war, but that one is on you, too. Add it to your list."

Roger mouthed 'Who?' at Charlie, but he ignored him.

"Don't worry about it, Brad," said Charlie. "I just talked to Avinashi an hour ago. She's fine."

"Don't try to bullshit me, Joiner. You're no good at it."

"I'd have you talk to her again, but I assume you'll understand if she doesn't completely trust you. They were having a little ice management problem, and she felt she could count on you to do the expedient thing. So she played a little trick on you. She feels really bad about it. I told her you would understand."

The line was silent. "Well, fuck me sideways," said Phelps. "Another Texso cowboy." The receptionist appeared with coffee. "Tell her I'm glad she's not dead."

"I'll do that."

"And tell me what the fuck is going on."

"I need the US to give the Lomonosov Ridge to the Russians," said Charlie.

"What?"

"We found it, Brad. We found the giant field Lazarev was looking for."

"One oil field ain't gonna get it done here, Joiner."

"How about two Ghawars? Maybe four."

"Okay, maybe."

"We need to give it to Chernov so he can use it to get rid of Lazarev. That's our best way out. We need to give them the Ridge."

"Okay, well I have two problems with that. First of all, how are you so sure that Chernov would or could do that? He seems more intent on saving his ass in London, raiding the minibar at the Connaught on NATO's tab."

"Don't underestimate him. He can do it. The military was never totally committed. You don't think some are getting cold feet, seeing that all holy hell has finally been unleashed? He'll get it done."

"Okay, fine. But second, you have absolutely no credibility when it comes to finding anything. There are people here that wouldn't trust you to find your own ass with both hands. You've got to understand that, right?"

"You don't have to take my word for it. Before you make the deal, I'll have proof. But if I can bring proof, I want you to tell me I can promise the Ridge."

"I would say no if I had anything else right now. But I don't, as I assume your mole Stoyan has told you. So I will float this insane proposition and call you back. But believe me, if we hadn't just gotten our ass handed to us in the Caspian and I wasn't desperate to change the topic I wouldn't waste my breath. Give me your number."

After a long ten minutes the phone in the conference room rang. Phelps.

"Alright. But it's gonna have to be rock solid. A picture of Ms. Sharma with her hand dripping with polar crude. Something like that. You've got two days. But let me just say that time is not your friend."

"Fine," said Charlie. "Roger will get back to you with what we need legally."

Phelps vanished back into the ether.

"Jacob, it's time to go see the Grey Cardinal," said Charlie. "Let's see what our little friar can do. Can you come with me? I need you to verify what Phelps told us."

Steve had to stop a block short of the Connaught, where the security checkpoints began. With the panic, this now meant tanks and soldiers, not just a few bobbies. Stoyan was able to get them through, but it took them half an hour to make it all the way through the cordon and up to the penthouse suite at the top of the hotel. Charlie had been there once before, on one of Jamilov's excursions to London to spend some of UKP's money. They were led into a large, elegant sitting room with floor-to-ceiling windows overlooking the Mayfair District.

"Gentlemen." Chernov breezed into the room, dressed impeccably in a navy blue suit with heavy, confident pinstripes and a silver tie. He embraced Charlie gently, kissing him on both cheeks. He wore cologne. Something sweet and smoky. "I am sorry for your suffering. So unnecessary." He invited them to sit, while a butler asked for their drink preferences.

"We found it, Viktor Ilyich," said Charlie. "We found the field Oleg Maksimovich was looking for. This could be a massive find. Out on the Lomonosov. And it could be Russia's, if you can handle Lazarev."

"What do you mean, it could be Russia's?"

"It's in the contested area. Which will not be contested if you can get rid of Lazarev. If you can use this to make a deal to get rid of Lazarev."

"So you understand he is vulnerable," said Chernov. "He always was. In fact, I never gave him much of a chance, but then I didn't anticipate your spectacular failure. But he never had time to get all his pieces in place. You rushed him too much, Charlie. Money has been lost. People that needed to be taken care of were not. The situation is very fluid. Yes perhaps, with the right incentives, we could see some reconsideration. So, what is the plan?"

"You have forty-eight hours. That's all I could get."

"Very well. But Charlie, back to what you said earlier. You said it could be a massive find?"

"Yes. It's one of the missing supergiants. A hundred billion barrels. Possibly two hundred."

"Well, that's a good conversation starter. I will see what I can do. You understand, of course, that you have a credibility problem, don't you? There may be some undiscovered tribes in the Amazon that would give you the benefit of the doubt, but the people I talk to will need proof."

"We are drilling as we speak."

"Very well. Let me make some calls. I am not sure there is anything I can do, but we must try."

London
Wednesday evening

Charlie went back to his office, partly by force of habit, partly to sit in his chair for one last time. He looked out the window as the sun set the City on fire, turning everything in sight a crimson red. He thought of Avinashi and Ted. Very close to the end now.

His mobile rang.

"Charlie, will you see me?" Shirin, her voice just a hoarse whisper.

"Meet me at the flat. I'm headed there now."

Charlie stood in the darkened library. He held a drink in his hand that would probably kill him if he added it to all the painkillers. Charlie set the glass down and flipped on the light. He kept a few pictures on the bookshelf. His parents. The whole family, Charlie about twelve. Sheila. The two of them and the baby. The buzzer sounded.

"Charlie, it's Duman." He buzzed him in.

Charlie opened the door and waited out in the hallway. He heard a single pair of heavy footsteps coming up the stone staircase. Around the corner of the railing came Duman, carrying Shirin. Gently, tenderly, slowly, like a grieving father with his little daughter.

"Duman," said Charlie. "What happened?"

The giant shook his head. Tears flowed from behind the dark glasses.

"Come in, put her on the bed," said Charlie.

Duman followed Charlie into his bedroom. Charlie pulled back the covers and Duman set her down.

The sight of her made Charlie physically ill. In three days, Shirin had nearly wasted away. Her skin was worn and yellowed and lay loosely over her bones like a collapsed tent. Her head was wrapped in a blue silk scarf, the beautiful hair clearly gone. She looked like an old invalid, trapped and tormented inside a body that refused to die. Only her eyes appeared as they did when he last saw her, except that now they overflowed with even more pain. Charlie pulled the covers over her carefully and knelt by her side.

"Charlie," she said. Her voice was faint and distant, like she was trapped at the bottom of a well, just out of reach. "Oh, Charlie. The doctors can't help me. But they wouldn't let me go. I asked Duman to find you. I have no right. But I am so afraid. It hurts so much. Why, Charlie? Why is there such suffering as this?"

"Don't be afraid, Shirin. I'm here."

She began to moan, with a long, low sound so alien and overpowering it seemed something had possessed her. After it passed, she was left crushed on the bed, making weak, quivering cries.

"So much pain, Charlie. Please help me."

He got up and went out of the bedroom. Charlie walked over to where Duman stood at the dining table, frozen. In front of him lay an open leather bag. Whatever he had been able to grab on their way out was dumped on the table. Some papers and a pile of vials, syringes and bottles. Charlie rummaged through it. He could hear Shirin moaning again from the bedroom.

The vials and bottles all bore the names of other patients. There were medicines for heart conditions and infections. No painkillers. All useless. He took one of the syringes and went to the bathroom. The Iranian doctor had given him a bottle of pills, but also a small bottle of morphine. Charlie filled the syringe with half the dose recommended for his own body weight. Shirin was calling for him now, more loudly.

He walked back into the bedroom. Her eyes were wide open, terrified. He pulled back the covers. She had soiled the sheets and there was faint, pungent smell like a baby. "Oh Charlie oh Charlie oh Charlie." He stuck the needle in the front of her thigh and pressed in the plunger.

After Shirin drifted off into unconsciousness, Charlie had Duman help move her back and forth on the bed so he could clean her and change the sheets. Then he sent Duman back to the Iranian doctor for more morphine.

He looked through the papers on the dining room table. There was a report on cheap printer paper. *Yazdani, Shirin. Hemorrhagic discharge in saliva and urine. Acute diarrhea and vomiting. Presence of Alpha emitters. Symptoms consistent with Polonium-210 exposure, one thousand to ten thousand times median lethal dose. Pain management initiated. Patient discharge request denied per an Inspector so-and-so.*

No wonder they would not let her go. Another Russian assassination. Perhaps not on UK soil this time, like Litvinenko, but now a British subject rather than Russian. She was evidence. But how could Lazarev have gotten to her so quickly? Charlie went back into the bedroom and sat in the chair. When his eyes adjusted to the dark, he was surprised to see her staring back at him.

"I wanted to say yes, Charlie."

He knelt back on the floor, right beside her. "I know."

"I couldn't. With what I had done."

"It doesn't matter."

"How could I have done this? I deserve to suffer."

"No. You did it for others. Not yourself. Your family."

"But I couldn't leave you there. They could not make me do that."

"No, you didn't leave me there."

"I couldn't."

He took her hand in his. "Say yes."

"Now?"

"If you will."

"Yes, Charlie. Yes."

"I'll never leave you."

"But here I am again, leaving you. I am so sorry, Charlie. We both know what that is like. My poor Adam. Your beautiful wife and son. And now I am leaving you all alone, again."

"Not yet."

As the room darkened, she seemed to be disappearing before his eyes.

"Shirin."

"Yes, Charlie?"

"I will not be all alone. There is still my son."

"Your son? Charlie, your son died with Sheila. I am so sorry, Charlie."

"No. My son is alive."

"Charlie, what do you mean? How could he be alive? He died in the explosion."

"No. Neither of them did. They weren't killed by the bomb."

"What do you mean? I don't understand. It's the medicine, Charlie. Please tell me, but slowly. I want to understand."

"I couldn't get them out. They were caught. There was fuel everywhere, and flaming pieces from the bomb and the car, but the gas tank still hadn't ignited. Sheila was screaming at me to get the baby out. He was screaming, too. We could see his foot was crushed. I pulled on his belts but I couldn't get them unstuck. We both did. She was trapped, and she still kept trying to help me with the baby's straps. I told her to get out but she wouldn't listen. I had a knife, I always had a knife, and I cut the straps. I had to yank his foot out. The foot was really bad, and he stopped crying. Sheila made me get the baby out and then it was too late. I barely got the baby out. It was so hot."

"Oh, Charlie. But you got the baby out. The two of you. You and Sheila. You got him out."

"But Shirin, it was all my fault. They told me to get out. To get Sheila and the baby out. There were threats. But I cared more about Alif. I thought no one could do it right but me. My conceit killed Sheila. My vanity."

"But Charlie, it was Lazarev, not these other threats. It was not your fault."

"But I shouldn't have had them out there. I was so ashamed. I felt I didn't deserve him anymore, that I couldn't keep him safe. That I was a danger to him. We flew back to Houston and I left him with friends. Close friends of ours. They had no children. They were happy to do it. I volunteered for Colombia. I thought all I was good for was work. The more dangerous the better, because deep down I wanted to die. Then I was kidnapped. By the time I got out I was in no position to be a father. And he seemed happy. I went to see him and he seemed happy. So were our friends. So I left him there. What kind of a father does this? Not a good father."

"Charlie, you did what you thought was best. That's what fathers do. You said he was happy."

"He was, for a time. I was so proud of him. But not of myself. So I went away again for a while. But he started having problems. He was different from our friends, and they started to fight. Our friends didn't want to talk about it. They were defensive. We had a falling out. They asked me not to see him. I did anyway, and they didn't stop me. I tried to help. But I was still gone. Too much. Then everything started to go bad in the Caspian. I was so ashamed. I didn't want him to be ashamed, too. So I couldn't say anything. And now. It's only worse."

"No, no. He would be so proud of you, Charlie. I am proud of you. You must go to him, Charlie. You must tell him. This is my final wish, Charlie."

"I can't. Because Lazarev has taken him."

"Charlie, how is that possible?"

"Because Ted Crawford is my son. Ted is my son, Shirin, and now he is gone. I've failed him again."

He was too tired to cry. He felt not so much sorrow as shock at what his life had become. He wanted so much to go back. To go all the way back to Houston. To stay home like Stan and watch over his son.

"No, Charlie, this is not your fault. You are not the one doing these things. It's them. These mad, insane people. This is who you are, Charlie. You couldn't be anyone else. And look, you will save us all. And Ted will be proud. You will get him back. You will think of something. I know you will, Charlie. I know you will. That is who you are. This is who you are supposed to be."

"I don't know, Shirin. I don't know how."

"Charlie, you must have faith. Do not despair. I will always believe in you." Her voice trailed off. Then another moan took hold and Charlie filled the syringe. "No, no, not yet," she said. "I can make it a little bit longer. I don't want to leave you. Not yet. I can stand it. Lie down with me, Charlie. I want to lay with you here. Will you lay with me here? Until it is over? But you must not touch me again. They said you could be hurt if you touched me. I am so cold now. Please don't leave me, Charlie, please don't leave me."

He pulled the blanket up over her. He pulled over another pillow and slid in next to her. He leaned over and kissed her on each cheek, over her protests. Then, as they lay together in the darkness, he whispered to her about how he felt when he first saw her, and then when he proposed to her. He told her how nervous he had been to call her up and ask her to go to Umbria, but how he could not stop himself. The very first day when they went for a bike ride and he kept trying to steer the tandem from the back. The wild rumors in the village about their trips, the grocer promoting the torrid, once-a-year standing affair and the priest swearing they were a secret agent and her love-struck source.

Towards the end she became very nauseous again. Then Duman arrived back at the flat. He had a whole box of morphine vials, which Charlie doubted the doctor had parted with willingly.

Shirin had stopped vomiting. Charlie lay on his back and stared into the darkness.

"It's too painful, Charlie," she said. "I need you to release me."

"I can't, Shirin. I can't do that."

"It's okay. I'm not afraid anymore." Her body tensed. "We are married now, aren't we Charlie?"

"Yes. I think we are."

"I love you, Charlie."

"I love you, too, Shirin."

He refilled the syringe and slid the needle and the morphine into her arm. Then he picked her up and held her. With the full box of narcotics, he kept her in the gray area between unconsciousness and death until she finally slipped away from him just before dawn.

When the sun started to creep into the room he went out to wake Duman to tell him she was gone. Duman said he would call her family. Charlie realized he would not have even known how to get a hold of any of them.

The line in Charlie's flat rang.

"Hold, please." A voice, Russian accent.

"Charlie," said Lazarev.

"You killed her."

"I did not kill her, Charlie. She betrayed me but I did not kill her. Your brother Chernov killed her. Because she was helping me. And because he was jealous. These are the masters you serve."

Another day was brightening over the Thames, oblivious to the suffering on its banks.

"Have you found it, Charlie?"

Charlie hesitated. "Yes, I think so."

"Have you told anyone? Other than the traitor Telnov and the others on the boat?"

"No."

"Then you must not, and you must come to me immediately."

Suddenly, Charlie was standing under a shower of cold fear. "Why would I do that?"

"Because I have your son, Charlie."

"My son? My son is dead."

"Not your fictional son. No, this Ted Crawford. Is that his real name? You abandoned him so many years ago, Charlie, I am not sure if you feel for him like a son. We shall find out. Because if you do, you must come to me now."

Charlie's heart was pounding so hard he wondered if Lazarev could hear it. "No. You won't hurt him, you need him. For Firebird."

"I don't think so. He's already told us so much. I'm not sure what there is left to tell. You do not care if he continues to suffer?"

"You make me weigh the fate of the world against that of my son?"

"You don't care about the world, Charlie. Nothing in your life would suggest that. The only question is whether you care more about your son, or yourself. But even the devil cares about its offspring, in his narcissism. So, Charlie? Will you come to save your son?"

Charlie turned his back on the rising sun and went over to stand in the door of his bedroom. He could see Shirin lying dead on his bed, in the shadows.

"I will come."

"Of course."

"But only if you release him. I want him at the border crossing near Kirkenes. My people will deliver the location and proof of the field to Chernov and the Americans, unless I tell them not too. Which I will do only if they confirm to me that my son has been released to them at Kirkenes unharmed."

Lazarev hesitated. "I am not like you, Charlie. So I will agree to this. And I will give you my word that you will be safe with me as long as no one knows anything more about the field. In fact, I will hold you only as long as necessary. Perhaps you will even be able to see your son again. Not for a long time, but perhaps someday. Unless we find out that anyone has learned of the field. Are we in agreement?"

"How did you know, Olezka? How did you know he was my son? No one knows this."

"You should not have gone home, Charlie. Of course we were listening to you. But I see even you make mistakes, Charlie. We will have someone there soon. Be ready." He terminated the call.

Duman told Charlie that her father was coming in from Esher. The family was distraught. Charlie told Duman he needed to leave, now. Stop her father, and take Shirin to Esher. Charlie went to the window and looked out over the street. Traffic was already busy. He saw no one obviously looking back at him.

His mobile phone rang again. The connection was faint, but he could hear Avinashi yelling on the end of the line. Yelling with joy. He told her to hang up and he would call her back. He took a fresh mobile and went out of his flat and across the hallway to the stairwell that led to the roof. He climbed the stairs to the top. Out in the fresh morning air, he dialed her back.

Arctic Ocean
88 degrees North
Thursday morning

"Charlie, we did it, we did it!"

Avinashi stood on the platform of the *Sevmorput* with her nose and cheeks daubed in black crude. She was yelling unselfconsciously into the satellite phone, smiling at Zubov, as he smiled back at her. They were all deliriously happy.

"It's beautiful, Charlie. We're 2500 meters into the oil column and we're still going. The rocks are so porous and permeable you could probably see through them. They measured out at eighty milli-darcies, which doesn't even seem possible, so they're testing it again. And the natural pressure is so high, they're worried about the blow-out preventer. We're working up a rough estimate of oil in place. Charlie, it's perfect, and it could be huge."

"Avinashi, have you called anyone else about this?" asked Charlie. "Anyone at all?"

"No, Charlie," she said. "We've been running a tight hole. Total blackout. Just like you asked. I wanted you to be the first to know."

"That's good, Avinashi. Because we can't tell anyone. Ever."

"What? Charlie, that's crazy. Why can't we tell anyone?"

"For Ted, Avinashi. They learned a secret about Ted. That he's my son. They will give him back if we don't tell anyone. Avinashi, we can't let anything happen to him."

She grabbed onto the rail. "Oh, Charlie. Oh no. What can we do? There has to be something we can do. Right?"

"I have nothing left, Avinashi. Except this. I can do this for Ted. I can go back. To Russia." Charlie went silent. At the end, nothing but the dull static of the satellite connection. No more planning. No more last minute gambles.

He continued in a somber tone. "Here's what I need you to do. Once I tell them where the field is, they'll want proof. They'll want to talk to you. Pull together what you can to convince them. All the details. Once they know, they will want to erase all traces of what you've done. They will kill everyone on that ship. You'll need to get off, out onto the ice. I will send someone for you. You have the beacons. They'll find you."

One beacon, she thought. But billions could die. How could Charlie do this? How could she do this?

"No, I can't," she said. "There's no way off the ship. Charlie, don't let them kill me. Please."

The line was silent again. "You're a good person, Avinashi," he said. "So I know you have to try that. But I know you can figure it out. You always do. I have to go."

"No, Charlie, stop. Ted wouldn't want you to do this either."

"I can't fail him again, Avinashi. I just can't do that. This play didn't work. Maybe the two of you can figure something else out."

"What? Charlie, what can we do? This was it, this was our best chance. There's nothing else."

"Avinashi, I have to go. You need to go. Now. Get off that ship."

CHAPTER 22

END TIMES

Arctic Ocean
88 degrees North
Thursday

"Escape?" said Rubin. "Are you mad? We're thousands of kilometers away from anywhere at all."

Avinashi had called Rubin down to the drilling platform and pulled him inside the door of the mud pump room. The pump was still working hard. They were 3500 meters into the oil column and would continue now until they hit bottom or the drill stem snapped.

"Lazarev is going to find out about us," she said. "Probably as we speak. Then it's just a matter of how fast they can fly out here. He will kill us all. I know he will kill me. I don't know why he wouldn't. It's the only way he can keep it. My only chance is to get out onto the ice. I think someone will be looking for me."

"You think?" said Rubin, throwing his hands in the air. "And just what if they don't? Oh, what have we done, what have we done?" He plastered his hands on his face and bent over at the waist. Then back up again. He peeked out again from behind his hands.

"You are certain?" he said.

"Enough to go myself."

He covered his face again and moaned. "Alright. Come with me."

They were deep in the hold. Rubin was running his flashlight back and forth over a machine that looked to Avinashi like one of those old World War I tanks, the kind where the track seems to run in a huge oval around the entire side. It looked like two of these tanks connected together with a rod, end to end, like circus elephants connected trunk-to-tail.

"It came into our possession in Arkhangelsk," said Rubin. Yes, thought Avinashi, it just dropped out of the same generous sky as my mud pump. "The captain was fascinated by machinery of all types," he said. "He was very happy it ended up with us."

The topside surface of each unit was entirely covered by a suspended metal deck, with a chest-high tubular metal railing all around. At the front, poking up a few feet between the tracks of the first tank, and through a notch in the deck, was a windowed cockpit, just large enough for a single driver. There was a similar structure on the second unit, at the very back, but this one was filled with what appeared to be a snorkel for the engines. The whole affair was wrapped in a tangle of cables, like a giant beast caught in a net.

"An Arktos escape vehicle," said Rubin. "Designed for the North Caspian, where they need to be able to drive off drilling platforms right into 4/10 to 6/10 ice coverage. In case of fire, or an explosion. This is the only vehicle that can climb up out of the water right onto pack ice. Oh yes, it floats. And it can make four or five knots in the water, but I wouldn't recommend it over long distances. It's not entirely stable in the open water. Part of the reason is that it's fully articulated in the middle. There's a universal joint in the middle between the two. This allows the front half to pull itself out while the back half pushes from the water. Then the front half pulls the back half out. Ingenious."

Avinashi frowned. "It doesn't look very fuel efficient," she said. "Didn't the captain like snowmobiles?"

"This we never discussed. But these are designed to carry sixty men on their backs. Or twenty-five barrels of fuel, I would estimate. If we load it up we may just be able to get over the horizon. Also, each half has space inside for ten men. This will provide shelter while we wait for this supposed rescue."

"Okay," she said. "But how will we get it down to the ice?"

"The toolpusher Rostov has a man scheduled to be in the crane …" Rubin checked his watch. "In forty-three minutes. To move additional drilling pipe up to the derrick. But this man's first order of business, as the Second Mate will inform him, is to offload the Arktos for testing. Two unfortunate souls will be inside. There was great difficulty preparing the Arktos to be lifted, particularly in the dark. Fortunately, as you can see, we left our lift cables in place for future deployment. It is difficult to see, but the Arktos is sitting on a steel plate. The cables are connected to the plate. Once we are set on the ice, we drive off. I believe there is a slight chance we will be gone before they are roused to action. So, do you agree is this our least worst alternative?"

They would be like bank robbers attempting their getaway in a tractor, she thought. "It's bright orange," said Avinashi. "They could spot us ten miles out. Can we camouflage it?"

"Hmm. Perhaps. Now, go collect your things and meet me back here in thirty minutes."

Her new survival suit fit perfectly over the three layers she had put on underneath. The warm, cozy feel gave her a much-needed boost in confidence. She was back in the darkened hold, with Rubin and four roustabouts. They had loaded the decks with fuel drums and loaded other supplies inside. The Arktos had a good enough coat of new white paint. Avinashi had her radio beacon. They were ready to go, right on time.

"You will ride on top," said Rubin. "On the fuel drums."

Her confidence evaporated. "You're joking," said Avinashi.

"I do not have time to teach you to drive," he said. "And someone was to be on top to keep the cables from fouling when we drive off the plate." She would be totally exposed and sitting on top of a bomb. "Here, use this," he said, handing her a crowbar.

Even if she were inside, one shot into a fuel barrel and they would both be incinerated. Probably melt right through the pack ice and lie forever on the ridge.

"Okay, fine," she said. He helped her through the tangle of wires onto the top of the barrels.

The hatch covers groaned open. Steel gray light flooded the hold, and Avinashi could see the low clouds still overhead. Rubin had started the big diesels of the Arktos. They rumbled loudly, filling the hold with exhaust. Then the cables around her rustled to life, grabbed the Arktos and yanked it skyward.

Right away she fell and almost rolled off the barrels. Only a cable stopped her, right in the back. Rubin pounded on the window of the cockpit and made grabbing motions, as if around the cable. Thanks for the tip, she thought. She grabbed hold and got to her knees. Faster than she would have preferred, they were up and out of the hold and swinging over the deck.

The view from atop the Arktos, suspended high over the ship, made her stomach jump into her throat. But there was no one out on the deck. No one shouting, pointing. They swung out over the side, over the ice, and started down.

They were partially afloat, the front of the plate pitched sharply up. Rubin gunned the engine and the Arktos lurched forward. The only thing keeping Avinashi upright was the cable, but now it was ripped from her hands as the heavy cables whipped by her head. The front half of the Arktos was already out on the ice, dragging them forward. But the back was fouled. Cables were wrapped around the rear cockpit. Avinashi crawled to the rear and pulled on the cables. They were rock solid, as if they were stone. She looked up at Rubin in the cockpit.

"Back up, back up," she yelled. He turned and shook his head. He couldn't. He couldn't lose his grip on the ice upfront. She would have to get them free.

Shouts from above. Yelling for the Chief Mate. Someone telling them to stop. The cables tightened. They were trying to pull them back up. There was only one chance.

"Faster, faster," she yelled at Rubin. The engine screamed louder and pulled harder on the cables. Avinashi worked the edge of the crowbar under the lip of the rear cockpit where it was riveted onto the deck, and she pulled. As hard as she could.

The yelling from the deck was louder. *Vintovka.* Rifle.

She would not stop. She could not stop. It would all end for her here, if that was to be.

And with a metal scream, the cockpit ripped off the body of the Arktos and banged down into the icy water, snared in the cables. The rear unit of the machine plunged down into the water, no longer held by the wires. Until the Arktos worked its magic and pulled her out. And started rumbling across the pack ice.

Up on the deck stood a seamen with the rifle. Standing next to Telnov. The seamen aimed the rifle at Avinashi.

Until Telnov put his hand on the rifle, and pushed it down.

Priozersk
Thursday evening

The iron hand gripped Charlie's neck and was shoving him forward over uneven ground. Charlie stumbled because his head was inside a bag, where it has been ever since they pulled it down over his eyes in the library of his flat, snuffing out the picture of Sheila and Ted. He tries to stay calm because the cloth is so thick that if he starts to panic or when they hit him in the stomach where he was cut he can hardly breath. But then the earth itself sways under his feet and he falls. But he is caught on a hard cord across his chest, so the iron hand can easily reach over to hit him hard on the back of the head before it pushes him forward, back onto the rough ground.

They stop and old hinges groan loudly, the kind that support heavy doors. Then in one long motion the hand pushes him forward several paces then yanks him back off his feet onto a chair. His hands are unshackled, but only so his bloody wrists can be yanked around the high back and squeezed again into the metal rings. The hand grabs the bag and tries to pull it off. But the hand also grabs a fist full of hair, and the bag is still fastened around Charlie's neck, so that his head is as likely to come off as the bag. The hand cuts the back of his neck as it slices off the bag, and Charlie can feel the blood running down his back. Then the bag comes off, but it is still dark. By the time his eyes adjust, the hand is gone and Charlie is alone. He is in a round room made of stone. The door has been closed. High above him, small openings admit the last faint red light of day.

It is dark before they come. A young boy in a long black tunic enters carrying a pitcher and a lamp, both of which he sets on the floor. He goes out and brings back a second chair which he places across from Charlie. Then the boy picks up the pitcher and lifts it to Charlie's lips. He is allowed a few gulps but is left thirsty. The boy opens the door and sits on the ground behind Charlie.

Lazarev has to duck to enter the room. When he straightens up again, he seems to tower over Charlie. No longer any Western dress. He wears a green tunic, with black breeches and high black boots. The tunic is simple, with a gold braid across the right breast and a single ribbon over the left, a ribbon with a double-headed eagle medallion. He holds his hands behind his back, and his face is composed. Too peaceful in the midst of so much chaos and despair, thought Charlie.

"Do you remember this place?" said Lazarev, looking about the tower. "In its darkest hour, Russians pledged on this sacred ground to defend their land to the last soul. And now, four hundred years later, Russia is being called again to make a final stand, to defend our land, the Church, Christian civilization itself. You are making a sacrifice, Charlie. But we are all being called to sacrifice. You are not used to this, I know."

Charlie stared into the light of the lamp, hardly hearing a word.

"I would not expect you to understand," said Lazarev. "So. Where is my field?"

Charlie snapped back to the present. He stared at the tall man with the white hair, asking about oil. "They lied to you, Oleg Maksimovich," said Charlie. "They lied to protect the drift stations. And to protect other lies. You were on the Lomonosov Ridge."

"The Lomonosov?" said Lazarev. "How is that possible?"

"You didn't cross five hundred kilometers of ice, Olezka," said Charlie. "You crossed eleven hundred kilometers. How you did it, I have no idea. You are the only one who could know."

Even now the pain was written on Lazarev's face. "I was not alone," he said. "I know that now. It was God's plan."

"Yeah? Then he needs a new fucking plan."

"Still the blasphemer," said Lazarev. "Well, see where that has gotten you. And so, the details now, please. What is the play? Azolla source rock, certainly. So it is true?"

"No, it's not true. Not for this field, anyway. And it couldn't have been, not for a field this large."

"What do you mean?"

"There's not enough sediment. Since the Eocene. Not enough to bury and cook a supergiant, I don't care how green it was up there. Just look at the sediment maps and just try to draw in a hundred kilometer field near the ridge. I can't."

"But then how?"

"It had to be deeper. In older rocks. The Lomonosov is a continental margin, rifted away from Northern Europe by the spreading Gakkel Ridge. A field that large had to be below the Eocene. In older rock, laid down when this was the edge of a large continent, with the heavy sediments you would see with a traditional passive continental margin."

"But that's impossible. The region hasn't been stable enough for the oil to survive through that period, through the rifting. Impossible!"

"But it was the only way. I assumed you were right, that it was possible. Then I set about to figure out how. Don't you see, Olezka? It was you, you were the one that showed it was possible. I only had to figure out how. You were the one that provided the hope, if you could have just believed in it. If you wanted to believe in it. And I did. So I started looking. And I found it. It took me a while, but I found it."

"So, again, where?"

"Where we found the next-largest Arctic field. And before that East Texas. In a strat trap. The kind that hides big fields. An angular unconformity. It was there, in the seismic traces. Just a handful of pixels from the whole image, but I could feel it. I could see it. I just knew it was there. You know how it is. You look at hundreds of thousands of rock samples, pore over hundreds of miles of seismic, suddenly you know what the structures are from a few clues, the way you recognize your wife from the sound of her footsteps. You know how that is, don't you?"

Charlie could see from the look on Lazarev's face that he did not, and that it angered the Russian.

"It's on the Makarov Basin side, eighty-eighty degrees North," said Charlie. "And do you know what the ironic part of this is, Olezka? Run the geology backward millions of years, before the continent rifted away. Whose shoreline was that? Before it was pushed out into the middle of the Basin?"

"I have no idea," said Lazarev, irritated. The serene tsar was giving way to the awkward, frustrated geologist, once again.

"The Swedes," said Charlie. "It's Norway now, but of course Norway just being a little part of old Sweden. So there. Now you've taken something back from them. Something rather substantial. So perhaps now we can let bygones be bygone."

Lazarev face reddened with anger. "Never," he said. "That you would believe this only proves that you still think only in economic terms. That you are still half a man, if that." He took a deep breath and pulled down the front of his tunic. "So, I shall need proof. To know this is not just one of your schemes. Before I release your son."

"Avinashi can send you the location and the well logs. I can give you her number."

"Very well, I will return if they are confirmed."

The air at the bottom of the tower was still and damp. Beardless Aleksei watched him silently. Lazarev returned.

"So we're good?" said Charlie.

"Your son was released."

"Okay, now I want proof, or the same information goes to the Americans, and Chernov. Give me a phone."

The boy had one. Charlie gave him the number. The boy dialed and held the phone to Charlie's ear.

"It's me," said Charlie. The man on the phone provided Charlie with the prearranged code word. Then he gave his own. "Sac fly." He listened further. "No, you know what to tell him. I have to go. No. I have to go." Charlie nodded his head. The boy terminated the call and sat back against the wall.

"I am not a monster, Charlie," said Lazarev. "But I am called to do difficult things. Like you. Which brings me to my real purpose for being here, Charlie. A gesture of goodwill. In fact, I wanted to offer you encouragement at what I am sure is a moment of deep despair and confusion. It may be a simple matter of biology, of blood, that requires you to reverse course at this moment, to take this very human act. But let us hope this is the result of some ember of Christian goodwill and understanding that has not been smothered out by years of materialist striving, of ambition. Something that will provide this hope you prattle on about, something for you to build on. You have much to answer for Charlie. To God, to your family, to all the people who you have caused to suffer. That will now suffer. Should you choose to seek redemption, it will not be an easy path. But I do hope you ask for God's mercy. All things are possible with Him. Perhaps even you will achieve some measure of salvation. Not in this life, but perhaps the next."

Lazarev stood up.

"As I agreed, you will be released after your confinement is no longer necessary. Of course, this will not be for many years, if at all. Try to see this positively. Use the time. Spiritual guidance is freely available in the Gulag, as we say. Then perhaps you will benefit from the spaces of the North, as I did."

Lazarev turned to go.

"You wanted me to fail, didn't you?" said Charlie. "With Firebird. You are doing all this because we don't have enough oil. But you still didn't want me to find any. Is this about oil, Olezka, or something else?"

Lazarev seemed to honestly consider the question. "No. I expected you to fail. And then you did. Don't feel badly, Charlie. Mankind was destined to fail, you were simply its instrument. And failed only if we measure by your terms, Charlie. Not my terms, where your so-called success was just an illusion. But still, you played a small role in finding my field. You should take some comfort that hundreds of years from now, Russians will burn that oil. In a much different world. A world remade."

Charlie raised his head. "I expect it will be sooner than that."

"No," said Lazarev. "We shall not need it before then. And nothing can be done until the West falls."

"I don't know about the West," said Charlie. "But Texso isn't going anywhere. Except to eighty-eight degrees North."

Lazarev stiffened. "What are you talking about?"

"I made a deal, Oleg Maksimovich," said Charlie. "Texso did, with Chernov. He used this field to buy back Titov. The deal was done, they were just waiting for the proof. And my contact is now sending them the same package you just got. If I were you, I'd keep an eye on the news. The plan was to immediately announce a major Russian find and a conspiracy to hide it from its rightful owners, the Russian people, all for one politician's personal gain. Which politician is to be arrested and tried for treason. That's what they told me."

Lazarev had lost any color but the yellow from the lamp. He wobbled around the chair on weak knees and fell into it.

"No. You wouldn't do all that, not knowing I had your son. You wouldn't risk him."

"That's why I had to get him back. Using the only leverage I had."

Lazarev rolled his head slowly as if awakening from a trance. Charlie knew that a devastating realization was dawning.

"The location of the field was the only thing that I had of value," said Charlie. "But why would I agree to keep this secret to save one scientist? I had to make you think I would do this. I had to make you think it was your idea. So I told you that Ted was my son."

"That night in your flat. You knew we were listening," said Lazarev, speaking mostly to himself.

"You're always listening," said Charlie. "It's so damn predictable."

"But you came here. You knew what your fate would be."

"You know, you're the one that needs some time for reflection, Oleg Maksimovich. After all these years, you don't understand me at all."

Giant meet stone, thought Charlie.

"Do you think that this field changes anything?" said Lazarev. "It doesn't matter if it's two hundred billion barrels, the age of oil is still over. Growth has ended."

"The oil was never going to last forever, a child could see that. You're right, this doesn't change that. But it could be a bridge to a brighter day, and we just need to keep going over it for a little longer. What's your plan? Hunker down in the muck and pray until we get wiped out by a plague or a meteorite? That's not a winning plan. We just need to keep going. So, the way I see it, I don't have to stop Peak Oil. I just have to stop you."

Lazarev was up and manic now, yelling. "What do you believe, Charlie? Anything? Or do you just mindlessly destroy? The times of trouble are coming and all you can do is destroy me. I am the one that knows how to help them through these coming days. The people need their faith, Charlie, they need a strong leader, and I am that man. God has chosen me, he led me out of the Arctic to lead his people, but all you can do is destroy me."

"What do I believe? I believe that our imaginations can shape our reality, and that our moral obligation is to twist that reality into the world's biggest goddamn pretzel before we let a billion children starve. I don't know when we'll run out, and neither do you. We'll know it when we see it through our rearview mirror. Until then, let's just keep looking. Who knows? Maybe the world's biomass of mice is greater than the biomass of elephants. And maybe Ted can round them all up. With Firebird."

"You are a conceited fool. A talented man, fooled by his own gifts."

"No, conceit is to think you know what the future holds. To think reality is going to play out according to some static plan. A plan that says more about you than reality. Trying to fix an insurmountable problem, searching for solutions you might never find, risking complete failure, that requires humility."

"Look at you. You are like a child, with your simple optimism. America has not suffered, like Russia, so you do not understand."

"Stop it. Just stop it. You're not pilgrims bred for some post-apocalyptic wasteland. Your suffering is more tragic than you realize, because it was pointless. You need to wake up. The nightmare is over, no one is trying to steal your land anymore, they just want to pay you handsomely for drilling rights. Bargaining for a PSA isn't the same thing as riding in on a pony and pillaging your cities. It's time for you to join the civilized world, maybe make a positive contribution instead of just threatening it with enslavement or annihilation."

"The problem is Charlie, that you have not known true suffering."

"I think I've suffered a bit. Thanks to you."

"No, Charlie, you haven't. You know nothing of suffering, yet. But now you will. You will now know suffering, Charlie. And for what? So that by some miracle this disaster might be avoided?"

"I don't know what will save us. But something will. It might be a bunch of small things. More likely it's one idea that looks ordinary but blows up, becomes big. That's not wishful thinking. That's the way the world works. We need to keep the system working, with enough degrees of freedom, with enough favor, for it to live. Our world is defined by those few big ideas. Those giants. That's the way nature works. That's the way God works." Charlie paused. "Perhaps He is calling you through me, Olezka. It is not too late. For you."

Lazarev stared blankly ahead.

"I am not your enemy, Oleg Maksimovich," said Charlie. "And you are not mine."

Charlie slid forward on his chair. He stood and leaned forward. He kissed Lazarev on one cheek, then on the other. The cheek is cold, thinks Charlie. Cold and dry, like Arctic ice.

Lazarev got up from his chair. He listed to a side and the boy rushed forward and caught him. He helped Lazarev make his way toward the tower door. Before he left, Lazarev whispered in Aleksei's ear.

Alone together, Beardless Aleksei stares deeply at Charlie. He lifts the chain holding his spoon over the top of the head and smiles. As in centuries past, the red tower is filled with the screams of man as blood is shed and vengeance is meted out.

CHAPTER 23

FINAL PLAY

Priozersk

After taking his eyes Beardless Aleksei dragged Charlie back across the bridges to the asylum, to a small room on the second floor. He cut Charlie's hands free and locked him inside. Charlie stumbled around the room in darkness and pain. The only furniture was a bed with no mattress, only ropes strung across the frame. The room had no windows and a metal door. Time passed, but he had no real sense of it other than how thirsty he became. By that measure it was two or three days before two men opened the door and found him, laying on the ropes. They gave him water but no food and kept him locked in the room. Again, time passed before another soldier returned and dropped a chair on the stone floor. Shortly after he left, a single set of footsteps entered the room and a man sat down on a chair. A sweet, smoky scent filled the room.

"So here you are, I have been looking for you" said Chernov. "Sorry about your eyes."

"Where's Lazarev?"

"Dead, finally. He holed up in Kogalym with his Neftepolk. We had to send in Titov with his Tamanskaya jackals. Very messy job, I am told. His people did worship him, I will say. They fought to the last child. But Titov's people, they get the job done. Not a soul left." He sighed. "What trouble he caused, our Oleg Maksimovich. The world is better for his passing. I expect you would agree."

"Shirin. You killed her, too."

"Such a whore, you should thank me. She was working with Lazarev, you know, against you. You should have done it yourself but you are too weak. She was a beautiful woman, Charlie, and she used it against you. You are like the stupidest cypher clerk caught in a honey trap because some two-kopeck whore gave him the time of day."

"One of my people was on the *Sevmorput*. I want her back."

"Yes, Ms. Sharma. Most unfortunate. Lazarev reached the ship before we could stop him. Apparently, in addition to nuclear devices the Neftepolk also possessed Tu-95 bombers. Who knew? All gone. The only evidence the *Sevmorput* ever existed are the well logs from Ms. Sharma. I know you told Stoyan to look for Ms. Sharma, but there is no chance that she survived. So you see there is nothing we can do. And now the Lomonosov is Russian territory, so it is my decision, and I have forbidden it. Dickinson agreed. I must tell you though if she does appear, I may shoot her myself. We can't afford another Lazarev."

"Get me out of here."

"I am sorry, Charlie, but that is not convenient right now. I need to get the right deal. Your friend Roger is so much more agreeable than you would be, Charlie, don't you think so? Particularly with Dickinson at his shoulder. What a pair. There is much for me to do as the situation stabilizes. I can't have you making trouble for me right now. Fortunately, as far as anyone knows, Lazarev disposed of you. So I think you will just stay here for a while."

"You bastard."

"I also need to get rid of some generals. They have proven they can't be trusted. And maybe Titov, too. He is a bit too effective."

"They were also promised a cut."

"Yes, but they clearly didn't earn it with their traitorous behavior with Lazarev. A deal cut in a moment of weakness. What choice did I have? They do not deserve it. I will be making some changes."

"More for you."

"Mm, yes. Someone needs to control the gold, Charlie. You let the House of Saud get rich, why not the House of Chernov? Rest assured, Charlie, I will sell the oil. That's all you care about in the end, right? Always focus on the most important objectives. I backed you, you backed me. And it was win-win, as you like to say, right?" He laughed.

"I have been talking to Dickinson and Stoyan," said Chernov. "We have a plan for getting this situation settled down. It's in good hands. Your friend Karim and his tribe they killed that damn Arab, too, the butcher. Animals. Best thing for all would be if that country ran dry, but they tell me unfortunately that will not be the case for some time. The markets have settled down. Oil is still at two times what it was, and I don't see that changing soon. But that's good for everyone, right?"

"Certainly good for you."

"Provided I can get this field on line in the foreseeable future. So much to do. But, what would you think? If we made it a real priority? Five years? Seven? Texso is so good at what they do. Even for fifteen percent. Yes, I decided that thirty was too generous and Dickinson and Crawford agreed."

Charlie dropped his head. "Have you read any stories about the first Grey Cardinal, Viktor Ilyich?"

"Such nonsense, these fairytales. There is no Grey Cardinal."

"You know, that's what he would have said, too. Father Joseph, the simple monk in the plain gray robe. Richelieu sends Father Joseph across the border to Regensburg. The Germans were going to sit down and see if they could work something out between their Catholics and the Protestants. So they didn't have to kill each other over fine points of doctrine. Richelieu said the good Father would be just an observer, nothing more. Ready to help, if asked. And in fact Father Joseph just whispered in a few ears and quietly returned to France. After which the Germans set upon each other with swords and pitchforks and about a third of the country was wiped out. From the violence, from famine, from disease. Being an ally of Germany, the Austrian Emperor was beside himself. How could this have happened? Inquiries were made. In the end, he confided to his ministers that he believed a poor monk had defeated the Germans with only a rosary."

"Are you trying to flatter me, Charlie?" said Chernov. "I do not think this is a flattering comparison."

"Then tell me this wasn't your plan all along. How did Lazarev get all those votes in the first place? And whose idea was it to give him the Ministry of Natural Resources? How did Titov get the Tamanskaya and the Moscow Military District? You said it was Putin, but all I know is what I hear from you. You got out to London, but not Putin. And where is Putin now? Tell me you didn't bring civilization to the brink of collapse just to advance your career."

Chernov smiled. "Did you think Volodnya was ever going to retire? I didn't."

"Lazarev was right," said Charlie. "The devil exists. The only question is whether you will recognize him."

Charlie heard Chernov get to his feet.

"I do like you, Charlie. It would pain me to say goodbye. I am not as sentimental as Lazarev, you may have noticed, but perhaps I will keep you around."

Chernov pounded on the door. "Oh, I nearly forgot," he said. "Titov sent you a gift."

Charlie heard the jingle of metal falling on stone. He knew what it was and left it lying there. A jagged spoon.

"I know it won't bring your eyes back," said Chernov. "But do try to be happy with what you accomplished. After all, you won."

Arctic Ocean
Unknown position

Avinashi sat on the fuel drums while Rubin drove until the *Sevmorput* was a small dot. Then there were distant, thunderous explosions and plumes of smoke and the ship vanished from sight.

Without the rear exhaust, the noise from the rear engine of the Arktos was deafening. But she had been unable to avoid it because she had to keep pumping fuel from the barrels into the tanks.

She pounded on the cockpit window. When Rubin cut the engines, she took a deep breath and sighed her relief. But then she looked around them at the vast distances, and at the overcast skies, and she was afraid.

Rubin opened the hatch and poked his head out. "See anything yet?"

"It might be a while."

He crawled out and sat with her on the fuel drums.

"How many left?"

"Two."

"It doesn't matter. Your beacon is on?"

She patted her chest pocket.

"We should put it out on the ice," he said. "Away from the metal."

He taped two life vests together to make a little platform. They climbed down and walked a short distance out on the ice. He laid the vests down. She stood the beacon upright on top, the base stuck between the two front halves of the top vest. The stared silently at the tiny device.

"We are just delaying the inevitable," said Rubin.

"Someone will find us," said Avinashi. "I don't know how I know, but I do."

"Telnov let you go," said Rubin. "Why?"

"He owed me."

"I hope you have other friends. We should get inside. It is cold."

The skies cleared and for many times the sun traced its circle in the sky but no one came. They had brought what they had thought was more than enough food but it was nearly gone. They drank filtered water from the sea and it was freezing them from the inside out. After two days the battery indicator on the beacon lit up so she had to turn it off. Left on their own, they would drift with the transpolar current down towards the East coast of Greenland. She reckoned it was a thousand kilometers until they reached open seas. If they didn't freeze or starve to death first, sometime in the next two months the pack ice would break up underneath them in the warmer waters and the Arktos would sink to the bottom.

Rubin just sat in the belly of the Arktos berating himself endlessly. She could not bear to listen, so she sat by herself in the rear unit with the empty boxes of food. She was afraid to fall asleep because she might not wake up. But in the cold, and with the loneliness, sleep was unavoidable.

One bright night she had a dream that Rubin finally stopped talking. She went in to check on him and found him unconscious. In a panic, she went into the cockpit and tried to start the engines. She cranked the engine over and over. Then the Nganasan, Tubyaku Porbin, appeared out on the ice. Holding two polar bears on leashes. She tried to call out to him but she was so tired she couldn't move her lips. She leaned her head back on the seat and just watched him. He wrapped her feet in warm bear fat and then tied up the two bears to the front of the Arktos and jumped on one of them. Then all twenty or so tons flew up into the air. She was surprised to see bears fly.

She woke up with a start, both startled and embarrassed. That was the type of dream Porbin was supposed to have, not her. After he had been dipping into his plastic bag. Then the ice crackled, followed by a low, deep thumping, like someone was plucking an electric bass with the amp off. She knew what had woken her. She threw open the hatch and scrambled outside. Rubin was already on top of the front unit, looking ahead.

At open water.

"No, no," he said. "How is this possible?"

The sea was the color of the deep blue sky. The wind was up, and she thought she could see swells, even some waves breaking on the edge of the pack. And out beyond the edge, broken ice. And, almost to mock her it seemed, fate presented her with another rare tabular iceberg, a beautiful, angular shape, being blown rapidly by the strong winds.

No, she thought. Moving up into the wind. East.

Frantically, she dug the beacon out of the pocket of her suit and turned it on. Battery low. But it was on.

"Hold this," she said, slapping the device in Rubin's hand. "Up high."

"Did you hear something?" he said, looking around the sky. She was already inside the front unit. She locked the hatch then moved up into the cockpit. Rubin was pounding on the thick windows and shaking his head at her. He was as safe out there as inside, she thought. This time the engines started right up.

Avinashi jammed down on the throttles and the Arktos lurched forward. It did not have tremendous acceleration, but enough to throw her off the seat and to make Rubin yell louder from the back. She got back in the seat and steered the vehicle towards the open water. They might very well die in the attempt, she thought, but the only scenario in which they lived involved her driving this machine off the edge of the ice and after that ship, and that is what she was going to do.

They were less than a hundred meters from the edge. There was significant swell, at least four or five feet. The Arktos was not designed for those kinds of seas, and they were missing the rear snorkel. How long would it be before the rear unit flooded and dragged them down with it? Less time than for the entire unit to capsize? Rubin was apparently wondering the same things because he was pounding frantically on the cockpit. She looked back only to motion that he should hold the beacon up. He just stared at her wide-eyed like she was crazy. Then about five meters shy of the edge the front unit crashed down through the ice.

The machine pitched down sharply as it plunged into the sea. She felt they were headed straight for the bottom, but she kept the throttle down all the way. The rear unit worked its magic, pushing them free of the pack and into the sea.

But she could not see. So she could not steer. There was no longer anything to be done. Wave after wave pummeled the cockpit, and she only had brief glimpses of sky from the bottom of the swells. Rubin was screaming. The Arktos kept clawing its way through the icy water. She knew that in minutes the rear unit would be flooded. Avinashi had no more tears. She just kept her hand down hard on the throttle, fixed her eyes on the last bit of sky and asked her mother to pray for her.

Then the white boat was on top of them, its tower rising high above the water. She has seen this boat before, in pictures, and she wonders if she ever woke up from her dream. But then she sees men throwing lines from the stern and suddenly she panics and thinks she will not get out in time. But the hatch swings open, and her face is bathed in icy seawater. She fights her way out of the hold and over the barrels and jumps into the water, towards the boat. She tries to grab a line but her hands are too cold and the line is stiff and cuts her hands. She sinks below the surface and looks up at the light, so bright, so cold. Then a hook slips under her arm and she is pulled up through the water. She holds onto the pole with all the strength she has left, until two tattooed arms reach down and pluck her from the water. And hold her as she does her best to fill the sea with her tears.

When Avinashi awakens she thinks she must have died because the first person she sees is Wayne Parsons. But then she realizes it is a picture. One of a whole series hung up along the wall. She also recognizes Halbouty. And Pratt. Masters. The great oil finders. In the middle there is a gap, where a picture must have fallen. Probably in heavy seas. Sleeping next to her on the bed is a pocket-sized Norse god, his blond hair splayed across the pillows. A man wearing a puffy parka pokes his head in the door. She tries to get up.

"Easy now," said Rod. "Just lay there until I can get another look at you. You can't be too right in the head trying to cross the ocean in that tractor. Damn thing sunk about one minute after you jumped.

Good thing you came after us, though. We didn't pick up your signal until you got in the water." He looked closely into her eyes. "No headache? Don't feel like you bumped it on anything?"

"No, I don't think so."

"Okay. Got your friend out there, too. We had recently instituted a 'No Russians' rule on the boat, but I've made an exception for him," said Rod. "He also appears worse for the wear. Keeps telling me he's the new harbor pilot for the Port of Los Angeles."

"His name is Rubin," she said. "He's fine." He would be, with no more long trips through the ice. Lots of family time. House on the beach.

"Thanks," she said. "But what is going on here? How in the world did you find us?"

"Amazing what you can do when you abandon your common sense," said Rod. "All it took was prowling the Arctic Ocean for two weeks in a fiberglass hull. After his trip to Iceland, Charlie stashed the *Final Play* in Kirkenes. 'Just in case,' he says. I thought he was punishing me for losing this big fish. Like the Gulag. But it wasn't a bad place. Kind of pretty. You should have seen the look on their faces when I showed up and asked what the billfish were hitting on. After I picked up Ted at the border we went straight to sea to look for you. Ted was convinced he could find you with his voodoo math. Didn't rest for two whole weeks, spent all his time analyzing weather and current data and making expensive satellite calls to some guy named Dieter parked in front of a supercomputer at Stanford. Said he had a 90 percent confidence level you would pop out where you did. I played along because he was so miserable and it made him feel like he was doing something, but the idea that it was some goddamned math is ridiculous. It was the *Final Play*, that I can tell you with 100 percent confidence level. She always raises the big fish. Don't know how she does it, but here you are. Can't argue with success. Don't ask too many questions, just count your blessings and try not to mess anything up. Got that? Little advice from old Rod. Ride a good thing when you got it."

Rod pulled out a watch cap from his pocket and pulled it on, then raised his hood and tied the drawstrings.

"And now, we are getting the hell out of here," said Rod. "And never coming back.

"Where is he?" said Avinashi. "Where's Charlie?"

"Don't know," said Rod. "He gave himself up. For Ted. Lazarev is gone, but we don't know what happened to Charlie. Chernov has them all looking."

Rod sighed. "Just have to do it myself. But I'll get him. *Final Play* always raises the big fish. Can't explain it."

When Avinashi woke again she climbed up to the bridge. A young man named Ryan was at the helm, carefully picking his way through the ice headed south and west. Ted was in the cockpit in the fighting chair, and she went down to join him.

He drew her up into his lap and held her tight. Tucked under his chin she peered south towards a distant coastline. "That's the last of Russia," said Ted. "The Kola peninsula."

She turned to him and looked up. "Charlie never had a chance to talk to you. He told me something you should know. The last time we spoke."

"Rod told me." He shrugged. "It didn't feel like a surprise. I think I always knew." He lifted his eyes and looked to Russia. "Seems a little bit selfish to be upset. But I'll give him hell when we find him."

CHAPTER 24

A WORLD OF HIS MAKING

They flew him far away and threw him in a concrete cell with an iron door. Charlie did not go quietly. He cursed Chernov. He cursed Lazarev. He cursed his jailors. He cursed the holes in his face that burned and dripped foul pus. He cursed the darkness and the cold. They beat him for it but he just cursed them all the more. Finally they came into his cell and stuck a needle in his thigh. After that he could no longer yell. He could barely sit up. They stabbed him again and again. He lost the ability to connect his thoughts, to make sense of sounds. Only animal instinct kept him alive, making him crawl across the floor for his bowl, blindly shoveling into his mouth whatever the pigs refused to eat that day. There were no days or nights, no beginnings or ends, no time at all. Conscious or unconscious, it was all the same. Nothing but endless pain and misery and blackness.

But Charlie refused to die.

Eons later the drugs stopped. As his mind cleared he became aware of the patterns. Winter's ice followed by summer's biting flies. Spring cleaning when they would blast him with a hose, holding his head against the wall while they flushed the eye sockets. The footsteps in the hallway once a day that brought him the garbage he lived on but not anyone who would speak to him. And the truck that drove once a week up and down the road on the other side of his cell wall. With the engine so loud he could just hear it through the concrete.

A diesel engine.

One day like all the others footsteps came and slid open the panel in the door, but no bowl came through. Two sets of footsteps. One set walked back down the hallway. The other just stood and watched him through the opening. After several long minutes a familiar smell entered his cell. A sweet, smoky scent. He dragged himself over to the door and lunged through the slot, but he was too slow. He grabbed at air as he screamed Chernov's name. Without reply, the footsteps turned and walked back down the hallway and were gone.

A few days later they came with his new eyes. They flushed his sockets with the hose and vodka and then tried to force the hard round orbs into place. They were the wrong size so they finished the job with a hammer. The bones in his face healed after a few weeks and the infections subsided as well.

Just counting the time of which he was conscious he had been banished to the north for many years. One decade at least. Two or more very likely. Years spent inside himself, loosely tethered to this world.

Well into this time Sheila finally found him. She entered his room like sunshine through the window he did not have. She lay down next to him, her warm cheek against his. She had looked for him long and hard she said, but the north was vast and empty and he was well hidden. She was tired and weak but that did not matter now because she had found him. She thanked him for saving their son. She told Charlie that Ted had married, and they had a grandson. This had given her great joy and had relieved her sorrows. She was leaving now and wanted him to know that she loved him always. Then she was gone and he was alone again.

He remembered the night with her in Yemen after he had hit at Alif. They lay on the sand out back of the house and stared up at the stars. In a fit of cocky euphoria he was rattling on and on about Kings and Queens and Mandelbrot and fractals and Zipf and how hell no they were not going home he was going after the two at the top and their life would be one long, grand adventure she would see. The woman he loved who only wanted to get back safely to Houston but could not because of his hubris smiled at him then so proud and sad at the same time. Teasing him she said you know the monks discovered fractals long before Mandelbrot, it was true she had read it. At least one of them did this monk called Udo who loved to play with numbers. He would do the math by hand with a quill and a scroll, a human computer with the patience of Job. He thought he calculate whether a soul could reach heaven by iterating the sacred and profane number pairs until they converged into a Mandelbrot set or diverged into the abyss. 'Each person's soul undergoes trials through each of the three-score years and ten of allotted life, its own nature diminished or elevated in stature by others it encounters, wavering between good and evil until it is either cast into outer darkness or drawn forever to God.'

At the time he had no idea what she meant and then a week later she was dead.

Charlie hung on. He hung on and kept listening for the truck.

Two pairs of footsteps. The panel shot open and then nothing. Someone watching again.

"*Da. Da, eto on. Otkrojte dver.*" Russian. With a Texas drawl.

The iron door swung open. The footsteps of the guard walked back down the hallway. The visitor stood silent. Then something clattered to the ground. Something heavy. Wooden. Hickory with a helping of lead, if he had to guess.

The visitor walked over and knelt on the ground. Long, thin arms wrapped around Charlie and pulled him close, burying his face in puffy nylon. The man shook and sobbed. After a while the man put his neck under Charlie's arm and lifted him to his feet.

"C'mon, Charlie. Time to go home."

"Charlie. It's me, Rod. Can you hear me?"

He had gone from the cell to a gurney to a van to an airport and on to a plane. Up a short flight of stairs and then around a very tight corner to where they lashed down his bed. He picked up the sweet aroma of aviation fuel. Someone checked his vitals and then they shot into the sky with a roar.

"Holy Mother of God, what did they do to you in there?" said Rod. "I thought I looked bad. What did they do to your eyes?" Rod pulled up a lid. "Two big black marbles. You look like a goddamn fish. Christ, can you hear me at all?" He was leaning in close and Charlie could feel Rod's breath on his ear. It had been years since he had spoken. Charlie was not certain he could remember how. He just lay on the bed, wondering if it was all a dream.

"I never gave up on you, buddy," said Rod. "You know that, right? Been looking for you this whole damn time. We all have. Me, Avi and Ted. They kept tellin' us you were dead. Just one more body. Whole country's a human compost pile. They got me on TV a few years ago. Had me pose with the priest. I thought, whatever works, you know? Get the word out. Then they turned it into a joke. Made me look like a crazy person. But it became my trademark. Opened doors, loosened tongues. And here you are. So the joke's on them and they can all go straight to hell."

The were at altitude and the cabin air was cool but the blanket must have been electric because he felt warm all over. Rod asked the attendant if he could have one of those little sandwiches so they wouldn't all go to waste. And a non-alcoholic beer if she had one.

"Chernov did help," said Rod. "I'll give him that. Gave me two men, and this special pass. Got me on planes and trains and all that. Made it a lot easier in the beginning. Before I knew my way around, knew the language. The three of us went everywhere. Hate to tell you this but we were even out here once. Years ago. Didn't go in your building though. The operator told us it stored toxic waste. Lying bastard. Anyway, that all ended when Chernov died. Almost two years ago. Been on my own since then."

The attendant brought Rod his dinner and he continued his one-sided conversation while he chewed.

"Get this. Chernov put up a statute of you. Big bronze thing, right in the goddamn center of Murmansk. Friend of Russia, the great oil man Charlie Joiner. You'd like it, you're all decked out in your rock gear. Except it doesn't look like you at all. Better lookin', like Dennis Eckersly. Anyway, that's where I was, handing out flyers with your real picture on it when this guy comes up holding one and starts asking me about the reward money, real Russian-like. Right away I know he knows something. Turns out he's in town for his mom's funeral but he lives out at the edge of the universe where he's a cook at this special camp where I've already been but where he swears he's seen this guy in the picture. An American. Been there forever. No more Chernov so I call Avi to get a ride and she sends me a Texso jet no questions asked. Ten hour flight and then what do I find. Guess I better pay the man his money."

Rod leaned over to look out the window. "Christ, black as pitch out there. Godawful country. No, I am not coming back." He went to use the head, while the attendant brought Charlie an extra pillow and checked the IV in his arm. Rod returned crackling and crinkling. A bag of chips. He pulled up close to Charlie again.

"Murmansk ain't too bad. Probably a bit different than what you remember. Really getting built up. Like a frozen Dubai. You found a damn big field up there, I can tell you that. They run pipes out of Murmansk down to the Baltic that make Alaska's look like drinking straws. Bring it in under the ice in Texso submarines as big as aircraft carriers. Can you believe it? Didn't name it after you, though, if that's what you're wondering. Some Russian. It's all politics, you know. Colonoscopy. Kalashnikov. Something like that." Rod crumpled the bag and threw it away, then popped another near beer. Kolotkov, thought Charlie.

Charlie listened to the sweet, simple sound of a man chugging a beer after a good day's work. "Damn that Lazarev," said Rod. "Can't make his piece of hell hot enough for me. Whenever I got to Peter I used to road trip up to Priozersk with a big bottle of water just to piss on his grave. Finally got wise to me and started posting a guard."

He belched like an old man. "Made you miss about a hundred World Series. Wish I could say you missed a bunch of Aggie titles, but they haven't done a goddam thing since the dinosaur age. Little Charlie's still dead set on pitching for them, of course. Where the hell else is a Joiner gonna play? He's got six pitches, can you imagine that? Two of 'em he made up and I still can't figure out how they work. Goddamn nearly unhittable. Must be something I taught him, but I just can't remember." Rod's mind wandered down some unseen path, before snapping back.

"That's Avi and Ted's little kid, did I mention that? Not that little anymore. Not that big either." He sighed. "He's done fine so far, but probably gonna be too small to pitch at the next level. And of course he bats nine because he tries to rip everything over the fence just like granddad. Haven't had the heart to tell him he's got to play within his limits. Don't relish that conversation. Stubborn as all hell. Maybe you could tell him. You two deserve each other.

"Be better if I was there all the time. But I've been out here, so he stays with Avi's dad. Deepak's great, but doesn't know a damn thing about baseball. Crazy shot, though. Since Avi became CEO she's off kissing kings and queens and Ted and Liang are in Chile half the time, flying back and forth to penguin land. Ted's convinced that's where they'll find the other one. The one at the very top." He punched Charlie's shoulder. "Sorry bud, Ted says yours was only number two. Number one is gonna be his."

Rod groaned as he leaned over to look out the window. "Well, will you look at that. That's more like it. Which city is that?" The attendant patiently told Rod they were approaching Stockholm. "Look at all those lights. Far as you can see. Beautiful sight." He grunted as he sat back down. "You know what it reminds me of? Gettin' lost on that little skiff that one time. Remember that? You hooked up on that big ol' blue right before dark and got us towed halfway across the Gulf. Wouldn't let go, of course. Damn thing was bigger than the boat, nearly sunk us haulin' it in. There we were, motoring around the Gulf in a rowboat with a big ass fish hanging over both sides, no compass and the night as black as shit. Couple of knuckleheads we were, natural selection should have kicked in right there. You wouldn't say it, but I know you were scared shitless. Then we came across the absolute sweetest sight I ever saw. That trawler, bound for Galveston, dragging a net right through a soup of that day-glo plankton. The yellow brick road, right in front of us. We caught up and you started whipping the boat back and forth in their disco light wake, whooping like a dumb ass. Followed her all the way home." He sighed. "Out of the valley of darkness. Something like that." He sniffed. "Christ, I need some shut-eye. We'll be home soon. So quit your gabbing." In a few minutes he was snoring.

Charlie remembered. He reached out and took hold of his friend's gnarled hand.

And so Charlie went back to see the world, a world of his making. A world of giants. Where he kept throwing such stones as he could lift, until one bright day when God Himself pried Charlie's hands loose from this life and carried him home, to His hall of heroes.

Clouds are not spheres, mountains are not cones, coastlines are not circles, and bark is not smooth, nor does lightning travel in a straight line.

—Benoit B. Mandelbrot
from *The Fractal Geometry of Nature*

Imagination, then, is an indispensable quality of the petroleum geologist. The world's future supply of petroleum is as dependent upon the imaginative powers of the petroleum geologist as on the presence of favorable rocks—of which there appear to be an abundant volume.

—A.I. Levorsen

Michael Troy is the pen name of an American businessman.

Author's Notes

The famed geologist Kenneth S. Deffeyes noted that Zipf's law suggested the possibility of two large undiscovered oil fields in his book *Hubbert's Peak: The Impending World Oil Shortage* (2001). Though he did not consider any such discovery likely, he leaned towards the South China Sea as the potential hiding spot and so used the placeholder names "Ho Chi Minh" and "Imelda." But that would have been a much different story.

The most revealing and moving memoir that I discovered during my research was John Masters' *Secret Riches: Adventures of an Unreformed Oilman* (2004). Masters truly takes you inside the mind of an oil finder. He also shares very freely both his successes and his setbacks, many of the latter involving personal tragedies, in a way that reminds us that life is always a balance of the two. Masters would also put up his feet on the desk when he needed to think.

To learn more about life on the ice, read William F. Althoff's *Drift Station: Arctic Outposts of Superpower Science* (2007). This definitive history has everything, from polyarniks to gravity readings to tabular icebergs to murder. In real life it was raisin wine that provided the motive. He quotes Papanin: "We live as if on a powder keg, for at any moment an ice jam may occur, the ice floe crack apart and capsize, and draw us down with it to the depths."

Lest you think Ted is being too hard on Russia and its geographical challenges, read Fiona Hill and Clifford Gaddy's *The Siberian Curse: How Communist Planners left Russia Out in the Cold* (2003). Combine too much cold and space with central planning and you get a slightly suboptimal outcome.

To learn about the oil weapon coming out of the American scabbard in the '80s, I recommend Peter Schweizer's *Victory: The Reagan Administration's Secret Strategy that Hastened the Collapse of the Soviet Union* (1994).

For the full story on Azeri oil in the '90s and the blow-by-blow battle for the 'Contract of the Century,' see Steve LeVine's *The Oil and the Glory: The Pursuit of Empire and Fortune on the Caspian Sea* (2007). For additional historical backdrop and further insight into the explosive mood on the ground, be sure to read Thomas Goltz's *Azerbaijan Diary: A Rogue Reporter's Adventures in an Oil-rich, War-torn, Post-Soviet Republic* (1999).

Finally, a word on business conduct. The spread of global anti-bribery laws, including the US Federal Corrupt Practices Act, has been an unequivocal boon to society and the public good and deserves our full support. Charlie and Avinashi make mistakes, which they admit and pay consequences for, and their having done so in this story should be in no way be construed as an endorsement of such activity. Had they had better counsel at the time, I expect it could have all been avoided. So, seek good counsel, follow the law, in letter and spirit, and consider a contribution to Transparency International (www. transparency.org).